Trevillion dragged himself to his feet. "Tara! What in blazes?"

She sped back to his side. "Are you all right?" Her voice died away. "Oh, gods," she whispered, looking past him. Icy-hot chills raked her flesh. "Natiere."

Head and shoulders above the rest, the Butcher stood, watching her. A satisfied smile softened the ragged scar ruining his face. He was so close. His black eyes locked with hers. In that instant, she sensed his pleasure, his approval. Her mind slipped deeper into his and felt anguish, the pain of a life as tortured as his victims. Surprise crossed Natiere's face.

Trevillion gripped her arm. "Tara!"

Tara's story continues in

TROUBLE BY ANY OTHER NAME

Coming soon

From

Lori L. MacLaughlin

Lady, THY NAME IS TROUBLE

LORI L. MACLAUGHLIN

Book and Sword Publishing

Lori L. MacLaughlin/Book and Sword Publishing, LLC
Vermont, USA
www.bookandswordpublishing.com

Publisher's Note: This is a work of fiction. Names, characters, places, and incidents are a product of the author's imagination. Locales and public names are sometimes used for atmospheric purposes. Any resemblance to actual people, living or dead, or to businesses, companies, events, institutions, or locales is completely coincidental.

Cover Design: North 100 Design and Lori L. MacLaughlin
Cover Art: © FreeImages/Leroys; FreeImages/AssassinM;
iStock/Mikesilent; iStock/anton-tokarev; iStock/Byshnev
Book Layout © 2014 BookDesignTemplates.com
Map: © 2015 Lori L. MacLaughlin

Lady, Thy Name Is Trouble/ Lori L. MacLaughlin. -- 1st ed.
ISBN 978-1-942015-00-0

Book and Sword Publishing

ACKNOWLEDGEMENTS

This journey began many years ago when a young girl read others' books and was inspired to create stories of her own and give life to the characters clamoring in her head. My dream of being a published author has become a reality, and I would like to thank those who were instrumental in helping me along this journey: my writing group, the ELFS — particularly Kari Jo Spear and Jody Wood — for their insightful comments and suggestions; freelance editor Meg Brazill for her judicious "red pen;" Lo Alvarez-Thamm of North 100 Design for the beautiful cover; Pat Goudey O'Brien and the League of Vermont Writers for advice and inspiration; and all my wonderful friends for their encouragement.

Most of all, I wish to thank my parents, who always encouraged me and gave me wings to fly. None of this would have been possible without their unfailing love and support. I am forever grateful.

For My Parents

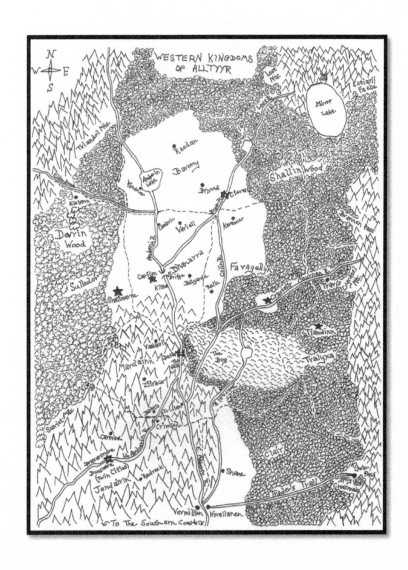

Lady,

THY NAME
IS
TROUBLE

CHAPTER 1

Tara Triannon sat in the window seat, staring out into the darkness. Something was terribly wrong. An unnatural silence, taut and disturbing, gripped the air, as if it would strangle anyone who ventured into it. Tara sensed the danger. The icy chills goose-pimpling her skin told her the threat was near. She felt trapped, vulnerable.

She shook her head to clear it; her eyes searched the shadows of her cramped, darkened chamber for... what? She didn't know.

Thunder rolled, not far in the distance. A storm brewed in the west. *More than one*, she thought grimly. Blood would spill before morning as sure as Haedis was god of the Abyss.

She rose and paced the length of the room. The banked fire glowed dimly, succumbing to the smothering darkness. Her sword-belt lay nearby on the neatly-made bed. She buckled it on, adjusting the scabbard so she could draw her sword easily with her left hand. She was glad she hadn't bothered to undress when she'd turned in for the night some hours before.

A clock chimed, and she jumped, her sword half drawn out of reflex. One hour past midnight. She caught a glimpse of herself in the mirror that hung between the bed and the fireplace. Silver-blue eyes stared back at her, more silver than blue in her agitation; silver-blonde hair flowed in waves down her back. She looked beyond her reflection, searching the room behind her but saw nothing out of the ordinary.

Sheathing her sword, she returned to the window and opened the casement. She needed fresh air. A cool breeze drifted in, soothing her nerves with its sweet fragrance of damp earth and spring flowers. She sat back against the cold stone wall and drummed her fingers on the seat. Oh, to be free of this confounded castle with its narrow hallways and confining rooms. She frowned. If only Laraina would end her dalliance with the Dhanarran prince. Her older sister's affairs didn't usually bother her, but this one had dragged on too long.

Thunder rumbled, closer this time. Tara shivered, her sense of foreboding growing sharp as the edge of her blade. Wiping sweaty palms on her brown leather leggings, she looked out the window once more. Bright shafts of moonlight filtered through the heavy overcast, reflecting off the white stone buildings of the city below. From her tower window she could see the entire city of Carilon, the Dhanarran capital, spreading across the valley to the west, pure and pristine like a city of the gods. Beyond the valley and the sweep of grasslands shrouded in darkness lay Sulledor. She would not be surprised if trouble came from that quarter. Sulledor was a rocky, forested kingdom with scarce land for agriculture. Sulledorn kings had turned greedy eyes and restless swords on neighboring lands many times. Only a life-or-death situation or a great deal of money would convince her to set foot there. She had no wish to tangle with its current leader, the brutal General Caldren and his nightmarish executioner, Captain Natiere, or "The Butcher," as he was more often called. The Captain's penchant for torture was well documented by the mangled bodies left in his wake. The new peace treaty Laraina's prince had brokered with the General was worth less than the ashes it would burn into. Tara, however, hadn't been able to convince anyone of this. The people of Dhanarra clung stubbornly to their illusion of peace. They considered their Prince Kaden a hero.

Tara fingered the hilt of her sword, tracing its well-worn lines to ease her annoyance. Prince Kaden was a fool. She had no use for him, and she knew he had none for her. He didn't trust her. He thought her cold-blooded and arrogant and blamed her for making Laraina's life one of constant trouble. She dismissed his complaints. She didn't care what Kaden thought. She and her sister were swords for hire, soldiers of fortune; trouble came with the profession. They both accepted that. If the prince didn't like it, that was his problem. And yes, Tara may have taken some risks, perhaps more than were necessary, but what was life without a little excitement? She pictured the tall, brown-haired prince with his usual glare of disapproval. What Laraina saw in him — or with the countless other men she'd been with — Tara would never know.

Another face, jaunty and handsome, flitted through her mind, teasing her with a rakish smile. Her fingers curled into a fist, and she slammed the door on the memory. She'd been burned once, badly. Never again.

Shoving aside her unpleasant thoughts, she leaned back and closed her eyes, inhaling the cool night air. She had to calm down.

A faint sound formed in the cloying darkness. Icy coldness shot down Tara's spine — her danger sense warning her of immediate peril. She bolted upright, listening, hearing only the ominous silence and the booming of distant thunder. Yes, there it was again, outside, a faint rustling like the tread of a night wolf stalking its prey.

Cautiously, she peered over the edge of the stone sill. There — slipping across the inner courtyard, obscured by the murky darkness — a mass of moving shapes. Lightning flashed, revealing a troop of soldiers, fully armed, their swords drawn. Emblazoned on their shields was the eagle and crossed swords of Sulledor.

Stifling a curse, Tara dashed out of her room and down the torch-lit hall. She had to find Laraina. They had to get out. She came to a cross corridor, hesitated, changed direction. She should warn the Dhanarran king.

She rounded a corner and slammed into something huge. Hands of iron gripped her arms, holding her. She gasped, recognizing the hulking giant in her path. Captain Natiere. The Butcher. His black eyes stared down at her, inscrutable. A long, gruesome scar snaked down the left side of his face from his cragged forehead to his stubbled chin. Blood stained his shirt. Fresh blood. Tara pulled away but couldn't break his grip.

A look of shock crossed the Butcher's face. "*Silvestri witana*," he whispered. Then recognition lit his eyes. "I know who you are." His voice was as rough and gravelly as his face. "You're one of the Triannons." He smiled. "Your reputation does not do you justice."

Tara stopped struggling, her eyes drawn to his. His gaze held her as strongly as his hands. She could not move or breathe.

"*Mi achina*," he said softly and released her.

Tara fell backward, catching herself against the wall.

"I look forward to our next meeting." He strode down the hall and disappeared around a corner.

Tara sank to a crouch, her heart hammering in her chest. She looked down and saw blood on her clothes. Blood. The king. She jumped to her feet and ran.

****

"Kaden, wake up!" Laraina Triannon shook the man sleeping beside her. "Wake up!"

Prince Kaden of Dhanarra stirred and shoved his tousled brown hair out of his eyes. "All right, I'm awake. What is it?"

Laraina sat up, her long red curls falling over her shoulders and concealing her voluptuous figure. "I heard someone shouting."

"At this time of the night?" Kaden rubbed the sleep from his eyes. "Are you sure it wasn't a dream?"

"I'm sure. Listen!"

The muffled beat of running footsteps pounded the air, then more shouting, screams of pain, and the unmistakable clash of weapons.

Prince Kaden jerked upright.

Laraina slid into a robe and snatched up a candle, lighting it from the embers in the fireplace. Tara had said something terrible was going to happen. No one had believed her. How had she known? "I have to find Tara. I hope she's all right." *And not in the middle of the conflict*, Laraina added silently. Knowing her sister...

The bedroom door flew open. Tara burst into the room and closed the door behind her.

"Tara!" Laraina cried. "Thank the gods you're all right!"

"Sorry to barge in on you like this," Tara said as she ran to the dressing table and began throwing clothes at them, "but we're under attack and we've got to get out of here!"

Prince Kaden yanked on his clothes. "Who's attacking us?"

"Keep your voice down," Tara warned. "The Sulledorn army has breached the castle. I don't know how they got in, but they're here, and if you don't hurry up you'll be meeting them personally!"

"That's impossible. They signed the peace treaty less than three weeks ago."

"They took you for the fools you were," Tara said in disgust. "Since when has Sulledor ever honored a treaty?"

The roar of battle grew louder. Tara cracked the door open and peered out into the corridor.

Laraina dressed hurriedly. "How many are there?"

Tara shook her head. "I don't know. Too many. More than we can handle."

"Did you see my father?" Prince Kaden stomped into his boots. "Has he summoned the Guard?"

Tara hesitated, then turned toward him. "Your father is dead. I'm sorry."

"Dead?" Kaden whispered.

Laraina gasped, noticing the blood stains on Tara's shirt. She hadn't seen them before in the dim light. She ran to her sister. "You're bleeding! Are you all right? What happened?"

Tara waved her away. "It's not mine. I'm fine." She turned back to the door. "The army hasn't reached this level yet, so we may still have time to escape."

Prince Kaden seized Tara's arm and pulled her around to face him. "How do you know my father is dead? Just whose blood is that all over you?"

Tara wrenched out of his grasp and shoved him against the wall. "Don't ever do that again."

Laraina stepped between them and glared at the prince. "Are you accusing her of —"

"She's a sell-sword, she's covered in blood, and she hates me. What am I supposed to think? Someone had to let the Sulledorns in. None of my men would betray me."

"I'm a sell-sword, too. Does that make me a traitor?"

"No." Kaden ran his hand over his face. "Raina, I'm sorry. I didn't mean —"

"We don't have time for this," Tara snapped. "I know your father is dead because I saw him — *after* he was murdered. In fact, I ran into his killer, literally."

"Who did it?" Kaden demanded. "I will tear his guts out with my own hand."

"No, I don't think you will," Tara said grimly.

The clash of battle began to fade.

Tara headed for the door. "Now is our chance to escape. This is not the time for vengeance. There are too many of them. We need to get away and warn Faragellyn. I doubt the Sulledorns intend to stop here."

Kaden pounded the edge of his fist against the wall. "I will not be driven from my own castle!"

An ear-splitting scream rose above the battle sounds.

"Aurelia!" Prince Kaden cried.

"Wonderful. That's all we need." Tara whipped out her sword and dashed into the corridor.

Kaden grabbed his broadsword and followed with Laraina right behind him.

*****

Tara raced down the dimly lit corridor, fuming over the prince's accusation. Of course, he would blame his father's murder on her, rather than admit it was the result of his own stupidity. If he laid a hand on her again, she wouldn't answer for the consequences.

Reaching the end of the passageway, she peered around the corner to her right. About halfway down the hall, she spied three Sulledorn soldiers. One of them was dragging a diminutive, but well-rounded girl in a pink nightgown out of a room.

"Let go of me! How dare you touch me!" the girl demanded. The top of her head barely reached her captors' shoulders. "If you don't let go of me, I'll turn you into a goose!" She babbled a nonsensical phrase. One of the soldiers disappeared, and in his place stood a towering moose. Its antlers scraped the stone ceiling. The moose bellowed and galloped off down the hall.

The two remaining soldiers gaped.

The girl stamped her foot. "I said goose, not moose!"

One of the soldiers grabbed a handful of her short blonde hair. "Witch! What did you do to him?"

"Ouch! That hurts!" She dug her heel into his foot. "I am *not* a witch. I am a *sorceress!*"

He howled and raised his hand to strike her.

Shaking off her surprise at the appearance of the moose, Tara charged around the corner, brandishing her sword and yelling like a madwoman. The startled Sulledorns released the girl and drew their own weapons, but not before Tara was upon them. She swung her blade and sliced a deep gash across the ribs of the nearest soldier. He stumbled back with a cry, his sword clattering to the floor. Tara ducked as the second soldier's blade whistled by her ear. She dealt him a swift kick in the belly that doubled him over, then brought the hilt of her sword down on his head. He staggered, groaning, and sprawled at her feet.

Clutching his wounded side, the first soldier fled. A well-thrown dagger brought him down. Tara retrieved the dagger, wiped it off, and tossed it back to Laraina, who, with Kaden, had arrived moments before.

"Well done, sister," Tara said with a smile. "Now let's get out of here." Her smile faded as a troop of Sulledorn soldiers appeared at the end of the hall behind them.

"There they are!" the Sulledorn leader shouted and broke into a run.

"To my father's bedroom! Quickly!" Kaden caught Aurelia's arm and dragged her down the corridor at a dead run.

The Sulledorns charged after them.

Tara and the others scrambled around a corner and raced down a darkened hallway, the Sulledorns hard on their heels. At the far end of the corridor they slid to a stop in front of the king's bedroom. Kaden kicked open the door and they dashed inside, slamming the door shut and bolting it just as the Sulledorns reached it.

The king's bedroom was cold and dark, its cavernous interior lit only by the embers still smoldering in the fireplace on the far side of the room. Prince Kaden crossed to the hearth. He reached toward the mantel, then froze.

"Father," he whispered.

Sprawled on the bed beside him, eyes open in the stare of death, lay the blood-drenched corpse of the King of Dhanarra. His throat had been cut.

Tara clamped her hand over Aurelia's mouth to silence her scream.

The sharp crack of splintering wood roused them to action as a battle axe smashed into the chamber door behind them. His jaw set in a grim line, Prince Kaden twisted one of the candlesticks on the mantel. With a grating sound, the fireplace swung outward into the room, filling it with smoke.

"Follow me." The tall prince took Laraina's hand, stooped low, and stepped into the passageway.

"Wait for me!" Aurelia cried, grasping Laraina's other hand. Tara brought up the rear. The fireplace swung shut behind them, plunging them into darkness.

*****

With a splintering crash the door fell from its hinges, and the Sulledorn soldiers stormed into the king's bedroom. Smoke billowed around them, blinding them. Coughing and choking, they retreated to the corridor. As the smoke cleared, the soldiers rushed back into the room, only to find it empty.

"They're not here, sir," said one of the soldiers.

"I can see that, you dolt!" said the lieutenant in command. "There must be a secret passage." He whirled on his men. "Find it! Or I'll feed you to Captain Natiere!"

The soldiers blanched. They fanned out and searched the room.

The disgruntled lieutenant turned on his heel and strode out the door. "Sulledorn idiots. How difficult is it to capture one man? My guard would have had the prince's head in no time." He tugged nervously at his goatee. The General wouldn't like this. But, the lieutenant reasoned, it wasn't his fault the castle was full of secret passages. He didn't know what the General wanted Prince Kaden for anyway. The prince spent more time in the bed chamber than the council chamber.

The lieutenant descended the long, winding staircase to the main floor of the castle and turned into the east wing. His footsteps echoed in the silent corridors. The sounds of battle had long since died away. The castle guards, taken by surprise, had been easily overcome.

He rounded a corner and froze in his tracks. Beside the door to the General's newly-acquired headquarters stood a giant of a man. He was well over six feet tall and nearly as broad as the door itself. Black eyes stared straight ahead. Thick black hair lay in a short braid down his back. Torchlight flickered over the gruesome scar on his face and on the blood staining his clothes. Cloaked in black fur, the General's Executioner looked more beast than man.

The lieutenant swallowed the lump in his throat and forced himself to continue. *When I am king, the first thing I will do is get rid of him*, he vowed silently. He strode to the door, saluted the Butcher, who ignored him, and rapped sharply.

"Enter," commanded a smooth voice from inside.

Assuming an air of confidence, the lieutenant swung open the heavy wooden door and marched in. A lone figure stood behind a table in the center of the small room. Tall and muscular with pure white hair and a short clipped black mustache, General Caldren was strikingly handsome. However, those good looks masked a dangerous man, one who had ruled Sulledor with an iron fist ever since the mysterious disappearance of the rightful king twelve years before.

The General did not look up as the lieutenant entered, but continued to study the map in front of him.

The lieutenant saluted. "Lieutenant Phelps reporting, sir!"

"And what have you to report?" the General asked without looking at him.

"The castle is secured as per your orders, sir."

"And the prince?"

Phelps shifted uncomfortably. "Um... the prince has... er... eluded us for the moment."

The General raised his head. "Eluded you?"

"Er... yes. He and the girl — his cousin — escaped with the Triannon sisters through a secret passage."

The General's eyes narrowed. "I see."

Fear crawled over the lieutenant's flesh, turning his knees to water. "We will find them momentarily, I assure you. A unit of men has already been dispatched to search the area, and I will join the search myself and make certain they are captured."

The General smiled. "That won't be necessary. *Captain!*"

The lieutenant cringed as Captain Natiere and two sentries appeared beside him. Terror gripped him. "Sir, I —"

"Silence!" bellowed the General. He motioned to the sentries. "This man is of no further use to us. Get rid of him."

The sentries grabbed the lieutenant's arms and propelled him toward the door.

"Lock him in the dungeon," said Captain Natiere. "I'll see to him shortly."

"No! Wait! Please!" The lieutenant thrashed wildly. "I can be of help to you!" His voice rose to a wail as they dragged him out the door. "No! I opened the gates for you! You said I would be the new king of Dhanarra!" His shouts echoed through the stone corridors, then abruptly ceased.

A cold silence descended.

General Caldren turned to the Captain. "It seems we will not be able to use the prince as a hostage as I had planned." He waved his hand dismissively. "No matter. The remaining towns can be taken just as easily by force." He fixed his eyes once more on the worn map spread out on the table before him. A smile played over his handsome features as he traced his finger across the map, plotting an imaginary trail of destruction. "And it will be much more pleasurable." He turned back to the Captain. "The fool informed me that the prince has escaped with the Triannon sisters. Take some men, find them, and kill them. I don't want word of our attack to spread."

With a curt nod, The Butcher quit the room.

CHAPTER 2

"Where are we?" Tara whispered as she stepped out into a narrow ravine overgrown with brush and briars.

Kaden shifted the tangle of bushes to conceal the entrance to the secret passage. "About a mile south of the castle."

Tara peered into the darkness. *Half the Sulledorn army could be hiding out here and we'd never know,* she thought. She relaxed her mind, sifting through the myriad auras of the living creatures around her. She sensed no immediate danger.

Laraina came up beside her. "See anything?"

Tara shook her head. "No. I'll scout around. Keep an eye on them." She nodded toward Kaden and Aurelia.

"All right, but be careful," Laraina warned.

Tara set off through the dense underbrush.

****

Prince Kaden breathed in the darkness around him, still numbed by the night's events. He felt lost, cut adrift from all he had known. His father — dead. How could this have happened? Could it be that the treaty for a lasting peace he'd worked so hard to secure was only a web of empty promises? And like a spider's web, so easily torn. He gritted his teeth. Tara had been right, curse her. She'd said they were fools to trust General Caldren. Sickness churned in his stomach. How many people had died because of his mistake? The thought horrified him. And how many more would fall before he could set things right? He steeled himself — for set things right, he would. Even though his sword had never touched an enemy blade, he would take back his castle and send the General to the Abyss with his own hand. But how to do it? He needed a plan.

Aurelia suddenly screeched.

Kaden whirled.

"Look at this!" Aurelia displayed a huge tear in the sleeve of her pink nightgown. "My new nightdress is ruined! Just look at this!" She stood on her tiptoes and thrust her arm in front of his face. "Do you know how long it took me to conjure this?"

Kaden let out a breath and tried to calm the fear that clenched his gut. "Yes... no... I see it. Please keep your voice down."

"Why should I keep my voice down? I am a member of the Royal House of Dhanarra." She spun on her heel and stalked away from him.

"Aurelia, you must be quiet. Where are you going?" Kaden followed, nearly running her over as she turned on him.

"Back to the castle. And you are going to take those soldiers and bury them in the dungeon — after I turn them into worms!"

"Aurelia —"

"Attacked in my own room! They hurt my arms, tore my gown, pulled my hair." She rubbed her sore scalp, then stamped her foot. "I will not stand for such an outrage! Where were all the guards?" She scowled at the dense thickets. "And why in the name of the gods did you drag me out here? It's freezing!" She clasped her arms around herself and rubbed vigorously. "Will someone please tell me what is going on?"

Kaden gripped her shoulders. "If you will be quiet for a minute, I will explain."

*****

Tara dashed back across the ravine toward the prince and his cousin. *Those idiots! Didn't they know any loud noise could mean capture and torturous death?* She burst through the underbrush in front of them. "Be quiet — both of you — before I stuff gags in your mouths. No one knows where we are right now. I'd like to keep it that way."

"Don't threaten me!" Kaden snarled.

Aurelia grasped Kaden's shirt. "My uncle... the King... is he really... dead?"

Kaden stared at Aurelia as if she had struck him. "Yes," he whispered.

Aurelia burst into tears and threw herself against him.

Tara rolled her eyes.

Kaden embraced Aurelia, his face grief-stricken. Laraina laid her hand on Kaden's shoulder and squeezed it gently. He met her gaze, then brushed his lips across her hand.

In the midst of her weeping, Aurelia glanced up and frowned at their silent exchange. Sobbing harder, she moaned until Kaden turned back to comfort her.

Tara stepped forward. "You little —" She bit off the epithet as she caught Laraina's glare. "Fine. If you don't care, I don't care. I'm going up to the top of the ravine. Keep them quiet till I get back. Strangle her if you have to."

Laraina nodded.

Tara crossed the ravine again, slipping soundlessly through waist-high brush and bracken. That brat was going to get them all killed. She should have gagged Aurelia the minute they stepped from the secret passage. Prince Kaden wouldn't have approved, not that Tara cared about that either. Seething, she climbed the rocky slope.

A faint breeze grazed her skin as she reached the top. The air lay moist and heavy with a strong odor of mint. A pale crescent moon slipped in and out of the black clouds, casting long, uneven shadows over the landscape like so many wandering ghosts. The eerie silence struck her again. Shrugging off her uneasiness, she crept forward until she saw the besieged castle.

High on a hill at the southeast end of the city it stood, stark and white, its towers and battlements etched sharply against the night sky. No lights gleamed in any of the windows. The city lay dark and silent, as if in peaceful slumber. It didn't look like a marauding army had just passed through. In fact, there was no sign of an army anywhere — no troops, no campfires — nothing.

That's strange, she thought. *Or is it?* Her eyes narrowed. What if the main army had bypassed the city entirely, knowing it would be an easy conquest? The Sulledorns could be halfway to Faragellyn by now. The rich timber and grasslands of Dhanarra's eastern neighbor were an obvious target. If she and the others escaped to the east, they'd walk right into the enemy camp.

Sensing a movement behind her, Tara turned and saw Laraina climbing the slope. Laraina reached the top and crouched beside her.

"I thought you were going to watch them," Tara said.

"They're fine. Where's the encampment? I don't see any fire glow or smell any smoke."

"There isn't any. The army's not here. I think they've gone on toward Faragellyn."

"Then they'll have taken the North Bridge. That limits our escape routes."

"It doesn't leave us with many choices." Tara studied a mental map. Their position lay on the west side of the rain-swollen Amberin River, which at this time of the year was impassable. The river bisected Dhanarra, running roughly north and south. The North Bridge provided the only means of passage to the east. They would have to go south into Mardainn.

Tara turned to go. "We need to get out of here."

Laraina stopped her. "You don't like Aurelia much, do you?"

Tara raised her eyebrows. "You have to ask?"

"Has she done something to you?"

"No, but only because I informed her what would happen if she did."

Surprise crossed Laraina's face. "What do you mean?"

"I mean that she is a spoiled brat whose only concern is getting her own way."

"I didn't think she was that bad."

Tara snorted. "Then you haven't seen her at her best. Who do you think put the sleeping powder in the drink of that servant she didn't like — which resulted in his dismissal — or put the burr under the saddle of the groom who wouldn't let her ride the horse she wanted because it was too wild for her — or conjured up the worms in Jenna's bed because Jenna was flirting with the boy she liked — or —"

"All right, all right," Laraina interrupted. "I see your point."

"She may think she is a powerful sorceress," Tara continued, "but in truth she is barely an apprentice. That makes her dangerous. She needs to learn discipline, and she needs to grow up if she wants to survive."

"I know," Laraina agreed, "but remember, she's only a child, and she just saw her uncle covered with his own blood."

"Only a child? She's fifteen years old, and if she felt half the sorrow she pretends to, I would sympathize with her. But she doesn't; she cares for no one but herself. I won't let her put us in danger with her nonsense."

Laraina considered. "I'll have Kaden talk to her."

"I doubt that will help much."

"Stop beating on Kaden," Laraina snapped, her green eyes blazing. "You're always criticizing him. There is more to him than you think. If you would look beyond a certain handsome face, you might see that not all men are jackasses."

Tara clamped her jaw to keep from saying something she would regret. She raised her hands in a gesture of peace. "Calm your temper. Now is not the time to discuss men's qualities, or lack thereof. We need to go." She headed down into the ravine.

Laraina followed. "Kaden and Aurelia are close. I wonder why Aurelia hasn't played any of her tricks on me, you know, out of jealousy?"

"We had a little discussion about that as well," Tara said over her shoulder.

"I see," said Laraina. "So that's why she's been so nice to me lately. You're very persuasive."

Tara smiled to herself and said nothing.

They made their way down to the choked floor of the ravine. Kaden and Aurelia hadn't moved. The prince had his arm around his small cousin's shoulders, and she was dabbing her eyes with his silk handkerchief and looking up at him with a woebegone expression.

"The Sulledorn army is gone," Tara said. "I think they're headed east toward Faragellyn. The Faragellyn king needs to be warned. The Sulledorns will be guarding the North Bridge, and we can't cross the river anywhere else in Dhanarra with it as high as it is, so we'll have to head south into Mardainn."

"Then we'll head for Desta, the capital, and enlist their aid," Prince Kaden said. "The High Council —"

"We'd be wasting our time," Tara cut in. "The High Council of Mardainn is strictly isolationist when it comes to military matters. They'd likely arrest us for crossing the border and stirring up trouble. The only way to arouse them is to attack them. They wouldn't sign your peace treaty, would they?"

"No," Kaden admitted. "They were the only kingdom that wouldn't. They wanted nothing to do with me or anyone else." He shook his head. "But we still have to pass through Desta to reach Faragellyn. Desta has the only other bridge across the Amberin River."

"That's true," Tara conceded, "but we'll worry about that later. Right now we have to get moving. We've wasted too much time as it is."

"Kite isn't far from here." Laraina eyed Aurelia's thin nightdress and slippers. "We should be able to find some clothes and supplies there."

"In the middle of the night?" Kaden asked.

"That's the best time," Tara said with a smile. "Let's go."

"We don't need to," said Aurelia. "I can conjure up plenty of clothes and food." She began to chant.

Tara clapped her hand over Aurelia's mouth. "No conjuring! We've already seen what your conjuring can do."

Aurelia squeaked in fright.

Prince Kaden pulled Aurelia away. "Leave her alone."

Tara jabbed her finger toward Aurelia. "You had best keep her quiet, or —"

Laraina stepped between them, giving Tara an icy stare. "We need to get moving, remember?"

Clenching her teeth, Tara turned and led the way out of the ravine.

The terrain between Carilon and the Mardainn border was rough and rocky, scarred with ridges and gashed with deep gullies and ravines. Little vegetation grew, other than sparse grass, brush, briars, and occasional clumps of scrub pine and gorse. Wary of the uncertain footing, they traveled during the frequent breaks of moonlight, resting when darkness closed in.

They reached Kite about two hours before dawn. Located on the west bank of the Amberin River, Kite had a large port and a thriving trade with other river towns. Agricultural products and livestock from the rich northern farmlands of Barony, Faragellyn, and upper Dhanarra were shipped downriver to Kite and traded for gold, gemstones, forged tools, and weapons brought upriver from the mining towns buried in the mountains of Mardainn and Jendairin.

Tara surveyed the sleeping town. She could hear nothing above the roar of the swollen river. The wide streets near the marketplace and docks were well lit and usually well guarded, though at the moment there was no one in sight. The rest of the town lay cloaked in shadow lit only by a few widely-spaced oil lamps hung on poles. Where was the night watch? They had to be nearby. She let her mind probe the depths of the night, searching for danger, but found nothing unusual. She motioned for the others to follow and moved southward along the town's perimeter, keeping well out of sight behind the rocks.

A light rain began to fall as they circled around to the south side of town. They stopped near a broad avenue lined with small two-story houses constructed of rough gray stone.

"This rain should help cover our tracks," Tara said. Brushing back her damp hair, she turned to her sister. "We need supplies and horses. What's your fancy?"

Laraina studied the houses for a moment, then said, "I'll take the supplies. Kaden can help me."

Tara tried to keep the skepticism off her face. "Fine. I'll see what I can find in the way of horses and meet you back here."

*****

Prince Kaden watched Tara vanish into the rain and wished she was disappearing for good. She was going to get them all killed with her reckless attitude. Her condescending, know-it-all manner grated on his raw nerves. If it wasn't for Laraina, he would have tossed her out of Castle Carilon weeks ago. There had to be some way to separate them.

Aurelia sat down on a dry spot under a gnarled clump of pine trees. "My poor feet," she moaned, rubbing them gingerly. "My toes are scraped and sore, and my beautiful slippers are torn to shreds. I am of royal blood. My feet are not made to walk over these horrible rocks like a common person."

"Shhh! Quiet, please," said Laraina. "We don't want to alert the night watch. Don't worry, we'll get you some boots." She turned to Kaden. "Are you ready?"

"For what?"

"To help me get the supplies."

"You really intend to break into one of those houses?"

"Of course."

"Raina, in case you've forgotten, I am a prince. I'm supposed to uphold the laws, not break them." He stopped as a sudden realization shocked him. "My father is dead. I am no longer a prince. I am king." He swallowed the bitter taste in his mouth. "But king of what?" He scowled at his surroundings. "I'm skulking around in the dark like a common thief."

"I am *not* a common thief." The tone of Laraina's voice matched the ice in her eyes.

"No, I didn't mean that you were," Kaden said. "I meant that we should be fighting, not running and hiding from our enemies. My father deserves better from his heir."

He closed his eyes, racked by grief and guilt. He and his father, once so far apart, had been just beginning to come to terms, to understand and accept each other's differences. The king had been a stern, duty-driven leader, fully accepting his role as monarch in which personal wants and needs had little place. To Kaden, those wants and needs had been of utmost importance. He'd made no attempt to hide his extravagant tastes and bedroom appetite, much to his father's disgust. However, a recent illness had weakened the king, forcing Kaden to curb his habits and fulfill his role as royal heir. Stepping into a tumultuous political arena, Kaden had shown a diplomatic adeptness that had surprised everyone. Father and son had become allies instead of antagonists. Now everything had been ripped away.

Laraina's arms slid around him. "I'm sorry. I didn't mean to snap at you."

He pulled her onto his lap and hugged her. "I know. It's that red-headed temper of yours." He let her calming strength wash over him. It amazed him how a woman as fiery as she could be soothing at the same time.

"Can we save the reconciliations for later?" Aurelia said. "We're supposed to be getting food, which would be nice since I'm starving."

"Kaden and I will get the supplies," Laraina said. "And Kaden, we're not going to break any laws, we're just going to... bend them a little. Whatever you may think of our methods, we do not steal." She pulled a small bag of coins out of one of her belt pouches and balanced it in her hand, gauging its weight. "We pay for whatever we take." She dropped the bag back into her pouch.

"I still don't think it's a good idea," Kaden said.

Laraina raised her hands in a gesture of helplessness. "We can't knock on their front doors, now can we?"

He shrugged. "Why not? These people are subjects of the Royal House of Dhanarra. I am their Prince... er... King. They must give aid if it is needed."

Laraina nodded. "Yes, I know that. But we don't want anyone to know where we are. Secrecy is important. The Sulledorns can't pursue us if they don't know where to look."

"How do you know we're being followed?"

"Because General Caldren will be depending on the element of surprise in his attacks. He won't want us ruining his strategy by warning Faragellyn before he gets there. Now it'll be quicker and easier with your help, and we can't afford to waste any more time. Besides," she added with a provocative smile, "I like your company."

He hesitated. "All right," he said finally, unable to think of a more palatable way of obtaining the needed supplies.

"You aren't really going to leave me here alone!" Aurelia looked from one to the other. "Are you?"

"Only for a short time," Kaden said. "You'll be fine. You can sit right here under the trees and no one will see you."

"But what if a wild animal attacks me? A bear or wolf or —"

"There aren't any wild animals this close to town," said Laraina.

"What if you get caught?"

"We won't," Laraina said. "Just stay where you are. We'll be back soon."

Taking Kaden's hand, she led the way around the neat line of stone houses, approaching them from the rear. The steady rain poured down. She tried several windows and doors, but the results were the same.

"Locked!" she whispered in irritation. "Since when do the people of Kite lock all their doors and windows?"

"Probably since they've become acquainted with people like you," Kaden answered with a tense grin.

She made a face at him. "Very funny." She walked toward the next house. "We'll just have to force the... wait!" She halted. "Look! There's an open window on the top floor over there. Come on!"

She hurried over to the house, with Kaden following reluctantly.

"Help me up," she whispered.

He gave her a leg up. Standing on his shoulders, she could just reach the edge of the window. She caught hold of the sill, and with the agility of a cat, pulled herself up and over it.

Laraina had been in the house for several minutes when Kaden began to worry. Flattening himself against the wall, he cursed the rain and berated himself for letting her talk him into this. What had he been thinking? A flood of disasters that might have befallen her flitted through his mind. He was just about to go around to the front door and demand entrance when she appeared at the window. She let down a rope and motioned for him to come up. With relief and apprehension, he climbed the rope and joined her in the room. She pressed her hand to his lips, warning him to silence.

"There's someone sleeping in the next room," she breathed, "so be careful. See if you can find some cloaks in that closet." She pointed to a door on the far wall, then picked up a small, burning candle and tiptoed out of the room.

Kaden glanced around uneasily. A large bedstead with a bare mattress stood on his left, with a small chest of drawers against the wall facing him, next to the door. On his right he saw a table with another tiny lit candle and two wooden chairs. A spare bedroom. He crossed the room, pulled open the closet door, and rummaged through the contents.

A touch on his shoulder startled him half out of his wits. He glowered at Laraina, who had come up behind him, then showed her the two heavy cloaks he'd found. She smiled and handed him two more dark cloaks and a large, brightly-colored skirt and blouse.

"Take these to Aur —"

The bed in the next room creaked. Laraina motioned for silence as Kaden stared in alarm. The creaking grew louder, then ceased, only to be followed by the dull tread of heavy footsteps. Laraina grabbed Kaden's arm and propelled him toward the window.

"Go quickly!" she hissed. "I'll get the food and be right with you. Don't wait!"

She ran to the door.

"Raina!" Kaden whispered urgently.

She paused in the doorway and looked back.

"I can't climb down the rope and carry all this, and if I toss them out the window, they'll get soaked."

"Well... put them on," she suggested.

"You can't be serious," he whispered, but Laraina had disappeared.

The faint click of a doorlatch down the hall spurred him to action. Dropping the clothes in a heap, he sprang to the door and pushed it soundlessly shut. Then he pulled the skirt on over his trousers and tossed the blouse over his head. Shuffling footsteps sounded in the hallway as he fastened the heavy cloaks around his neck.

Sweat gleamed on his brow as the footsteps passed by the door, then stopped. With a silent oath Kaden clambered over the sill. He slid down the wet rope to the ground and ducked around the corner of the house just as a rumpled face appeared at the window. The figure peered out into the misty darkness, then Kaden heard a slurring sound as the rope was pulled up, followed by a thud as the window was closed and locked.

"Raina, I hope you know what you're doing," he muttered. He pulled one of the hoods up over his head and made his way back to where Aurelia waited.

*****

Shielding the candle flame with her hand, Laraina flew down the staircase to the kitchen at the rear of the house. She slipped into the pantry, pulled a well-worn sack from her pouch, and filled it with as many supplies as she could manage. With the sack tied securely to her belt, she drew out the small bag of coins and set it on a shelf in plain sight. Bowing to the empty room, she whispered, "Thank you very much," then sped back through the kitchen and around to the front door. Set neatly against the wall by the door, as she had hoped, were several pairs of boots. She heard the heavy thud of footsteps descending the stairs. Grabbing a small pair of boots, she let herself out the front door and slipped into the shadows.

*****

Returning from his first foray into house-breaking, Prince Kaden spied Aurelia in her pink nightgown, hunched under the twisted clump of trees, trying vainly to keep from being drenched by the rain. Her head bobbed back and forth as if she searched the darkness for some unknown assailant. Kaden hurried toward her, slipping on the wet stones as he fumbled with the catch of one of his cloaks.

As he drew near, Aurelia caught sight of him, scrambled to her feet and screamed. Kaden stopped short in surprise. He whirled around, expecting to see the entire night watch chasing after him. Seeing nothing, he turned back, perplexed.

Aurelia pointed at him and shouted something unintelligible. Kaden shivered, feeling cold rain splash against his skin. He looked down. He was naked. His hands dropped to cover himself, and he jumped behind a bush. "Aurelia! What in the Abyss did you do?"

Aurelia stared at him blankly. "Kaden? It's you? I thought you were a bear."

"Why in the name of Haedis would you think that?"

She stuck her hands on her hips. "You looked like some huge, lumbering beast coming at me. I couldn't see your face. How was I supposed to know it was you?"

Rain plastered Kaden's hair to his head. Goose pimples rose on his arms and legs. "You had best make my clothes reappear."

"Oh. Of course. I'm sorry. I don't know what happened. The spell was supposed to make bears disappear, but instead it made your clothes disappear, and — oh, I see. The spell invoked bare as in naked, rather than bear, the animal —"

"Aurelia!"

"Yes, yes. Let me think." She closed her eyes and put her hand to her forehead.

Kaden shivered again and tried to shrink into the bush.

"Perhaps you would like this," said an amused voice behind him.

Kaden spun around.

Tara Triannon stood behind him, grinning. She held out a horse blanket. Beside her, two horses stamped and snorted, held lightly by the reins.

Mortified, Kaden snatched the blanket and wrapped it around his waist.

Laraina ran up, clutching her bag of supplies. "What happened? I heard screaming!" She looked at Kaden. "What happened to you?"

"Let me guess," said Tara. "Aurelia cast a spell."

Laraina's lips twitched, and she put her hand to her mouth to hide a smile.

"I know!" said Aurelia. She pointed at Kaden again and blurted out a phrase.

Kaden's clothing reappeared on him, including blouse, skirt, and cloaks.

"It worked!" Aurelia clapped her hands with glee.

Tara raised her eyebrows. "Interesting choice of attire." She looked at Laraina. A chuckle slipped out and they dissolved into laughter. Covering their mouths to muffle the sound, they laughed until tears came to their eyes.

Kaden glared. "I see nothing funny about this." He stripped off the extra clothing.

"I'm sorry," Laraina said, regaining her composure, "but you just look so..."

"Matronly?" suggested Tara, wiping her eyes and grinning.

Laraina laughed in spite of herself. Still chuckling, she collected the cloaks, blouse, and skirt. "Dear Kaden, if you could only have seen yourself in a mirror."

He snorted and said nothing.

Laraina handed the skirt, blouse, and a cloak to Aurelia. "Put these on. And here are the boots I promised."

Aurelia examined the clothing with distaste. "I can't wear these. They're huge!"

"Put them on and be quick about it," snapped Kaden.

As Aurelia slipped on the blouse and skirt, Laraina donned a cloak and gave the remaining one to Tara.

They mounted the horses, Laraina and Tara on one, and Kaden and Aurelia on the other, and headed south toward Mardainn.

*****

Captain Natiere adjusted the saddle on his dark bay stallion as the cold light of dawn filtered through the drizzling rain. Ah, it was good to be back out in the field again — to breathe the chill, spicy air of spring, to taste the rain — to be away from the constraints of the army and the constant demands of General Caldren. The General had grown increasingly vicious and unstable. This war of his, this personal vendetta — the Captain wanted no part of it. His had always been a solitary existence.

For years Natiere had tramped the wilds alone, following an avowed path of vengeance, pursuing his own brutal form of justice. Faces passed before his eyes — men screaming, babbling, weeping — faces that once grinned and taunted and sneered at their victims' pain. He had made it his purpose to see them twisted and bleeding, wallowing in their own agony. The more they screamed and begged for mercy, the harsher their punishment; he had no use for cowards.

Fourteen years he'd spent scouring the kingdoms and territories from the lawless Eastern Frontier of his birth to the far reaches of the more civilized West, searching, tracking his prey.

His journey had ended in Sulledor some four years earlier. The fulfillment of his vengeful quest, however, had placed him at odds with General Caldren who did not take kindly to losing one of his men. They had come to terms when Natiere, now facing a life without purpose, agreed to serve as the General's chief executioner.

The partnership had been tolerable, even enjoyable at times depending on the assignment, but now it was beginning to wear. Restlessness welled inside him. The sounds and scents of earth and forest called to him. It was time to move on.

His mind shifted back to his present assignment — his last, he decided — to track down and dispose of the prince of Dhanarra and the Triannons. Natiere smiled. His wolfen spirit relished the hunt. He even had a worthy opponent this time. He had heard of the Triannon sisters. Who hadn't? Fire and Ice they were often called — Laraina, the redhead with her fiery temper and passionate love affairs, and Tara, the cold one, a left-handed swordswoman afraid of nothing and no one. They were smugglers, adventurers, soldiers of fortune. Their knack for doing the impossible — and living to tell about it — was legendary. And though the prince was his primary target, it was these two that interested him, or rather one of them. Tara Triannon, with her strange silver-blue eyes and long, silver-blonde hair...

The surrounding hills and darkened castle fell away, the gray sky fading to black as his mind's eye turned inward, and he saw once more the interior of a gypsy wagon, jumbled and cluttered in the faint light. Pain racked his fourteen-year-old body. His mind reeled from the horrific trauma he had endured. He wanted to die. A voice wouldn't let him. "Live. Fight. Be strong," it said. A face hovered over his, a man's face, old and wizened. Something was poured down his throat, a concoction, he learned later, of nyelil leaves, human ashes, and wolf's blood. "Vengeance will be yours," the man had said. "I have given you the means. The blood of the wolf will allow you to see that justice is done. But have caution. Your future will be grim and hard. Beware the silver-haired witch. She will be your redemption... and your downfall."

A vision of a woman with long, silvery hair — beautiful beyond description — coalesced in his mind. She stood straight and strong and wore a sword on her right hip.

Beware the witch...

Such had been the words of the craggy-faced gypsy warlock who had healed him after the horror that had ended life as he had known it. He'd spent eight years with the gypsies. It had taken him that long to recover mentally, to condition himself, to hone his skills for the task that lay ahead.

The rain beat harder, coursing down his furred cloak in rivulets. He pulled his mind back to the present, anticipation rising within him. He had been waiting for this moment, he realized, for the last four years.

Beware the witch...

His vision had a real face now. The witch of his dream had suddenly become flesh and blood. Her appearance in Castle Carilon had shocked him. He had never really believed she existed, that the silver-haired Triannon of whom he had heard and the silver-haired witch were one and the same.

The gypsy's warning whispered through his mind again, but he brushed it aside. He was beyond redemption. His fate would be as it would. The hunt was all that mattered to him now. He gazed out across the rugged expanse to the east. His quarry had a fair head-start, and this rain would obscure their tracks. He smiled again. So much the better.

Approaching hoofbeats interrupted his thoughts. Four men rode into view. Three of them stopped a short distance away. The fourth, a tall, wiry man with stringy blond hair and beard, drew his horse to a halt a few feet from Natiere.

"We got a report of a disturbance in Kite," he said. "Something about a woman screaming and some stolen property replaced by bags of gold."

The Triannon trademark. The Captain felt a sliver of disappointment. It would be too easy.

"So they have gone south," he said aloud, "hoping to enlist the aid of Mardainn, no doubt." He gave a short laugh. "Won't they be in for a surprise."

He mounted his bay, and the five galloped southward.

CHAPTER 3

"There they are, just beyond those scrub trees." Parting the brush at the top of the narrow ridge, Tara pointed toward the approaching riders who'd been pursuing them relentlessly for the past ten days.

Laraina nodded. "I see them. They're gaining."

"They're not more than an hour behind us, if that," Tara said. "We can't rest here long."

"But we have to rest," Laraina said. "The horses are about to drop."

"I know. They're spent. But we can't let those riders get much closer."

It was late afternoon. The storm clouds that had been gathering all morning were now amassing in earnest, promising a major assault.

Tara surveyed the surrounding area. The rough terrain had grown mountainous since crossing the Mardainn border the day before. The deep red rocks of the Scarlet Mountains towered over them like bloody sentinels, terrible reminders of an ancient war that had annihilated the two races of Dwarves that once dwelled there. The ridge where Tara and Laraina stood extended a short distance to the left before rising to a dizzying height. The scarlet face of the cliff gleamed dully from the intermittent rain that had plagued them ever since they'd left Carilon. Off to the right, the ridge fell away gradually, curling around until it reached the rock-strewn floor of the rugged valley below.

Tara's gaze settled once more on the riders. Far down the valley they came, weaving in and out of the rocks, unerringly following an invisible trail. She knew who pursued them, and the knowledge chilled her.

"About warning Faragellyn," Laraina said. "We don't have to talk to King du Mraine ourselves, do we? Kaden could warn him about the coming attack."

Tara pried her thoughts away from the riders. "Are you worried about Prince Fournier?"

"Well, we didn't part on very good terms," Laraina said.

Tara shot her a sidelong glance. "That's putting it mildly."

Their conversation ended as Kaden climbed up beside them. He stared out across the rocky expanse, watching the rapidly advancing shapes. "How could they have followed us so closely? The rain should have covered our tracks."

"It's going to take a lot more than rain to slow them down," Tara said grimly. "The Captain is well known for his persistence."

"Captain? You mean Captain Natiere? The Butcher?"

Tara nodded. "No one else could have followed us this closely. We need a better way to hide our trail."

Kaden wiped the sweat from his face with a handkerchief. "There is no trail. The rain washed it away. How can he follow something that isn't there?"

Tara shrugged. "I don't know. It's like he's part wolf. He can track anything, anywhere — and he never quits. I've seen his hand-iwork; it's not pretty."

"He leaves bodies in pieces," Laraina said. "We found one outside Vaalderin about seven years ago, just after we left Blackie de Runo and his band." She shivered. "Another body was found in Darbry." Tara nodded. "Natiere was like a shadow. He appeared, someone died, he disappeared. And it wasn't so much that they died, but how they died. Tortured beyond comprehension. The attacks seemed random, although they may not have been. Who knows?"

Kaden looked back at the riders. "You said you knew who had murdered my father. It was Natiere, wasn't it?"

"Yes."

"Then our course of action is clear. We let him come to us, and I'll kill him."

"Don't be an idiot," Tara said impatiently. "The Butcher is a master swordsman. *You* can't kill him." She tipped her head toward Laraina. "I'm not even sure we could. We'll have to outrun him until we think of something better."

Kaden bristled. "Is that your usual strategy — to run like a frightened rabbit?"

Tara's sword was at Kaden's throat before he could move. "You won't have to worry about the Butcher. I will kill you first."

"Tara! Enough!" Laraina grabbed Tara's shoulder and pulled her away. "If you can't respect him, you should at least respect his office. He is now king of Dhanarra."

"He's not my king," Tara retorted. "I'm not Dhanarran, and neither are you."

"We're not murderers, either." Laraina pointed at Tara's sword. "So put that away." She turned to Kaden. "Tara is right about outrunning them though. There are five of them and only three of us who can fight. If not for yourself, then think of Aurelia. Who will protect her?"

Kaden clenched and unclenched his fists. "What do you suggest?"

"We'll have to go where they can't follow, or at least where it will be a little more difficult." Tara sheathed her blade.

"You have something in mind?" Laraina asked.

"Yes, but you're not going to like it."

Laraina's eyes widened. "You're not suggesting..."

"You have a better idea?"

"Talk so I can understand you!" Prince Kaden demanded.

"She is suggesting we go into the Bog," said Laraina.

Kaden regarded them as if they had professed a desire to dive into a pit of quicksand. "You want to go into the Bog? We would die for certain!"

"Not necessarily," said Tara. "Vaalderin is only a couple of hours from here. If we could find someone who knows the territory to act as a guide —"

"Vaalderin! The city of thieves and cutthroats?" The tall prince sneered. "We might as well face the Captain and have done with it!"

"It's not that bad," Laraina said. "We've been in Vaalderin plenty of times without being attacked."

"And a few times when we have been," Tara added with a smile.

Laraina glared at her. "You're a big help."

"Even if you did find someone to act as a guide," Kaden said, "we'd never get through alive."

"That may be so," Tara countered, "but I would rather die in the Bog than be tortured by Captain Natiere."

Kaden didn't reply.

Laraina turned to her sister. "What's your plan?"

"I don't know yet, but I'll think of something." Tara glanced at the riders who were getting dangerously close. "We have to move. Now." She turned to go.

"But the horses," Laraina said, following after her. "Will they carry us that far with so little rest?"

"They'll have to," Tara said over her shoulder, "or we're in trouble."

They slid down the barren slope to the shallow gully where they had left the horses. Aurelia sat on a rock with her eyes closed and her cloak wrapped tightly about her. As Kaden and Tara untied the horses, she opened her eyes.

"What are you doing? We just got here!"

"We can't wait any longer." Tara mounted her horse.

"A few more minutes won't matter," Aurelia pleaded. "I'm exhausted, and I hurt all over."

"There's no time —" Prince Kaden began.

"Let me put it plainly," interrupted Tara as she pulled Laraina up behind her. "Either you get on that horse now, or we'll leave without you."

Aurelia got on the horse. Kaden swung up behind her, and they turned the animals' heads to the south, working their way through the rocks.

The going proved slow and difficult. Ragged peaks, deep red against the sullen sky, stretched away to the far horizon, broken by rocky slopes, shadowed canyons, and treacherous, steep-walled gullies. The exhausted horses stumbled frequently on the rough terrain. A sharp wind rose as they crested another ridge, piercing their heavy cloaks with its numbing chill. Tara kept a close watch behind them, expecting to see Natiere and his men at any moment, but an hour passed, then two, and still they did not appear.

At the edge of a narrow trail, Tara reined in her laboring horse. Pounded smooth by decades of travel, the well-worn trail curled lazily around through the scarlet rocks in the direction of Vaalderin.

"Look familiar?" Tara asked over her shoulder.

"Very," replied Laraina.

"I assume it goes to Vaalderin?" Kaden asked.

"That it does," said Laraina. "It's the roundabout route between Vaalderin and Desta —" She broke off sharply. "Did you hear something?"

Tara's eyes swept the path behind them. "I'm not sure, and I'm not staying around to find out."

She kicked her reluctant horse into a canter and plunged down the southward trail, followed closely by Prince Kaden and Aurelia. At the top of a deep, narrow gorge, Tara pulled up short.

Kaden drew alongside her. "What's wrong?"

"Finger Pass," said Tara. She scanned the shadowy floor of the defile for any sign of movement. "There are usually bandits at the far end. Collecting tolls you might say. Anyone who can't pay loses a finger."

Kaden grimaced. "Is there any way around it?"

"No, this is it," said Tara. "The quickest road to decadence you'll ever hope to find. Stay close and let us do the talking. And watch out for the bats."

"B-b-bats?" quavered Aurelia.

They picked their way down into the gorge. The shadows deepened, concealing the stagnant pools of foul green slime that marred the smooth floor of the gully. The moldy air grew chill and damp. A hollow silence descended, broken only by the splashing hoofbeats, the creak of saddle leather, and the incessant drip of water off the sheer vertical walls.

Tara's horse balked as the defile narrowed and veered to the left, the walls leaning in at the top to form a natural tunnel. Stroking her mount's lathered neck, she urged the skittish animal forward. They rounded the bend into dungeon-like blackness.

A sudden high-pitched screeching filled their ears. Something small and dark whizzed past them with a whisper of leathery wings.

Within seconds, the air swarmed with small, furry creatures darting in and out around them.

Aurelia shrieked. "Get away! Get away!"

"Quiet!" Tara ordered as she fought to control her shying horse. She dug her heels into her mount. She heard the clatter of hooves behind her as Kaden's horse followed. They charged forward toward the growing point of light that marked the end of the gully and the beginning of a small rock-strewn canyon.

A stabbing chill, sharp with warning, jolted Tara. At the head of the canyon, she reined in her horse and drew her sword. Laraina unsheathed hers as well. Kaden brought his horse up behind them and pulled his blade free.

"Stay close," Tara whispered.

She urged her quivering mount into the canyon. Boulders and brush obscured the path. An assortment of fingers, some bleached bone, some with flesh still attached, hung from the surrounding bushes.

They had taken only a few steps when a horde of shadowy figures encircled them.

Aurelia screamed. Kaden growled an epithet.

The bandits eyed them warily. A tall, scrawny man with a wild shock of dark hair strode out from behind a boulder and halted mid-step. A look that expressed an intense desire to be somewhere else flitted across his face. "Well now, the Triannon sisters. Been a long time."

"Not long enough," Tara said, recognizing him. "You'll get nothing from us, so either draw your swords or get out of the way. We're in a hurry."

The thief hesitated.

"Is it worth the number of men you'll lose?" Laraina asked, pointing her blade at the thief's men.

The bandits backed away.

Seeing his men retreating, the thief bowed low and gave his captives a wide, gap-toothed smile. "We will let you pass this once, for old time's sake."

He motioned to his men to withdraw. Two of the thieves removed a rope that had been strung across the canyon to unhorse anyone who tried to barge through without paying the toll.

The thief smiled and bowed again. "You are free to go."

"Thank you," said Tara dryly. "And because you have been so generous, I'll give you a piece of advice. Another party will be coming through here shortly led by Captain Natiere. If I were you, I wouldn't bother him."

Horror replaced the thief's smile. He bounded into the rocks. His men had already disappeared.

Laraina sheathed her sword. "That was nice of you."

"I wouldn't wish that fate on anyone, not even a bandit," Tara said.

"Who was that?" asked Kaden. "He seemed to know you quite well."

"His name is Rafflen," Tara said, "and he's just one of the friendly thieves and cutthroats that populate the fair city of Vaalderin."

"He's really not that bad," said Laraina.

"But don't worry," Tara added, "we'll find plenty more who are."

Prince Kaden glowered and said nothing.

The wind rose steadily, sending dark clouds of dirt and debris swirling around them as they rode on through the canyon. They passed dozens of hanging fingers, swinging in the stiff breeze. Aurelia shrank against Kaden to avoid being touched.

Tara glanced at the black sky. "Looks like we're in for it this time."

Laraina nodded.

They urged their sagging mounts forward up the winding trail that led out of the canyon. A few minutes later they emerged on top of a low ridge. In the rocky valley below sprawled the festering city of Vaalderin, its once beautiful crimson stone buildings now cracked and crumbling.

For decades, Vaalderin had been a highly prosperous mining town, but a massive earthquake had collapsed the mine, taking the lives of more than half the townspeople. The survivors had moved on, leaving it stark and abandoned — a ghost town. Shortly after, the looters had moved in, followed by vagabonds, gypsies, rogues and scoundrels, thieves and assassins — all the dregs of society. The city of Vaalderin soon became known as a haven for anyone who didn't belong anywhere else.

Tara and the others dismounted. A premature darkness was settling over the valley like a sinister shadow, making it difficult to see. Thunder rumbled in the distance.

"Phew! What's that horrible smell?" Aurelia wrinkled her nose in disgust.

"If you think it's bad now, you should be here in the summer," Tara said as she hooked the stirrup over the saddlehorn and began loosening the girth.

"Don't worry, you'll get used to it," said Laraina.

"We can't go down there," Aurelia said. "Those buildings look like they'll fall on our heads."

"Only during earthquakes," said Laraina.

"You can stay here if you like," Tara said, "and give my regards to the Captain when he comes through."

Aurelia brightened. "I know a spell that will —"

Tara whirled, her finger pointing in Aurelia's face. "If I hear any word from you that sounds like magic, I will gag you with a horse rag."

Prince Kaden stepped in front of Aurelia. "I told you to leave her alone."

Tara raised her eyebrows. "You would prefer she cast more spells? Perhaps you like being naked."

"There's no time for arguing," Laraina said. "We have to do something with these horses. They'll draw too much attention if we take them into town."

"We'll let them go now," Tara said. She turned back to her mount, pulled off the saddle and unbuckled the bridle.

"You did well, boy," she whispered, patting her horse's sweaty neck. "May you find a kind owner."

She hid the gear behind a tangled thicket of brush and briars. Kaden removed the tack from his horse and added it to the pile. Laraina slapped the horses on the flanks and sent them trotting off through the rocks to the west.

Thunder rolled ominously, much closer now, as Tara and the others half climbed, half slid down the steep rocky slope to the edge of the rotting city. Vaalderin was surrounded by a high stone wall, once impenetrable, but now filled with countless gaping holes. The once polished main gate creaked painfully as it rocked back and forth in the wind. When they reached the wall, Tara halted and pulled the hood of her dark cloak over her head to conceal her conspicuous hair. Laraina did the same, and then turned to Prince Kaden and Aurelia.

"Keep your hoods on at all times and don't talk to anyone. We don't want you to be recognized."

They adjusted their hoods and followed Tara into the city.

*****

Captain Natiere stood on the low ridge overlooking the squalid city, his memory stirring at the unpleasantly familiar sight. Many years had passed since he had been in Vaalderin. Judging from the smell, the quality of life there hadn't improved.

His mind slipped back, remembering with satisfaction a body left in pieces just outside the wall of the city, the gratifying results of a long chase. From the dead man's hand, Natiere had recovered his father's signet ring, an heirloom he'd thought irretrievably lost. The emerald green stone glittered on his own finger now, and a piece of the dead man's skull had been added to the ten others stored in the pouch at his belt. He'd added six more before he was through.

A wild howl rose into the sky, the cry of a wolf on the hunt. Natiere grinned as the sound echoed in his heart. *Well met, my Brother,* he said silently. *I, too, am on the hunt. How long it has been.*

The sound of shifting feet snapped his mind back to the present. His men were growing restless. He signaled them forward and started down the rocky slope.

*****

Confusion reigned inside the broken walls of the city. People shouted, fought, swarmed through the garbage-lined streets, heading for shelter, fleeing the approaching storm. Traveling black-marketers were closing up their brightly colored wagons and muttering about evil spirits in the air.

Tara scanned the crowd and, sensing no immediate danger, turned off the main thoroughfare into a narrow alley that reeked of filth and decay. She led them swiftly through a maze of darkened side streets to a dilapidated inn. Above the door, a wooden sign with a faded red rose dangled from one rusted hook.

Inside, most of the scarred wooden tables and benches were already filled. Tara led the way to the bar where the innkeeper, a dour-looking man with an enormous pot belly, was filling mugs with ale.

"Well, well, look who's here," the innkeeper said with a smile that transformed his face. "You want a room or you just passing through?"

"Yes," Tara said with a grin.

Laraina laughed. "A room and something to eat. And some supplies if you can manage it," she added in a low voice. "We may have to leave in a hurry."

He grunted. "As usual." He filled another mug with the sour-smelling ale. "Room's upstairs. Third on the left. Sheila'll bring you up something."

Tara placed a few extra coins on the bar. "Thanks, and keep your eyes open, will you?"

He scooped up the coins. "Don't I always?"

They climbed the creaky stairs to their room. As Kaden ushered Aurelia inside, Tara caught her sister's arm, detaining her. "Stay here and keep an eye on them. I'll see what I can find out about a guide."

"You sure you don't want me to come with you?" Laraina asked.

"I'm sure. Someone has to stay with them, and I would rather face an entire army than be cooped up with either one of them."

"All right, but be careful!"

Tara smiled. "Always. If I'm not back in an hour, leave town and head for the Bog. Don't wait for me." She skimmed down the back stairs and out through a side door.

It was pouring. Thunder cracked and lightning slashed the sky as Tara pushed her way through the dwindling crowd toward the center of the city. Pulling her cloak tight against the driving wind, Tara searched her memory for the locations of the most popular taverns. She rounded a corner and recognized a dingy alehouse, its doorway crammed with people.

That's as good a place to start as any, she thought. She ran across the muddy street to the door. She was just about to dash inside when she noticed a large figure with a slight limp hurrying toward the tavern from the opposite direction. He looked strangely familiar. As he drew closer, she saw that he was wrapped in a heavy cloak and had a battered, black tricorn hat jammed on his head.

It can't be, she thought. She stood on her tiptoes and tried to see over the throng that pressed forward into the tavern. She caught another glimpse of him as he neared the door. The rumpled black hat was unmistakable. Dominic! With an inward cry of joy, she shoved into the crowd, elbowing her way through in an attempt to catch him before he went inside. She broke out of the crowd, tripped over someone's foot, and nearly fell into his arms.

"Whoa, there!" he said in his booming voice as he caught and steadied her. "Are you —"

He gaped as her hood slipped back just enough to reveal a wisp of silver-blonde hair. "Well, I'll be a fried sardine!" He swept her up in an enormous bear hug.

"Hey, take it easy!" she protested, laughing. "At least let me breathe!"

He chuckled as he released her. "I don't believe it!" He glanced around. "Where's —"

Tara put her hand over his mouth. "Not here," she whispered. "Is there someplace we can talk? I need your help."

Dominic rolled his eyes. "In trouble again. I might have known." Smiling and shaking his head, he led the way back up the street. "This way."

They splashed through the growing puddles to a nearby inn. Dominic, a portly man with a balding pate, led them to a small room in the back sparsely furnished with a dingy-looking bed, a rickety table and chair, and a wash stand. Shaking the water from their cloaks, Tara and Dominic hung them on the chair next to the fireplace.

Tara sat on the bed. "I see you still have your lucky hat."

"Wouldn't be without it." Dominic brushed the rain off the well-worn hat and laid it on the chair.

"It's so good to see you again," Tara said with a smile. "What are you doing here? You're supposed to be a merchant now. You retired from adventuring, remember?"

"I'm on a business trip." The big man tossed some wood and kindling into the fireplace and started a blaze.

"To Vaalderin?" Tara asked dubiously.

"There are a lot of business people in Vaalderin."

"Yes, if you're a smuggler." Tara grinned. "I can't believe you're here. How long has it been? Four years?"

Dominic snorted. "Not long enough for me to have recovered from your last crazy scheme." He turned away from the fire. "I'll listen to your story, but you can count me out of the action this time."

"Oh come now," she teased. "Has retirement killed your sense of adventure? You used to love the thrill of danger, not to mention the rewards we picked up afterward."

"That was a long time ago," he said, but his eyes twinkled. "Besides, the last time you needed my help, we ended up in Lord Cranyl's dungeon."

Tara laughed. "What are you complaining about? We escaped, didn't we?"

"Escaped!" Dominic snorted again. "By the seat of our pants. And I've got these white hairs to show for it." He ran a hand over the tufts of white hair on his balding head.

"All right," Tara said, "I'll admit the plan might have been a bit risky —"

"A bit?"

"— but it worked, and you can't honestly say you didn't enjoy every minute of it."

Dominic laughed, his burly arms clasped about his considerable girth.

"You'll like this one even better," Tara added. "It's much worse."

"I'm sure it is," he said, still chuckling.

The fire burned brightly now, the leaping flames giving off a cozy warmth. Dominic limped to the washstand.

"Seriously, Dominic, I do need your help."

Dominic picked up a stained towel and wiped the rainwater from his face. "Who's after you this time?"

"Captain Natiere."

The towel dropped from Dominic's fingers. *"The Butcher?"*

Tara nodded.

"What in the name of the great god Azakai did you do?" He held up his hands. "Never mind. I don't want to know."

"I didn't actually do anything," Tara said. "General Caldren and his army have invaded Dhanarra, and I think they're on their way to Faragellyn."

"What?" Dominic shouted.

"Shhh! Not so loud," she warned. "Laraina and I were in the castle when they attacked."

Dominic made a wry face. "Raina'd taken a fancy to the prince, I'll wager."

Tara smiled. "How'd you guess?" She sobered. "The king was murdered. We managed to escape — 'by the seat of our pants' as you put it."

"Who's we?"

"Laraina and myself, the prince, and his cousin, Aurelia. We arrived in Vaalderin just before I ran into you. Natiere is right behind us. In fact, he's probably in the city by now."

"I see." Dominic's broad face was grim. "And just what exactly is it that you want me to do?"

"I don't want you to *do* anything. I just need to know if there's anyone in the city who knows the area well and would be willing to guide us over the mountains to Desta and then through the Bog into Faragellyn."

"The Bog! You can't go into the Bog. Not even you would —"

"What choice do we have?" Tara interrupted. "He'll follow us wherever we go. We can't risk an open fight with Kaden and Aurelia here, and we need to warn the Faragellyn king that the Sulledorns are going to attack. If we can reach Crystalir, we'll have the Faragellyn army on our side, and then maybe we'll have a chance. At least then, Kaden and Aurelia will be safe. But the only way I can see to get rid of Natiere and still get to Faragellyn is through the Bog. If we can't get anyone to take us, we'll just have to find our own way through."

Dominic guffawed. "And I thought you were crazy before."

"I'm not asking you to come with us. I just need a name."

"You're really going to do this."

"You have a better idea?"

He didn't answer. He picked up the towel he'd dropped and laid it on the washstand, folding it carefully. "There's only one man I can think of who might — and I emphasize the word *might* — be willing to take you, but it'll cost you plenty. How much have you got?"

She named a sum.

"It won't be enough."

"I'll worry about that later. What's his name, and where can I find him?"

"His name's Trevillion. Jovan Trevillion. He's most likely at the *Blue Swan.*"

"Trevillion. I've heard of him. A soldier of fortune. Handy with a sword, but unpredictable and a little crazy."

"A little?" Dominic laughed shortly. "He's as crazy as you are."

"Then we should get along just fine."

"More likely you'll be at each other's throats."

Tara ignored that remark. "What else do you know about him?"

Dominic scratched his head. "Not much. I've heard several stories. He had an older brother who was quite the troublemaker. Rumor has it they were somehow mixed up in the mysterious disappearance of the boy king of Sulledor twelve years ago — the missing King who was, by the way, General Caldren's younger cousin. In the chaos that followed, the General was quick to lay claim to the throne, and anyone who disagreed with him — zzzt." Dominic slid his finger across his throat.

"You said Trevillion had an older brother. Is he dead?"

Dominic shrugged. "No one knows. No one's seen or heard from him in twelve years."

"What makes you think Trevillion can help us?"

"Well, he's been in the Bog at least once. The stories are a bit mangled but from what I can put together, he forced a handful of men to go into the Bog with him to help search for his brother. What his brother was doing in there I have no idea. Trevillion was the only one who came back. Who knows what happened to the others. They vanished — along with his brother and the missing King.

"Trevillion dropped out of sight after that. Both Sulledor and the Mardainn council had warrants out for his arrest, but they couldn't find him."

"Did they have proof of his guilt?"

"No. They had nothing. I think the General himself was responsible for the king's disappearance — he and his Mardainn flunky Councilman Jarnik." Dominic spat out the name in disgust. "But there's no proof of that either. Jovan Trevillion was likely just a scapegoat, though his brother may well have been involved."

"What about Trevillion?" Tara cut in. "Is he still wanted?"

"Yes, by some people anyway. He resurfaced a few years ago. He took a lot of mercenary jobs, lived recklessly. It was like he was deliberately trying to get himself killed. Soldiers from Sulledor and Mardainn tried to arrest him but they were never able to."

Dominic chuckled. "It's ironic, but I think their constant pursuit brought him back from the edge. He stopped taking the suicidal jobs and instead made it his purpose in life to harass the people who were harassing him. He got so crazy that even the bounty hunters refused to go after him. But he's calmed down a bit, or so I've heard. They say, though, that there's still something eating away at him. Maybe he's still bothered by whatever happened in the Bog all those years ago."

Dominic paused, then continued. "He does have a reputation for earning his money, and he's the only man I know of that's gone into the Bog and come out alive. But whether or not he'd be willing to go back there is another story." Dominic hesitated. "I'm not so sure I'd want to be with him if he did."

Tara digested this information. "We'll just have to take the chance," she said finally. "It should be interesting to see if I remember my back alleys well enough to find the *Blue Swan*." She rose.

"You won't have to. I'll take you."

Tara frowned, noting the growing gleam in Dominic's eyes. "You don't —"

"I know I don't," he interrupted, "but I insist. One last fling for old times' sake." He banked the fire and retrieved their cloaks. "Coming?"

She laid her hand on his shoulder. "Thanks, but the *Blue Swan* is as far as you go. I don't want Natiere after you, too."

"I wouldn't mention the Butcher to Trevillion if I were you," Dominic said. "You'll be lucky if he takes it as it is."

They scanned the alley before going out into the darkness. It was still pouring. Driving sheets of rain pummeled the stony faces of the forlorn buildings, gathering in puddles at their feet like great pools of tears. The biting wind whipped through the deserted streets, scattering refuse in all directions, but the jarring crash of thunder and lightning had lessened considerably, giving evidence that the storm would soon be over.

Bending their heads against the wind, Tara and Dominic splashed through the dirty side streets, following a circuitous route to the far side of the city. Dim rectangles of light spilled across their path accompanied by raucous laughter, the cacophony of drunken singing, and the occasional smash of breaking furniture as they hurried past numerous inns and taverns.

Dominic signaled for a halt at the edge of the wide avenue that had once been Vaalderin's main thoroughfare. Lined with crumbling shops, temples, and public buildings that had all been converted to alehouses, the avenue ran the entire length of the city, from gate to gate, effectively slicing the city in half.

Tara moved close to Dominic's ear so she could be heard over the wind. "It's only a few blocks from here, isn't it?"

He nodded and peered around the corner to his left. He drew back sharply. "Someone's coming."

"Let me see." Tara pushed past him. She saw a figure, hunched against the storm, hurrying up the street toward her. An icy chill of warning crept down her spine, and even though she'd never seen any of Natiere's men before, she knew for certain that he was one of them. She glanced back down the long alley. There wasn't time to retreat. Better to attack while they had the element of surprise.

She flattened herself against the wall, her left hand curling around the hilt of her sword. Dominic tensed beside her. Carefully, she drew her sword from its sheath. The figure approached, his sloshing footsteps barely audible over the wind. They waited, poised for attack. The figure advanced until he was nearly abreast of them, then turned and vaulted up the steps of the tavern beside them. A harsh clamor burst out as he yanked open the door and went inside, then cut off abruptly as the door banged shut behind him.

Tara relaxed and sheathed her sword. Before Dominic could speak, she dragged him back down the alley. "That was one of Natiere's men. We'll have to cross further up. Quickly! Come on!"

They hastened through several more streets thick with the stench of garbage and excrement. A few minutes later they arrived once more at the brink of the wide avenue. There was no one in sight. Only the dimly lighted windows stared back at them, revealing nothing of the nightmarish hunter harbored somewhere within. Dominic glanced at Tara. She nodded and they sped across the avenue into the shadows of a rotten alley. The *Blue Swan* lay only a block or two away. They rounded a corner. Tara slid to a halt as an icy chill gripped her.

"Dominic, look out!" she cried.

A pair of hooded thieves leaped from the shadows in a sinuous blur of motion, their dark cloaks billowing, their knives held high. Tara kicked the knife out of the first one's hand, while Dominic grappled with the second. Then she smashed a wicked left cross into the startled thief's face. The thief staggered back, flailing as he slipped in the mud. Tara sprang forward, grasped his arm, and swung him headfirst into the wall. He crumpled to the ground. She turned in time to see Dominic lay his man out flat with a nasty uppercut. She clapped him on the back as he stood rubbing his knuckles.

"I see you haven't lost your touch."

He grinned, looking extremely pleased with himself.

Tara bent down and examined the unconscious thief.

"Not one of your... um... friends, is he?" Dominic asked.

"No, just one of the locals." Another icy chill stung her and she whirled, her hand flying to her sword. There was no one there.

"What? What is it?" Dominic cried in alarm.

Tara glanced around, searching the shadows, then focused again on the alley behind her. "Someone was watching us. Come on!"

They raced down two more streets, fleeing the terrifying shadow that Tara knew was close behind them. There was very little time. She wished Dominic hadn't insisted on coming. If anything happened to him...

"There it is!" Dominic pointed to a decayed building just up the street. They ran to the tavern and ducked around the far side. Tara looked back the way they'd come but saw no one following. Dominic pulled open the door and a blast of stifling heat from the huge roaring fire struck them, mixed with the smells of sweat and sour ale.

A boisterous crowd filled the tavern. Dominic squeezed his way through the closely-packed tables and headed for the bar. Tara followed, readjusting her hood to conceal her face and hair. Dozens of conversations, punctuated by laughter and curses, jumbled together around her.

"You want anything?" Dominic asked as she came up beside him.

She grimaced. "No. Is he here?"

Dominic turned to the bartender and said, "Just two," and dropped some coins on the counter. "Table in the far corner," he whispered out of the side of his mouth as the bartender poured the drinks.

Tara took in the whole room, her eyes catching on the man at the corner table. She caught her breath. He was dark-haired with a few days' growth of beard, broad shouldered, well-muscled, and without a doubt the best looking man she had ever seen.

"Great. That's just what I need," she muttered. She'd had enough of roguishly handsome men.

"Did you say something?" asked Dominic as he picked up the drinks and turned away from the bar.

"No," she grumbled.

He glanced at her quizzically. "You'd better let me do the talking."

Tara started to object, but Dominic was already threading his way through the crowd. With a sigh of exasperation, she followed, and, glancing at the man in the corner again, she had the distinct impression he was watching them over the rim of his mug.

Dominic proceeded directly to the corner table and, without ceremony, plopped one of the drinks down in front of the man sitting there.

"Mind if we join you?" Dominic sat down without waiting for an answer.

Tara sat beside him, positioning herself so she could watch both the front and back doors.

"Not at all," Jovan Trevillion responded with amused sarcasm, picking up the full mug and indicating with a wave of his hand the seats they had already taken. "What can I do for you?"

Dominic took a large swig from his mug and wiped his mouth on his sleeve. "I'll come right to the point because time is short. We want to hire you as a guide to take us through the Bog to Faragellyn."

"We?" asked Tara.

"What?" Trevillion asked simultaneously.

"Yes we, and you heard me," replied Dominic, addressing first Tara, then Trevillion.

"Dominic —" Tara began.

"I'm coming with you," he stated firmly.

"You want me to do what?" Trevillion asked again.

"We want you to take us through the Bog to Faragellyn," Dominic repeated.

Tara scowled at Dominic. "You're not going."

Trevillion held up his hands for silence. "You want me to take the two of you —"

"Four of us," Tara corrected.

"Five," said Dominic. "Two men and three women."

Tara glared at Dominic, and Trevillion regarded them dubiously.

"Do you want to die that badly?"

"Some adventurer you are," Tara said.

Trevillion laughed humorlessly. "Going into the Bog with an old man and three women would be suicide."

"Two of those women can handle a sword as well as you can, if not better," Tara retorted.

"Indeed." Trevillion smiled with amusement. "Now that I would like to see."

Dominic gave a sigh of resignation and sat back with his drink.

"I'd be more than happy to demonstrate," Tara said, "but we're in a bit of a hurry. Since you're obviously not interested in this little adventure, we will leave you to your drink. I apologize for wasting your time."

She began to rise, but Dominic pulled her back down.

"Not so fast. We can't go into the Bog on our own. We know nothing about it."

"Don't tell me what I can't do," she snapped.

Trevillion stared at her. "And they said *I* was crazy. Two men and three women, and you've never even been in the Bog? You wouldn't get two miles."

"Well, if you aren't there you won't have to worry about it, will you?" she shot back.

She turned to Dominic, then suddenly froze, cold jabs cutting through her. She dragged him to his feet. "Find Raina and get out of town! She's at the *Red Rose*. Don't wait for me, I'll catch up when I can. Go!"

She shoved Dominic toward the back door just as two black-cloaked figures entered the front.

CHAPTER 4

"Tara, wait!"

Dominic's urgent whisper fell on deaf ears. Tara was already gone, slipping through the crowd toward the new arrivals. "Just like old times," he grumbled. "She never listens to me."

"Does she listen to anyone?" Trevillion asked, watching Tara progress through the crowd.

"No." Dominic tossed his empty mug onto the table. He nodded to Trevillion. "Another time."

Keeping his head low, Dominic squeezed along the wall to the back door. He stopped with his hand on the latch and looked back to see how Tara was faring.

The newcomers had reached the bar and were standing with their backs to it, their hooded eyes sweeping the crowd. Tara upended a table, showering them with stew and ale. Seizing a chair, she smashed it over the first one's head; she threw the remnants at the second one along with plates of food, mugs, bottles, and anything else she could lay her hands on. Her hood fell back, revealing her silver-blonde hair. Dominic heard Tara's name whispered in recognition; the murmur swept through the room. Several patrons, half-drunk and angry at losing their meals, upended more tables, greasing the floor with splattered food and ale as they lunged for Tara and the two black-cloaked men. Fights broke out amid yells and curses.

Dominic watched Tara battle her way to the front of the tavern, dodging brawlers and flying utensils, the two men in pursuit. A reeling man slammed her into the wall. Catching his arm, she braced herself, swung the man around, and threw him backwards at the large front window. He crashed through it, shattered glass exploding in all directions. Tara bounded through the gaping hole and disappeared into the stormy darkness, followed by the black-cloaked men.

"Confound it, Tara. You're going to get yourself killed," Dominic whispered. Cold wind and rain blew in through the broken window, soaking tables and brawlers. *How many times have I said that before*, he wondered. He eased out the back door into the rain.

Seeing no one about, Dominic limped down the alley and hurried toward the *Red Rose*. Tara and Laraina were in deep trouble this time. Captain Natiere would hunt them down until they were dead. Not only dead, but in pieces. He hoped that Laraina and her friends were still safe at the inn.

He turned a corner, tripped, and fell face first into the mud. Pain cracked through his ribs as a hard-toed boot kicked him up against the side of a building. Two men hauled him to his feet. One punched him in the belly. He doubled over with a groan.

Suddenly, the hands that gripped him were wrenched away. Dominic fell to his knees. One of his assailants spun across the alley, crashed into the opposite wall, and collapsed without a sound. The second dropped to the ground, his head bent at a ghastly angle. A shadowy figure appeared and held out his hand.

"You!" Dominic took the offered hand.

Jovan Trevillion helped him to his feet. "You all right?"

"I've been worse." Dominic clenched his teeth, keeping one arm clamped around his badly bruised ribs. "Thank you."

Trevillion picked up Dominic's tricorn hat, brushed it off, and handed it back to him. "You're welcome."

Shouts erupted from somewhere beyond the *Blue Swan*. Dominic looked back and saw Trevillion do the same. "She's crazy, but she's good," Dominic said. "She'll get away." If he said it often enough, he might make himself believe it.

Trevillion eyed him, as if gauging the truth of his words.

May the great god Azakai keep you safe, my girl, Dominic prayed. He whipped his head around as movement from a nearby alley caught the corner of his eye.

Trevillion propelled him forward. "Come. I'll see you to the inn."

Dominic limped along beside the silent Trevillion, keeping up the swift pace as best he could. He wanted to ask what had prompted the mysterious soldier of fortune to help him, but didn't quite dare.

They reached the *Red Rose* without further mishap. The dilapidated building had weathered the storm well. The only casualty was the battered sign which had lost its tenuous grip on the rusted hook and now stood upright, half buried in the mud.

"Looks like a creepin' gravestone," Dominic muttered as he and Trevillion stepped into the building.

The inn was packed. Travelers and townsfolk alike, in a sea of rain-darkened colors, sat crammed at the tables or stood with plates in hand, gobbling down their meals. Dominic elbowed his way to the bar. Trevillion followed.

The innkeeper glanced at Dominic, then turned so quickly his huge belly bumped into the counter. "What is this — a reunion? I thought you were respectable now."

"I was," Dominic said with a tight grin. "Where is she?"

"Upstairs. Third left."

Dominic reached across the bar and clapped the innkeeper on the shoulder. "Thanks. Good to see you again."

The innkeeper nodded, gave Trevillion the once over, and went about his business.

Dominic led the way up the stairs and down the dingy hall to the third door. He tapped softly once, waited a moment, then made four quick taps. The door opened, and a cloaked figure peered out at them.

"Dominic!" gasped Laraina, opening the door wide to let him in. She threw her arms around him in a warm embrace, her hood falling back to reveal her riot of red curls. "Of all the luck!" She stepped back and looked him over. "You look great!" She hugged him again.

Dominic winced. "Easy, there."

She released him quickly. "Are you hurt?"

"Just a bruise." He massaged his sore ribs as he stepped into the small room. "You say I look great? Look at you. You're as gorgeous as ever."

Trevillion entered the room and closed the door behind them.

"Who is he?" Laraina asked, glancing from Dominic to Trevillion. She gripped Dominic's arm. "Where's Tara?"

"Now don't get your curls in a knot," Dominic said. "This is Jovan Trevillion. He's been through the Bog, and he's... um... decided to throw in with us." He watched for Trevillion's reaction.

Trevillion merely smiled and nodded to Laraina, open admiration in his eyes. "A pleasure."

"Thank you," she said, returning his smile. "I'm glad to meet you." She turned back to Dominic. "Where is Tara?"

Dominic hesitated. "She's... um... playing hide and seek with Na —," he caught himself, "your friends from Carilon."

"And you let her go?" Laraina cried.

"And just how did you expect me to stop her?"

"I'm sorry. I just..." Laraina took a deep breath. "I'll go find her and —"

"No." Dominic placed his hands on her arms. "She told me to get you out of town, and she'll catch up as soon as she can."

Laraina bristled. "We can't leave her here! You know what will happen if they —"

"Tara can take care of herself," he said gently. "You know that as well as I do."

"But —"

Dominic raised his hands in a gesture of compromise. "We can wait outside of town. She's not likely to come back here."

Laraina chewed her lip. "All right, but if she's not back with us in an hour, I'm going after her."

Aurelia rose from the cot at the back of the room and came forward. "Aren't you going to introduce us?" She gave Trevillion a radiant smile.

Laraina started. "What? Oh." Turning to Trevillion, she said, "This is Aurelia."

Aurelia curtsied and held out her hand. Trevillion took it and raised it to his lips. "I am honored."

She smiled again and batted her eyes.

Kaden stepped forward, glaring at Trevillion.

"This is Kaden," Laraina said.

Trevillion gave a brief nod. If he recognized the prince of Dhanarra, he gave no sign.

Kaden nodded curtly. "Let's skip the amenities and get out of here."

"Agreed," said Dominic. He led the way down the back stairs to the sweaty kitchen. Laraina and Kaden picked up the two generous packs of supplies left for them by the innkeeper and, with hearty thanks, strapped them to their backs.

Dominic peered out the back door. The rain had stopped; the storm-soaked alley lay silent, wreathed in shadows. It was still about an hour before midnight. Motioning for the others to follow, he started up the alley.

The small group hastened through the narrow side streets, their booted feet barely splashing as they neared the city's outer wall. The once-threatening clouds broke away, and a few stars glimmered in the night sky.

They had almost reached the outer wall when Dominic stopped and waved the others back into the shadows. Just off to his right stood a tall, gray-cloaked figure. Like a phantom the figure hovered in the middle of the street, head tilted as if he were listening to something. Slowly, the figure turned. Crouching behind a broken wall, Dominic drew back as the searching gaze swept over the back of their hiding place and passed on.

After several tense moments, the shadowy figure edged back toward the city. As soon as he was out of sight, Dominic signaled for the others to cross the open space. He held Trevillion back, motioning for him to follow.

With Trevillion behind him, Dominic slipped silently up to the point where he had last seen the mysterious figure. They reached the corner of a ruined building just as the gray-cloaked figure stepped out from around it.

"Ha!" he said as he spotted the others who were now in plain sight.

Trevillion belted him. The man staggered. Two more blows sent him diving into the mud, unconscious. Trevillion bent down and pulled off the man's hood, revealing a thin grizzled face with stringy blond hair and beard. Trevillion's mouth set in a grim line, but he said nothing.

Dominic peered around the corner. There was no one in sight. Leaving the man where he had fallen, Dominic and Trevillion hurried to catch up with the others, who were nearing the crumbling outer wall.

With Dominic in the lead, they scrambled through a wide gap in the wall and climbed up the steep slope into the blood red rocks, working their way around to the southeast side of the valley. They stopped in a small open space hidden from the malevolent eyes of the city by a massive rock formation.

"This is far enough," Laraina said. "We can wait here."

Dominic nodded.

"I'm going to scout around," Trevillion said and disappeared into the rocks.

Staring after him, Aurelia sighed rapturously. She sat down on a small boulder and tried to arrange her oversized clothing in a more becoming fashion. Kaden stood near her, as if on guard.

Laraina paced in the shadow of the huge outcropping of rock, stopping every few minutes to look down at the corrupted city now bathed in angelic silver moonlight.

"Stop worrying," Dominic said. "She knows what she's doing."

Laraina stopped pacing. "I know. If it was anyone else but... him... after us, I wouldn't worry so much."

"He won't find her. I'd be willing to bet on it." Dominic tried his best to sound convincing.

Laraina's eyes met his, and he knew they were thinking the same thing — that this time, Tara had taken on more than she could handle.

"If only she weren't so reckless," Laraina fumed.

Dominic was silent. Just like old times.

Prince Kaden joined them, a disgruntled look on his face.

"This is not a good idea," he said in a low voice.

"What isn't?" Laraina asked.

"Having that rogue for a guide. How do we know he won't run at the first sign of trouble and leave us stranded? Or for that matter, how do we know he won't hand us over to Natiere?"

"We don't," she said, "but I'm willing to give him the benefit of the doubt. I've heard he's unpredictable, but he has a reputation for earning his money — which reminds me." She turned to Dominic. "How much did you have to give him?"

Dominic rubbed his stubbled jaw thoughtfully. "Now that's the strange part. We didn't give him any. In fact, we never even discussed money. There wasn't time. The... um... men showed up while he and Tara were arguing." Dominic shrugged. "I really don't know why he's helping us, but he saved my skin earlier, so I'm willing to give him a chance."

"He saved your skin?"

"Two men waylaid me on my way to the *Red Rose*. He took care of them before I even knew what was going on. Then he came with me to the inn. I owe him one."

"Why didn't you say something?" Laraina asked. "Is that what happened to your ribs?"

"It's nothing serious." He patted Laraina on the shoulder. "I think I'll go sit down for a while, rest this old body." He limped away.

*****

Laraina turned to Kaden. "I don't see we have any choice but to trust Trevillion."

"Of course we have choices," Kaden said. "There are always choices. I don't trust him. And I don't like the way he looks at you!"

Laraina smiled. "I do believe you're jealous."

"Jealous? Of course I'm jealous. With your reputation and his looks —" Kaden ran his hand over his face. "I'm sorry. I didn't mean that."

"Yes, you did," Laraina said softly, "but I don't blame you. I earned that one." Her flash of anger had been frozen by the knowledge that he had every right to be jealous. She'd always flitted from lover to lover like a butterfly in a field of wildflowers, drawn away by someone more handsome, more exciting.

She faced Kaden squarely. "Trevillion may be good-looking, but I see no one but you — now or ever."

Their eyes held — his searching, almost desperate, hers honest and open. She let her love for him show through. He pulled her into his arms and kissed her.

When they finally drew apart, Laraina noticed Trevillion had returned. He was leaning against a rock, sharpening his knife. Prince Kaden slipped his arm around Laraina, and they stood side by side in the shadow of the outcropping, watching the city below.

*****

Tara peered around the corner of a half-crumbled, abandoned building. Nothing. The street was empty. She drew back, uneasy. She had lost track of her pursuers. She didn't like not knowing where they were. For more than an hour she'd been playing a deadly game of hide-and-seek, slowly working her way to the outskirts of the city, and praying to all the gods she could think of that Dominic had warned Laraina and gotten the others away safely. She glanced upward. At least the rain had stopped.

She peered around the corner again. Still nothing. She let out an exasperated breath. They had to be around here somewhere. She glanced down the alley behind her and the familiar icy chill of warning crept down her spine. Ah! They were behind her. She turned and felt another jolt. And to her left. Well, she knew where they were, now what?

She examined the ramshackle building beside her. The walls were full of cracks and crevices where the stones had shifted over the years. Easily finding hand- and footholds, she climbed up the side of the building and pulled herself onto the flat roof. Crouching low, she crept from roof to roof diagonally across the block, the houses on the outer part of the city being hunched together even more closely than those in the center. She reached the edge. A narrow alley separated her from the next block. Taking a few steps backward, she got a running start and leaped across, landing lightly on the other side and neatly pitching forward into a somersault to break the fall.

She rolled to her feet and surveyed the crumbling rooftops before her. This clump of decayed buildings was in even worse shape than the one she had just traversed. Holes gaped where roofs had caved in, and in some places, entire walls had collapsed. Moving carefully, she worked her way across until she could go no further. A yawning pit opened up before her — a drop of at least twenty feet. She backtracked a short distance, then bent down, grasped the rough edge of the roof, and lowered herself over the side. *Now I know what a spider feels like*, she thought as she climbed down over the wet, ragged stones. She reached the ground without mishap. The outer wall of the city loomed ahead of her. As she ran toward it, she could see in her mind's eye her tenacious pursuers converging on the corner she had left just minutes before. She smiled. *Not this time, Captain. Not this time...*

CHAPTER 5

General Caldren stood outside the village and watched it burn. He smiled with satisfaction as the raging fire engulfed the buildings. The thatched roofs, splashed with oil, generated dense smoke as they burned. He savored the moment, drinking in the acrid smells as the villagers' screams pierced the dawn.

Peasants, he thought. *Witless peasants.* They were hardly worth killing.

"General Caldren, sir!"

The General scowled at the intrusion.

A young soldier saluted crisply. "The area is secure, sir."

"And the peasants?"

"The survivors are being held in a corral on the south side of the village, sir. They're mostly women and children."

The General nodded. "Excellent." He rubbed his jaw, relishing the feel of the rough stubble. It had been a long time since he'd enjoyed the rigors of the field. "How many more villages between here and Belgarde?"

"Three, sir. According to the scouts, they are as yet unaware of our presence. No one has escaped to warn them."

"Good. Prepare to move out."

"Um... sir, what should we do with the captives?"

"Kill them."

The soldier blanched. "All of them?"

"Yes, all of them." The General stepped toward the soldier. "Do you question my orders?"

"No, sir." With a hasty salute, the young soldier fled.

The General spat in disgust. "Idiot." He surveyed again the burning village. Twelve years he'd waited for this — longer even. Since the death of his father twenty-two years ago he had planned for this. Revenge. Revenge for his father, Rhaygarn, who was denied the throne of Sulledor simply because he was the second-born twin. Thirteen minutes were all that separated him from his brother, Rhalinyr, yet it was enough to deny him the throne.

All the bitterness, all the anger that had driven his father echoed inside his son. Caldren recalled his father's humiliation when Rhalinyr died in a hunting accident, and Rhalinyr's five-year-old son ascended to the throne instead. The leaders of all the other kingdoms endorsed the child king and pledged their support. Rashly, Rhaygarn had tried to assassinate the young king. He was caught, tried by the Court of Kings, and executed as a traitor to the crown. He'd been branded a traitor, when all he'd ever wanted was a chance to lead Sulledor to new fields of prosperity. The injustice of it rankled. They would pay, Caldren had vowed. They would pay, if it took every breath he had.

As a young man, Caldren had kept a low profile. He joined the military and rose through the ranks. For ten long years he'd waited, forming his plans and laying the groundwork in secret. He kept his seething emotions hidden behind an innocuous mask, disguising his intentions until it was too late for anyone to stop him.

Then he had struck. Caldren disposed of the young king in such a way that no one could connect him with the crime. As next in line for the throne, he assumed power. After six months passed with no word of the vanished ruler, Caldren used his executive powers to declare the boy dead and took his rightful place on the throne. Any objections had been quelled. He spent the next twelve years plotting revenge on a much grander scale, refining his strategy, nurturing his hatred until it burned like a poison in his blood. He lulled the other kingdoms into a false sense of security. Then he struck again.

Now, Carilon was his. The fortress at Belgarde soon would be. All the villages in between would be reduced to ashes. The Faragellyn border was not far beyond. His massive army would cut a swath of death and destruction all the way to the Cyranel Mountains. He would not be stopped.

More screams erupted from the south side of the village, then went still. Caldren smiled. The silence indicated his orders had been carried out. Excellent. He turned his back on the annihilated village and strode away.

*****

The three-quarter moon shone like molten silver in the midnight sky, its glow bright after the oppressive blackness of the storm. Laraina Triannon paced across the small open space, clenching and unclenching her fists. *Sister, where are you?* she wondered for the thousandth time.

Prince Kaden stepped in front of her. "Will you please stop pacing?"

With an effort, Laraina stood still. "I can't help it. She should be here."

Dominic rose stiffly. "She will be."

"And how long do we wait?" Laraina lowered her voice. "She said to give her an hour. An hour has come and gone."

"We can't all go back into the city." Dominic limped over to her. "If they do have her, they'll be waiting for us."

"I agree," Laraina said. "Jovan Trevillion can take the three of you on to Desta. I will find Tara and —"

"You're not going back there alone," Kaden said, his face resolute.

Laraina shook her head. "You can't come with me."

Trevillion silenced them with a wave of his hand. "Someone's coming. Get out of sight."

Laraina herded the others behind some boulders, then watched through a cover of brush.

Without a sound, Trevillion moved to the edge of the massive outcropping that rose between them and the moonlit valley below. He stood with his back pressed against the stone, his hand resting lightly on his sword.

The soft scrape of booted feet on stone drifted like a whisper on the night wind, drawing steadily closer to the edge of the outcropping. Laraina held her breath. The intruder stopped. Trevillion tightened his grip on his sword.

A soft tapping broke the stillness — one tap followed by four quick taps. After a moment, the combination was repeated.

Laraina sagged with relief. "Thank the gods!" She rapped three times on the rock with the hilt of her dagger. Trevillion stepped back as she rushed forward and embraced her sister.

"Where have you been?" Laraina demanded.

"I'm sorry," Tara said, "but they were rather persistent. I only just got rid of them. You shouldn't have waited for me —" She broke off as she caught sight of Trevillion. "Well, well. What are you doing here?"

"I came to watch you get yourselves killed." He gave her a roguish smile. "Vaalderin is short on amusements."

Laraina watched Tara and Trevillion stare each other down. She had obviously missed something, or else Dominic had left out some details about their meeting.

"Jovan helped us get out of the city," Laraina said. "He's already scouted around."

"I see." Tara eyed him coldly. "Then I must thank you."

"You're most welcome." He answered her cool tone with an exaggerated bow. "Shall we go?"

"After you," she said with a wave of her arm.

Trevillion led the way southeast through the silver-splashed rocks.

*****

They traveled in single file. Aurelia stayed close behind Trevillion, followed by Laraina, Prince Kaden, and Dominic. Tara kept rear guard. They made good time, and Tara had to admit Trevillion seemed to know the area well.

Shortly before dawn, heavy gray clouds rolled in from the north, blotting out the moon and forcing them to halt. As soon as it was light enough to see, they moved on again. They stopped briefly midmorning and again in the early afternoon to rest and eat a meager meal, then continued, climbing through the blood red rocks toward Desta and the only bridge across the Amberin River.

By evening, the mountain air had grown frosty. Tara shivered, but not from the cold. The Butcher was back on their trail. She knew it as surely as if she could see him scaling the craggy bluffs they had climbed scant hours before — a nightmare, blacker than the twilight shadows that spread across the rocks. They needed to move faster.

But speed proved impossible. The trail dwindled to little more than an animal track, winding through a dense maze of scarlet cliffs, narrow defiles, and thorn-filled gullies, and Tara began to wonder if Trevillion had lost his way.

At the top of a steep incline, Trevillion paused, surveying a shallow gully that led into a wide, windswept canyon.

"Can we stop now, please?" Aurelia said, drooping against him. "My legs ache." She drew her skirt up to her knee to show off her shapely calf. "And I'm hungry."

"Not here," Trevillion said. He reached out to steady her. "Perhaps on the other side of the canyon."

Tara glanced at Trevillion, her eyes drawn to him. Her breath caught at the sight of his broad-shouldered frame silhouetted against the darkening sky. She gritted her teeth. Curse it all! Why did he have to be so confoundedly good-looking? Aurelia sidled closer to Trevillion, and Tara had a sudden urge to shove her down the bank. Angry with herself, she turned away. Aurelia could hop into his arms for all she cared. Despite her efforts, Tara found her gaze sliding back, lingering on Trevillion. He was tall, though not as tall as Prince Kaden, who towered over everyone, but Tara could see by the well-formed muscles rippling under Trevillion's tight leather tunic that he was by far the stronger of the two. Surprised and dismayed at where her thoughts were leading, she barged forward.

"Why are we stopping? We need to keep moving." She climbed to the front of the line.

"Shhhh!" Trevillion raised his hand for silence as he studied the gully.

Tara cleared her mind, opening her senses to the surrounding sounds and smells. A faint chill shivered through her. Danger lurked, but she didn't feel any serious threat.

"Let's go before it's too dark to see," she said.

Trevillion shot her a glance. "What's the hurry?"

Tara glimpsed Dominic's quick turn toward her to see if she would reveal the reason for their haste. "You came to see us get ourselves killed," she said smoothly. "Why delay the entertainment?"

"You don't believe in caution, do you?" He shook his head. "I'm surprised you've lived as long as you have."

He started down into the gully before Tara could reply. The others followed. Grumbling, Tara resumed her position at rear guard. A breath of wind brushed their faces like ghostly fingers. High above, a mountain hawk called, its harsh cry echoing across the lonely reaches.

They made their way through the gully and into the high-walled canyon. A faint scrabbling noise whispered through the semi-darkness as a multitude of small, dark shapes skittered across the canyon floor.

"What was that?" Laraina asked.

More scratchings, tiny claws on stone, sifted through the stillness.

"Mice," said Dominic. "Lots of them."

"As long as they're not spiders," Laraina said. "I can stand anything but spiders."

"What's wrong with spiders?" Kaden asked.

"I hate them!" Laraina shuddered.

"Someone dumped a jar of spiders over her head when she was younger," Tara explained. "Needless to say, he never did it again."

"Not after you got through with him," Laraina said.

Tara kicked at a small, gray rodent that tried to chew on her boot. More mice swarmed around her feet. Their high-pitched chittering grated on her nerves. "Can we speed it up, up there?" she called ahead to Trevillion.

"Not unless you can see better than I can," he said.

Tara squinted, barely able to make out the shapes of rocks and brush that littered the canyon.

A squeal rent the air. Kaden danced to one side. "Stepped on one. They're all over the place."

Aurelia screamed as a mouse scampered up her leg. She swiped it off and clambered up onto Trevillion's back, wrapping her arms and legs around him. "Keep them away from me!"

Trevillion staggered forward, plowing into a thick tangle of brush. "Aurelia, let go!"

"*Deleri disparano!*" Aurelia shouted.

Dead silence froze the air; a freezing chill whipped down Tara's spine. The silence fractured as feral screams raked the canyon. Lithe shadows appeared out of nowhere, leaping across the floor of the canyon. With terrified squeals, the mice scurried away as dozens of wildcats pounced on them.

Tara yelled and brandished her sword at a cat that bared its teeth at her. The wildcats only stood about knee height, but they were vicious.

Kaden cried out as one of the wildcats leaped off a boulder onto his back. Its claws sank into his backpack. The cat's weight dragged the pack off his shoulders, and both the pack and the cat fell. The cat twisted its lean, muscular body to land on its feet, then bounded away into the darkness. Kaden caught his breath. "Aurelia, what did you do?"

"The mice were supposed to disappear!" Aurelia cried. She slipped down off Trevillion's back.

"They disappeared, all right," Tara snapped. "Right into those wildcats' mouths, which is where we're going to be next!"

"Back against the canyon wall! Quickly!" Trevillion ordered.

Kaden grabbed his pack, and they scrambled out of the open space, putting their backs to the rock wall.

"This way," Trevillion said. "Hurry, but don't run or they'll chase you." Keeping one hand on the wall to find his way in the near-dark, he led them at a fast walk toward the end of the canyon.

Tara noticed the mice had stopped squealing. They'd either been eaten or had burrowed themselves into holes out of reach. The wildcats prowled the canyon, searching for more prey. She sensed the cats stalking them, the beasts' hunger almost palpable.

Laraina halted. "Wait!"

The others stopped.

"What are you doing?" Tara hissed. "Those cats are about to eat us."

Laraina snapped some branches off a scrub tree beside her and handed them to Tara and Dominic. "Hold these." She dropped her pack, snatched out a piece of cloth, ripped it into three pieces, and tied them to the ends of the sticks. The smell of good brandy tickled Tara's nose as Laraina poured the liquid over the cloth.

"Here." Trevillion had caught on to Laraina's idea and already had flint and steel in his hands. He ignited the brandy-soaked cloths. Light flared, illuminating a ragged space around them and five wildcats poised to attack. Trevillion grabbed a torch from Dominic, and they waved the flames in the cats' faces. Yowling, the wildcats bolted, racing away toward the canyon entrance. The other cats followed.

Dominic let out a breath. "Whew!"

Tara smiled at Laraina. "Well done, sister."

Laraina picked up her pack. "Like I said, I can handle anything but spiders. However, partial credit must go to Boris and Sheila of the Red Rose for packing a flask of Cierran brandy."

"That was Cierran brandy?" Dominic grimaced. "What a waste."

"Let's go," Trevillion said. He headed for the end of the canyon.

"I don't understand why my spell didn't work," Aurelia complained as she followed after him. "I focused the elemental energies correctly. It should have worked."

"Just like the last one?" Tara asked, unable to keep the sarcasm out of her voice.

Laraina swatted her, a "stop picking on her!" expression on her face.

Aurelia threw Tara a dark look.

"What do you mean 'elemental energies?'" Laraina asked.

"Everything around us — all the elements — give off energy," Aurelia explained. "My teacher, Mage Dralain, said some people, like me, are sensitive to it and can tap into that energy and, with the proper incantation, use it to create magic spells. I know how to do it. I don't understand why it didn't work. Maybe I just used the wrong word."

Tara clenched her fists, anger and bitter memories threatening to leak through the cracks around some of her locked mental doors. She didn't want to hear any more about magic. "I don't care what the problem was. Just don't do it again."

Laraina glared at her. Kaden didn't intervene, and Tara wondered if Aurelia's conjuring of the wildcats had unnerved him.

Aurelia shot Tara another furious glance, but said no more.

They left the canyon and traveled in silence, journeying with the intermittent moonlight. Black clouds scudded across the sky. Rain threatened, but held off.

Two hours later the moon disappeared for good. Trevillion took the first watch as Tara and the others bedded down beneath a sheltered outcropping. More than once, Tara felt Trevillion's gaze on her as she lay, pretending to sleep. His attention was disconcerting. Why was he watching her? The knowledge stirred feelings she had no intention of exploring. She forced them out of her mind and willed herself to sleep.

The next day, Tara avoided Trevillion and spoke little to anyone, concentrating on the rocks ahead of her. The black clouds thickened, settling so low that Tara felt as if she had to walk hunched over to keep her head out of them. Captain Natiere still followed. She sensed his presence behind them, gaining ground, but whenever she looked over her shoulder, she saw nothing.

By the third day, the Scarlet Mountains had grown more treacherous. The group struggled over wildly uneven terrain that one moment soared above them in towering, insurmountable cliffs and the next, dropped away into veils of mist. Jagged peaks pierced the sky like bloody teeth, giving Tara the impression she'd stumbled into a dragon's maw.

The rain began shortly before dusk. They took shelter in a small, dry niche in the rocks protected by a large overhang. Bone weary from the hard climb, they settled down for the night.

*****

On watch, Tara sat with her back against the damp wall of stone and stared into the gloom. Silence, deep and oppressive, lay over the mountains like a sodden blanket. The torrential downpour had subsided, leaving behind a fine gray mist that swirled like a tortured phantom in the breeze.

Tara tipped her head back and closed her eyes, trying to still the rampant whirl of disturbing thoughts. Trevillion. She couldn't stop thinking about him. There was something strange about him that she couldn't quite put her finger on. She was attracted to him, though she would sooner cut off her arm than admit it. But it wasn't that. There was something deeper, something hidden behind his heart-stopping good looks and roguish manner. Who was he really? And why had he agreed to come along on this suicidal adventure?

What did he hope to gain by it? She felt a pang of guilt and wondered if he would have come if he had known about Captain Natiere. Natiere. Now there was another problem...

Shaking with a sudden chill, Tara rose. Her eyes searched the darkness. Nothing. There was no one there. Stepping around the prone bodies of her sleeping comrades, Tara groped her way a few steps back along the path from which they'd come. The hooded mountains rose up before her like sentient beings ready to pronounce judgment. Tara wished she could see through them. Natiere was out there somewhere. She could feel his terrifying presence reaching across the distance. He was close... too close...

"What do you see?" asked a soft voice beside her.

Tara started violently, her sword half drawn, before she realized who it was.

She glared at Trevillion. "That's a good way to get killed."

"You didn't answer my question," he said, unruffled.

Tara wrestled with her conscience. They needed his help to get through the Bog, yet it wasn't fair to him...

"We're being followed," she said, avoiding his eyes.

"I haven't seen or heard anyone."

"Nor have I, but he's there, and he's not far behind us."

"Who?"

The question hung in the air between them like a drop of water suspended over a still pool.

Tara met his gaze. "Captain Natiere."

"Natiere?" Trevillion echoed in surprise. "The Butcher? What does he want with you?"

Tara briefly explained.

Trevillion was silent. "That raises the stakes a bit, doesn't it?" he said at last with an unreadable expression. "Were those his men in the tavern?"

Tara nodded.

Trevillion smiled grimly. "You play a dangerous game."

"You know what they say about old habits. However, this time I have little choice. If Kaden and Aurelia weren't here we could do something... find a way to fight him. But we can't risk their falling into his hands, so for now we'll just have to outrun him."

"That has never been done."

"Then we shall be the first." Tara dared him to contradict her. He said nothing.

She turned to go back, then stopped. "I'm sorry I didn't tell you before. I shouldn't have asked you to come without telling you what you were getting into."

Their eyes met once more, and Tara's heart skipped a beat.

"It would not have made any difference," he said softly.

Tara tore her eyes from his face and headed back to the camp, forcing herself to walk normally as if her emotions were not in a wild state of confusion. Wrapping her cloak around her, she lay down and closed her eyes, but it was a long time before she drifted off to sleep.

*****

The morning dawned bright and clear. Tara awoke to the piercing cry of a mountain hawk gliding on the rising air currents, its dark wings reflecting the pale rose of the sky. She sat up, inhaling the cool, crisp air. She knew without looking that Trevillion was not in camp. Kaden, Aurelia, and Dominic were still asleep, wrapped warmly in their heavy cloaks. Laraina was off to one side, fishing their breakfast rations out of one of the packs. Putting Trevillion forcibly out of her mind, Tara rose, crossed to her sister's side, and sat down.

"It's about time we had some good weather," she said as Laraina handed her a portion of bread and cheese.

"No argument from me," Laraina said with a smile. "After all the rain we've had, I think we've earned a little sunshine. By the way, you don't know where Jovan went, do you? He was gone when I awoke."

Tara stiffened at the mention of his name. "No."

Laraina frowned. "What's the matter with you?"

Tara looked away. "There's something about him that's not quite right."

"About Jovan?"

Tara nodded.

"In what way?"

"Well, he's not who he says he is. I mean he is, but he isn't."

"Now, that makes a lot of sense." Laraina looked skeptical.

Tara scowled. "Well, you wanted to know what I was thinking."

"All right, I apologize, but what exactly do you mean?"

"It's hard to explain." Tara tried to put her thoughts into words. "I sense that he is a man with many secrets, even beyond those that have to do with his brother and the missing king of Sulledor."

"What's this about a missing king?"

Tara recounted what Dominic had told her about Trevillion's possible involvement in the disappearance of the boy king of Sulledor.

"That's interesting," Laraina mused. "I wonder how much is truth, and how much is hearsay."

Tara shrugged. "I don't know. I can't read him. He hides everything behind that expressionless mask." She took another bite. "I would like to know who he really is, and why he's helping us." She paused. "I have the strangest feeling that we didn't meet by accident. Like we were meant to come together. I've never felt anything like it." She turned to her sister. "Do you believe in Fate?"

Laraina thought for a moment. "I believe in Fate in that I believe people die when it is their time, but I also believe that people's life paths are formed by the choices they make, not by some preordained plan. Why?"

"I don't know. It just seems like we suddenly have very few choices, as if our path is being directed for us. We are being driven toward some unknown end by the events happening around us."

"By who?" Laraina glanced upward. "The gods? I didn't think the gods intervened in people's lives unless asked in prayer and even then only if it suited their purposes. I suppose they might intervene if they were angry with someone." Her eyes narrowed. "You haven't provoked any gods, have you?"

"No, of course not," Tara said. "At least, not that I know of. I can't explain it. It's like in a card game. No matter what cards I had in my hand, when the gold was on the table, I always felt like it was mine to lose. I was in control. *We* were in control. Now we're not. Not since the attack on Castle Carilon. But it's more than that. Do you understand what I mean?"

Laraina shook her head. "I never understand you when you start talking in riddles. And I think you're making too much of this. We were simply in the wrong place at the wrong time."

"Were we?"

Laraina gave an exasperated sigh. "Just answer me this — is Jovan Trevillion a danger to us?"

Tara considered. "No, I don't think so." *At least not in that way,* she thought.

"Then let's not worry about it. We have enough trouble as it is." Laraina started to rise, then sat back down again. She lowered her voice. "Oh, and one other thing. You need to stop criticizing Aurelia so much. I know she's having trouble with her spells, but jumping down her throat every time isn't going to help."

"Someone has to stop her before she does some serious damage."

"Maybe not. Maybe she just needs some encouragement —"

"No. Definitely not."

Laraina squeezed Tara's arm. "I know the villagers treated you horribly because they thought you had magic, but you shouldn't take your anger out on her."

Tara's jaw clenched, vitriolic memories spilling into her mind in spite of her efforts to keep them locked away. "That's not what I'm doing."

"Isn't it?" Laraina squeezed her arm again in sympathy. "Please think about what I said and don't be so hard on her. All right?"

Tara kept silent, not trusting herself to speak. Yes, it rankled that those with magical talent were accepted and even celebrated in the more enlightened cities, instead of being reviled and persecuted as they were in outlying villages like the one in which she was born, but that had no bearing on her treatment of Aurelia. Aurelia had so many irritating qualities, Tara didn't need that reason to dislike her.

Laraina patted her arm and went to wake the others. Just then, Trevillion returned. Thoughts of Aurelia flirting with him slid through her mind before she could stop them, deepening her foul mood. Tara forced herself to finish eating. As soon as the others were done, they broke camp and traveled onward.

Just past midday, a sudden vigorous tremor in the ground under their feet brought them up short. The tremor only lasted half a minute. Off in the distance, they heard a loud rumbling.

"Rockslide." Trevillion gazed in the direction of the sound.

Aurelia, standing next to him, put her hand to her forehead. "Oh, I don't feel so well." She closed her eyes and swooned into his arms. He caught her and set her down gently, propping her against a rock. Her eyelids fluttered open. "What happened?"

"Here, drink this." Trevillion held a water flask to her lips.

She drank a little, then brushed her hand over her eyes. "Thank you. I'm so sorry. I've never felt dizzy like that before."

Kaden knelt beside her. "How do you feel now?"

"Much better. I'm all right, really I am." She smiled up at Trevillion. "Thank you so much."

"I'm going to be sick," Tara muttered under her breath.

Laraina swatted her.

Kaden and Trevillion helped Aurelia to her feet.

"We should keep going if you're up to it," Trevillion said.

"I'll be fine. If I just had something to hold on to..." She smiled at Trevillion again, hopefully.

Kaden intervened. "You can hang onto my arm."

"Oh... thank you," she said, looking vexed, "but I wouldn't want to hinder you."

"You won't." The prince offered his arm, and they followed after Trevillion, who had already started across the rocks.

As Tara fell in behind the others, her mind slipped its tight rein, and a sudden image of Trevillion bending over her, instead of Aurelia, his hand on her shoulder with care and concern, slid into her head. A tremble shot down her limbs, and she missed a step. Her cheeks grew hot. Fuming silently, she whipped her errant thoughts back into their cage.

When the late afternoon sun began to dip below the scarlet peaks, the weary group stopped to rest at the bottom of a rock-strewn gully. Trevillion left to scout ahead. Tara and the others clustered together on low rocks, eating dried fruit, watching as the golden glow of the setting sun flared into a fiery orange-red. The burning rays blazed across the mountainside, painting brighter and brighter shades of scarlet until it seemed the whole mountain had caught fire.

An icy jab of warning struck Tara with a suddenness that startled her. She leaped up. All at once, the ground began to tremble. The others rose hastily, but before they could take a step, a violent quake ripped through the gully, knocking them to the ground. A deafening roar filled their ears. The ground writhed beneath them like a wounded animal in its death throes. They scrambled to their feet as a mass of dirt and rocks thundered down the slope toward them.

"Run for it!" Tara pointed to a large overhanging rock thirty yards away.

They raced across the convulsing floor of the gully. Stinging pebbles pelted them like hailstones. Boulders hurtled past as if flung by a catapult. Aurelia reached the overhang first, then Laraina and Kaden. Tara ran beside the limping Dominic.

"Dominic! Look out!" Tara cried, as a cabbage-sized rock flew at him. She shoved him forward out of the way, but in doing so put herself in its path. She tried to dodge it, but the rock struck a glancing blow on the back of her right shoulder, spinning her around. Pain tore through her, and then she was engulfed in a smothering cloud of dust and dirt.

CHAPTER 6

Dizzy with pain, Tara fell to her knees. Small rocks and pebbles bombarded her; dust clogged her eyes and nose. She heard someone screaming her name. Blinded and breathless, she crawled toward the sound.

Strong arms snatched her up. She was carried a few steps, then swung gently to the ground. A warm body covered her. A masculine scent filled her senses. She recognized it immediately: Trevillion.

He curled his body around her, his chest against her back, his muscles tense as he shielded her from the rockslide. Heat rose within her in spite of the pain in her shoulder.

Beneath her, the floor of the gully rocked like a bucking horse. Tara clenched her fist against the pain. Just as she thought she could stand no more, the rocking ceased.

Trevillion pulled away from her. "Where are you hurt?"

The anxiety in his dark eyes surprised her. "My shoulder, mainly." Gingerly, she sat up. She sucked in a hissing breath as pain knifed through her right shoulder.

"Easy. Let me look at it." Trevillion raised the back of her shirt and ran gentle fingers over her shoulder blade.

A tremble shivered through her at his touch. Her breath came faster and sparked a fit of coughing.

Trevillion pressed a water flask into her hands. "Drink."

She took a long draught. The cool water soothed her gritty throat. "What about you?" she asked when she could speak again. "Are you hurt? You must have been hit."

"Nothing serious."

She eyed him doubtfully. "Are you sure?"

"I should know."

She suddenly remembered Dominic. Shoving the flask at Trevillion, she struggled to rise. "Did Dominic make it to the overhang?"

Trevillion pulled her back into a sitting position. "I don't know. Hold still and let me look at this."

Tara clenched her jaw as he examined her injured shoulder. His fingertips on her skin sent tingling shudders through her. She did her best to stifle them.

"I think your shoulder blade is broken," he said. "There's not much I can do for it out here but wrap it and make a sling."

"Are you a medic?"

"No, but one learns to do what is necessary in the field. Do you hurt anywhere else?"

"Not badly."

Trevillion tore a length from the bottom of his cloak and wrapped it around her chest, arm, and shoulder, fashioning a sling.

Tara wiped the dust out of her eyes. A thick haze hung over the gully in the wake of the rockslide, obscuring the overhang where she hoped her sister and the others had found safety. She and Trevillion were sitting in a shallow depression at the base of the slope, protected by large stones embedded in the hillside and by the shape of the slope itself. Most of the rocks must have bounced right over them. She pictured herself lying in the depression with Trevillion close against her. Her face flushed, and warmth spread through her again. She shook her head to banish the image and gasped at the spasm of pain in her shoulder.

Trevillion slipped his arm around her, supporting her. He cupped her cheek and turned her face to his, his eyes holding hers, as if gauging her stamina.

"You need a medic. You can't go through the Bog like this."

Tara pulled away, annoyed at the butterflies cartwheeling in her stomach. "Don't tell me what I can't do. It's my right shoulder that's hurt. I'm left-handed. I'll be fine."

Laraina's strained voice broke through the stillness. "Tara! Can you hear me?"

"Over here!" Trevillion called.

Tara heard the sound of running feet, and then Laraina, tears running down her cheeks, appeared in front of her, followed by Dominic, Kaden, and Aurelia.

"Tara!" Laraina dropped to her knees beside her and embraced her. "We thought you were dead!"

"Not so tight," Tara pleaded, gritting her teeth.

Laraina released her. "You're hurt! How bad is it?"

"I'll live." Relief spilled through Tara at the sight of Dominic. "Are you all right?" she asked him anxiously.

Dominic snorted. "Am *I* all right? I'm fine, thanks to you." He shook his head and laughed, wiping away what looked suspiciously like tears. "You get yourself half killed, and you ask if I'm all right."

Trevillion handed Tara the water flask again. "We'll stay here tonight. We can camp beneath that overhang."

"What about... um..." Dominic hesitated, glanced at Trevillion.

"He knows," said Tara. "I told him." She looked back up the ravine, mentally scanning the rough terrain through the dusty haze, searching for sources of danger. She felt none near. "We should be able to rest for a couple of hours, anyway. Natiere is still following, but he's not as close as he was."

"How do you know that?" asked Kaden.

"Yes, how do you know that?" said Trevillion.

Tara avoided his gaze. "I just... know."

"Perhaps he ran afoul of a rockslide, too," said Laraina.

A low rumbling started up again, this time some distance below them. The ravaged ground shook faintly. Trevillion scooped Tara up in his arms before she realized what he was doing and carried her toward the overhanging shelf.

"Hey! I can walk," she protested.

"So can I. Now hold still. And don't argue," he added, just as she thought of a suitable retort.

When they reached the overhang, he set her gently on her feet. She winced and, seeing his look of concern, said, "I'm all right... and thanks. I owe you one."

"I'll remember that," he said with a smile that quickened her pulse. He began setting up camp.

Tara watched him for a moment, lost in thoughts of how he might collect that debt. Then reason cracked its whip, and she turned away, scolding herself.

Daylight faded, the air growing cooler as the rest of the group gathered under the rim of the large rock. Tara found a comfortable spot and eased herself to the ground.

Laraina knelt beside her. "Let me see what you've done to yourself this time."

"It's not that bad."

"You'd say that if you broke every bone in your body. Now let me see it."

"Yes, Mother."

Laraina raised the back of Tara's tunic. She gasped. "Look at this! It looks like half a cantaloupe sticking out of your back." She probed the swollen area.

Tara flinched. "That hurts. Stop poking me." She pulled her tunic back down. "What did you expect?"

Laraina turned to Trevillion. "Can you find us a medic in Desta?"

"You know that's not necessary," Tara cut in. "Now stop worrying. It'll be fine in a few days. Let's get some sleep." She lay down on her side with one of the backpacks for a pillow.

Laraina covered her with a cloak. "I'll take the first watch. Someone else will take yours. You are not to get up. Is that clear?"

Tara snorted. "Yes, Mother."

Aurelia stepped forward. "I'll do it."

The others stared, shocked into silence.

"Aurelia, I applaud your courage," Prince Kaden said, sounding surprised and impressed, "but I'm sorry. It's much too dangerous."

"Nonsense," she retorted. "How hard can it be? You look and you listen."

"I will take the second watch," said Trevillion in a voice that brooked no argument. He smiled at Aurelia. "But it was brave of you to offer. Thank you."

She blushed. "You're welcome. I only wanted to help. You must teach me what to do so I can help."

"I think it would help if we could all get some sleep," Tara said irritably.

They bedded down and were asleep within minutes.

*****

Laraina stayed close beside Tara, keeping the first watch. She sat cross-legged with her sword balanced on her knees. She felt safer with her weapon near at hand. Tara had said the Butcher didn't pose an immediate threat, but that could change quickly.

The moon had risen, gilding the mountain in silver light. Thin clouds slipped across the night sky.

Laraina glanced at her sister from time to time, but Tara seemed to be sleeping soundly. Brushing back her tangle of red curls, Laraina sighed. One of these days, Tara was going to get herself killed. Or get them both killed. She thought back over their many adventures, seeing them now through eyes grown wiser with age and experience, and was amazed she and her sister had survived. Her hot temper and Tara's cold pride — Tara's stubborn refusal to admit that something couldn't be done — had landed them in so much trouble. But somehow they'd always survived. No matter whose dungeon they were in, or in what war they fought, or whose enemy they were, they survived. The tension and strain of constant danger had driven Laraina into the arms of many men. Though brief, these passionate affairs had given her a release. Tara, however, never seemed affected by the tension. She thrived on the adrenaline rush of danger and constantly sought it out.

For Laraina, though, adventure had lost some of its allure. During the two months she had spent with Prince Kaden before the Sulledorn invasion, she had become acutely aware of the benefits of a settled life. Perhaps it was Kaden's love. The thought of it warmed her. Or perhaps she was just tired of the endless traveling. Judging from the castle gossip, the prince had changed a great deal from his earlier days of promiscuity and negligence. The mantle of responsibility had straightened his shoulders, strengthened his character. Laraina, too, had changed. In the past, Tara's welfare had been her only concern. But having watched Prince Kaden and his now-deceased father manage the welfare of the entire kingdom of

Dhanarra, she had begun to think of life on a much larger scale. This new perspective fascinated her, and she wanted to learn more. One thing stood in her way. She glanced down at her sleeping sister and drew in a troubled breath. If she were to give up adventuring, make Dhanarra her home, what would Tara do?

*****

"We will camp here for the rest of the night," said Captain Natiere, studying the midnight sky. Faint stars blinked back at him, made pale by the brightness of the moon.

"But they can't be much beyond the next ridge," argued one of his men. "Let's get 'em and have done with it before there's any more of those cursed earthquakes."

"We will pick up the trail at dawn." Natiere's menacing glare ended the discussion.

The four bedded down without further comment.

A few yards away, a small stream tumbled down through the rocks. Soundlessly, Natiere crossed the distance and crouched beside the streambed. Dipping his hands into the icy water, he scooped up several handfuls and drank deeply, then splashed some on his face. The coldness of the water stung the tender flesh edging the ragged scar. He ran his fingers over the disfiguring gash and remembered the pain when the razor-sharp blade had sliced open the left side of his face. A hideous wound inflicted by his own hand, a reminder to himself of the suffering he had witnessed, worse even than the suffering he had endured. Such heinous crimes...

Laughter filled his ears, evil, taunting. Screams of agony from his tormented parents, his five brothers and sisters. No one to hear, no one to help. Seventeen men, roving bandits, had attacked their small farm, viciously slashed, tortured, left them to die. He alone had survived, found and retrieved from the edge of death by a passing band of gypsies.

More memories crowded around him. He saw himself standing before the mirror in what had once been his parents' bedroom. Eight years had passed since the slaughter of his family; he had grown to manhood in that time. The gypsies, who had taken him in, had told him there was nothing more they could teach him. He must walk his own path. His footsteps had led him back here. Staring at his reflection, he had pulled out a well-honed knife and cut the side of his face. As the blade sliced downward, he'd uttered a vow – the beginning of his quest for revenge. Seventeen men. He would not stop until he had tracked them down and torn them apart. The scar on his face would be a reminder. Every time he touched his face or saw his reflection he would remember what had been done to his family. There would be no pity, no mercy for those responsible – only slow, torturous death. He hadn't bothered to sew up the gash on his face; he had left it ragged and raw, the mark of the damned.

Events from his past swept through his mind, acutely clear. He saw the flames as they licked up over the dilapidated farmhouse, burning to ashes his childhood home. That life had been stripped from him. He saw himself walking to the grove of willow trees where his butchered family lay buried in unmarked graves. Taking a cloth soaked in his own blood, he had wrung out several drops over the ground and repeated his vow. Then he'd turned on his heel and strode away. He did not look back. The hunt had begun...

Captain Natiere splashed more water on his face and shook his head, surprised by his thoughts. It had been years since he'd remembered his childhood. Now the memories were coming back to haunt him. Why? They'd first started troubling him at the beginning of this last chase, after running into Tara Triannon in Castle Carilon. Thinking about her, with her long, silver-blonde hair and strange beauty, had reminded him of the gypsy's warning. *Beware the silver-haired witch*, a raspy voice whispered in his mind.

He rose to his feet and stared into the night. He felt her presence in a way he felt no other. He sensed her pain. She had been injured in some way. He would give her this night to recuperate. She had earned that much by eluding him in Vaalderin. This chase was turning out to be highly entertaining. At dawn, the hunt would begin anew.

*****

Tara Triannon woke just before dawn, feeling confused and disoriented. Her head hurt, and her mouth felt as dry as dead leaves. Where was she? She'd been in the middle of a strange and terrifying dream, one that had vanished the instant she awoke. She tried to recall it, sensing it was somehow important, but only succeeded in making her headache worse. She sat up carefully to avoid paining her shoulder.

Laraina, who was already awake, crossed to Tara's side and sat down. "Are you all right?"

Tara rubbed her temples. "My head hurts."

"Not another dream?" Laraina asked, her brows knit with concern.

Tara nodded. "Worse."

"And you can't remember it."

"No."

"There must be some explanation. It's been quite a while since the last one."

She fell silent as Dominic sat up slowly and stretched. He shook Kaden and Aurelia awake. Trevillion was nowhere in sight.

"How do you feel?" Dominic asked Tara as he and Kaden handed out breakfast rations.

"Stiff and sore and hungry," she answered.

"Is this all we get?" Aurelia said, with a sour look at her meager portion.

"We're almost out of food," said Kaden.

"But I'm starving. This is hardly a quarter of a breakfast."

"I'm sorry. That's it."

Aurelia brightened. "I could make us some food. It would be very easy. Some nice hot oat bread with honey would be perfect right now."

"No," said Tara. "We discussed this before. No magic."

"You mean, *you* discussed it," Aurelia grumbled. "I don't recall having any say in the matter." She turned her back on the others and ate in silence.

"I hope we get to Desta soon," Laraina said.

"We should be there in another day or so," said Trevillion, coming up behind them, wet canteens slung over his shoulder. "There's a small stream beyond those rocks if anyone's interested." He indicated a pile of boulders a short distance up the gully.

Laraina slid around behind Tara and raised the back of Tara's tunic, inspecting her bruise. She shook her head in bewilderment. "I don't know how you do it."

"Do what?" asked Tara between mouthfuls.

"The swelling is half gone."

"I told you there was nothing to worry about."

Trevillion looked at the bruise. "She's right. It's half healed." He looked at Tara questioningly.

"I've always been a quick healer," Tara said, irritated by the scrutiny. "And now, if you don't mind, I'm going to go find that stream."

Trevillion gave her a hand up.

"Thanks," she said as she brushed herself off. She removed her makeshift sling and gave it back to Trevillion.

He accepted the length of cloak without comment and stuffed it into a backpack.

Tara walked up the gully, noticing a clear sky through the rosy glow of dawn. *Where was the Butcher,* she wondered. Why hadn't he attacked? Her sense of danger would have prodded her awake if he had come near in the night.

She found the stream, washed her hands and face, and ran damp fingers through her hair. After drinking her fill, she rose and stood for a moment, listening to the burbling of the brook and the warbling of some distant bird. Then she turned full circle, opening her mind to the living auras around her. An icy chill shot down her spine. He was coming.

Tara raced back to camp.

"What's wrong?" Laraina demanded.

"Natiere is coming. We have to move out. Now."

CHAPTER 7

They threw their gear together and shouldered their packs.

"Tara, you're up front, behind me," Trevillion said. "Laraina, you take rear guard."

"But —," Tara and Aurelia said simultaneously.

"He's right," said Laraina. She held up her hand to stem any discussion. "You're hurt. I'm not."

"But that's my spot," said Aurelia with a stamp of her foot.

"I'm fine," Tara said. "I don't need to be babied."

"No arguments," said Laraina. "Let's go."

Trevillion headed down the ravine.

Tara hesitated. The last thing she wanted was to be near Trevillion.

Laraina pointed down the path. "Go."

Cursing under her breath, Tara followed after him.

Aurelia stomped along behind her. "It's not fair," she muttered.

"Believe me, I don't like it any better than you do," Tara said over her shoulder.

Dominic, Kaden, and Laraina fell into place behind them. They caught up with Trevillion at the end of the ravine. Trevillion climbed the steep, head-high bank, then leaned down with his hand outstretched. Reluctantly, Tara took his hand. The strong, calloused grip warmed her skin and sent her stomach butterflies into a tizzy. She allowed him to help her up the bank, then pulled her hand away with a mumbled thanks and moved away from the edge, away from him. He turned back to help Aurelia. Aurelia grasped his hand with both of hers. She clambered up the bank, falling against Trevillion as she reached the top.

"Oops," she giggled. She smiled at him as he steadied her.

Tara felt the stab of an emotion she refused to put a name to. She looked away and glared at the surrounding rocks, squelching the feeling as she would stomp out an errant flame. When she looked back, the others were up and ready to go. She rejoined the group, willing her shoulder to heal faster.

Trevillion set a rapid pace across the blood-red rocks, leading the way through a series of shallow canyons that opened out onto rough, rocky ridges. Tara tried to stay back, away from him, but Aurelia kept forcing her closer, trying to get close herself. His nearness teased Tara's senses. She was aware of every move he made. When the climbing grew arduous, he helped her over the difficult places with surprising gentleness. She refused his help as much as possible. The touch of his hand jangled every nerve in her body, stirring emotions she couldn't quite suppress. She tried to ignore them, but it was a losing battle.

The air grew colder as the day wore on. Dark clouds gathered, massing for another storm. Tara watched the lowering overcast. They were in for a drenching.

Around midafternoon, Trevillion finally stopped at the base of a steep, jagged incline. Slabs of scarlet rock, shrugged off by the taller mountains, had piled in jumbled layers to a height of thirty feet.

Tara looked up at the nearly vertical slope and knew it would be a hard climb. Her shoulder throbbed just thinking about it. Her injury had healed quite a bit, but she had abused her shoulder unnecessarily by forcing herself to climb in places she should have accepted help — places like this one.

"We have to climb *that?*" Dominic said, coming up beside her. He pulled off his hat, wiped his brow with his sleeve, then crammed his hat back on his head. "Great gods alive. My toenails are worn clean off from the last climb."

Trevillion gave Dominic a sympathetic smile. "Sorry, old man. It's either climb it or spend half a day going around it."

Dominic sagged against a boulder. "What I wouldn't give for a shot of Cierran brandy."

Tara patted him on the back. "Me, too."

He turned to Laraina. "Did you have to dump it all on those torches back there?"

Laraina shrugged. "It seemed like a good idea at the time."

Aurelia plopped down on a rock. "I need a rest. And some food." She fingered her travel-stained clothes and wrinkled her nose. "And a bath."

Tara laughed. "You'll get a bath soon enough when the rain hits." She studied the sullen sky. "We'll be drenched before the day is out."

"Why don't we rest here for a few minutes before we attempt the cliff," said Laraina. "Tara should rest her shoulder."

"My shoulder is fine."

"It is *not* fine, so stop saying that it is," Laraina retorted.

"We can rest at the top," said Trevillion. "It's a plateau, and there is good cover, so we won't be seen." He faced the steep pile of rock. "I will go up first and throw down a rope."

Choosing his hand- and footholds carefully, Trevillion made his way up the slope. Scatterings of rock broke off under his feet as he climbed. He reached the top and disappeared over the edge. A minute later, he reappeared and tossed down a rope.

Tara rolled her aching shoulder to loosen it up, then grasped the rope.

"Tie it around you," Trevillion called down. "I'll pull you up."

Grumbling to herself, Tara tied the rope around her waist, looping it through her sword belt to keep it from riding up around her arms. Gripping the rope with her left hand, she dug her toes into the slope and climbed as Trevillion pulled. She tested each step, searching for crevices in the brittle rock, wary of the narrow ledges that crumbled under her weight. She kept her right hand against the rock face for balance.

As she neared the top, a tremor shuddered through the mountains. Above her, a slab of red rock broke loose.

"Tara, look out!" Laraina yelled from below.

Tara caught the rope with both hands and swung out of the way to her left. The quick movement wrenched her shoulder. She bit back a cry of pain. The rock hurtled downward and smashed into the ground below.

Trevillion appeared, looking over the edge of the cliff, leaning against the pull of the rope, which he'd wrapped around a boulder. "Are you all right?"

"I don't need to worry about the Butcher," Tara said as she regained her footing. "These mountains are going to kill me first."

Trevillion pulled her the rest of the way up, lifting her over the edge as if she weighed nothing. Tara leaned into him, let the strength of his arms support her until she realized what she was doing. Flustered, she straightened up and pulled away. Moving to the side, she sat and cradled her arm, trying to shake off the burning pain in her shoulder. "I'm fine."

Trevillion eyed her dubiously. "Should I repeat what your sister said?"

Tara heard Laraina's voice calling from the base of the slope. Tara nodded toward the edge. "You should get them up here before we have any more tremors." She worked at the knot in the rope around her waist.

"Hopefully, there won't be any more," said Trevillion. He moved her hand aside, loosened the knot, and removed the rope.

Tara steeled herself against his touch.

"Stay here," he said. He went back to the edge and called down to Laraina.

Tara closed her eyes and concentrated on slowing the rampant wingbeats in her gut Trevillion's nearness had caused.

Trevillion pulled Kaden up next, and then the two of them brought the others up without mishap.

Laraina knelt beside Tara. "Don't say you're fine."

Tara opened her eyes and smiled faintly. "It hurts. Is that what you want to hear?"

Laraina shook her head. "I know it hurts. I want to know how much."

"It's tolerable. Not as bad as before."

"There's a hollow in the scrub trees and brush over there where we can rest for a few minutes." Trevillion pointed to his right. "It looks like there's water there, too."

"Just a few minutes?" Aurelia asked plaintively.

"We can't stay long," Trevillion said gently and headed toward the hollow.

Tara rose, with Laraina's help, and after scanning the ridges behind them and seeing no sign of Natiere, she followed the others to the grove of stunted trees.

Nearby, a large pool of water, a rain-filled depression in the surface of the plateau, beckoned. The dark, wind-rippled water reflected the gray sky.

Trevillion knelt, scooped up a handful, and tasted it. "It's fine," he said and filled his water flask.

The others did the same. Then they washed the sweat and grime from their hands and faces and went back to the grove.

Bending low, they stepped into a cave-like space and settled among the trees beneath a canopy of tangled branches. Trevillion posted himself at an opening in the side of the hollow. Tara sat near the entrance, away from the others, where she could see back across the plateau. Though she hadn't seen Natiere, she knew he was still close. And it wasn't just that she could sense his presence as a source of danger. She could sense *him*. Strongly. She could feel his mind, almost as if he were reaching out to her. That both puzzled and alarmed her. She could generally sense people she knew, in terms of knowing their proximity. But the only other person she could sense that strongly was Laraina. And Trevillion, she amended with a grimace. She was always acutely aware of him. Why would she have this odd connection to the Butcher? She had run into him once in Castle Carilon on the night of the attack, and then only for a few moments.

She shivered and glanced back toward the mountains they had crossed. Somewhere, beyond her scope of vision, he stalked them. They shouldn't be sparing this time to rest. But not everyone could take the hard pace they'd been keeping. She looked back at the others. Dominic sat down heavily. The rough terrain was taking its toll on him, and she knew he was reaching the limits of his endurance. Aurelia, too, drooped with exhaustion. Kaden looked weary, but, she admitted grudgingly, he was holding up a lot better than she'd expected.

Laraina handed out the last of the food. "That's it." She turned the pack upside down to shake out any last crumbs. "I hope we'll be able to get more supplies in Desta."

"We will," said Trevillion. "I have a friend there who can get us whatever we need."

Aurelia fingered her piece of stale bread with distaste. She opened her mouth to complain, glanced at Trevillion sitting nearby, and closed it again without speaking. She took a bite and chewed in silence.

Laraina gave Tara a portion and sat down beside her.

Tara toyed with her bread. The pain in her shoulder and her constant battle with her emotions had stolen her appetite. A face crept into her thoughts, roguishly handsome. A memory long locked away slipped to the surface. A soft summer evening... tall grass and daisies and buttercups tossed by the breeze, fireflies bright against the dusk in the field where they had first shared their love. Myles. She heard his voice, seductive and seemingly sincere, comparing her beauty to the stars. "As long as those stars shine I will love you," he had said. More memories burst forth – his hearty laugh after playing a joke on fellow traveling companion, Xavier; the crash as he fell to the floor after losing yet another drinking duel with Dominic; his shout of triumph after their "seat of the pants" escape from an impregnable castle. They'd retrieved a jewel there, which a viscount claimed had been stolen from him. Myles' need for the adrenaline rush of danger had been as great as hers. He'd been willing to chance almost anything, and the viscount had been willing to pay dearly for the jewel's recovery. They had partied well that night. She remembered the touch of Myles' fingers brushing her face, his blue eyes warm and beguiling as he gave her that crooked smile he saved only for her.

Then the smile faded, replaced by a look of revulsion in those same blue eyes when she told him she, Laraina, and Dominic had been exposed to the black fever. "Sorry, my love," he had said. "All bets are off. Catch you in the next life." The words echoed through her head, and she saw him running away, to be anywhere but with her. Then the Lord Marshal had appeared with his soldiers to escort them to the local dungeon. It seemed a price had been placed on their heads by the noble whose castle they'd robbed. Later, she'd discovered that Myles had been the one to turn them in. He'd made a tidy sum on the deal. A mercenary to the end. If she ever ran into him again, he would wish he'd died of the fever.

Trevillion's voice broke in on her thoughts, scattering them. He had moved closer and was now sitting beside Dominic; he and the old adventurer were conversing in low tones. She couldn't hear what they were saying, but she didn't need to. The sound of Trevillion's voice was enough to cause the now familiar tightness in her stomach. Her hand balled into a fist, crushing the bread.

"What's the matter with you?" Laraina asked. "Are you sure you're all right? Maybe you should lie down and rest."

"I'm fine," Tara said, annoyed. "Will you please stop fussing over me like a mother hen?"

Laraina regarded her silently, then shook her head. "I swear, sister, your temper is getting to be worse than mine. You will notice that I haven't lost my temper since we left Kite."

Tara looked at her. "You haven't, have you? To what do we owe this extraordinary occurrence?"

"I think perhaps it's because I'm in love," Laraina whispered.

Tara felt a sliver of apprehension. Her one fear was that her sister would lose her heart to a scoundrel and get hurt as she had. "I've heard that before," she said dubiously.

Laraina looked away. "I know, but I think maybe this time I mean it."

Tara stared, suddenly aware of a change in her sister's whole demeanor. Angry with herself for not noticing sooner, she turned Laraina around to face her and looked long into her eyes.

"Well, well," she said finally. "May I be the first to congratulate you." She embraced her, summoning a smile to hide her misgivings.

Laraina smiled back. "Just think, now that I've got my love life straightened out I can work on yours."

"Oh, no," Tara retorted. "If you even think of such a thing, I'll —"

Laraina laughed and jumped to her feet, keeping her head low. "I was only joking." She started back toward the others, then stopped and turned around. "Of course, there's always —" She dodged as a ball of wet, half-rotted leaves whizzed by her. Still laughing, she walked over and sat down beside Kaden.

*****

"They're quite a pair," Dominic said, watching the sisters fondly.

"That they are," Trevillion agreed.

"I can still remember the day we met," Dominic continued, settling back with a faraway smile. "Whooo, boy, what a time that was! It was about seven years ago — in Vaalderin, no less. I was sitting in a tavern when Tara walked in. Now I don't need to tell you that with her looks she turned every head in the place. At the other end of the bar sat a man by the name of Lars Barstow. I don't know if you know him or not."

"We've met," Trevillion said in a tone that told exactly what he thought of Lars Barstow.

"Yes, well, Lars walked over to her and said, 'I've got a room upstairs. Let's you and me go have some fun.' Tara looked him up and down and said in a voice that would freeze a bonfire, 'You touch me and I'll knock your teeth through the back of your head.' Lars lost his temper. He grabbed her and pulled her off the stool.

"Well," Dominic paused, chuckling, "she turned around and let him have it!" Dominic pounded the palm of his hand with his fist. "She belted him a good one. Knocked him flat on his back over a table. I swear I've never seen such a nasty left cross on a woman.

The whole place went quiet. There wasn't even a peep. Tara stood by the bar watching him. He took one look at her and pulled himself to his feet. He had the ugliest look on his face. I mean even uglier than usual. Then he said some things I won't repeat and lunged at her, and I, chivalrous fool that I am, I stepped in front of her and tackled him." Dominic sighed happily. "That was the beginning of the wildest bar brawl I've ever had the pleasure of fighting in." He laughed. "And Tara was right in the middle of it, slugging away, throwing bottles and chairs and — well, you saw her at the *Blue Swan*."

"I did indeed," Trevillion said softly.

Grinning broadly, Dominic continued. "This had been going on for quite some time when Laraina walked in. She just stood there for a minute with her hands on her hips, shaking her head. Then she fought her way into the middle of it, grabbed Tara, and dragged her out the back door. Now by this time I had two black eyes, a bloody nose, and a few less teeth, and I decided that they had the right idea, so I followed after them. I hadn't gone more than a few feet out the back when, lo and behold, they appeared in front of me. Tara thanked me for my help and offered to bandage me up. We went to my room. While they were fixing me up, the two fellows I was traveling with, Myles and Xavier, came in. We found out that we were all going in the same direction, so we decided to travel together.

"Things happened fast after that. Those two could get into more trouble. I could tell you stories. You wouldn't believe some of the things they did." Dominic chuckled and shook his head. "But they always managed to come out of it in one piece." He smiled to himself.

Trevillion studied the plateau beyond the side opening in the grove, then looked back at Dominic. "What happened then?"

Dominic started. "What? Oh, well, about four years ago we were traveling in Barony when Xavier lost his head over a girl from Brynnd. Well, not literally." Dominic laughed. "They got hitched, and he went to work on her father's horse farm." Dominic grew sober. "A few months later, Tara, Laraina, Myles, and myself were hired to steal a jewel from some high and mighty noble in the Twin Cities. I don't remember much about it. I came down with black fever. Myles bolted faster than a rabbit with ten foxes on his tail. He was scared to death that he was going to get it. I haven't seen his skinny hide since. Tara took it hard. She and Myles had been more than friends, if you know what I mean. Somehow, we ended up in a dungeon. I was in rough shape for a while, thought I'd seen the end of this life. Tara got us out of the dungeon. I don't know how. I recovered, and I don't know how that happened, either. Black fever is usually fatal. About that time I decided I was getting too old for the adventure business. A friend offered me a partnership in his merchant trade, so I took him up on it. Tara, Raina, and I said our goodbyes and went our separate ways." His voice grew softer. "I didn't realize just how much I missed them. They've always been like family to me." He fell silent again.

Trevillion finished his bread, drank a few swallows, and dropped the canteen back into his pack. "What about your partnership?"

"It was boring. Sitting around all day taking inventories, sorting, stocking shelves, selling boring goods to boring people. I stuck with it as long as I could, but the day finally came when I just couldn't stand it anymore. I took a good look at myself and said, 'What am I doing here? I'm an adventurer not a businessman, and I'll be damned if I'm going to do this just so I can live longer and end up deaf, blind, and toothless in some old home for the useless somewhere. I'm an adventurer, and by the gods, I'm going to die like one.'

So I quit and headed for the open road." He smiled. "It was the happiest day of my life."

*****

Tara wiped the crumbs from her hands and looked out at the glowering sky. She had the feeling this storm would be worse than the last one. Her eyes searched the ridgeline behind them, straining for a glimpse of the hunter who dogged their steps like some ghoulish hound. Nothing moved but what blew in the wind. All around, the brooding mountains loomed like hulking giants, their barren peaks obscured by the restless, shifting clouds.

Aurelia rose. "I'll be right back," she said and disappeared behind a clump of trees.

Stifling a shiver, Tara opened her mind and scanned the nearby canyons and ridges. *I know you're out there*, she thought, *but how close?* Icy fingers chafed the back of her neck. She sensed danger, but not from the direction she expected. She sprang to her feet. "Aurelia's up to something!" Tara had barely taken a step when a familiar screech raked her ears, coming from outside the grove. Tara raced out of the hollow onto the open plateau, the others right behind her.

Aurelia darted into view, waving her arms over her head and screaming as if all the demons from the Abyss were after her. Tara and the others ran toward her. Then they saw the bees.

"Ow! Ow! Ow!" Aurelia shrieked. "Get them off me!"

"Into the water!" shouted Trevillion. He scooped Aurelia up in his arms and ran toward the pool. The others followed, cursing as angry bees swarmed around them.

"*Deleri dispranis!*" roared a gravelly voice from somewhere above and behind them.

The bees vanished. A dull echo reverberated through the hooded mountains like a death knell. Tara and the others whipped around, searching for the source of the voice.

"*Dispranis,*" Aurelia muttered as Trevillion set her down and pushed her behind him. "That's the word."

"There! I see him." Tara pointed. "Up on the ridge."

The others followed her gaze. High on a cliff, a scant canyon-width away, a dark figure stood, blurred against the leaden sky.

"Oh, gods! The Butcher!" Laraina whispered.

"Falling a little bee-hind, are you?" the wind-blown voice taunted. Grating laughter filled the distance, bouncing off the surrounding rocks. The figure turned and disappeared from view.

"We've got to get out of here!" Laraina cried.

Trevillion drew his sword. "Follow the path to the edge of the plateau. Once you're down, keep due east. Desta is two hours from here." He started back the way they'd come. "I'll slow Natiere down and —"

Tara caught his arm. "No! You can't! You'll be killed!" She held him back, suddenly seeing in her mind Trevillion lying dead on the ground.

"Thanks for the show of confidence."

"It has nothing to do with your skill," Tara said quickly. "It's just that sometimes I know things, and I know for certain truth if you go out there now Natiere will kill you!"

"You can't know —"

"I do know."

"She does know," Laraina said. "Don't ask me how. We'll get the packs." She raced to the grove with Kaden on her heels.

Trevillion shook his head impatiently. "I don't see —"

"Trust me. Please." Tara felt the blood rising in her face as Trevillion's eyes held hers. She let go of his arm and stepped back.

Aurelia slipped between them and threw her arms around Trevillion. "Jovan, you must come with us. You must! I'm frightened."

Trevillion gently disentangled himself. "All right, all right. You've convinced me."

Laraina and Kaden dashed back with the gear. Tara let out a breath of relief as Trevillion sheathed his blade.

"This way." Trevillion set off across the plateau.

Clamping down an urge to toss Aurelia into the pool, Tara ran after him. She kept her right arm against her chest to ease the pain in her shoulder. *I only wanted Trevillion to come with us so he could get us through the Bog,* she told herself. *Otherwise, I wouldn't care.* She cursed herself for blushing. These reactions were getting out of hand. "It won't happen again," she said under her breath. She glanced behind her to make sure the others were keeping up.

They grouped around Trevillion at the east rim of the plateau. He snatched a rope out of Kaden's pack.

"Please hurry!" Aurelia said.

Tara peered over the rim. A rugged cliff stretched downward into a gloomy valley, its hidden depths shrouded in mist and lengthening shadows. She suddenly felt cold all over.

"Tie this around you. We'll lower you down," Trevillion said to Tara. He held out the rope.

"What's down there?" She took the rope and tied it around herself.

"Rocks, brush. Why?"

She shivered. "I'm not sure. It feels... menacing, somehow."

Trevillion stayed her hand and undid the rope from around her waist.

"What are you doing?" Tara asked, perplexed.

Trevillion handed the rope to Laraina. "You and Kaden go down first." He wrapped the other end of the rope around a stout rock.

Tara bristled. "There's no reason —"

"Don't argue," Laraina said. She secured the rope around her waist, then gripped the length and lowered herself over the edge, pushing away with her legs as she descended.

When she reached the bottom, Kaden started down.

Tara fidgeted with the pommel of her blade as she watched Laraina standing below with sword drawn, but nothing swept out of the mist to attack.

"You're next," Trevillion said.

Ignoring the ache in her shoulder, she tied the rope about herself and climbed down. As soon as her feet touched level ground, she shrugged off the rope and drew her sword. The rasp of the metal blade barely penetrated the deadening mist that crept over the rocks like a predator. Tara moved away from the cliff and joined Laraina and Prince Kaden.

"I can't see a thing," Laraina whispered. "How about you?"

Tara shook her head. She let her eyes blur into the mist, trying to sort through the tangle of auras she felt. She sensed anger, hatred — cold, violent, merciless — as ancient as the rocks themselves. "Something happened here. Something terrible."

"It's creepy down here." Aurelia appeared beside them, her voice loud in the damp stillness.

Tara jumped. Her eyes snapped back into focus. "Quiet!" she ordered.

Aurelia stamped her foot. "Must you always yell at me?"

"I'll stop yelling at you when you stop doing things that require yelling about," Tara retorted in a low voice. "You need to learn to keep your voice down." She noted the many red swellings on Aurelia's face. "What happened with the bees?"

Aurelia stiffened. "They came out of nowhere and attacked me."

"Out of nowhere," Tara repeated. She scanned the silvery mist but saw nothing. "You conjured, didn't you."

Aurelia hesitated. "Yes, I did." She lowered her voice. "I was so hungry. I just wanted some oat bread and honey. I was going to make enough for all of us."

"What happened?" Laraina asked. She pulled a small brown container from her belt pouch and handed it to Aurelia. "Rub some of this on your stings. It will ease the pain."

Aurelia took it gratefully. "Thanks." She dug out a glob of waxy salve and gingerly covered her numerous welts. "The oat bread was easy. I made a huge loaf. Then I started conjuring the honey."

"And you got bees instead," finished Tara.

Aurelia's shoulders sagged. "Yes."

"What happened to the bread?"

"I dropped it when the bees attacked me."

Tara shook her head. "Why do you think I keep telling you not to conjure?" She looked back up at the cliff face. Dominic had reached the ground and was disentangling himself from the rope.

"I can conjure very well," Aurelia snapped.

Tara shot her a look of disgust. "Yes, you have certainly demonstrated that." She ignored Laraina's glare.

Aurelia tossed her head. "Mage Dralain told me I'm one of the best apprentices he ever had."

"Did he now." Tara tightened her grip on her sword. "Well, remember this, the next time you think about conjuring. If the Butcher hadn't gotten rid of the bees, we would have been too distracted to fight him, and he would have caught us. Instead of standing here complaining, you could be having your toes cut off, one by one."

Aurelia glanced at her feet, then leaned into Kaden. "He wouldn't do that... would he?"

Kaden hugged her, his face grim. "He would. And worse."

"Why did he get rid of the bees?" asked Laraina.

"He probably wanted to torture us himself," said Tara. "Can't let the bees have all the fun."

"He used magic," Laraina said. "That must be how he tracks so well, but why hasn't he used his magic on us directly?"

Dominic hurried over to them. "I need some help holding the rope so Jovan can climb down."

Laraina and Kaden followed Dominic back to the cliff, leaving the question unanswered. Aurelia tagged along after them, still applying the salve.

"Who knows," Tara said to no one in particular. She stepped closer to the mist and thrust her sword into it, swirling it around. Nothing happened. *He used magic.* The words stuck in her mind. Magic. She remembered running into the Butcher in the hall of Castle Carilon while on her way to Prince Kaden's father's room. What had he said to her?

"Aurelia," Tara said, turning around.

Looking apprehensive, Aurelia came over.

"Do you know the phrase, *Silvestri witana?*"

Aurelia's eyebrow arched upward, and her mouth quirked. "I believe it means 'silver-haired witch.'"

Tara kept her expression neutral. "How do you know?"

"It's from an Eastern gypsy language. The gypsies had some powerful magic-users. I studied them a few months ago as part of my training."

"I see. What about *Mi achina?*"

Aurelia thought for a moment. "It's an endearment. It means 'my heart,' 'my soul' — something like that." She stopped. "Are you all right? You look sick."

"I'm... fine," Tara managed to say. She tried to erase the stunned expression she knew must be on her face.

"Where did you hear it?"

"I heard someone say it some time ago. I was just curious. Thanks."

Tara turned away, her mind spinning with confusion. Why would Natiere have said that to her?

Trevillion strode up beside her and held out a length of rope. "Hang on to this and don't let go of it. I don't want to lose anyone."

She took it without speaking. The others stood close in a line and grasped the rope. Holding the leftover coil, Trevillion led them into the mist.

CHAPTER 8

A clinging fog billowed around the group as they followed Trevillion deep into the valley. Earth and sky disappeared. Tara could hardly see Trevillion in front of her. Rounded boulders, beaten smooth by the elements, and patches of brush appeared and disappeared like spectral beings in the mist.

Tara gripped the rope, her left hand hovering over the pommel of her sword. Cold prickles raised goose bumps on her skin. She looked around, casting outward with her mind. Faint whispers curled around her, fading in and out of the fog. Harsh murmurings — the clash of weapons, battle cries, and screams from wounded men she couldn't see — began to swell and ebb in nightmarish confusion. She pulled back on the rope to stop Trevillion.

Aurelia ran into her. "Hey!"

Tara pushed her back into Kaden and drew her sword. She let go of the rope and whirled around, trying to pinpoint the origin of the sounds, but they seemed to come from everywhere.

Trevillion appeared from the mist. He caught her sword arm. "You're going to kill one of us."

Tara snatched her arm away. "Don't you hear it?" She searched the mist but couldn't see beyond the end of her blade.

"Hear what?"

"I don't hear anything," said Laraina, coming forward.

"Me, neither," said Dominic.

"The sounds. The voices." Tara snapped her head around. "There is a battle going on right here... somewhere."

"There is nothing here," said Trevillion. "It is a trick of the mist. Take the rope. We need to keep moving."

Air whistled past her head as if a sword blade had swung and missed its mark. She jumped backward.

"Your 'nothing' just swung at me." She backed away, feeling the press of unseen enemies. The mist closed around her. She heard Trevillion cursing and giving orders to the others. Ghostly figures formed around her, some short and thick-bodied with long hair and beards, some taller with shorter hair and long moustaches. They all wore heavy armor and spiked helmets. Back and forth they fought in hand-to-hand combat, their battle axes clanging against metal and thudding against bone.

Tara stared as the battle raged all about her, yet did not touch her. The combatants either didn't see her or were ignoring her. *Dwarves*, her mind registered. They were Dwarves, ghosts of the two races that had once lived in these mountains. Their catastrophic battle, centuries ago, had killed every last one of them.

A battle axe cleaved through the helm of one of the Dwarves, and he stumbled backward, falling into her. She felt a stinging cold as his spectral body fell right through her to sprawl on the ground.

The attacking Dwarf now stood in front of her, his teeth bared, his dead eyes locked on her. He swung the axe at her head. She dodged the blow and stabbed him with her sword. Her blade passed through him as it would through smoke, with no effect.

Something grabbed the back of her tunic and yanked her away from the Dwarf, who had raised his axe to strike again.

"Don't provoke them," Trevillion said roughly. He held her in an iron grip as he pulled her through the mist. "They will ignore you if you stay out of their way."

"You *do* see them," Tara said. "Why did you say there was nothing there?"

He didn't answer.

Tara stumbled over an upturned helmet, which appeared and then was swallowed up by the mist.

"How do you even know where we're going?" she demanded.

"I have a good sense of direction."

"So do I, but not in this." She stopped, nearly running into Laraina.

"Thank the gods," Laraina said. She gave Tara a quick hug. "I didn't think he'd be able to find you."

Laraina and the others stood huddled together. They had tied the rope around their waists to keep from being separated.

"Did you see or hear anything?" Tara asked. "Any of you?"

Laraina, Kaden, Aurelia, and Dominic all shook their heads.

"All I see is this miserable fog," said Laraina. "What did you see?"

"Ghosts. I saw ghosts of ancient Dwarves killing each other." She looked at Trevillion. "I want to know why we see them and they don't."

Trevillion released her. "I don't know." He picked up the rope and slipped it around her waist, tying a knot that she could easily undo. "I didn't want to do this, because it will limit our mobility, but it seems it is necessary."

Tara forced herself to stand still as he adjusted the rope, neither pulling away nor moving toward him, both of which she wanted to do. The voices still whispered, teasing her senses. She saw movements in the fog and knew the battle still seethed around them.

"And will you put that away?" Trevillion nodded at her sword. "It will do no good here."

Tara reluctantly sheathed her blade. Taking the end of the rope, Trevillion set off into the mist. Tara and the others followed, pulled along at a fast pace.

Thunder rumbled, and a cold drizzle began to fall, damping down the fog. Jagged lightning ripped through the heavens, and the drizzle became a downpour. Tara threw her hood over her head and wrapped her cloak around her to shut out the driving rain. The mist thinned, revealing more of the barren valley, but nothing of the Dwarven battle. The ghosts had disappeared, their voices lost in the storm.

The mist dissipated as they left the valley and worked their way down a gentle slope. The rain stopped. The sky cleared, the purple-gray of twilight settling over the mountains. Ahead lay another deep vale, this one wide and fertile with patchwork fields of new grass and tilled soil ready to plant. The Amberin River surged down the center of the valley, which angled away from them, following the southward course of the river. At the far end of the vale, they saw the crimson bulk and gleaming lights of a walled city.

Trevillion slid to a halt at the bottom of the hill. He nodded toward the lights. "Desta. The gates close at dark. If we get there before that, entering the city will be easy. If not, it becomes a little more challenging. Untie the rope. It's fairly easy going from here."

"It's almost dark now." Tara worked the wet knot free with bone-cold fingers.

Aurelia sneezed. "I can't get this off. I'm so c-cold!"

Trevillion helped her loosen the rope. "We'll be where it's warm soon."

"I could use a fire and hot food to warm these old bones," said Dominic. "They're stiff as tree trunks."

The others untied themselves and Trevillion stowed the rope in Kaden's pack. "Let's go."

The lights of Desta grew brighter against the darkening sky as they descended into the valley. The capital city of Mardainn straddled the boisterous Amberin River, the two halves of the city connected by three wide arching stone bridges. A high rock wall encircled the city, broken only by the tall archways where the river flowed through. The roar of the rushing water drowned out every other sound.

They crossed the valley floor, trusting in the darkness to hide their approach. As they neared the wall, some marshy hillocks provided cover, well beyond the range of the watchlights. Tara could see only one gate leading into the city, and it stood closed.

"The gates won't open until dawn," Trevillion said.

"Gates?" Tara asked.

"There are two, one on each side of the river. Both are well guarded."

Tara noted the soldiers patrolling the perimeter wall at close intervals. The gate itself was a massive structure of close-set wrought iron bars, backed by a solid sheet of iron. A narrow corridor of light spilled through the bars on the left side of the gate. The solid iron panel had not been closed completely. "What is that light on the left?" she asked, pointing.

"The traveler's gate. They are still open for late travelers," said Trevillion, "but you have to persuade the guards to let you in."

"If I go up to the gate and demand entrance, they will let us in," Kaden said. "We can speak with Councilman Jarnik."

"Who will throw us in the dungeon," Trevillion said curtly.

Kaden bristled. "That's ridiculous. Why would he do that?"

"Because you threaten Mardainn's neutrality. He will not risk bringing war to his country by picking a fight with Sulledor, which is what you'd be asking him to do."

"Once he knows what General Caldren has done, he will have to give aid."

"He won't," Trevillion said. "He does as he pleases. The council will not challenge him. And you can be sure he already knows what the General is doing. Jarnik has many spies."

Kaden took a step toward Trevillion. "I am a reigning prince. He can't just ignore me."

Trevillion didn't move. "He won't have to ignore you. He'll have you killed."

"He wouldn't dare."

"He would, if it would be to his advantage. If he thought killing you would buy the General's good graces, he would lock you in the dungeon and let you rot. It wouldn't be the first time he's had a hand in such things."

Tara glanced at Dominic, remembering the story he had told about Trevillion, his brother, and the missing king of Sulledor. Dominic had said he thought both General Caldren and Councilman Jarnik were involved in the boy king's disappearance. And in the disappearance of Trevillion's brother. She wondered how much Trevillion was risking, entering Desta.

Kaden faltered. "His life would be forfeit. The Court of Kings would convict him."

"Who would know?" Trevillion asked. "No one would be around to tell them what happened. We'd be dead, too. Besides, if the other kingdoms fall to Sulledor, there will be no Court."

Tara stepped between Kaden and Trevillion. "We don't have time for this." She faced Kaden. "Our goal is to warn Faragellyn of the coming attack. The only way to get there is over the Desta bridge. Then through the Bog to get rid of the Butcher."

Kaden raked his hand through his hair and turned away, cursing.

Tara looked back toward the mountains. With a strange chill, she sensed the presence of Captain Natiere. The Butcher was very near. Yet, her danger sense was not warning her of a dire threat. Instead, she felt something she couldn't describe, even to herself. She'd never felt anything like it. "We need to get inside. Can't we bribe the guards or something?"

"You can if you have something to do it with," said Trevillion.

"How much will it take?"

"That depends on who's on duty."

Tara eyed him questioningly. "You know them?"

Trevillion gazed at the city once more, his face expressionless. "I've met some of them."

"What if I talk to the guards?" Dominic stepped forward. "They wouldn't recognize me. You could all wear your hoods and be anonymous."

Trevillion shook his head. "No. I can get us through with the least amount of questioning."

Tara pulled a small coin pouch from her pocket. She knew Dominic must have been thinking along the same lines as she had, and she wondered at Trevillion's motives. She had the feeling he was risking a great deal, entering Desta openly. Why was he doing it? A knot of foreboding twisted her stomach. She dropped the pouch into his hand. "Here, take this. Use what you have to and keep the rest. We owe it to you anyway."

Aurelia grabbed the pouch from Trevillion's hand. "I'll go first. They don't know me, and they can't refuse a lady in distress." She sped toward the gate.

"Aurelia, no!" Trevillion ran after her.

Tara and the others quickly followed. Tara flipped her hood up over her head, masking her face as much as possible, and gestured for the others to do the same. She glanced up at the perimeter wall as she ran, expecting to be spotted by a patrol. Luckily, the patrol was just rounding the bend, heading away from them.

Aurelia reached the gate first. "Hello in there," she called out.

Trevillion caught her and pulled her back away from the gate. "Aurelia, listen to me. You have to let me deal with them."

"Someone's coming," Tara whispered as the group gathered behind Trevillion and Aurelia.

"What's going on out there?" demanded a gruff voice from inside the gate.

"We need shelter," Aurelia began.

Trevillion held up a finger for silence, and Aurelia closed her mouth. Trevillion surreptitiously took the coin pouch and dropped it in his pocket.

A guard appeared at the gate. "What's the matter? Can't control your woman?" He gave an ugly laugh.

Tara appraised him quickly — short, square, all muscle, and not friendly. He wore a metal helmet and leather armor over chainmail. Gripped in his hands was a nasty-looking poleaxe. He leered at Aurelia through the bars.

Aurelia straightened and tossed her head haughtily. "Stop staring at me."

Tara's hand slid to the hilt of her sword hidden beneath her cloak. Her eyes shifted to the guardhouse, which stood just inside the gate. Through its open door she could see one other guard, an older man with gray-streaked hair, sitting at a table, rocking his chair back on two legs, a fan of playing cards in his hand. He looked toward them as if weighing whether or not it was necessary for him to get up.

Trevillion stepped forward, easing Aurelia behind him. "I thought you two had sworn off card playing after that last trouncing I gave you."

The guard with the axe looked closely at Trevillion, recognition dawning on his face.

Inside the guardhouse, the chair came down with a crash. The older guard strode toward them. "Jovan Trevillion! Great Azakai's balls, are you out of your mind?"

"Nice to see you too, Gustav," Trevillion said. "Now open up. We're in a hurry."

"I can't do that." Gustav eyed Tara and the others. "Jarnik will skin us alive if we let you in without arresting you, not to mention what he'll do to you if he finds you here."

"We're only passing through," Trevillion said. "We'll be in and out before anyone knows we've been here."

The younger guard continued to ogle Aurelia, who was peeking out from behind Trevillion. "Who's that you've got with you?"

"A fellow traveler." Trevillion moved to block his view.

"You leave her with us and we'll let you in, no questions asked." The guard licked his lips. "What do you say, girl?" He winked at his cohort. "We treat our women nice."

Aurelia's lip curled. "I can't think of anything I would find more revolting."

"A spitfire, eh?" The guard turned to Trevillion. "I like this one." He unlocked the gate. "She stays. The rest of you can go on through."

"Sorry, Randel. I can't do that," Trevillion said. "She is under my care."

Randel snorted. "I'll bet she is."

Aurelia gasped at the implication. "How dare you!" She pointed at him and spoke some foreign-sounding words.

Trevillion caught her wrist and in one smooth motion, lowered her arm to her side and covered her mouth with his other hand. "Not now, please." He handed her back to Kaden. Kaden's cloak slipped back as he drew Aurelia beside him, revealing his scabbard. The watchlight glinted off the bright metal. The guards' eyes narrowed.

Tara gripped the hilt of her sword, forcing herself to remain still and wait for Trevillion's lead. She found it hard not to tell the guards that they were welcome to keep Aurelia.

Trevillion took the coin pouch from his pocket and dumped a few coins onto his palm. Both guards' eyes flew to the glittering gold.

"Well, now," said Gustav. "Whose pockets have you been fleecing lately?" He strode forward and fingered the coins. "This should do fine. Pay us back for all the card money you took from us."

"I won it from you fairly," Trevillion said.

"I want the girl," Randel whined.

"Forget the girl," said the older guard. "You can buy ten girls with your share of this."

Randel grunted and banged open the traveler's gate. Tara saw the cold speculation in his eyes and knew he was considering taking both Aurelia and the gold.

Trevillion motioned for the others to pass through the gate behind him. Tara walked through the gate, baring her scabbard as she moved. If the guards thought they were all armed, they might think twice about provoking a fight. The others followed. They regrouped inside the wall, keeping Aurelia safely encircled. Aurelia pulled her hood up to hide her face. Trevillion stepped through the gate last, then dropped the coins into Gustav's hand.

Randel grabbed his share. He gestured with his head toward the city. "Get going." He fastened lusty eyes on Aurelia. "Before we change our minds."

"Don't get caught," Gustav warned. "Jarnik will have your liver on his dinner plate."

"He'll have ours, too," said Randel.

Trevillion dropped two more small coins from the pouch into his hand and tossed them to the older guard. "Don't worry. We won't be here long."

Gustav eyed the coin pouch. "Want to play some cards?"

Trevillion smiled and slipped the pouch into his pocket. "Another time." He clapped Gustav on the shoulder. "Thanks. I won't forget it." He ushered the others forward into the city. Tara kept an eye on the two guards until they were out of sight. She noted that Trevillion did the same.

Once they were beyond the view of the gate, Trevillion took the lead. "Keep your eyes out for patrols. You won't hear them over the river."

"You should have let me turn him into a goose," Aurelia grumbled.

"I would have been happy to let you do so," Trevillion said with a half-smile, "but it would have drawn a little too much attention to our presence." He turned off the main route, and they hastened through a series of empty, lamp-lit streets. The houses, temples, and places of business were all tightly shuttered, with only the noise of the river filling the deserted spaces.

"Where is everybody?" Tara whispered to Trevillion.

"Curfew," Trevillion said. "Strictly enforced. Everyone must be off the streets by sunset."

Tara glanced around as they hurried deeper into the city, taking in the ornate crimson stone buildings and the scrupulously clean avenues. She'd never been to Desta and she couldn't help comparing it to the filth and ruin of Vaalderin. As they neared the center of the city, the steady drone of the river rose to a thundering roar. More than once, the sudden appearance of a two-man security patrol sent them scurrying down vacant side streets, barely escaping detection. After several such detours, they reached the inner edge of the city. Here, the line of buildings ended in a wide, flat docking bay that extended to the river bank.

Trevillion halted in a shadowed alley beside what looked like a warehouse. The others crouched, away from the slant of light that fell across the alley from the street lamps along the dock. Tara inched forward until she had a good view of the docking bay. Just off to the right, a high stone bridge rose upward, arching across the river like a crimson rainbow. Beneath it, and all along the edge of the river, small boats bobbed fiercely in the current, tugging at their moorings as if trying to escape. The river itself was dangerously close to overflowing its banks.

Tara swept her gaze over the dock area. So much open space to cross between the line of buildings where they stood and the edge of the bridge, with no cover. And then another wide expanse on the other side. Could they cross it without being seen? Tara looked back at the bridge. They had little choice. She hoped their luck would hold.

"My friend lives just on the other side of the river," Trevillion whispered. "If we can get across the bridge, it won't take long to get there."

Tara pointed out a patrol on the far side of the river, heading for the bridge. Trevillion nodded.

The patrolmen, looking bored, walked slowly over the bridge, stopping momentarily at the highest point to gaze at the river. One of them pointed at something in the water. The other nodded in agreement. Then they continued on, moving in a leisurely manner. They reached the end of the bridge and stepped out onto the smooth surface of the dock.

Tara tensed, ready to dash back down the alley as the patrol headed toward them.

A voice called out from somewhere off to their right. The sentries stopped and turned. One of them called back and raised his hand in greeting. Tara and the others sank lower in the shadows, not daring to move. The second patrol stepped into view. The four sentries gathered a short distance away and talked heatedly among themselves. One of them gesticulated furiously and pointed back toward the part of the city Tara and the others had come through. Glancing over their shoulders, the patrolmen hurried away to the right, disappearing down a distant street.

Tara let out a breath of relief. "I wonder what that was about."

Trevillion looked around the corner. "Follow me."

They sped across the open dock and dashed over the high, arching bridge, reaching the line of buildings on the far side of the river without incident. Keeping a sharp watch for the ubiquitous patrols, they dodged through the eastern half of the city.

The moon had risen, its bright fullness spilling silver light along the immaculate streets, accentuating their shadows. Trevillion led them down a side street that branched off a wide avenue lined with shops. Halfway down the block, he halted at a door and motioned to Laraina and Kaden to keep watch at the corners. Laraina nodded, and they went to stand guard. Trevillion rapped softly. After a moment, Tara heard someone moving about inside the building.

Laraina ducked back around the corner and waved at them. She raised two fingers and pointed up the street, indicating an approaching patrol. Trevillion knocked again, more urgently. There was a soft rattling as someone fumbled with the lock.

Tara moved swiftly to her sister's side.

"Back me up," Laraina whispered. Grabbing her water flask, she staggered drunkenly around the corner and crashed into one of the patrolmen. "Oh, I'm... shorry." She took a wobbly step backward. "I didn't... didn't know you were there."

Tara peered around the corner as the disgruntled sentry righted himself and caught her sister roughly by the arm as she tried to step past him.

"Not so fast, wench."

"Wench!" Laraina yanked her arm out of his grasp. "Who are you calling a wench?"

"Listen, *wench*." The sentry seized her arm again and pointed to the night sky. "It's past sunset. You're breaking curfew. You'd better be nice to us or we'll turn you over to Councilman Jarnik. A few days in his dungeon and you won't be looking so nice."

Both patrolmen now had their backs to the side street.

"I beg your pardon," Laraina said, "but I'll do nothing of the sort." She punched the patrolman in the nose and elbowed him in the side.

Tara poked the other sentry in the back. He whirled around, and she kicked him in the stomach. Then she and Laraina brought their knees up hard under their respective patrolmen's chins. The two patrolmen snapped over backward in unison, landing in the street with a thud. The sisters regarded them disdainfully, then turned and shook hands.

"Well done, sister," said Tara, smiling.

"The same to you." Laraina grinned.

Trevillion and Kaden, swords drawn, appeared behind them.

Kaden ran to Laraina. "Are you all right?"

"I'm fine, as my sister is always saying. Help me, will you?"

Laraina grasped one of the unconscious patrolmen by the leg and gestured for Kaden to take the other leg. Trevillion grabbed the second patrolman, and they dragged them around the corner and down to where Aurelia waited. Tara followed. Dominic kept watch at the other end of the street. They dropped the men in front of the door Trevillion had knocked on, which now stood open.

A short, stocky man with thick gray hair and beard stared out at them. "Jovan! What are you doing here? Jarnik will —"

"Yes, I know," Trevillion said. "Beldon, we need your help. May we come in?"

"You are always welcome here." Beldon's gaze shifted to Tara and Laraina, and Tara saw recognition in his eyes. "The Triannon sisters." He bowed low. "I am honored."

"Thank you," Tara said.

Laraina flashed him a smile. "What should we do with them?" She nodded at the unmoving sentries.

"Leave them. My sons will take care of them. Please, come in." Beldon stepped back, and with a wave of his arm, bid them enter. Then he turned and called softly into the house. "Bryon! Rogan!"

Two sturdy blond youths hastened into view from another room.

"Would you get rid of the garbage, please?"

"Yes, Father," said Bryon. Each hefted a patrolman over his shoulder.

Aurelia stared after them, a rapt expression on her face as she watched them hurry away.

Beldon closed the door, making certain it was securely locked before ushering his guests further into the house.

*****

Captain Natiere strode through the billowing fog, ignoring the Dwarven conflict, his mind on his quarry. His men followed, unaware of the battle raging around them. The pouring rain had stopped, and the ghostly war had resumed with the resurgence of the mist. The moldy smell of age and death clung to the blood-red rocks in the wake of the storm.

Natiere smiled with satisfaction. He was very close. He would have his prey. Soon.

Three spectral Dwarves charged across his path, brandishing axes and shouting battle cries. He deftly sidestepped, holding his arm out straight to herd his shivering men away from the onslaught. The Dwarves hacked at their ancient foes. Natiere continued onward, clashes and screams rising and falling around him. His men stumbled after him, muttering. He cuffed the man behind him.

"Quiet!" Natiere ordered. The muttering stopped.

He smiled again as they wended through mist and rocks and combatants. The Triannons had led him on a wild chase — one far better than he had hoped for. The silver-haired witch had even managed to elude him in Vaalderin. He had to give her credit for that; her reputation was well deserved. If this was to be his last hunt he couldn't have chosen a better opponent. He sighed in regret. Unfortunately, all hunts must end.

They emerged from the mist and descended into the dark valley where the city of Desta lay in torchlit silence, all sounds engulfed by the roar of the river. As they crossed the flat to the city, the Captain could see that the traveler's gate still stood open, though barred. He shook back his dark furred cloak and hood as they approached the wall and stepped up to the gate. He could see the sentries in the guardhouse, playing cards.

"Open the gate," Natiere demanded.

"State your business," said one of the guards, a stocky man with a poleaxe leaning against the wall behind his chair. Neither guard looked up from their game.

Natiere rattled the gate. "I said open it."

The guard threw down his cards in disgust. Shoving back his chair, he caught up the poleaxe and stomped toward the gate. "You'll have to make it worth my while. Got any women with you?" The guard glanced up as he spoke. The words died in his throat.

"No, I don't," said Natiere, "nor would I give them to you if I did. Now open this gate, or I will rip it off and wrap the bars around your neck."

"Ca-Captain Natiere," the guard stammered, frozen to the spot. "Sir!" he added hastily, saluting.

The other guard sprang to his feet, his cards flying through the air. He stayed in the guardhouse, keeping the table between himself and the open door.

"Well, don't just stand there babbling like an idiot!" roared Natiere. "Open the gate!"

"Yes, sir! Immediately, sir!" The guard dropped his axe and with trembling fingers, unlocked the gate.

Natiere entered and halted before him. "Now you listen to me. No one, and I mean *no one*, passes through this gate without *my* permission. Is that clear?"

The guard nodded vehemently. "Yes, sir! Very clear, sir! No one, sir!" He slammed the gate shut and locked it with a loud click.

"Good." Captain Natiere and his men walked into the silent city.

They strode through the empty streets, wending their way to the Council Building, which stood near the center of the western half of the city. Natiere curled his lip in scorn as the patrols they encountered either reversed their course or scurried to the far side of the street as they passed.

The Council Building was an imposing structure three stories high, with a grand red-and-white marbled staircase leading up to an intricately-etched wrought iron door. As the Captain and his men mounted the stairs, the sentry snapped to attention. He saluted crisply.

"Open it," ordered Natiere.

"Yes, sir!" The sentry unlocked the door and threw it wide.

Natiere and his men stepped inside. The door whisked shut behind them.

Natiere scanned the ostentatious entry hall. As he had expected, there was no one about. His gaze slipped with disgust over the profusion of cheap statuary, hideous artwork, and gaudy ornaments displayed in every available crack and crevice. Councilman Jarnik was a fool. However, he did have one redeeming quality: he kept a dungeon well-stocked with interesting instruments of torture. The Captain smiled as he pictured the plump councilman manacled to one of his own devices.

Turning his mind back to the business at hand, Natiere took a last look around. At the far end of the hall, a wide carpeted staircase led to the upper floors.

He gestured to his men. "Wait here."

He crossed the room and bounded up the stairs, taking them three at a time. At the top floor, he turned right and strode down the wide corridor to the largest suite, which he knew Councilman Jarnik kept for himself. Noiselessly, he opened the door and entered the darkened room. The odor of incense clogged the air. He whispered a word and the glowing embers in the fireplace burst into flame.

A loud snore emanated from the far corner of the chamber. Peering into the gloom, Natiere spied the rotund councilman lying in his bed asleep. With a fiendish smile, Natiere slammed the door.

The councilman jerked upright, thrashing as he tried to untangle himself from the covers.

"Who's there?" he demanded in a high-pitched voice. "Foss, is that you?"

Natiere ignored him and went to the window.

Councilman Jarnik succeeded in extricating himself from the bed clothes. "Answer me! Who is there?"

Captain Natiere pulled back the heavy drapes hiding a tall, arched window. He undid the lock and threw open the casement. Cold air and moonlight flooded the room.

"Natiere!" the councilman gasped, squinting against the light. "What are you doing here?"

Natiere turned away from the window but said nothing.

Jarnik frowned. "Savage," he muttered under his breath. Rising quickly, he slipped a dark robe over his ample frame and smoothed down his graying hair.

"Well, what do you want?" he asked impatiently.

Natiere eyed the councilman with contempt. "A group of fugitives has just entered the city."

"That's impossible," Jarnik declared. "The gate guards —"

"Are worthless," interrupted the Captain. "Order a lockdown. No one is to enter or leave the city until I find them."

"I will not," the councilman blustered. "I am in charge of this city, and I —"

"You will do as I say," Natiere cut in sharply, "or you will find yourself in a very unpleasant position. It might interest you to know," he continued more calmly, "that a man by the name of Jovan Trevillion is with them."

"Trevillion!" The councilman's face turned a deep shade of reddish-purple. "That's impossible! He wouldn't dare!"

"He is here!" Natiere snarled.

Councilman Jarnik took an involuntary step backward. He tugged on a bellpull hanging beside the bed. A moment later the door opened and a man in uniform appeared.

Drawing himself up with dignity, the councilman addressed the sentry. "I am ordering a complete lockdown. The gates are to be barred, and no one is to pass in or out of the city until further notice. Is that clear?"

"Yes, sir."

"Inform Major Laudring to assemble the men in the square, and that they are to follow the Captain's orders."

"No," said Natiere. "I do not want your men. I will find the fugitives myself."

"Then why the lockdown?" asked the councilman. He thrust out his chest, trying to reassert his importance. "That's not very sporting of you."

"I wish to see how resourceful they can be."

"Just who are you hunting?"

"That is not your concern." Natiere strode to the door.

The sentry backed away and flattened himself against the wall of the corridor.

Natiere paused with his hand on the doorlatch and turned to face the councilman. "I will give you Trevillion. You can deal with him as you choose. The others are mine." He gave a contemptuous nod and went out.

*****

Tara finished stuffing supplies into her backpack, then turned to help Laraina and Dominic.

"Beldon, are you sure you can spare this much?" Trevillion asked.

Beldon nodded. "Of course, Jovan. We have plenty."

"We'll find a way to repay you," Laraina said.

The old man held up his hands and shook his head. "You are my guests, and my friends. It is no trouble."

The door burst open and Beldon's sons dashed into the house, flinging the door shut behind them.

Tara's hand flew to her sword. "What's wrong?"

"Councilman Jarnik has ordered a lockdown," the elder son gasped, catching his breath. "The gates are barred, and his men are searching the city."

Tara and Laraina glanced at each other in alarm.

"Natiere must be here," Tara said. "We need to leave. Now."

Beldon paled. "Captain Natiere? The Butcher?"

Tara nodded.

"He is," said Rogan. "Sergeant Blaine told us that he forced Jarnik to order the lockdown but told him not to send his men out. Jarnik sent his army out anyway." Rogan looked at Trevillion. "He wants you."

"Then we must move quickly," said Beldon. "You will have to use the smuggler's gate."

"The what?" Tara and Trevillion asked simultaneously.

"The smuggler's gate," Beldon repeated. "It was put in by Blackie de Runo several months ago."

"Blackie de Runo?" Tara echoed in surprise.

"Yes. Do you know him?"

Tara and Laraina grinned at each other.

"That we do," said Laraina. "We'll have to remember to thank the old pirate."

"The gate is in the northeast wall," Beldon continued. "Bryon will show you." He turned to the youth beside him. "Do you have the uniform?"

"I'll get it," Bryon said. He vanished into another room.

Tara and the others grabbed the gear and went to the door. Bryon reappeared moments later, looking unchanged. Tara cocked her eyebrow, but didn't ask.

Trevillion embraced his old friend. "Thank you for your help."

"You're welcome. Farewell, and good luck to you," Beldon said as they followed his son out the door.

A full moon lit the city as the small group headed toward the northeast wall. They kept to the shadows, slipping unseen through the narrow, empty streets. Hoarse shouts echoed nearby. The sound of fists pounding on doors mingled with the heavy thud of swiftly marching feet as the army swarmed over the city. Bryon quickened his pace, hardly stopping to check at the corners before dashing around them. They were nearly to the wall when a shout told them they'd been spotted.

Tara looked behind her and saw a large troop of soldiers several blocks back, shouting, drawing weapons, and racing toward them.

"Run!" Bryon cried.

They ran. Bryon dodged around a corner and slammed into a group of a dozen patrolmen, responding to the alarm. Aurelia screamed. Bryon fought and kicked as the sentries tried to grab him.

Trevillion lowered his shoulder and charged into them, bowling several of them over. Swords flashing, Tara and Laraina pulled Bryon back behind them, then attacked the patrolmen still standing, felling four of them with quick strokes. Trevillion took out three more, clearing a path for the others to follow.

"This way!" Bryon cried, taking the lead.

Kaden pushed Aurelia ahead of him through the tangle of fallen sentries. Dominic followed on his heels. Tara smashed the hilt of her sword into the face of another patrolman and, levering her foot against his side, shoved him out of the way.

Aurelia shrieked as one of the sentries on the ground grabbed her ankle. Hearing her cry, Trevillion whirled and, with one slash, cut the man's arm off. The patrolman howled and writhed. Aurelia stared at the blood spurting from the dismembered arm still clutching her ankle, then swayed and collapsed in a heap.

"Aurelia!" Kaden ripped the hand away, then scooped her up in his arms.

"Go!" Tara cried. She shoved Kaden and Dominic ahead of her.

They raced through the last of the twisting streets, the pursuing soldiers barely two blocks behind them.

Suddenly, Trevillion broke away from the others.

Tara skidded to a stop. "Where are you going?"

"They'll come after me," he shouted, crossing to the left. "Escape while you can!"

"No!" she cried.

Laraina grabbed Tara by the arm and yanked her back out of sight. The pursuing soldiers swept around the corner. They spotted Trevillion and plunged after him.

"Come on!" Laraina dragged Tara after Bryon and the others. At the wall, Bryon dropped to his knees and slid his hands over the rough stones until he found the catch. A small door about two feet square popped open, revealing a rough-hewn tunnel. Dominic wriggled through first. He turned back and grasped Aurelia as Kaden handed her through. Then Kaden crawled into the tunnel.

Laraina sheathed her sword and crouched by the opening. She turned to Bryon. "Are you sure you'll be all right? What if they recognized you?"

"I'll be fine," he said. He shucked off his shirt and trousers, revealing a patrolman's uniform. He tossed the outer clothing into the tunnel.

Tara looked back, hesitating. *Let him go,* her mind said. *He means nothing to you. You should be glad to get away from him.*

Laraina's brow furrowed. "What's wrong?"

Cursing, Tara tore off her pack and cloak and tossed them to her sister. "I'm going back."

Laraina caught them and fell back. "You're what? Why? Jovan drew them off so we could escape!"

"At the expense of his life?" Tara shook her head. "I can't live with that. I owe him."

"What about us? What about them?" Laraina pointed in Kaden's direction.

"They'll be fine with you. Head for the Bog. We'll catch up as soon as we can."

"You're going to be *dead!*"

"Trust me." With a quick thank you to Bryon, Tara ran back up the street, away from the smuggler's gate.

*****

Laraina stared after her sister.

Prince Kaden poked his head back through the door. "What's going on out here? Why aren't you –?" He stopped. "Where's Tara?"

"She went back," Laraina said helplessly.

"She did what? Of all the hare-brained...!"

Laraina threw the pack and balled-up cloak into the tunnel. "She's going to get killed!"

Kaden shoved the stuff behind him. "That's her choice. You're *not* going after her." He pulled Laraina into the tunnel and gestured to Bryon. "Shut the door!"

"Good luck to you!" Bryon locked the door in place.

*****

Tara raced down the moon-silvered streets, following the clash and clang of weapons. Shutters cracked open, then slammed shut as the city dwellers glimpsed what was happening. Up ahead, a snarling knot of soldiers blocked her path. She dodged into a side street. The soldiers chased after her, following a parallel course. Somewhere to her right, near the docking bay, she heard a shout and recognized the voice. She charged forward.

She found Trevillion with his back to the wall, the councilman's soldiers closing in around him. Trevillion fought them off, but was impossibly outnumbered. Tara ran toward him. With another shout, Trevillion leaped into the surrounding troops, sword flashing, and Tara lost sight of him. Just as she reached the mob of soldiers, Trevillion staggered out of the melee and fell, clutching his right side. Tara swept past him, yelling and launching a vicious attack on the nearest soldiers that had them backing away like rats from a flame.

Trevillion dragged himself to his feet. "Tara! What in blazes?"

She sped back to his side. "Are you all right?" Her voice died away. "Oh, gods," she whispered, looking past him. Icy-hot chills raked her flesh. "Natiere."

Head and shoulders above the rest, the Butcher stood, watching her. A satisfied smile softened the ragged scar ruining his face. He was so close. His black eyes locked with hers. In that instant, she sensed his pleasure, his approval. Her mind slipped deeper into his and felt anguish, the pain of a life as tortured as his victims. Surprise crossed Natiere's face.

Trevillion gripped her arm. "Tara!"

She blinked, wrenched her eyes away. She saw the regrouping soldiers coming at them.

"This way!" With his arm clamped to his side, Trevillion ran.

Forcing her limbs to move, Tara followed. Soldiers attacked from all sides. Ducking and slashing, they fought through them and kept running. Tara felt the Butcher coming after her, gaining. She heard a voice like grinding rock barking orders, and the soldiers backed off.

With startling suddenness, Tara and Trevillion burst out into the open. In front of them lay the swollen river. The councilman's troops swarmed out onto the docking bay on either side of them. Tara and Trevillion raced to the river's edge and jumped.

CHAPTER 9

The muddy surge whisked Tara downstream, tossing her about like a stray leaf. Coughing and choking, she fought to keep her head above water. Her sword hampered her movements, but she refused to let go of it. The thunderous roar of the river filled her ears. A chill of danger swept over her as the sound rose to an even more deafening height.

The Falls! She had no time for more than a flicker of dawning horror before she was catapulted over the edge. Blinded by mist and spray, she plummeted over twenty feet into a deep, roiling pool. The relentless pounding of the falls drove her to the bottom. Dazed, she struggled out from under it and frog-kicked her way to the surface. She burst into the clear, gasping for breath.

Wiping her hair out of her face, she glanced about. Bright moonlight gilded the rippling water and gleamed off the wet scarlet rocks encircling the pool. She couldn't see Trevillion. Shivering, she floated onto her back and sheathed her sword. Her muscles ached from the cold. Willing her arms and legs into motion, she swam toward the east bank of the pool. The current tugged at her, pulling her toward the lower falls — a sheer drop of a hundred feet to the rocks below.

Something brushed against her. She swung around and found Jovan Trevillion beside her, half-swimming, half-floating, his lips tinged with blue.

"Hurry," he croaked. "The lower falls..."

Tara threw her arm about him, and they kicked their way to shore. They dragged themselves onto the rocky bank and collapsed.

Tara rolled onto her back, content to just breathe.

Trevillion, lying prone beside her, coughed and cleared his throat. "You all right?" He levered himself up on one elbow.

She nodded. "You?"

"Fine."

She laughed. "What a ride!"

Trevillion stared at her, incredulity on his face. Then his expression changed. She sensed regret, resignation, and something else. She caught her breath. Trevillion raised his hand and traced the line of her cheek, then slid his thumb over her parted lips. Heat shot through her, setting every nerve on fire. She felt as if the wind had been knocked out of her, her bones melting into mush. She wanted to move, to look away, to do anything, but she couldn't tear her eyes from his face. He leaned over and brushed his lips across hers. She closed her eyes as sensual explosions rippled down her body. She found herself reaching for him.

Stabbing cold ripped down her spine. Startled, she rolled away and bolted upright. "We have to move!" she gasped. She pulled Trevillion to his feet. They stumbled farther up the bank, behind the rocks, out of sight of the upper falls.

Struggling to calm her reeling senses, Tara peered up through a crevice toward the head of the falls. Several soldiers on horseback appeared, some on each side of the river. They looked down into the churning pool. Three or four dismounted and searched the ground along the river. One of them pointed toward the base of the lower falls. The soldiers remounted their horses and disappeared from view.

Tara let out a breath. "They're gone for the moment." She turned around. Trevillion lay flat on his back, eyes closed, his arm clamped to his side. Her gut clenched as she spied blood oozing between his fingers. She dropped to her knees beside him. "I thought you said you were fine!"

"That's what you always say, isn't it?" He coughed, leaving a trace of blood on his lips. "You should not have come back for me."

Tara pushed back his sodden cloak and eased his torn shirt away from the wound. "No, I shouldn't have."

"Why did you?"

Tara was silent. Why had she? The answer that presented itself was not to her liking. "I owed you one."

"Where are the others?"

"Hopefully, on their way to the Bog."

Trevillion curled onto his side, racked by another fit of coughing. His breathing grew ragged. Tara hurriedly cleared away the rest of the fabric.

"Oh, gods," she whispered. She had pulled away the cloth to reveal a deep gash across his ribs cut clear to the bone. The gash stretched from the middle of his belly to just under his armpit. The lower part of his rib cage was crushed inward. She saw the jagged bone of broken ribs, threatening to pierce the skin.

Tara sat back on her heels, at a loss. She knew he had been wounded in the fight with the soldiers, but it hadn't seemed like a severe injury. He must have hit the rocks when he went over the falls. She shook her head. What did it matter how he was injured? He was alive, but he wouldn't be much longer if she didn't do something. Seizing the remains of his tattered shirt, she pressed it against the wound to stem the bleeding. Trevillion's face contorted in pain.

"Why didn't you say something?" she demanded.

He coughed again and spit out blood. "What was there to say? It's a death wound." Sweat beaded on his brow; every breath seemed torturous. He clenched his fists. "Go. Before the soldiers get here."

"I'm not leaving you here."

"Well you can't carry me, and even if you could, I'd bleed to death long before you got anywhere."

"If you think I went through all that just to let you die —"

Trevillion pounded the ground with his fist. "Blast it, Tara! There's nothing you can do. Now go!"

She stared at him in silence. He was wrong. There was something she could do. But it would mean revealing her deepest, most closely held secret, a secret she had shared with no one, not even her sister. Was she willing to risk it? *He's just a man,* her mind said. *Men are selfish, spineless, betraying.* Memories of Myles swirled around her, leaving an angry, bitter taste. Then images of Trevillion, showing care and concern, helping her through the hard climbs despite her reticence, filtered into her mind. She felt his kiss once more on her lips like a sweet, tingling draught. He had saved her life, and he had been willing to sacrifice himself so she and the others could escape. How could she not help him?

She swallowed a curse. "Lie flat." She put her hands on his shoulders and eased him onto his back.

"Tara, I told you to go."

"I don't follow orders. You should have figured that out by now." She drew her dagger.

"What are you going to do with that?"

"Relax. I'm not going to use it on you." She ran the blade over her thumb, testing its sharpness. Then she sliced a gash across the palm of her left hand. Dropping the dagger, she placed her bleeding hand over the open wound in his side and closed her eyes.

A surge of warmth and strength coursed through her body like a fiery river. The pain of Trevillion's wounds knifed through her, then was swept away by the burning, white-hot rush of power. Harnessing that power, Tara opened her mind and searched deeply, probing the injury, carefully mending broken bones and torn flesh. She sensed the nearness of Trevillion's soul and felt a yearning to merge with it, to be one. She caught herself and pulled away. Slowly, she withdrew. She opened her eyes. Her head felt like she'd been spinning in circles. Trying to focus, she looked down at the wound. It had healed completely, without a scar.

Trevillion sat up. He caught her hand as she removed it from his side and held it, sliding his thumb gently over her palm. The gash in her palm was fully healed, as well. At his touch, she looked up.

Trevillion stared. "Your eyes..."

"What about them?" She turned and looked closely into a small pool of moon-bright water trapped by the rocks. "Oh." The silver-blue color of her eyes was swirling to match her still spinning head.

"How did you do... what you did?"

She rubbed her eyes. "It is a gift I was born with. I can't explain it, and I would ask that you not tell anyone — not even Laraina."

"She doesn't know?"

"No one does. You see, in Wyndover, the village where we grew up, such a talent would be considered witchery." A deep-seated hostility seeped into Tara's voice. "The Elders feared any sort of magic and considered it evil. I got enough suspicious glances because of my hair and eye color. The only reason the townspeople tolerated me was because my parents had been respected members of the community. If they had known about this, I would have been thrown to the wolves."

"You have my word," he said softly.

Tara held his gaze. Then she nodded. "Thank you."

"No," he countered. "Thank *you*."

Tara smiled. "Now we're even."

Trevillion smiled back. "What else can you do?"

"Nothing that I know of, except that I can usually sense when danger is near." She wiped off her dagger and slid it back into its sheath. Her dizziness eased. "We should get out of here before the soldiers come back."

Trevillion rose and gave her a hand up, steadying her.

"I'm all right," she said, stilling herself mentally.

Trevillion removed what little was left of his shirt and tossed the remnant into the river. It swirled in the current and disappeared over the edge of the lower falls. Scooping up handfuls of water, Tara and Trevillion washed away the blood staining the spot where Trevillion had lain. Then they made their way through the rocks to the northeast.

*****

"They're gone, sir." The sentry spoke from the edge of the doorway to the massive torture chamber housed on the lowest level of the Council Building. He had come to an abrupt halt after seeing the erstwhile west gate guard, stripped of his axe and armor, being chained to a giant spit by Captain Natiere.

"That is quite obvious," observed Natiere.

Councilman Jarnik glared at Natiere, then turned back to the sentry. "What about the boy who was with them?"

The sentry fidgeted. "The man, Beldon, and his family who aided them have disappeared as well."

"Have they?" Natiere grunted. "What a surprise."

"You don't seem very upset," Councilman Jarnik said peevishly.

"Upset? Why should I be upset?"

Jarnik stared at him, arms akimbo. "Your quarry has just escaped from under your nose. I should think you'd be furious."

Natiere snorted. "Hardly." With flint and tinder, he lit a fire in the fire pit and built it up, ignoring the cries from the guard chained to the spit. "I am impressed by the Triannons and their resourcefulness. This hunt has turned out to be quite entertaining, much more so than I had anticipated." He rose and began turning the spit. "To show my appreciation, I'll give them another hour or two's head start before I track them."

The councilman laughed shortly. "I'm sure they'll be appropriately grateful. I, however, intend to do no such thing. My soldiers are already searching the area. The fugitives will be found and brought back here within the hour."

The Captain smiled with amusement. "I highly doubt it."

"You will see," the councilman said with a sniff.

"Excuse me, sir," ventured the sentry, "but there's a messenger here from General Caldren."

Councilman Jarnik frowned. "Great gods, what does he want now?"

The sentry moved aside and another man, dressed in peasant garb, stepped forward. "The General requests more men for the ambush at Relic," he stated impassively.

"More men!" The councilman threw his hands up in disgust. "I've already sent an entire battalion. They were dispatched two weeks ago. Now he wants more? What does he think we are, his personal army reserve?"

"I wouldn't know, sir," the messenger said, his face still devoid of expression.

"Well, you can tell the General his request is denied. I can spare no more men."

A loud guffaw from Captain Natiere startled the councilman, and he spun around. "What are you laughing at?"

"You." Natiere chuckled. "General Caldren never 'requests' any-thing. If you take it as such you're more a fool than I thought."

"Now look here." The councilman drew himself up to his full height. "You're overstepping the bounds of your authority."

"Am I?" The Captain assumed a look of penitence. "Forgive me."

"I also have a message for you, Captain, sir," said the messenger, who was starting to lose his composure as the cries of the roasting gate guard grew more shrill.

The Captain bent down to poke up the fire. "What is it?" The pungent smell of burning flesh permeated the air.

The messenger choked on his words. "He requests that you abandon your pursuit of the fugitives and accompany the second battalion to Relic to aid in the ambush."

"No!" The Captain snapped upright. "I am too close to give them up now."

Both the sentry and the messenger bolted from the chamber.

Natiere slammed a log down into the fire pit. Sparks flew as the fire blazed. With an effort, he reined in his anger. He was still hon-or-bound to serve the General. But he had no intention of giving up his prey. He felt again the remembered touch of Tara's mind in his, vibrant, yet cool and calm. The deeper touch that had brushed his blighted soul was inadvertent, he was sure, but it had surprised him. He had been able to sense her presence. It seemed that she could sense him, as well. Strangely, the idea that someone else, even for a moment, had shared the misery he had endured made him feel al-most human again. The thought intrigued him. He was not *alone* anymore.

Natiere tossed another log onto the fire. He had made an agreement with General Caldren; now he would end it. Four years in the General's service was more than enough penance to pay for killing one of the General's murdering, thieving men. He would go to Relic and inform the General that he would no longer be his exe-cutioner. Then he would be free to continue his pursuit. He would find her. He didn't care about the others. He would kill them quick-ly and discharge his final duty to the General. Killing them slowly in his usual manner no longer interested him. But the silver-haired witch he would not kill right away. Not until he felt her cooling touch in his mind again.

The gate guard screamed and begged for mercy. Captain Na-tiere tossed more wood into the pit.

Councilman Jarnik, who had moved to the other side of the chamber, eyed the Captain warily. "You laughed at me for presum-ing to oppose the General. Will you?"

Natiere glared at the councilman. "Assemble another battalion in the square."

The councilman eased toward the door. "Will you be following the same route as the first battalion — south to the Amberin fork, then north along the bank of the Nournan River through the Bog?"

"No. We will cut through the mountains. There are many passes that will get us to the Nournan much more quickly. From there we will go up through the Bog along the riverbank. We will leave in an hour."

"An hour," spluttered the councilman. "That's not nearly enough time —"

"Stop babbling and do as I say!" roared Natiere.

The councilman's mouth closed with a snap and he fled the room.

Captain Natiere turned back to the groaning gate guard, grasped the spit handle, and rotated it vigorously.

*****

Tara and Trevillion traveled continuously for the next two days, heading northeast toward the Bog, sometimes going miles out of their way to avoid the persistent sweep of the Mardainn soldiers. Someone was determined to find them, but whether it was Captain Natiere or Councilman Jarnik, they did not know. Tara no longer felt the chill of Natiere's presence and began to worry that he had gone after Laraina and the others instead. Laraina, Kaden, Aurelia, and Dominic, escaping northeastward out of Desta, should be nearing the Bog by now, if they had avoided pursuit. She figured she and Trevillion were about half a day behind them.

The second night was dark with clouds. When they could no longer see their footing, they took shelter in a small cave in the rocks. They rested on a pile of wind-blown leaves that had collected at the back of the cave.

Tara took the first watch. Trevillion slept beside her. Beneath them, the crushed leaves gave off a faint earthy odor. Tara stared out at the darkness and listened to the stillness of the night. Even the roar of the Amberin River had faded into the distance. She tried to relax and rest her aching muscles, but the possibility of her sister being in Natiere's grasp kept her nerves taut. Her stomach growled. They had no supplies. She had given her pack to Laraina, and Trevillion had shed his when battling the soldiers. There wasn't much food to be found in this rocky country. She rubbed her belly. Thoughts of meat and bread and cheese made her mouth water.

Trevillion stirred in his sleep; he turned onto his side, facing her, his head pillowed on his arm. She looked at him in the faint light, at his dark, sleep-tousled hair, the short beard covering his strong jawline, the well-muscled chest only half covered by his cloak. The urge to touch him, to run her hands over those muscles and through his hair was almost overpowering. Her stomach butterflies began their dance, and she swallowed hard. And the thought of him doing the same to her... The butterflies flew into a frenzy.

She tipped her head back against the cave wall. What was there about dark-haired rogues that she found so irresistible? Myles had been handsome, but it was his devil-may-care attitude that had drawn her. That and the fact that he had truly seemed to want her. He had been young then, brash and arrogant. She had been young too, and so used to people spurning her because of her strange coloring that she found his attention intriguing. Even so, they had flirted for a long time before she had finally let him into her heart. A mistake, she knew, but she had ignored the warnings of her conscience. She had been so taken by his whimsical courting that she had let herself be blinded to his faults. Myles was a mercenary, and she had known deep down that his main priority was himself. She had never completely trusted him. He had not the strength of character she sensed in Trevillion.

She looked down again at Trevillion and wished she knew more about him. She knew nothing in truth, only the story Dominic had told her. Why was he helping them? She wanted to ask, but there really hadn't been an opportunity. They had kept silent, rarely speaking over the last two days to avoid detection by the Mardainn patrols. Not a word had been said about the healing, or the kiss. She blushed as she thought of how his lips had touched hers, if only for a brief moment. Why had he kissed her? Did he really care that much? She didn't allow herself to follow that line of thought. If they survived the Bog and the General's war, she might think about it. But then, who knew if Trevillion would still be with them at that point? They had only asked him to guide them through the Bog.

Trevillion stirred again, rolling onto his back. Tara quickly looked away. Her cheeks grew hot once more, and she was glad for the dimness of the cave. Trevillion roused and sat up. "Your turn to sleep," he said.

Her stomach grumbled. "Good. I need to stop thinking about food," she said, seizing on her original train of thought to hide her emotion. She lay down and closed her eyes.

*****

A persistent numbing chill prodded Tara awake. Something was wrong. Dead wrong. She sat up and instantly regretted it. Her head felt like it had been hit with a sledge hammer. She closed her eyes and reopened them, trying to make sense of the scene before her. She was sitting on the cold stone floor of a long, dimly lit hallway. How had she gotten here? Where was here? And where was Trevillion?

Ignoring the pounding in her head, Tara rose to her feet and looked around. The hall appeared to be hewn out of solid rock. Thick, yellowish slime splotched the dark gray walls. A dungeon, perhaps. But whose? Masses of cobwebs hung from the low ceiling. Four torches in bare metal sconces spaced several feet apart provided the only light. At the far end of the hall stood a massive iron door. She stared at it uncertainly, then looked behind her. A deep, impenetrable blackness met her gaze. She rubbed her throbbing temples. She had the strangest feeling she'd been here before. A vague unpleasant memory flitted through her mind. She tried to grasp it, but it slipped maddeningly away.

An odd scraping noise, like someone or some thing, walking, dragging a damaged leg, emanated from deep in the blackness. She smelled the faint odor of carrion. A death-like cold crawled over her skin, sending warning chills through her blood. The scraping sound drew closer, mingled with the rasp of labored breathing. She sensed a presence, vile, malevolent, murderous.

Fear tightened her chest until she could barely breathe. She reached for her sword. It wasn't there. She rifled her clothing. She had no weapons of any sort. Heart pounding, she grasped one of the burning torches. Holding it in front of her as a weapon, she backed toward the door. Her breath caught in her throat. One by one, the remaining torches flickered and died, as if snuffed out by an invisible hand. Tara whirled in a panic and leaped to the door. She tore it open and dashed through, not caring what dangers lurked on the other side. She only knew that she had to get out of there.

Halting breathlessly, she found herself in another torchlit hallway, this one lined with doors. She glanced behind her. The iron door she had passed through stood open. The hall beyond was pitch black. She slammed the door shut, but saw no way to lock it.

Clutching the torch, she ran down the narrow corridor, passing countless hallways that branched off in every direction, each lined with identical iron doors. She darted into one of the passages that veered to the left. The passage soon branched out into still more passages. She halted. Which way?

Torn by uncertainty, she crept to one of the doors and tried the latch. The door swung inward, pulling her with it. She fell forward and nearly plunged headlong into a yawning pit of blackness. The torch slipped from her grasp as she clawed at the latch to save herself. Hanging over the void, she gripped the door handle and swung her body back and forth until she caught the edge of the hall floor with her toes. She flung herself back into the hallway, pulling the door shut after her. She rolled onto her knees, shaking.

A door opened and closed somewhere behind her. The odd scraping echoed harshly in the stone corridor. Bitter cold washed over her, like plunging through ice on a frozen lake. Not daring to seize another torch, she leaped up and ran, twisting blindly through the endless maze of passages. Thick cobwebs dangled in front of her like gauze curtains. She tore them aside without stopping. The hideous scraping sounds hovered just on the edge of her hearing, gnawing at her sanity. She ran on and on and on until she could run no more. Her lungs burned like fire, her breath coming in short gasps. She stumbled to a halt. Crouching with her back to the wall, she tried to beat down the hysteria that had seized her mind. She had to calm down and concentrate and find a way out. She looked at the door across from her. There were a million doors in this dungeon. One of them had to be an exit.

The door beside her opened. A bloodcurdling hiss shocked her to her feet. Hot breath scorched her cheek; the stench of rotting flesh gagged her. Something seized her from behind. She screamed. A hand clamped over her mouth. She opened her eyes to moonlit darkness. She was lying on the ground. She scrambled to her knees, fighting the hands holding her.

"Tara, stop! Wake up!"

Jovan Trevillion's voice cut through her terror. Her mind clung to the familiar sound. She stopped struggling and sank back to the ground.

Trevillion slid his arms under her and carried her to the mouth of the cave, setting her down in a damp splash of moonlight. He knelt beside her. "Look at me." He cupped her face. "The color of your eyes is swirling again."

"Is it?" Her head ached like it was stuck in a vise and she couldn't stop trembling. She was so cold. She clasped her arms about herself and rubbed weakly. "I'm fine." Her voice sounded strange to her, faraway.

Trevillion frowned. "You're white as death, and you're shaking worse than any earthquake I've ever felt."

"I'm cold."

Trevillion sat behind her. He slipped his arms around her and drew her to him, lifting her onto his lap, enfolding them both in his worn cloak. She didn't resist. She leaned back against him and rested her throbbing head on his bare shoulder. He held her close, cradling her in his arms, his body warming her.

The moon shone down, bright in its fullness. The smell of earth and damp leaves filled the night air. Tara took several deep breaths and tried to clear her head of the disturbing remnants of her dream. A small voice in the back of her mind told her to get up, to move away, but she didn't want to listen. Resting in Trevillion's arms this way she felt protected — safe, in a way she'd never known.

"It must have rained," she observed.

"A storm blew through while you were asleep," Trevillion said. "Tell me what happened."

Tara massaged her aching temples. "Nothing really. It was just a dream." She stopped, thinking. "Strange..."

"What is?"

"I've been having nightmares off and on for a while now, but in the past, I couldn't remember what happened in them."

"You mean you've had this dream before?"

"Yes. I'm sure it's the same." Though she wasn't sure how she knew.

"Tell me."

Tara closed her eyes and let the dream replay itself in her mind. She saw again the blackness, felt it closing in on her. She watched herself running through the endless maze of door-lined corridors. She heard the creature, whatever it was, dragging after her, then springing out of the door next to her. Cold panic whipped through her and her eyes shot open. She fought down the urge to bolt.

Trevillion's arms tightened. "Easy. You're safe. I'm here."

She beat on the pommel of her sword with her fist. "I don't understand it. I have never been afraid of anything. How is it that something that doesn't even exist can fill me with such mindless terror?"

"It must have something to do with your... gift."

Tara turned sharply. "Why do you say that?"

"Your eyes did the same thing both times."

Tara turned back around. Why would that be?

"How did you know you had this healing power?" Trevillion asked. "And how did you know how it worked?"

"I discovered it by accident when I was about thirteen. Laraina and I were rock climbing one day, looking for a cave that smugglers used to stash their goods. Laraina fell and hit her head. The wound bled all over the place. Before I realized what I was doing, I had knelt beside her, pulled out my knife and cut my hand open. The pain shocked me. I remember staring at my bleeding hand and thinking I had gone mad. But, somehow, I knew what to do. I put my hand on the wound and healed it."

"Did she know?"

"No. I moved her away from the blood on the ground and washed the blood from her face and hair before she came around. I didn't dare to tell her. I thought the Elders must be right. They were always calling me a witch-child. I didn't want Laraina to think the same and turn away from me. I also didn't want word of what I had done to slip out. Raina's not always good at keeping secrets. If any-one found out, I'd be dead."

"How many people have you healed?"

"Three, not counting you. The second was Blackie de Runo."

"The smuggler?" Trevillion asked, surprised.

Tara nodded. "It was his stash Raina and I had been trying to get into. He helped us escape from Wyndover after the Elders found out I'd been hiding him and came for us like an angry mob. But that's another long story. The third person I healed was Dominic."

"When did you first start having the dreams?"

Tara thought back. "The first time I remember having it was four years ago — the night I healed Dominic of the fever." She paused, a chill running through her. "Black fever is fatal if it's not caught quickly. Dominic came down with it. We ended up in a dungeon — please don't ask — and Dominic was dying, so I risked using my healing powers. Laraina was asleep. She never knew. But he was so far gone it took all the strength I had to pull him back. I had to reach deep inside both of us." She trailed off, remembering the toll it had taken.

"He recovered quickly after that," she said finally, "but I didn't. That night I had the dream. I woke up screaming, terrified out of my wits, but I couldn't remember what the dream was about. I've had it several times since then. I never noticed a pattern." She thought for a moment. "The night after the rockslide, when my shoulder was hurt, I had the dream."

"You were healing yourself," Trevillion said. "There has to be a connection."

Tara scowled. She couldn't deny it. The evidence was too great. What did it mean? What was happening to her?

"I wonder if Laraina has powers like yours but just doesn't know about them," Trevillion said.

"She doesn't."

"How do you know?"

Tara shrugged. "I just know."

"Tell me about the dream," Trevillion said again.

Tara hesitated, loathe to recall it.

"You're awake now. It can't harm you."

"Why do you want to know?"

"In case I can help in some way."

Tara glanced back at him. "How could you help?"

"I don't know. I can't tell without knowing the dream."

She quickly described her nightmare. Trevillion listened without comment.

"Does it mean anything to you?" Tara asked.

"No," he said, but he seemed lost in thought.

"Why are you helping us?"

"Why?" Trevillion repeated as if not understanding the question.

"You risked your life for us in Desta. Why?"

"You are enemies of General Caldren. I'm willing to risk quite a bit to confound his plans."

"But you didn't know that when we talked to you in Vaalderin. We only said we wanted you to guide us through the Bog. We didn't say why."

"As I said before, Vaalderin was short on amusements."

Tara swallowed her frustration. She had seen the unreadable mask come down and knew she would get no more answers. If she antagonized him with persistent questioning, he might change his mind about leading them through the Bog. She still thought she and the others could get through on their own, but their chances would be better with him along. She drew away and forced herself to rise. "There's enough light now. We should get moving."

Trevillion rose and led the way across the ghostly silver rocks.

CHAPTER 10

"They should have been here by now," Laraina Triannon fretted as she paced back and forth in a small woodland clearing. The ground under her feet was spongy, matted with moss and dead leaves. The odor of rotting vegetation permeated the moist air.

Prince Kaden caught her arm. "You have to stop pacing. You're driving yourself, and me, crazy."

She stopped, shivering. Off to her left, not a stone's throw away, lay the Bog.

Shrouded in mist, its brooding presence filled her with dread. She had brought the others this far, but had dared go no closer. The damp air reeked with the musty smell of age and something sinister. Within its foul borders time ceased to exist. From the earliest remembrances, the Bog had struck terror into even the most stout-hearted of men. It seemed alive — a living, breathing entity with a mind of its own, twisted and malevolent, as if presided over by a demon, and the passing of centuries had neither brightened nor dimmed its perpetual gloom.

Dominic rose stiffly from where he knelt, taking inventory of their supplies. "He's right, Raina, calm down. Give them time. We've been running hand over foot for three days now, and they have a lot more ground to cover."

Prince Kaden looked at him blankly. "Hand over foot? What in the Abyss does that mean?"

Laraina pushed her hair away from her face. "What do you mean 'more ground to cover'?"

"Well, the way I see it," Dominic said as he lurched over to a nearby tree and lowered his massive frame to the ground. He settled himself as comfortably as he could against the rough bark. "They only had one way out — the river. As high as it is, they would have been swept halfway to Darbry before they could get to shore —"

"Yes, and right over the Falls," Laraina interrupted. "That is, of course, assuming they got to the river."

"Of course they did." Dominic scratched his back against the rigid bark of the tree. "Now as I was saying, they would have been carried who knows how far downstream before they could get to shore. That means they'll have to cross a pile of rugged territory just to get back to where they started. Add to that the fact that Captain Nightmare and his ghoulish friends will be looking for them. It'll be another day at least before they catch up with us."

"If they catch up with us," Laraina muttered. She started pacing again. She saw Kaden glaring at her and forced herself to stand still. He turned his back and sat down on a dry patch of moss next to Aurelia who lay curled up with her eyes closed, trying to sleep.

The weary group had entered the misty primeval forest of Shallin Wood early the day before. Vast and largely unexplored, the ancient forest was a tangled mass of towering hardwoods, dark evergreens, and thick budding undergrowth. Dormant vines, some as thick as a man's arm, crisscrossed through the close-set trees to form a natural ceiling. All manner of birds and wildlife flourished in its trackless depths.

Laraina wiped her brow and looked around the clearing. What if Tara didn't show up as Dominic predicted? What if she and Trevillion were dead? What if...? There were so many possibilities; all of them bad. *They have to be alive*, she told herself firmly. *And if they're not back by this time tomorrow, we will go after them.* She glanced at Kaden and knew that would likely be a battle. Kaden would be happy to have her sister out of the way, and that bothered her. She hated the animosity between them. It seemed so senseless. They both needed to change their attitudes.

The late afternoon sun filtered through the dense network of vines, tracing an intricate pattern on the floor of the glade. A deep silence surrounded them, broken only by the occasional harsh croak of a raven. The natural forest sounds had dwindled as they'd neared the Bog.

More croaks rang out, followed by the rustle of wings.

"Ravens." Kaden let go of his knife. "A sure sign of bad luck."

Dominic scoffed. "A raven never hurt anyone. Now if it was a vulture, I'd be worried. Vultures are nasty creatures. At least, the ones around Vaalderin were." He stretched out on the soft ground, tipped his hat down to shade his face, and closed his eyes.

"Ravens, vultures. I don't care what they are," Kaden fumed. "I still say this is an insane idea and we shouldn't be here."

Laraina had to admit she was beginning to agree with him. At first, Tara had convinced her that going into the Bog was the only way to escape Natiere's dogged pursuit. But now that she was here, there was something about this place that scared her as much as the Butcher did.

She sat down next to Kaden. "What else could we have done?" she asked, half to herself as she sought another plan of action. If she could come up with something else before Tara returned, they wouldn't have to venture into the Bog.

"We should have talked to the Council at Desta," Prince Kaden said. "I've met with Councilman Jarnik in the past. He wouldn't sign the peace treaty, but he couldn't refuse to help a neighboring country against an act of war."

"How do you know that? Tara said —"

"I don't care what Tara said. Your sister is a lunatic. She doesn't always know what she's talking about. It's time you realized that."

Laraina jumped to her feet. "She is *not* a lunatic. Her quick thinking has gotten us out of more trouble —"

"It was her lack of thinking that got you into trouble in the first place."

"Will you stop arguing!" Aurelia sat up and rubbed her eyes. "I can't sleep." She edged closer to Kaden, drew his arm around her, and huddled against him.

Laraina noted Aurelia's pale, drawn face and the fearfulness in her eyes as she looked toward the Bog.

"Must we be so close to it?" Aurelia asked. "It gives me the creeps!"

Another raven burst out of the trees, startling them with its strident croak. The black bird swept through the clearing and circled over their heads. Kaden sputtered an oath as he and Laraina ducked. Aurelia squeaked and cringed against Kaden's side.

"I have had enough of this insanity." Kaden stood, pulling Aurelia up with him. "We're going back. Are you coming with us?"

"Back where? Desta?" Laraina asked. "Natiere is back there."

"We'll take our chances." Kaden gestured toward the Bog. "The gods only know what's lurking in that cursed place."

"We can't leave. Tara will be looking for us here."

"Then stay."

Laraina froze, anger and dismay warring within her. "You would go back without me?"

Prince Kaden raked his hand through his hair. "Raina, I don't know what else to do. My father is dead." His voice broke, and he looked away. When he looked back, he had himself under control. "I am now King of Dhanarra. I have to think beyond myself, beyond us. My responsibility is to the people of Dhanarra. I must find allies to help defeat General Caldren and the Sulledorns. Yes, King Du Mraine of Faragellyn could help, but the Bog stands between us and him. If we go into the Bog, we'll die. Councilman Jarnik has a large army under his command. I will *make* him help me."

Angry tears filled Laraina's eyes. He was asking her to choose between the man she loved and the sister she had vowed to protect. The oath she'd sworn to her father long ago rang in her ears. She willed her tears not to fall. "How will you find your way to Desta if I stay?"

"I can find the way back," said Aurelia. "There are spells for such things as finding directions. We won't need your help."

"Raina..." Kaden's voice had grown rough. He took a step toward her. "I want you to come with me."

Laraina stood her ground. "Tara expects me to wait for her here. I will not turn my back on my sister."

"But you would turn your back on me."

"No, you know I wouldn't." She flung her hands up. "You are forcing me to choose between you and I can't."

Kaden crossed the distance between them and pulled her into his arms. "If she can find you here, she can find you there." He looked down at her, brushed her red curls back from her face. "Raina, I love you. But with or without you, I must go back. You have to understand."

"We had best stick together," said Dominic, sitting up with a grunt.

A throaty growl from the surrounding forest brought Dominic to his feet. "What was that?"

"I don't know." Laraina stepped away from Kaden and drew her sword. "It didn't sound friendly."

Another growl answered from across the clearing. They heard the faint swish of moving brush.

"Everybody up in the trees," Laraina ordered. "Now. Climb!"

A feral scream tore through the silence, sending shivers up and down her body. A wolf-like beast, black as death, eased into the clearing. Golden eyes stared at her as the creature bared its teeth.

"Oh, gods," Laraina whispered, eyeing the beast's finger-length claws and fangs. She gripped her sword and backed slowly away from it, glancing toward the others.

Kaden had shoved Aurelia up into the nearest tree, a tall hardwood, and was boosting Dominic up behind her.

Laraina heard a metallic rasp as Kaden started to draw his sword. "No, Kaden, don't." She kept her voice low. "Get up in the tree. I'll need you to pull me up." She waved her sword in front of her. The beast crouched, its pointed ears flattened against its skull, a ridge of hair rising along its back. It growled low in its throat. She heard Kaden cursing and sheathing his blade. She backed up more quickly.

The beast howled and leaped forward. Laraina turned and ran. Out of the corner of her eye, she saw something large and black lunge at her from out of the forest. She swung her sword on instinct and lay open the second beast's side as it bowled her over. It screeched and twisted away. Laraina scrambled to her feet, dropped her sword, and launched herself at the tree. Kaden caught her hand and pulled her up. Her toes scrabbled on the rough bark as she clambered up next to him. The first beast leaped at her, clawing at the thick trunk. Hanging onto a branch with one hand, Laraina pulled her knife out of her boot and swiped at the beast. The beast snapped at her as it dropped back to the ground.

Laraina and Kaden climbed higher to where Aurelia and Dominic stood clinging to the branches. The wounded beast licked at its bleeding side, then disappeared into the undergrowth. With a snarl, the other wolfen creature loped out of the clearing.

Laraina sagged against the tree. "Is everyone all right?"

The others nodded.

"What were those things?" Dominic asked.

"I don't know," said Laraina. "They looked like wolves, but they were bigger than any wolves I've ever seen."

"We have to get out of here," Kaden said. "A lot of good we're going to do stuck in a tree."

"What if they come back?" Aurelia asked in a strained whisper.

"I think we're safer up here," Laraina said. "We wouldn't be able to cover much ground before nightfall. There may be more of them, and I don't want to be caught on the ground in the dark."

"We could build a fire to keep them away," Kaden said. "There's plenty of brush for firewood."

Laraina shook her head. "A fire would lead The Butcher right to us."

"We don't know that he's out there."

"We can't assume that he isn't."

"I can make light," Aurelia said brightly.

"I don't know if that's a good idea." Laraina squinted into the settling dusk. She couldn't see anything moving.

"Let her try," said Kaden. "We need to see, so it's either that or build a fire."

Laraina looked at Aurelia. "Can you do it?"

Aurelia pushed away from the trunk. "Just watch me." She sat down on a branch. "I need something round." She checked her clothing and pockets.

"I might have a coin." Laraina dug into her belt pouch, but came up empty. She turned to Kaden and Dominic. "What about you?"

They shook their heads.

"I have an idea," Aurelia said. She pulled out a strand of her hair and placed it in her palm in the form of a circle. "This should work." She waved her other hand over it, then lowered her hand, palm down, bending her fingers until they formed a cage over the circle of hair. "*Millonnen luminestera*," she whispered. Nothing happened. She repeated the words. The hair began to glow with a soft, yellowish radiance. She smiled and bounced with glee. "It's working!"

The faint light brightened and grew to a glowing ball in her hands. Then, suddenly, the light poofed inward toward Aurelia, racing up her arms, over her head, and down until her whole body glowed with warm, yellow-white light. She raised her skirt up above her knees and looked at her glowing legs. "That wasn't supposed to happen."

Everyone stared at her, speechless.

"Are you all right, cousin?" Prince Kaden ventured.

"I'm fine. I just don't understand what happened."

"It must have been because you used your hair," Laraina said.

"Maybe, but that shouldn't have mattered."

"Can you turn it off?" Kaden asked.

Aurelia shrugged. "I don't know. I can try again with something else."

"No, let's leave things as they are for now," said Laraina. "We have light without having to worry about a fire. We can douse you, if we have to, by covering you up. Thanks, Aurelia. I'm sorry I doubted you."

Aurelia sat up straight, a smile on her glowing face. "You're welcome."

Laraina looked down at the ground. "I'm going down. I want to grab my sword and the packs before anything else attacks us."

"I'll do it." Kaden climbed out of the tree and dropped to the ground.

"Kaden, be careful." Biting her lip, Laraina climbed down after him, stopping at the lowest branch, her head swiveling as she watched the surrounding forest. Kaden handed her sword up to her, then dashed over, grabbed the packs, and ran back. Laraina sheathed her blade, caught the packs as he tossed them up, and helped him back up into the tree. They climbed to where Aurelia and Dominic waited and settled in.

Darkness fell rapidly and with it the temperature. Sleep did not come easily. Where the ghostly woods had been silent during the day, they roared at night. Snarls, hisses, peeps, and wild shrieks echoed and re-echoed through the inky darkness. Aurelia kept her hood down, her glowing head providing enough light to keep the night creatures at bay. She sat, shivering, with one arm around the trunk of the tree, and batted at moths. Laraina and Kaden stood with swords drawn, whipping around at each new sound. Dominic sat nearby, knife in hand.

The noises continued, shrill and terrifying, like the disembodied voices of lost and tortured souls. Laraina sighed wearily. It was going to be a very long night.

*****

The sky was as black as a bottomless pit when General Caldren reached the broad walkway along the eastern parapet of the hulking fortress of Belgarde. He stood at the edge in the shadow of the watchlight and gazed out into the thick darkness, gloating over his latest victory. Belgarde was his. It had fallen as easily as Carilon. His man on the inside had performed flawlessly.

As soon as light appeared in the eastern sky, he and his army would march on to the Faragellyn border town of Relic. More villages would be burned and more peasants massacred. He looked down at his hands as they gripped the rim of the parapet; blood stained them. The enemy's blood. He raised them high.

"This is for you, Father. See them bleed!"

A soldier approached from the north parapet. General Caldren lowered his hands and turned toward the advancing figure.

"General Caldren, sir." The soldier saluted. "The fortress is secured, sir."

The General nodded in satisfaction. "And no one escaped?"

The soldier cleared his throat. "A few made it outside the castle, but I think we caught them all."

"You *think*?" General Caldren whipped out his knife and slashed the soldier's cheek.

The soldier yelped and clutched his bleeding face.

"I will not stand for incompetence!" the General bellowed. "Report back when you are certain."

The wounded soldier stumbled away in shock.

*****

Tara looked around the small forest clearing, searching for signs of her sister and the others. The midmorning sun spilled through the lace of vines crisscrossing the branches overhead, and splashed in odd patterns on the forest floor. The resilient moss didn't hold footprints, but some scuffed spots that could have been made by boots were visible. Moving to the edge of the clearing, she walked the perimeter and inspected the dense undergrowth. A broken leaf caught her eye, and she bent for a closer look. A faint trail, much like an animal path, led off to the southwest toward Desta. She recognized her sister's handiwork in disguising her back-trail.

"Look at this," Jovan Trevillion said from the other side of the clearing.

She crossed the glade to where Trevillion crouched, examining the soft ground. He pointed to a partial paw print molded into a patch of moist dirt.

"Wolf tracks," he said.

Tara squatted beside him. "That's a wolf? It's huge."

"Bog wolves. Looks like two of them. They're much bigger than the average wolf." He touched the ground with his fingers and came up with a reddish-brown smear. "Blood."

Tara's chest tightened. "Whose?"

"Good question." He followed the tracks to the edge of the clearing. "There is more blood here. I would guess one of the wolves was injured."

Tara looked at the tall hardwood tree next to her. She could see where chips of bark had been scraped away. "Someone has been climbing trees. Can you give me a leg up?"

Trevillion came back to where she stood and boosted her up into the tree. She climbed upward, noting broken branches and a few cloak threads stuck on a twig, but no blood. Relief washed over her. "I don't see any blood up here." She climbed back down the tree and jumped to the ground.

Wiping her hands on her leggings, she looked around the clearing again. "They were here. These signs are only a few hours old. Why didn't they stay?"

"Maybe they didn't think we were coming."

"I told Raina to head for the Bog and wait for us there. We would catch up as soon as we could. The only path I see out of this clearing leads back toward Desta. It hasn't even been three full days yet. She has never doubted me before. Why would she go back and risk running into the Butcher? Why wouldn't she wait for me?"

"Perhaps she couldn't. Perhaps Natiere found them and took them back."

"No." Tara shook her head. "He's nowhere near. I haven't felt his presence since we left Desta. They left on their own, for whatever reason."

"They can't be that far ahead of us."

"No, but by the time we find them and get back here, we'll have wasted a whole day." She strode across the glade and ducked into the faint trail she had found. She heard Trevillion following.

They traveled swiftly through the forest, stopping only once to drink from a small stream. Tara's anger overruled her weariness and gave her speed. She knew exactly where the problem lay — with one tall, brown-haired prince. Kaden must have convinced Laraina to go back. *How could she believe him over me? He's going to get her killed.* Tara's hands balled into fists. *Unless I kill him first.*

Just after midday, Tara slowed her pace as she and Trevillion approached another small clearing. She held up her hand and stopped, listening as the murmur of hushed voices mingled with the songs of the thrushes and warblers and the chittering of squirrels. She recognized her sister's voice, but couldn't tell what Laraina was saying. Then Kaden spoke, his heated words cutting through the trees, insisting they continue on. Tara's eyes narrowed, her fingers curling around the hilt of her sword. Sensing no danger, she motioned to Trevillion and moved forward.

"I wish there was a better way to disguise our trail," she heard Laraina say. "The Butcher could find us so easily."

"The Butcher wouldn't need to follow a trail," Tara said as she and Trevillion stepped into the glade. "All he would have to do is listen. I could hear you clear back in the woods."

"Tara!" Laraina ran forward and hugged her hard. "Are you all right?"

"We're fine."

Aurelia ran to Trevillion. "Jovan! You're back!" She threw herself into his arms.

Tara turned on Aurelia, then swallowed what she'd been about to say. "Another spell gone bad?" she asked instead.

Trevillion extricated himself from Aurelia's embrace and looked at her glowing face and hands. "It looks like you captured the moon."

Aurelia smiled and lifted her chin. "We needed light, so I made light."

Dominic clapped Tara on the shoulder and swept her into one of his crushing bear hugs. "I knew you would make it. How did you escape? The river?"

Tara hugged him back. "Yes," she said, when he let her breathe again.

"How did you avoid the Falls?" Laraina asked.

"We didn't," Tara said. "We went over the upper part. We managed to drag ourselves out before we reached the Lower Falls." A sudden memory, Trevillion's lips on hers, sent heat rushing through her body; blood rose in her face. She abruptly changed the subject. "We found where you camped near the Bog. Why didn't you wait for us?"

Kaden stepped in front of Laraina, his chin raised in challenge. "We are going back to Desta to get help from Councilman Jarnik, as we should have done in the first place."

"And whose decision was this?" Tara demanded.

"Ours." Kaden swept his arm around Laraina and drew her up next to him.

"He and Aurelia were going back with or without me." Laraina's hand flew out in a gesture of frustration. "I couldn't let them go on their own."

"Well, thank you for the support." Kaden pulled his arm from Laraina's shoulders. "You wanted to get away from the Bog as much as I did."

"Yes, but I wanted us *all* to discuss the matter first."

"If we had stayed, we would have been wolf fodder."

"As I said before, Jarnik won't help you," Trevillion said. "He will either throw you in his dungeon or hand you over to General Caldren."

"And how do you know this?" snapped Kaden.

"Councilman Jarnik and the General have been in league for years," Trevillion said. "The Mardainn council claims to be neutral, but they are not. They support whoever pays them the most."

"Again, how do you know this?" Kaden's eyes narrowed. "Are you in league with them too?"

"Believe me or not, as you choose. I will take you through the Bog if that is where you wish to go. If not, I will say goodbye." He stepped away as if to leave.

"No!" Aurelia linked her arm in his. "You can't leave."

"Wait, Jovan, please," said Laraina. She turned to Kaden. "Why would Jovan have helped us if he was working with the General? It doesn't make sense. He risked his life for us. He has done everything he said he would do."

Kaden gripped Laraina's shoulders. "You are taking your sister's side again."

She shrugged him off. "I'm not taking anyone's side. I'm trying to find the best way to keep us all alive." She turned to Trevillion. "It would help to know why you agreed to come with us."

"You are enemies of General Caldren," Trevillion said. "He and Jarnik and I have a long history. Anything that would confound them is worth a little risk."

"You call going into the Bog a *little* risk?" asked Kaden.

"My reasons for going into the Bog are my business," said Trevillion.

"I believe him," said Dominic.

"So do I," Tara said. She remembered the story Dominic had told her about Trevillion, his brother, General Caldren, and the missing king of Sulledor. The General was somehow involved in the disappearance of Trevillion's brother and the boy king. She sensed there was no love lost between the General and Trevillion.

Prince Kaden crossed his arms in front of his chest. "Well, I don't."

Laraina looked from Kaden to Tara and back.

Tara kicked her heel into the dirt. "We're wasting time. The way I see it, Dhanarra is lost. By now, the General will have most of it under his control and will be heading toward the Faragellyn border. If we can get to King du Mraine in Crystalir and warn him of the General's advance, we might be able to save Relic and some of the other border towns. If we go back, even if Jarnik agreed to help, he would only give token support. He would keep his main army near to protect his own kingdom. By the time we got back to Dhanarra, Faragellyn would be overrun, and we would have no chance of defeating the General. Can't you see that?"

"She's right," said Trevillion.

Laraina took Kaden's hands in hers. "Kaden, please. I see the sense in what she is saying. Getting through to King du Mraine is our best chance to regain Dhanarra."

"We are going to die in the Bog," Kaden said flatly.

Laraina turned to Trevillion. "Is there no way around it?"

"You could go south around the edge of it and come up through the middle along the banks of the Nournan River. The ground is more stable there. It's less dangerous, but it would take days."

"We have to go through," Tara said. "It is the shortest route, and hopefully, it will throw Natiere off our trail."

"If Natiere was still following he would have caught us by now," Kaden said.

"Just because we haven't seen him doesn't mean he isn't out there," Tara said.

"He is probably amusing himself with Jarnik's torture chamber," said Trevillion.

"He has one?" asked Tara.

"He does." Trevillion's tone closed the subject.

Laraina looked at Kaden. He returned her gaze, then took his hands from her clasp and folded his arms across his chest again. "Fine." He pinned Tara with a glare. "We will do as you say. But our blood will be on your head when we die."

Tara glared back. "So be it."

Dominic picked up the packs and handed one to Tara and one to Trevillion. "There's food in there if you're hungry." He gave a pack to Laraina and then shouldered one himself.

"Food. Yes, we need some. I'm starving." Tara pulled out a breadstick. "We can eat on the way."

Trevillion dug some cheese out of his pack and headed back up the path. Aurelia, Kaden, and Dominic followed, with Laraina and Tara bringing up the rear.

Laraina hung back beside her sister. "Are you sure this is the right thing to do? The Bog seems such a frightening, evil place."

"I don't see any other way," Tara said. "We can't go back. Natiere is still out there. Have you seen any sign of him?"

"None. I thought he must be after you and Jovan."

"We haven't seen him either." Tara hesitated. "I saw him in Desta, right before we jumped into the river. He was quite close. He caught my eye and, for a moment, our eyes locked, and I couldn't look away. I somehow sensed his thoughts. And then I sensed in him a terrible pain."

"You mean he was injured?"

Tara ducked under a low branch. "No. It wasn't a physical pain. It was more like mental anguish, as if he had suffered a horrible trauma that had blackened him forever. Then something happened, and we broke eye contact, and I lost the connection. It was the strangest thing. I've never had that happen before, even with you, my own sister."

Laraina studied the ground in front of her moving feet. "What do you think it means?"

"I don't know. Nothing is making sense anymore."

Laraina avoided her gaze. "I have never understood how you sense things and know things you couldn't possibly have any way of knowing." She pushed a red curl back from her damp forehead. "Perhaps whatever tragedy Natiere suffered gave him his scar." She fell silent.

Tara sensed an awkwardness between them she had never felt before, a strangeness she did not know how to bridge.

Laraina finally looked at her. "I'm sorry we didn't wait for you. Kaden was determined to go back whether I went with him or not." She looked away, tears in her eyes. "I didn't want to leave because I knew you would be looking for us, but Kaden said you would be able find us if we went back. I couldn't let him and Aurelia go off by themselves. Especially after we were treed by those wolf-like creatures last night. And I was frightened by the Bog. There's something about it that just..." She stopped and faced Tara. "I don't know what else to say. I'm sorry."

Tara buried the hurt she felt and hugged her sister. Then she turned her around and gave her a gentle nudge forward. "We need to catch up with the others."

Laraina wiped her eyes on her sleeve and hurried up the path.

Tara watched her a moment before following. She had never seen her sister in such a state. None of the men Laraina had been with had ever come between them.

I think perhaps it's because I'm in love. Laraina's whispered words came back to her, and realization struck her like a hammer blow. She was losing her sister. The one person she trusted, the one who had stood by her through so much. A sharp ache settled around her heart. What would she do without her? Tears burned her own eyes. *Kaden, you had best not break her heart, or you will answer to me.*

They reached the clearing at the edge of the Bog about an hour before nightfall. Trevillion gestured to the hardwood tree they had vacated earlier. "I suggest we spend the night in the tree. Sleep if you can. We'll leave at dawn."

Wordlessly, Prince Kaden helped Aurelia into the tree and climbed up after her.

"We need to empty two of the packs." Trevillion set his pack on the ground.

Tara, Laraina, and Dominic brought their packs over and set them next to his. Trevillion dumped the contents of his and Tara's packs into the other two.

He handed Tara an empty pack. "Fill this with moss. I'll fill the other one." He gave the supply packs to Laraina and Dominic. "You two up in the tree." Trevillion began digging up the greenish-brown moss that covered the ground.

Tara put the moss in her pack. "What is it for?"

"To burn," Trevillion said. "It gives off a little light and a lot of smoke, and it smells bad. It will cover our scent and keep away the spiders."

"Spiders? Laraina will love that," Tara said.

They finished filling their packs and climbed up into the tree. Kaden, Aurelia, Laraina, and Dominic slept in twos, the watcher making sure the sleeper didn't fall out of the tree. Dusk drifted over the glade, erasing the shadows and leaving the group in blackness. Aurelia's glow cast the only light in the dark woods. Growls and chirps and rustlings stirred the silence, growing more boisterous as the night deepened. An owl hooted and swept past the tree.

Tara leaned back and settled herself against the thick trunk. Trevillion climbed over and sat on a branch next to her. She could just see him in Aurelia's glow.

"You should get some sleep," he said. "I'll take the first watch."

Tara looked down. The ground below lay hidden in darkness. "I have to admit I've never slept in a tree before."

"It's an interesting experience." He sounded amused. Then he sobered, his voice growing soft. "I won't let you fall."

Warm tingles shivered down Tara's spine. She tipped her head back against the tree, cursing and enjoying the feeling at the same time. "Thanks. Wake me when it's my turn on watch." She closed her eyes.

*****

A bestial howl nearly jumped Tara out of her skin. Somewhere above her, Aurelia screamed. Tara reached for her sword, felt her balance shifting, and suddenly remembered she was in a tree.

Trevillion steadied her. "Sit still." His voice rose, so the others could hear. "It's on the ground. It can't reach you."

Another howl rose from the base of the tree. Four pairs of golden eyes looked up at them.

"What are they?" Tara asked as the eyes circled the trunk.

"Bog wolves," Trevillion said. "Aurelia, can you give us more light?"

"Yes, I think so." Aurelia rolled up her sleeves and hiked her skirt up. Yellow-white light from her glowing arms and legs spread throughout the tree and shone down to the ground. "Does that help?"

"Yes, thank you."

"Those are what treed us last night," Laraina said.

"I'm sure glad they can't climb," said Dominic.

The wolves circled the tree several more times before disappearing into the forest.

"You can douse the light now, Aurelia," Trevillion said. "Thanks."

"You're welcome." Aurelia rearranged her clothing, and the light dimmed.

"What happens when we meet those wolves in the Bog?" Laraina asked. "Head for the nearest tree?"

"No," said Trevillion. "You do *not* want to climb the trees in the Bog. Better to fight with the wolves. I'm hoping we can avoid them. They generally only prowl at night."

"What's in the trees?"

"Spider nests."

"*Spiders?*" Laraina made a strangled noise. "You're joking, aren't you?"

"I'm not joking. The spiders in the Bog are deadly, as are most of the other things we'll run into there. The Bog is an evil place. Dark magic rules it from an ancient source no one remembers. We'll be lucky to come out alive."

"Why are you willing to go back in?" Tara searched his face in the dim light. Their eyes met and held. A wave of unbearable guilt, horror, and pain flooded Tara's senses, left her reeling. The feelings vanished as abruptly as they'd come.

"I have unfinished business," Trevillion said, his face and voice expressionless. He lay back against the tree and closed his eyes.

Tara stared at him, her blood throbbing in her temples. It had happened again. Just like with Natiere. Though, this time, Trevillion had somehow shut her out of his mind. How had he done that? She didn't even know how she had gotten in.

"Lunatics! I'm surrounded by lunatics," she heard Kaden say above her. Laraina said something in reply, but Tara had stopped listening. She replayed the last few moments in her mind. One minute she was looking Trevillion in the eye, and the next, she was feeling what he was feeling. How was that possible? They'd looked at each other before without it happening. What was different this time? She considered demanding an explanation. He must know something, or he wouldn't have been able to close her out like that. And why hadn't he said anything when it happened?

Tara looked at Trevillion again; her eyes lingered on his ruggedly handsome face. He would likely refuse to answer if she questioned him. She decided to leave him alone. He would need all the sleep he could get if the Bog was as deadly as he said.

She looked toward the Bog and opened her mind to the aura surrounding it. Malevolence, hatred, death. The power that fueled the Bog reeked of it; she felt the strength of its black grip. She kept her mind open, probing deeper. Whispers swirled and ebbed in an endless flow. She tried to decipher them, but couldn't. Another aura from out of the Bog slipped into her consciousness, a pure evil without form, drawing near.

Shocking cold shot down her spine; her mind snapped shut. She straightened with a jerk and nearly fell out of the tree. As she regained her balance, she felt the evil aura dissipating, melting back into the black depths of the Bog. The threat of danger faded. Her heart pounded in the silence. Silence. She looked around. The night sounds...

"What happened to all the noises?" Dominic echoed her thoughts.

"What did you do?" Trevillion's voice startled her. She turned and found him watching her.

"I don't know. I was looking at the Bog. I felt an evil presence. It seemed like it was coming toward me. It felt somehow familiar, though I don't see how it could be. I sensed danger, and I... don't know what happened." She shrugged. "It's gone now."

"The presence or the sense of danger?" Trevillion asked.

"Both."

"Well, whatever you did, don't do it again. At least, not until we're out of the Bog."

"The presence — what was it?"

"I don't know." Trevillion lay back and closed his eyes again.

Tara shot him an irritated look. She was sure he knew a lot more than he was saying. Why did he have to be so secretive?

Tentative squawks and chirrups broached the silence. Squeaks, snarls, grunts, and growls followed, swelling into a cacophony as the night creatures resumed their activities.

Tara stared into the darkness. She had so many questions — about Trevillion, about the Bog. What did Trevillion mean by "unfinished business"? What did he hope to accomplish? What was the presence she had sensed, and why had it seemed familiar? She had never been near the Bog before. She took a deep breath and wondered that she had already grown used to the smell of rot and decay. Why did she have the feeling she'd been driven here, to a place so loathsome that no one in their right mind would go near it? Something strange was happening to her and to the world as she knew it.

She wondered, again, if there really were gods of Fate directing people's paths, drawing her toward an unknown future she was sure she was not going to like.

She swept her long hair back behind her, her hand falling lightly to the hilt of her sword. In a few hours, dawn would grace the forest, and they would begin their journey into the Bog. Then maybe she would get some answers.

*****

Early the next morning, they packed up their gear and gathered around Trevillion. The eerie sounds of the night had given way to an uneasy silence. Trevillion picked up a stick and drew a map in the soft moss.

"This is Desta," he said, marking a spot on the ground. "This is the Bog." He moved his stick up and to the right and scratched out the boundaries of the Bog. "And this is the Nournan River." He drew a long, sharply curving line starting in the northeast corner and then veering south through the heart of the Bog. "Now, we are here." He pointed to a spot about halfway between Desta and the river. "The best way to go is northeast until we hit the river." He traced a line along the route he had indicated. "It shouldn't take more than three days, and if we're still alive by then, we'll follow the river into Faragellyn and on up to Crystalir. The riverbanks are firm, and it will be much easier traveling."

Trevillion tossed the stick away and erased the map with his foot.

"Before we go," he cautioned, "there are three things you have to remember. Rule number one: don't trust your vision. Any place that looks solid enough to build a house on is probably bottomless. Rule number two: do not disregard anything you hear. If you hear any noise, no matter how slight, or even if you just think you hear something, tell me. Rule number three: don't touch anything unless absolutely necessary. The plants can be as dangerous as the animals."

Trevillion shouldered one of the packs and led the way to the edge of the Bog. "Stay in single file, but stay close, and step only where I step."

With that, he turned and entered the Bog.

CHAPTER 11

Captain Natiere strode through the early morning mist toward the head of the halted battalion, grinding his teeth in anger at another delay. They had been on the march for three days. That his troops did not want to go on this mission to Relic was becoming more and more obvious. "Cowards," he muttered to himself. "An entire battalion of fools and cowards. A gaggle of geese has more backbone."

As he approached the front of the line, a small man with lieutenant's bars on his uniform hurried back to meet him. Trailing behind the Mardainn lieutenant, his arm locked in the lieutenant's grasp, was a frightened scout.

"I'm sorry for the delay," the lieutenant said crisply, "but there seems to be a problem."

"Explain," ordered Natiere.

The lieutenant thrust the cowering scout forward. "Scout Romar says that a rockslide has blocked the trail."

"So find another."

"But there are no others," the lieutenant protested. "We'll have to turn back."

"There are dozens of others," snarled Captain Natiere. "And we are not turning back — for any reason." His black eyes swept over the battalion. "And for those of you entertaining thoughts of desertion..." His voice rose to a thunderous level. "Any man who so much as steps one foot out of formation will be profoundly sorry."

As if on cue, a chorus of fierce howls rose from the surrounding rocks. A large, black wolf, lean and shaggy, appeared on a shelf of rock above the startled troops. Baring its teeth, the wolf uttered a long savage howl, then vanished into the shadows.

The Mardainn soldiers exchanged fearful glances.

Captain Natiere surveyed his troops, and when no one spoke, he nodded curtly. "Good. Consider yourselves warned. Fall in." He strode to the head of the line and led the way into the scarlet rocks, bearing southeast.

*****

With a keen sense of foreboding, Tara watched Jovan Trevillion step into the Bog. Aurelia followed right behind as if glued to him, with Prince Kaden, Dominic, and Laraina trailing closely. Tara moved in after them. The yellowish mist, thick and foul-smelling, swirled around their knees, making it difficult for them to follow in each other's footsteps. A pervasive odor of decay choked the air. Tara searched the gloom for any movement. Lifeless trees, black and twisted, rose from stagnant pools of muck, their tortured limbs groaning under the weight of the greenish-black moss and vines that draped to the ground. Spider webs stretched from tree to tree overhead like gossamer curtains, spreading here and there between the trunks of the trees below. A heavy silence lay like a shroud over all.

Tara felt the Bog closing in around her. A deep cold settled into her bones. Shivering, she eased her sword from its sheath.

"What's wrong?" Laraina whispered, hesitating in front of her.

"Nothing, yet," Tara whispered back. "Keep going."

An hour passed, or was it two? Tara had lost all sense of time. Aurelia shrieked, and Tara jumped, her heart hammering. Trevillion whirled as Aurelia clutched his arm in a death grip.

"What happened?" he demanded.

"S-s-snake," Aurelia stammered. "H-huge, t-touched my foot."

"Did it bite you?"

"N-no." She swayed and nearly fell.

Trevillion caught her. "Don't faint!"

"I'm sorry," she squeaked. Tears filled her eyes. "I-I'm frightened."

"I know," Trevillion said more gently, "but you must be brave."

Aurelia nodded, sniffling.

"Things should get more interesting from here on in," Tara said as the group started forward again.

"Why do you say that?" Laraina asked over her shoulder.

"Because she just told every hungry monster within five miles right where we are."

"That's a pleasant thought," Prince Kaden grumbled.

They pressed onward, but the Bog remained silent. A flash of movement caught Tara's eye. She stopped. "What's that?"

Trevillion halted. "Where?"

"In the top of that tree." Tara pointed to a blackened, moss-covered tree off to her right.

Trevillion craned his neck. "I can't see it from here. Describe it."

"It looks like a stick with legs. It's about four feet long and it just went around the other side of the tree."

Kaden turned to Trevillion. "What is it?"

"I haven't the slightest idea." Trevillion moved forward again.

Kaden clenched his fists. "Wonderful. This is just great."

"Maybe it will stay up there and not bother us," Laraina said.

"It's probably gone to inform its relatives that dinner has arrived," said Tara. She kept her eyes fixed on the spot where she had last seen it.

"You're just full of pleasant thoughts today, aren't you?" Kaden snapped.

Tara smiled and said nothing.

The ground grew softer as they went on. Muck and slime sucked at their boots as they sank in over their ankles. Trevillion slowed his pace, testing each step before putting his full weight on it. The mist flowed around them, concealing the treacherous footing. They skirted countless pools of quicksand, the velvety surfaces deceptively smooth. Laraina gasped as she spotted skeletal hands protruding from the edge of one. The bony fingers, stained greenish-gray, clutched a tree root.

Kaden looked at Trevillion. "A friend of yours?"

In a move lightning quick, Trevillion grabbed Kaden by the throat. Kaden grappled with Trevillion, but couldn't break his grip.

Laraina tried to pull them apart. "Stop it! Stop it!"

Dominic forced his burly body between the combatants. Trevillion released Kaden and took a step back. Cold fury burned in his dark eyes.

Dominic pushed them an arm's length apart. "There are enough things in this Bog trying to kill us without us doing the job for them."

Prickles of ice slid down Tara's spine. Her skin crawled. She looked up and saw black blobs, some as big as her hand, moving in the trees, creeping along the spider webs. "We need to move."

Trevillion's gaze followed hers. The others looked up.

"Oh, gods," Laraina whispered. "Not spiders."

Trevillion cursed. "Follow me. Hurry."

They slogged after him, slipping and sliding through the muck in their haste. Laraina suddenly disappeared below the waist-high mist.

"Raina! Where are you?" Tara cried.

Kaden whirled around. "Laraina?"

"Here. I'm stuck." Laraina's voice rose. "Get me out."

Tara sheathed her blade. She flailed through the mist until she found her sister's hand reaching up. Kaden grasped Laraina's other hand, and they pulled her out of the mire.

Kaden hugged Laraina. "Are you all right?"

She nodded.

"What happened?" asked Trevillion.

"I took a wrong step and sank in up to my hips," Laraina said. "I couldn't get out." Her eyes widened. "Dominic, don't move."

"What? What is it?" he cried in alarm.

Laraina pointed at Dominic's arm.

He looked down and froze. A large, hairy, greenish-black spider crawled down over his shoulder. Another clung to his cloak. "Somebody get them off me!"

Tara drew her dagger and flicked them off.

Dominic let out a long breath.

Laraina screamed as another fist-sized spider dropped in front of her, brushing her face. She leaped back, lost her balance, and sat in a pool of muck. Kaden and Dominic helped her up.

"Follow me!" commanded Trevillion. Covering their heads with their arms, they plunged further into the Bog as hundreds of spiders, on strands of spun silk, dropped from the trees around them.

Tara felt something scrabbling up her sleeve and flung her arm out, sending several spiders flying. She heard wingbeats, and a shadow swooped by her, trailing the stench of carrion. A memory of dark walls and fear triggered at the smell, but she couldn't place it. The shadow caught one of the spiders in midair and gulped it down. More shadows, a flock of monstrous black birds, their wrinkled heads and necks devoid of feathers, swept through the trees, picking spiders out of the air and off the mossy branches. Tara ducked as one of the birds flew at her head. Its curved talons raked her hair. She whirled and saw it had a wriggling spider clutched tight. The bird lit in a tree, gobbled down the spider, and then launched into the air again.

Glancing around, Tara realized the spiders had disappeared. They were no longer dropping from the branches. Stabs of ice spun her around again. One of the birds swooped toward her, talons extended. The other birds followed.

"Look out!" Tara cried, drawing her sword. She swung at the nearest bird, and it veered away, squawking. Another flew by and clawed at her clothing.

Trevillion, Laraina, and Kaden pulled out their blades and swung at the attacking raptors. Aurelia screamed and ducked into the mist. Dominic fought with his long knife. He yelled as one of the birds caught his cloak, nearly pulling him over. Trevillion skewered the bird, then swung his sword in an arc. The dead bird slipped off the end of his blade and landed in a spider nest built low in the crotch of a tree. Spiders swarmed over the carcass and dragged it down into the trunk.

They brandished their weapons as the vile raptors dove at them, sharp beaks and talons wide. Wielding her sword with both hands, Tara cleaved through several more birds before the gruesome flock ceased their attack and flew off into the Bog. As soon as the birds were gone, the spiders crept once more along the tree branches.

"This way!" Trevillion said. "The dead birds should occupy the spiders for a little while."

They all hastened after him. Trevillion sliced through a mass of cobwebs blocking their path. Tara reached the broken strands of web, hanging like torn lace on either side of her, and hesitated. A cold uneasiness slid over her. There was something so familiar about this place. She dug into her memory, trying to find the connection.

"Tara, come on," Laraina said, somewhere ahead of her.

Shaking her head in frustration, Tara hurried to catch up.

Trevillion led them a short distance further, then stopped. "Was anyone bitten?"

They checked each other over, looking for spiders or spider bites, but didn't find any.

"What were those birds?" Tara asked. "They looked like huge vultures."

"They are," Trevillion said. "They're carrion hunters."

Dominic clapped Prince Kaden on the shoulder. "What did I tell you? Vultures are nasty. And you were worried about ravens."

Kaden scowled darkly and muttered something unintelligible.

Trevillion opened Laraina's pack and handed out portions of bread and cheese. "We'll eat as we go," he said.

Aurelia refused her ration. "I'm not hungry," she said with a grimace.

"You have to keep your strength up," Trevillion said.

She wrinkled her nose. "The smell makes me sick."

"You'll get used to it."

"I've heard that before."

He looked at her quizzically.

"Vaalderin," Tara said.

"Ah, I see," Trevillion said. "Please try to eat something."

Reluctantly, Aurelia took some bread and nibbled on it.

They trudged onward, sloshing through scum-covered pools, sinking in over their knees at times. The only sound was the squelching of their boots in the muck. Aurelia stayed as close behind Trevillion as she could, stepping in his tracks almost before he'd stepped out of them. Laraina scanned the trees around them, jumping at any shadow resembling a spider.

A faint chill raised the hairs on the back of Tara's neck, and she searched the gloom. Something watched them, but she couldn't tell from where. She started to cast out with her mind to locate the source of danger. The chill deepened, rippling over her body like a wave of ice water. She slammed her mind shut, remembering Trevillion's warning. The gripping cold eased.

"We're being watched," she said.

"Do you see anything?" Trevillion asked.

"No. I feel it."

"You didn't..."

"I started to. I think it's the same presence I felt last night."

"That's all we need." He set a faster pace.

"What's out there?" Tara asked.

"As I said before, I don't know."

"You do know," Tara shot back. "At least, you know something about it. Why not tell us?"

Trevillion stopped and turned, anger smoldering in his eyes.

Dominic held up his hands. "No fighting! We can discuss this later. Keep moving." He pointed toward the front of the line. "I don't want any more spiders crawling on me."

"Neither do I," Laraina echoed.

"Fine. Go," Tara snapped, stung by Trevillion's animosity.

They pushed onward. The gloom darkened as the day faded, shades of gray deepening to black. The damp air grew cold.

"As soon as I find a good place, we'll set up camp," Trevillion said.

"Camp? In this muck? You can't be serious," Kaden said.

"If you want to wander around in the dark, you're more than welcome to," Trevillion said.

"What dark? We have Aurelia to light our way," Kaden argued.

"Unless Aurelia would like to disrobe, there won't be enough light to travel, and I wouldn't ask that of her."

Aurelia looked coyly at Trevillion. "Well, I suppose I could, if it would be helpful."

"No, but thank you. It would still be too dangerous."

"Where do you camp in a place like this?" Laraina asked.

"If you're lucky you can find some firmer ground at the base of a tree," Trevillion said.

"What about the spiders?" Laraina looked up.

"We'll burn the moss. The smoke should keep them away," Trevillion answered.

He moved on, stepping carefully in the near dark. He stopped in front of two great trees, grown close together. Gnarled roots spread out two or three feet before sinking down into the muck. The ground between the roots was spongy and moss-covered and relatively dry.

"This looks as good as any," Trevillion began. Aurelia squealed as an enormous green-and-black-striped snake dangled in front of Trevillion's face. He grasped it by the neck and twisted. Bones crunched, and the snake's head drooped lifelessly. Trevillion yanked the snake's considerable length out of the tree and tossed it into a pool of quicksand; it was swallowed up with a slurp.

"As I was saying, we'll camp here tonight." Trevillion stripped off his pack and dug out the rich brown moss. "All of you stay close to the tree." He placed the moss in a loose circle around the base of both trees, enclosing Tara and the others. Using the flint from a tinderbox, he sparked a fire. He lit the circle of moss and fanned the small flames until they burned steadily. Acrid smoke billowed upward, obscuring the upper branches of the tree. "Stay inside the circle," Trevillion warned. "We'll set a double watch. I'll take the first with one of you. I want to keep an eye on this fire a while longer."

Knowing that the others were exhausted, Tara volunteered. She shrugged off her pack and perched on a massive tree root. Dominic sank down beside her, squeezing into a mossy spot between two roots. Laraina, Prince Kaden, and Aurelia sat on the other side of the trees.

Dominic's labored wheezing filled the dank stillness.

Tara laid her hand on his shoulder. "Are you all right?"

He nodded. "Just in need of a rest," he puffed between breaths. "And a drink." He lifted his battered hat and swiped his sleeve across his brow.

Tara helped him off with his pack and handed him a water flask.

"That's not the kind of drink I meant." He grinned. "But it will have to do." He took a long swig.

"You shouldn't have come," Tara said.

"I wouldn't have missed it," he said. His breathing grew calmer. "Who else will be able to say they went into the Bog and survived?"

"We're not out of it yet."

"We're not dead yet, either. That's something."

"We've been lucky."

"You always were a lucky one." A fond smile lit Dominic's face. "I still don't know how you did some of the things you did."

Tara eyed him soberly. "I'll never forgive myself if anything happens to you."

Dominic covered Tara's hand with his. "It was my choice, and don't you forget that. I'm a big boy." He settled his hat more firmly on his head and sat back. "Besides, what's to worry? I've still got my lucky hat."

Tara shook her head. "You and that hat."

"This hat has gone everywhere I have." Dominic looked at the pack beside them. "Any food in there?"

She dug out some dried fruit and meat, and they both ate. Then Dominic wrapped himself in his cloak, tipped his hat forward, and closed his eyes.

The darkness settled over them like a wet, clammy blanket. Smoke from the burning moss curled upward, stinging Tara's eyes and throat. The yellowish mist writhed around the trees and choked her with its fetid odor. She drew her knees up and pulled her cloak more tightly around her to shut out the chill.

Fingering the pommel of her sword, she thought back, remembering the adventures she and her sister and Dominic had shared. They'd been through so much together. And he was right. She had been lucky. She could have been killed many times over, but she'd always managed to come out unscathed. They all had.

Restless chills slid over her skin, raising goosebumps on her arms and legs. She squinted into the dark. Something still watched them, but whatever it was seemed to be hovering at a distance, neither drawing nearer nor moving away. She could hear nothing, save for Dominic's snoring and the quiet movements of Trevillion as he tended the fire. She wondered if Trevillion was still angry with her. It annoyed her that he would not share what he knew about the Bog. She wanted to pursue the subject further, but he didn't come near. She watched him furtively as he worked, stoking the fire with more moss, his dark features shadowed in the faint light.

All at once, he stopped what he was doing and stood motionless, as if listening. Tara heard a sniffling noise like someone crying. Trevillion moved around to the other side of the tree. Tara heard voices, Aurelia's and Trevillion's, talking in low tones. When Trevillion came back around to Tara's side of the trees, he wasn't wearing his cloak. His bare torso drew her eyes like a magnet.

With an effort, she looked away. She closed her eyes and took a deep breath to cool the heat rising through her body. Why did he give his cloak to Aurelia? She already had a cloak. The last thing they needed was for him to get sick from the cold and leave them stranded out here. In her mind's eye, she saw Aurelia flirting with Trevillion and throwing herself into his arms. Tara's hand clenched around the hilt of her sword. She opened her eyes and found Trevillion very near, crouching with his back to her as he added moss to the fire. The firelight played over his rippling muscles, touched his dark hair with gold. A heady mix of lust and jealousy surged through her. She balled her hand into a fist so hard her fingernails drew blood.

Trevillion rose without looking at her and moved around to the other side of the tree.

Tara sat still, not trusting herself to move or think. After a few minutes, the pulse pounding in her head began to subside, and she could breathe again. She rose, slipped off her cloak, and stepped around to where Trevillion crouched, watching the fire. She dropped the cloak into his hands. "So you don't freeze." She hurried back to her post on the other side of the tree before he could say anything.

It was near the end of their watch when a cold shock brought Tara to her feet. Something approached from off to her left. Several somethings. She could feel them slinking through the dark like deadly shadows in the mist. She drew her sword.

"Dominic, wake up!" She shook him awake.

Trevillion appeared beside her. "What is it?"

"Something's coming," Tara said. "I can't tell how many."

They woke the others. A low growl pierced the darkness.

"Bog wolves," Trevillion said grimly. "Form a circle, backs to the tree. Aurelia, get behind us and stay there." He handed her a knife. "Here, take this, but be careful what you do with it."

Aurelia's hands shook as she took the blade from him.

Several pairs of golden eyes appeared through the smoky haze.

"Bang your swords together," Trevillion ordered. "Yell, scream, make as much noise as you can!"

Aurelia didn't have to be told twice. She let out a piercing shriek that would have shattered every window in Carilon. The others joined in, screaming and shouting and clanging their swords together until it sounded like they were fighting a bloody war at the base of the tree.

The golden eyes vanished. Trevillion motioned for quiet. The last echoes faded away, replaced by a tense silence. They remained with their backs to the tree for several more minutes, watching, waiting, but the wolves did not reappear.

Tara let out a long breath. "They're gone."

"But will the noise bring others?" Laraina asked.

"A calculated risk," Trevillion said. He sheathed his blade. "If we have to fight them, we're dead, so I'd rather not try."

The others sheathed their weapons.

"And if they come back?" Tara asked.

Trevillion smiled grimly. "Our fate will be as it may."

"Here is your knife," Aurelia said. "I'd rather not keep it." She handed Trevillion the knife and unfastened her outer cloak. "And thank you for letting me borrow this. I'm much warmer now." She stopped, confused. "Oh, you have one."

Trevillion took his cloak from her. "Yes. Thank you." He turned to Tara and swept the cloak around her shoulders, his fingers brushing her throat as he fastened the clasp. "And thank *you*," he said softly. Their eyes met for a moment, and Tara's resident butterflies took up their mad dance in her stomach. Then Trevillion turned away. "We may as well try and get some sleep while we can. Laraina, will you and Kaden take the next watch?"

Laraina nodded. "We will."

They settled down again. Out of the corner of her eye, Tara caught Aurelia glaring at her. She smiled to herself as she went back around to the other side of the tree. She sat on the root and gathered Trevillion's cloak around her. His cloak was thicker and warmer than the one she had been wearing, and it smelled of... him. She caught herself drinking in his scent. Temblors shivered over her body. She glanced at Dominic who had resumed his seat between the roots. He sat with his eyes closed, trying to go back to sleep.

This has got to stop, Tara scolded herself. She touched the small metal clasp at her throat, her fingers tracing over the design. It felt like a bird of some sort with two lines crossed below it.

She froze. She undid the clasp and held the cloak down near the embers of moss until she could see the design more clearly. It was the eagle and crossed swords of Sulledor.

CHAPTER 12

Tara sat back, gripping the clasp. Why was Trevillion wearing a Sulledorn cloak? From what Dominic had told her, she thought General Caldren and Trevillion were sworn enemies. Trevillion himself had said he was helping them because they were fighting against Caldren and the Sulledorns. Was he working with the General in secret, to lead them into a trap? Caldren wanted them dead, or he wouldn't have sent the Butcher after them. She forced herself to stay calm. If Trevillion's mission had been to lose them in the Bog and get rid of them that way, he could have done so before now and had an easier time escaping. Why lead them so far in, where he would be less likely to survive himself? It made no sense. Was Trevillion to kill them if Natiere failed? That didn't make sense either. Unless Trevillion wanted their help with his "unfinished business" in the Bog, and then planned to dispose of them. She shook her head. No. The whole idea was ridiculous. If Trevillion was a danger to them, she would have sensed it.

She considered discussing her thoughts with Laraina, but decided against it. Laraina would likely tell Kaden. If the prince found out that Trevillion might be associated with those who had murdered his father... No, she couldn't talk to Laraina. She ran her thumb over the raised emblem. There was only one way to find out what she needed to know.

Refastening the cloak about her shoulders, she glanced to her left toward the far end of the other tree where Kaden sat on watch. She could just see him in the dim light. He didn't appear to be looking her way. Silently, she rose, slipped around the trunk to her right, and slid onto the root next to her sister.

Laraina jumped. "You startled me. Is something wrong?"

Tara shook her head. "Sorry. I can't sleep. Why don't I take the rest of your watch? There's no need for us both to be awake."

"Are you sure? You must be just as tired as I am."

"I'm sure. Why don't you take my spot over beside Dominic? It's more comfortable than this."

Laraina looked at Tara more closely. "What's bothering you?"

Tara avoided her eyes. "It's just this place. I'll be happy when we're out of it."

"So will I." Laraina yawned. "You really can't sleep?"

"No."

"All right. Wake me when you get tired." Laraina rose stiffly and went around to the other side of the tree.

Tara gave her sister time to fall asleep. She didn't like not being able to talk to her about this. They always discussed everything. Well, almost everything. She looked across to where Trevillion slept with his back against the further tree. Aurelia lay just on the other side of him. She hated to wake him, but she had to know. She waited a little longer, then crept to Trevillion's side and touched his shoulder.

He woke instantly, his hand on his sword.

She held a finger to her lips and motioned for him to follow her back to where she'd been sitting. They crossed the intervening roots and sat down. Trevillion eyed her questioningly.

"I need to ask you about this." Tara unfastened the cloak and laid the clasp in her open palm. She tried to keep the accusation out of her voice.

Trevillion looked at the clasp, not understanding, then comprehension dawned in his eyes. The expressionless mask slid over his face. "My brother gave me that cloak. He was a member of the Sulledorn army."

"Were you?"

Trevillion took the clasp and studied it. "For a time. Many years ago."

Tara ran her hand over the soft fabric. "This cloak doesn't look that old."

Trevillion met her gaze. "Do you trust me?"

She looked into his eyes but could feel nothing of his thoughts, as she had the one time before. "Should I?"

"That, my dear, is a question only you can answer." He held out the clasp.

She looked down at it, the symbol of her enemy. Her instincts said Trevillion was trustworthy. She wanted to believe that he was. But could she chance being wrong? *Our blood will be on your head when we die.* Prince Kaden's words echoed in her mind. Reluctantly, she took the clasp, fingered it. "I need to know more."

"What do you want to know?"

A raindrop splashed on Tara's hand, dripping over the clasp like a tear. More followed, sizzling in the moss fire. Trevillion cursed and dropped down beside the dampening moss, trying to keep the fire going. Tara ground her teeth. Of all the times for it to rain. She donned Trevillion's cloak and pulled the hood over her head as the black sky opened in a deluge.

Aurelia dragged herself up with a moan. "Can this place get any worse?" She threw her arms up in the air, her hands and face glowing eerily. "I'm exhausted. I'm cold. I'm starving. And now I'm drenched. I want to go home!"

Kaden rounded the tree and slipped his arm around her. "I know, cousin. I do too."

Laraina and Dominic appeared, ducking their heads against the rain.

"If we all sit together, maybe we can stay warmer," Laraina suggested.

"Aurelia, can you make us a shelter?" Kaden asked.

"No!" Tara and Trevillion said at the same time. They looked at each other.

Trevillion turned to Aurelia. "I'm sorry. No using magic in the Bog. Your words would be twisted by the evil that rules here. Any shelter you formed would likely be a man-eating one."

"What can we do?" Aurelia asked, shoving her wet, bedraggled hair back under her hood.

Trevillion stood, giving up on the fire. "Sit and wait until morning." He sat down with his back to the tree. Aurelia sat next to him and leaned on his shoulder. The others gathered in close. Tara squeezed between Laraina and Dominic.

The circle of moss smoked feebly, then fizzled out. Even the mist lay beaten down by the torrent. Soaked and shivering, unable to sleep, they huddled together to conserve whatever warmth they could muster.

The heavy rain continued all night. The moldy stench thickened the air until Tara felt suffocated. Surrounded by clinging blackness, she had the unnerving impression the Bog had swallowed them alive.

Dawn came, wet and gray. They ate quickly, picked up their gear, and set off into the murk. The Bog lay still and silent, save for the hiss of the rain.

Morning drifted into afternoon; the rain gave no sign of letting up. The dead trees seemed to weep as their limbs snapped under the weight of the dripping moss.

Around midafternoon, they stopped for a few minutes to rest and eat. Tara glanced at Trevillion from time to time, trying to think of a way she could continue their conversation. She wanted to do it covertly, but Aurelia never left his side. Jealousy burned through her again, despite the tight rein she held on her emotions. Tara did her best to douse the feeling, but she couldn't shake her dark mood.

They finished eating and reformed their line with Aurelia, Kaden, Laraina, and Dominic following after Trevillion, and Tara as rear guard. Tara started as a sharp crack sounded above her. A massive branch crashed to the ground right behind her, splattering her with muck and slime.

She grimaced. "Thanks a lot."

"Are you all right back there?" Laraina called.

"Fine. It missed me. I —" Part of the branch was moving. "Forget what I just said. We may have a problem here." She drew her sword.

Dominic turned, then stumbled back, bumping into Laraina. "Jumping jittlebugs! What is that?"

"What's wrong?" Laraina tried to see around him.

Tara eyed the stick creature warily. It seemed dazed. "Remember that stick-like creature I mentioned yesterday? Well, here's your chance to see one up close." The six-legged creature regained its balance and lunged at her. Tara leaped to one side and plunged up to her waist in a greenish pool of quicksand. The stick creature attacked, its pincer-like jaws snapping. Tara's sword flashed. A hissing screech shredded the air as her blade severed the creature's foreleg. The wounded creature reared back on its middle and hind legs, thrashing in the muck.

Weapons in hand, Dominic, Laraina, and Kaden sloshed toward it. Trevillion waded around Aurelia. The stick creature spun and launched itself at them. Laraina dodged, but her feet stuck in the mire, and she fell sideways, landing with a splash. Kaden swung his blade in self-defense and succeeded in knocking the creature away. Dominic rushed forward and brought his long knife down hard across the stick creature's back. It snapped like a twig.

Wheezing from the effort, Dominic stared at the unmoving creature as if he expected it to attack again. Kaden helped Laraina to her feet.

"Would somebody mind getting me out of here?" Tara asked. She had sunk up to her armpits in quicksand.

Kaden and Dominic slogged to the edge of the pool. Kaden took the rope out of his backpack and threw one end to her. Tara tossed her sword to Laraina and grabbed the rope. Kaden, Dominic, and Trevillion pulled. The quicksand sucked and slurped, reluctant to release its prey. Gradually, Tara emerged from the pool. When she reached the edge, Trevillion grasped her arms and pulled her up beside him.

"Thanks." She shook the muck from her hands.

Trevillion regarded her with one eyebrow cocked. "What was it you said, 'We might have a problem here?' My dear, you have a gift for understatement."

Tara smiled and tried to squelch the strange thrill running through her at his use of 'my dear,' the second time in as many days. "Let no one ever accuse me of exaggerating."

"Please, can we get out of here?" Aurelia begged. She stood rooted to the spot where they'd left her. "There are snakes over there. I saw them." She pointed a glowing finger toward a stagnant pool of water. The scum-covered pool rippled menacingly, then was obscured by the ever-shifting mist.

Trevillion resumed his place at the head of the line, and they moved forward into the gloom. Tara held out her arms and let the rain wash away the grime from the quicksand. Minutes slipped into hours as they struggled through the knee-deep mire. They saw no other creatures. Nothing moved but the falling rain.

Tara hardly noticed when dusk, like a black velvet cloud, settled over the Bog, dimming the already murky atmosphere. Trevillion called a halt at the edge of a wide, greenish-yellow pond, which extended forty or fifty feet to either side of them. Tara judged the distance across to be about half that. The water looked thigh-deep and was strangely devoid of scum.

She shivered as icy tendrils curled down her spine. "There's danger here."

"What kind of danger?" Trevillion asked.

"I don't know," Tara said. "Something to do with the pond. Did you see anything like this your last time through?"

"No."

"Can we go around it?"

Trevillion shook his head. "There's too much quicksand. We'd have to backtrack quite a ways."

"It's almost dark. Do we have time to go back and work our way around?" Laraina asked.

"No." Trevillion wiped the rain from his face.

"Why don't we camp somewhere around here for the night and either go around it or through it tomorrow when we can see better?" Laraina suggested.

"I haven't seen any good places to camp," Trevillion said. "The tree roots are all underwater."

"It looks like the ground rises on the other side," said Dominic. "Maybe we can find a campsite over there."

Tara slid her sword from its scabbard. "Let's go."

Trevillion did the same and stepped into the pond. The water rose to his hips, but the soft mud at the bottom came only to his ankles. He took a few more steps. Swords drawn, the others followed. Only the rain disturbed the pond's clean surface.

When they were halfway across, Aurelia stopped and pointed. "Look at the flower!"

A bright red flower on a yellow-green lily pad floated on the surface a short distance away.

"Where did that come from?" Tara asked.

"Good question," said Trevillion. "Keep moving. Hurry."

They leaned into the water, forcing their legs to go faster. The far shore drew closer, less than a dozen feet away.

"There's another one. And another," Aurelia said, as two more red flowers appeared on either side of them. "They're beautiful." More flowers surfaced around her. She bent down to pick one.

"Don't touch it!" Trevillion caught her around the waist and pulled her back as a bolt of needle-like darts shot out from the center of the flower. The darts whizzed past Aurelia's face and dropped harmlessly into the water.

"What a horrible place this is!" she cried.

"Hey! Something just grabbed my foot!" Tara pulled her foot out of the mud. Wrapped tightly around it was a thick yellow vine, anchoring her to the spot.

Prince Kaden stopped in his tracks. "I can't move." He pulled against the vines coiled about his feet and nearly fell.

Tara severed the vine that held her fast. A screech like fingernails on slate tore through the gloom, and the entire floor of the pond erupted with writhing, tentacle-like vines.

Aurelia screamed as the thick vines twined about her knees and pulled her over. Trevillion caught her as she fell. Dominic sliced through the vines that held her, twisting his body to avoid the stinging darts shot from a nearby flower. Aurelia screamed again and went limp. Trevillion picked her up and slung her over his shoulder.

Countless vines shot out of the water and wrapped around Dominic's arms and legs. The others, too, became swiftly entangled. Grabbing her dagger, Tara slashed at the vines with both blades. She fought her way to Dominic's side and sliced through the many vines that threatened to drag him under. Surprised by the sudden release, Dominic toppled over backward with a yell. Sticking her dagger in her belt, Tara pulled him, coughing and spluttering, to his feet.

"Kaden!" Laraina cried.

Tara whirled and saw Kaden go under. Caught fast by vines, Laraina couldn't reach him. With a primal growl, Trevillion pulled against the vine wrapped around his sword arm. It stretched thin and snapped. He cut through the rest of the vines around him. Then he crossed the few steps to where Kaden had gone down and, with one arm holding Aurelia in place, he sliced through some of the vines pinning Kaden. Dominic stumbled over to help. Between the two of them, they managed to get Kaden back on his feet. Tara ducked beneath a shot of flying darts and, sword and dagger in hand again, struggled across to free Laraina. They fought their way to shore and climbed up the shallow bank, out of reach of the vines.

Tara leaned against a tree to catch her breath. The screeching had stopped. The only sounds were the harsh gasps of the others and the patter of light rainfall. She looked back at the pond. The vines and flowers had disappeared. The rain-rippled surface looked calm again.

Prince Kaden took Aurelia from Trevillion, supporting her limp body with one arm while he patted her cheek with the other. Aurelia's face glowed faintly, a pale yellowish-white. Her eyes were closed. "Aurelia." Kaden lightly slapped her cheek again. "Aurelia!"

There was no response.

"She's not glowing as brightly as she was," said Laraina. "Would fainting cause that?"

"Bring her over here," Trevillion said. He had found a small patch of ground, wet, but firm, beneath a gnarled tree.

Kaden carried Aurelia over and gently set her down. Trevillion undid Aurelia's cloak and pushed up her sleeves, one at a time, examining her hands and arms. Tara squinted in the dim light. She saw nothing unusual. Trevillion slid Aurelia's blouse down over one shoulder, then the other.

Laraina gasped. Tara's stomach roiled, a sick feeling settling in her gut. Aurelia's right shoulder had swelled and turned an ugly shade of greenish-black. Four red dots, puncture wounds, stood out just below her collar bone.

"Oh, no," Laraina whispered. "The darts from the flowers! They must have been poisonous. What do we do now? We have no medicine."

Tara felt Trevillion's eyes boring into her.

Before she could move, Prince Kaden grabbed her arm and spun her about. "If she dies I'll hold you responsible."

Tara hit him hard across the jaw. Kaden reeled backward into a tree. She leaped forward and pressed the sharp point of her blade against his chest.

"No!" Laraina wrapped her arms around Tara, forcing her sword down and pushing her back. "Stop it, both of you. This won't help."

Tara stared at her sister, stung by the anger in Laraina's eyes.

Aurelia moaned.

Tara turned away from Laraina. She glared at Kaden, who was leaning against the tree, rubbing the back of his head. "I accepted responsibility for the decision to come here. I don't deny it now." She sheathed her sword, and knelt beside Aurelia. Trevillion crouched on Aurelia's other side, his hand on her forehead.

"Her fever is rising. She doesn't have much time."

Tara felt Trevillion's eyes on her again, but refused to meet his gaze. "You said no magic in the Bog."

"I know what I said. But you can't just let her die."

"Magic? What magic?" Laraina asked, coming closer.

Tara looked at Aurelia's swollen shoulder. She could almost see the poison coursing through the girl's body.

Trevillion reached over, turned Tara's face toward his. "You can handle the dream. I know you can."

Tara looked away. The last thing she wanted was to reveal her gift to more people. And then have to face the dream... But what choice did she have? Aurelia's face was pale and drawn, her magical light nearly out.

"Tara?" Laraina sounded confused and uncertain. "What is he talking about?"

"It's rather hard to explain." Tara hesitated, then drew her dagger. "I'm not sure how she'll take this, because of the poison. You may have to hold her down."

Trevillion nodded. "Dominic, hold her legs."

Dominic knelt and braced Aurelia's legs. He looked at Tara. "What are you going to do?"

"Just hold her," Tara said. With the tip of her dagger she cut a small gash on Aurelia's shoulder, directly over the four red puncture marks. Thick greenish-black pus oozed from the wound. Tara wiped the blade on a patch of wet moss, then sliced her left palm and placed it over the wound.

Dominic gaped at her. "What in the name of the great god Azakai are you doing?"

Tara took a deep breath and closed her eyes. Power shot through her veins, scorching in its intensity. She reined it in and sent it flowing into Aurelia. Pain, like tiny needle stabs, and waves of nausea washed over her. She doubled over, her stomach churning as she sought out the poison and purged it from Aurelia's system. Aurelia began to thrash and moan.

Kaden rushed forward. "What are you doing? Leave her alone!"

Tara opened her eyes. Putrid greenish-black pus poured from the wound beneath her hand. Dominic waved Kaden away. "Stay back. I don't know what she's doing, but I think it's working."

Kaden moved in close despite Dominic's admonition. Aurelia stopped writhing and lay still. Her swollen shoulder began to shrink; within minutes, it was back to its normal size. The flow of pus slowed to a drip, then ceased. Aurelia's shoulder gradually changed from greenish-black, to yellow, and then to a normal, healthy pink. The four puncture wounds were gone.

Tara removed her hand. Her head spun.

"Well, I'll be a fried sardine," Dominic breathed.

Tara pressed her fists against her temples, trying to slow the power still whirling inside her. She couldn't control it. She felt it getting away from her, as if someone or something was tugging at it. A blast of freezing cold numbed her senses. The presence approached, arrow-swift. Its evil aura crawled into her mind. She tried to block it out, but couldn't. Blackness swirled around her, pulling her in. Panic gripped her — the same panic she always felt in her dream. Realization hit her. The Bog had seemed familiar because her dream dungeon was here, somewhere, hidden within it. The presence and the creature in her dream were one and the same.

"Tara!" She heard Trevillion's voice distantly. His hands touched her face. Her eyes focused on him for a moment, and she caught a fleeting thought before his mind closed.

"You knew," she whispered, and then the blackness took her, and she knew no more.

CHAPTER 13

Tara screamed as the blackness engulfed her in a maelstrom of pain. The numbing cold sapped her strength. Icy fingers penetrated her mind, bringing forth images from her past. The memories flitted by in rapid succession, slowed at particular instances, then sped on, going backward in time. She watched herself healing Trevillion, Dominic, the smuggler Blackie de Runo, and Laraina. She had been so young then. Her life in between flew by in a blur. The presence sifted deeper, as if searching for some memory, long hidden, created before she was even aware of herself — embryonic memories of which she had no knowledge. The pain intensified as the presence ripped through her mind.

"Yes, yes, you are the one!" The crackling hiss seared her consciousness.

Clawing for a foothold at the edge of her sanity, she gathered what shards of control she could muster and thrust outward. "Get... out... of... my... head!" she shouted. The pain in her skull exploded; the black walls shattered. The world spun around her, then slowed and grew still. She opened her eyes. She lay in a long, dimly-lit hallway lined with doors.

An odd scraping sounded close behind her. The hall filled with the stench of carrion. A hissing shriek echoed in her ears as clawed hands grasped at her. She rolled away and staggered to her feet. Dizzy with pain, she fell against the wall, righted herself, and stumbled down the corridor. The creature followed.

Keeping her feet through sheer force of will, Tara ran down several passageways, tearing through cobwebs and the spiders that had created them. She ran until a fierce pain in her side forced her to stop. She lurched to a halt and rested her hands on her thighs as she sucked in air. She listened for the creature, but heard only her own harsh breathing. Hopefully, she had lost the creature somewhere in the maze of corridors. She rubbed her temples, then ran her fingers over her scalp. Her head hurt badly, but she found no sign of external wounds.

She looked down the hall at the line of doors. A flash caught her eye. On the floor against the wall near the end of the passage, something sparkled in the torchlight. She crossed the distance and knelt. Half-buried beneath a cobweb lay a ring — a man's ring, judging from the size. She picked it up and turned it over in her hand, wiping away the dust. A brilliant ruby in the shape of a beast with the head of an eagle and a lion's body — a griffin — stared up at her from a gold setting. She felt a glimmer of... something...

She heard the creak of a door open behind her.

"Give that to me!" the creature hissed.

Tara sprang away. The creature lunged at her. She jumped sideways and crashed into one of the doors. It popped inward, and she fell, screaming, into the void. Lost in a freefall, the blackness closed around her again, crushing the air from her lungs.

Something caught her hand, stopping her fall. A hand, warm and strong, grasped hers, and for a moment, she swung pendulum-like in the void. *I've got you. Hold on.* She heard the words, whisper-soft in her mind. Then she moved upward, and she could breathe again.

She opened her eyes. She lay in Jovan Trevillion's arms, her head against his shoulder, her hand gripped tightly in his. She saw the worried scrutiny in his eyes turn to relief. She looked down at their hands, felt the warmth of his clasp, and knew it was his voice she had heard. He somehow had entered her dream and pulled her out of the void. "How did you —"

Laraina knelt beside her, and Tara suddenly realized that the others were watching her, and that she was still cradled in Trevillion's embrace. She sat up slowly, mindful of the aching throb in her head. A light rain danced on her hood, and she smelled the rot of the Bog. The others sat or stood nearby, clearly defined in Aurelia's bright glow.

"Are... are you all right?" Laraina asked.

"I'm fine. My head hurts." Tara's eyes fell on Aurelia, who seemed to be glowing even brighter than before.

Aurelia cleared her throat. "I understand you saved my life. Thank you."

Tara swallowed her surprise. "You're welcome. I'm sorry you had to go through it."

"She doesn't remember any of what happened after stepping into the pond," Laraina said.

Tara looked away. She remembered very well.

"Tara, what did you do? How were you able to heal her?" Laraina asked.

"I don't really know," Tara answered. "I discovered a long time ago that I had this... gift. I think I must have been born with it."

"Why didn't I ever know about it? Why didn't you tell me?"

"I'm sorry," Tara said. The hurt in Laraina's eyes cut deeply. "I've only used it a few times."

Laraina gestured toward Trevillion. "He knew about it."

"He was one of those times," Tara said. "He was hurt during the fight in Desta."

"How long have you known about this?" Laraina asked.

"Since I was thirteen. I discovered it one day by accident. Raina, we were in Wyndover. You know how the Elders were. They already called me a witch-child. How long do you think they would have let me live if they found out I had some sort of magical power?"

"Who did you heal?"

Tara hesitated a moment. "You."

Laraina's eyes widened. "Me?"

"You were unconscious. We were rock climbing and you fell, and..." Tara took a deep breath. "It doesn't matter. Everyone in the village turned away from me because I was different. I was afraid you would, too, if you knew."

"Tara, I would never turn away from you. You are my sister."

"You healed me too, didn't you?" Dominic said. "When I had the black fever. One day I was dying, and the next I was recovering. That was you, wasn't it?"

"Yes, and that's when the dreams started."

"Dreams," said Laraina. "You did tell me you were having dreams — nightmares — but you couldn't remember them."

"I remember them now." Tara shivered. "They seem to be caused by the use of the healing power. I'm in a dungeon, and a creature is chasing me. I know now that the dungeon is real. It is here in the Bog, somewhere, and the creature is the presence I felt the night before we entered the Bog. The creature is trapped in the dungeon, but it can reach me through the dream. I don't know what it wants." She stopped, recalling the creature's words, *you are the one.*

"What is that in your hand?" Laraina asked.

Tara looked down. Her right hand lay curled around an object. "The ring!" She opened her hand. The gold and ruby ring lay in her palm. But how? Trevillion grew tense behind her. He took the ring from her hand.

"Where did you get this?" he demanded.

Tara glanced at him, surprised by his reaction. "It was on the floor in one of the passageways, hidden under the cobwebs."

He turned the ring over in his hand, then gave it back to her. "How did you get it out of the dungeon?"

"I don't know. I found it just before the creature found me. I had it in my hand when I fell." She stifled a shudder. "Have you seen it before? Do you know how it got there?"

"No," Trevillion said.

"May I see it?" Laraina asked.

Tara handed her the ring. Laraina held it up in Aurelia's light.

"A red griffin," Laraina said. "This is the insignia of the High Kings of Alltyyr."

"How do you know that?" Tara asked.

"I learned a lot of history from Prince Fourn —" She caught herself with a quick glance at Kaden. "— from when we stayed at Castle Crystalir last year. Crystalir is the former seat of the High Kings," she finished quickly.

"There hasn't been a High King in Alltyyr for over two hundred years," Kaden said.

"I remember seeing the griffin emblem on some of the shields and crests in the armory," Tara said. She looked at Trevillion again. "You really don't know anything about this?"

"No."

"And this has nothing to do with your brother and the lost king of Sulledor?"

"No."

She held his gaze, but his expression remained inscrutable. He knew something about the ring — she was sure of it. But she could think of no way to make him tell what he knew. "You are one of the most frustrating people I have ever met," she said and slipped the ring into the inner pocket of her tunic. She rubbed her eyes, exhausted, but she fought the urge to sleep.

Trevillion eased her back against him. "You should rest."

Tara forced her eyes to stay open. "The last thing I want to do is sleep."

"The dream is over. The creature shouldn't be able to reach you as long as you keep your mind closed."

Tara sat up again. "How do you know these things?"

Trevillion gave her an enigmatic smile. "As you once said to me — I just know."

"Do you have magic powers, too?" Aurelia said.

Trevillion shook his head. "No."

"Then how did you reach me in the dream?" Tara asked.

"I felt your need," he said softly.

She wrenched her eyes away as the butterflies tumbled in her stomach.

"You need to sleep," he said. "The worst of the Bog is yet to come. You will need all of your strength."

"You mean it gets worse?" Dominic asked.

"Much worse," Trevillion said.

"Wonderful," Tara muttered. She rubbed her aching temples. There were so many more questions she needed to ask, but her mind was fogging over. She couldn't think.

Sleep. You are safe. The whisper-soft words eased through her consciousness. Her eyelids drooped in spite of her resolve to stay awake, and she drifted into slumber.

*****

Tara woke with a start as a hand brushed her cheek. Jovan Trevillion's arms closed around her, held her still.

"Easy. It's morning. We need to move on," he said. "How do you feel?"

"I'm fine." She sat up, pulling away from his warmth. She must have slept in his arms again. She blinked a few times against the rain and brushed back a wet strand of silver-blonde hair, surprised to find that she really did feel fine. She had slept well for the first time in... she didn't remember when.

Laraina handed her a water flask and some hard biscuit and cheese, and gave some to Trevillion. Tara wolfed down her food and took a long drink. The others packed up to go. She looked around in the drizzly gray, wishing it would stop raining. *No*, she thought. They would likely be better off if the rain continued. The constant rainfall masked their scent and kept away the spiders. They were probably still alive because of it.

The group struggled forward into the nightmarish gloom, sinking knee-deep in the fetid ooze with every step. Thin trailers of mist, undaunted by the rain, flitted like ghosts among the lifeless trees. Fleeting movements — or were they only shadows? — tugged at the edges of Tara's vision. Globs of greenish-black moss dropped from the trees and splashed into the muck around them. The icy rain beat down on their heads as if it would drive them like nails into the soft floor of the Bog. The pounding of the torrent against the dead trees drowned out every other sound.

When the rain finally ceased, a brooding silence, thick and ominous, settled over the Bog. Odd whispers and murmurings assailed them from all sides.

"Do you hear something?" Aurelia asked in a low voice.

"What do you hear?" Trevillion asked.

"It sounds like very faint whispering." Aurelia looked around.

Trevillion stopped and turned. "Do you see anything?"

"No," she said.

Trevillion looked at the others. "Do you hear anything?"

Dominic, Kaden, and Laraina shook their heads.

"It sounds something like the Dwarven battleground in the Scarlet Mountains," Tara said, "only without the swordplay."

"Why would Aurelia hear it now, if she didn't hear it before?" Laraina asked.

"Tara healed her," Trevillion said. "Maybe some of her magic passed through."

"But Tara healed me, and Dominic too," Laraina said, "and we don't hear anything."

Trevillion shrugged. "Aurelia is a trained magic-user. Perhaps that is the difference."

"Then how do you hear it if you have no magic?" Tara asked.

Trevillion's eyes narrowed. "I didn't say that I did hear it."

"But you do, don't you? Just like you heard the Dwarves, and that was before I healed you, so you must have magic."

"I have no magic," he said curtly. He turned and started forward again.

"Why won't you admit it?" Icy shivers slithered over her skin. "What are those?"

Trevillion halted again. "Where?"

Tara pointed to her left, her voice dropping to a whisper. "Over there, moving through the trees."

Shimmering phantoms, mist-wraiths, like misshapen humans, drifted through the murk, but did not come near.

Aurelia's hands flew to her mouth to stifle a scream. "They look like ghosts," she squeaked.

"They are the souls of those who died in the Bog," Trevillion said, his voice grown rough, "trapped by the evil that rules here." He plunged forward into the muck. "Keep moving. Quickly!"

They slogged through the mire as swiftly as they could, angling away from the glowing apparitions. Whispering voices whirled around them, as if to alert the ghosts to their presence. Tara shivered, her body ice cold. The smell of death thickened the air until she could hardly breathe.

Then all at once, the air cleared. A new fragrance wafted in on a light breeze. Soft and strangely sweet, the faint perfume teased Tara's senses, evoking images of an exotic flower garden in riotous full bloom. Tara took a deep breath before she could stop herself. The air smelled so good, it was probably poisonous.

Banks of flowers appeared around them: orchids, lotus, honeysuckle. The fragrance grew stronger, the mix of scents like an opiate. Tendrils of mist caressed them, drawing them into the garden. Tara's weary, aching muscles relaxed; she began to feel weightless.

A glimmering shape appeared among the flowers — a twisted, deformed human. "Jovan," it whispered.

Tara saw Trevillion turn toward the sound, a horrified stare on his face. He tried to speak, but all that came out was a croak. "Jared."

The specter moved closer, its glowing greenish-yellow form gliding over the muck. "Wake," it said. "You must wake."

Tara tried to move, but couldn't. She looked at the wraith, saw through it to the flowers and trees beyond.

"Jared. Brother," Trevillion rasped.

"Foolish brother," hissed the wraith. "The Bog nearly devoured you the last time, yet you tempt it again." Its voice lowered to a sneering whisper. "But then you know you will live. The prophecy of Rinpool has not yet been fulfilled."

"The prophecy has nothing to do with this," Trevillion ground out. "I came here for answers."

"I justify my actions to no one," snarled the wraith.

"Why did you do it?"

"For the money, of course." The specter laughed, a hideous sound that froze Tara's blood. "And I could have had more. Young King Baynan offered me three times what General Caldren was paying me for the kidnapping if I would double-cross Caldren and take Baynan to Crystalir, instead of leaving him to die in the Bog. I agreed. My men and I followed the same path you are following now, and died in this same spot." Another bloodcurdling laugh echoed through the silent Bog. "I gambled and lost." The wraith spread its arms wide. "This is my reward. My men and I will dwell here for eternity."

"And the young king?"

"And the young king," whispered the specter. "He had courage for a boy. But he is still dead." The shimmering form shifted, grew more grotesque. "Your men are also here in the Bog, haunting the places where they died. You cursed them by following me, as you have doomed these here with you now."

Trevillion's fists clenched. "Those men are on your head, not mine. I believed you to be the innocent victim of a kidnapping scheme, but you were not innocent. You betrayed me, betrayed your king!"

"He was not my king," the wraith hissed. "I am my own ruler."

Tara's stomach knotted as the sweet fragrance grew nauseating.

The wraith floated up to Trevillion, hovered in his face. "You would condemn me! The brother who took care of you, saved your life many times. You owe me debts you will never be able to repay." The wraith smiled, its mouth a twisted, curving slash in the greenish-yellow glow. "I was going to save you yet again, but I have decided I will not. You and your friends will die here, and the prophecy will go unfulfilled — the prophecy of a future which should have been mine." The phantom passed through Trevillion and drifted toward the trees. "Poor, naive brother." The glimmering shape disappeared into a bank of wilting flowers.

Trevillion stared after the twisted wraith that had once been his brother. "Jared! Come back!"

Demented laughter floated back on a rill of mist.

"I will not die here!" Trevillion yelled. "Jared, do you hear me? You will suffer your curse alone!"

Tara started at Trevillion's shout. Shaking with a deathly chill, she shook her head and blinked... and realized she was chest deep in quicksand. There were no flowers surrounding them, and no phantoms — only mist and murk and black trees and death. The others, too, stood chest deep in the mire, their eyes vacant as if in a trance, except for Aurelia. With her hands clamped over her mouth and her eyes wide with fright, she stared in the direction the wraith had gone. A flock of hungry vultures landed in the trees above them.

Trevillion was still shouting. Tara yelled at him, but couldn't get either his or Aurelia's attention. She scooped up a handful of muck and slung it at him, hitting him in the shoulder. He stopped shouting, his head snapping around toward her.

"Wake up!" Tara cried.

A confused expression slid across his face, and he stared at the surrounding quicksand, comprehending their predicament.

"We need to wake the others." Tara stretched out her arms toward Laraina, but couldn't reach her. Picking up another handful of mud, Tara threw it at her sister.

With a startled cry, Laraina's head swiveled around. "What's happening?"

"Help us!" Trevillion ordered. He and Tara pelted the others with muck.

Laraina dug up handfuls of the slop and threw it. Aurelia was awakened first, then Dominic and Kaden. By now they had sunk up to their armpits in quicksand.

"Kaden, the rope!" Trevillion called. "Tie one end around yourself and toss the other end over that branch!" He pointed to one of the massive moss-covered limbs that stretched out over the quicksand.

Twisting around, Prince Kaden jerked his backpack out of the muck. He pulled out the rope and knotted it around his body. After two tries, he succeeded in swinging the loose end over the branch. The startled vultures rose as one, then resettled in the trees. The end of the rope dangled within Dominic's reach. He caught hold of it and ducked as one of the monstrous birds flew at him. The vulture snatched Dominic's hat, ripped it to pieces, and gulped down some of the shreds.

"Hey, you filthy sack of feathers," he cried. "You took my hat!"

The bird wheeled and flew at his face. The beating wings blinded him; the sharp talons dug into his flesh. Yelling like a madman, Dominic waved his arms over his head. Tara and the others watched helplessly, unable to reach him.

The vulture latched onto Dominic's forearm. Dominic brought his arm slashing downward and thrust it, bird and all, into the quicksand. Too late, the bird released him. Fluttering and croaking, the vulture struggled to escape. Dominic caught it by the neck and shoved it down into the muck. He held it there until it stopped moving. Then he yanked it out and waved it high over his head.

"Any other of you blasted carrion crows care to try your luck?"

Nothing moved. Not even a feather ruffled. The surrounding vultures eyed him hatefully.

Tara saw blood dripping from Dominic's temple. "Dominic, are you all right?"

He dropped the bird and wiped at the cut, smearing blood and quicksand across his forehead. "I guess so. It hurts, so can't be I'm dead yet." He shook his head. "I can't believe it ate my hat."

"Swing the rope over here," Trevillion said softly.

Keeping one eye on the vultures, Dominic tossed the end of the cord to Aurelia who grasped it and then swung it over to Trevillion. Wrapping his hands around the knotted cord, he pulled with all of his strength. His powerful muscles bunched and tightened. Slowly, he began to climb from the muck. The over-burdened limb cracked and groaned under the strain. Kaden rose a few inches, but remained stuck fast. Hand over hand, Trevillion climbed, tearing himself from the grip of the Bog. Moments later, he was free.

Using the rope, he struggled through the mire to the base of a tree. Tying the rope around the blackened trunk, he braced himself and pulled hard. Prince Kaden gripped the rope and climbed. Slowly, he emerged from the quicksand. A sharp crack echoed through the dead trees, and the supporting branch sagged to the ground. Black-winged vultures rose into the air. A few circled low, but Dominic waved the dead bird again, and they scattered. Kaden climbed up onto the branch and disentangled the rope. Spiders skittered out of the moss, scuttling toward him over the broken limb. With a yell, Kaden jumped off, back into the quicksand. Trevillion pulled him out. Fumbling with the knot, Kaden worked at untying the muck-covered rope from around his chest.

"Please hurry!" Laraina cried, eyeing the advancing spiders.

Trevillion pulled his knife and sliced through the knot. Together, he and Kaden rescued the others.

Weary beyond words, the muddied group stumbled away from the fragrant death trap, their singular thought to get as far away from it as possible.

Sometime later, they stopped, nearly dropping with exhaustion. Wheezing roughly, Dominic climbed up onto a raised tree root and sat down. Aurelia sank down beside him. The others gathered near, their harsh breathing rasping in the still air.

"How much farther?" Kaden asked between breaths.

"Not far," Trevillion said. "I think we are through the worst of it."

"You think? You don't know?"

Trevillion didn't answer.

"Stop complaining," Tara said. "We're still alive."

"And how many times have we almost been killed?" Kaden demanded. He glared at Trevillion. "I thought you were supposed to know the way through this cursed place."

Trevillion regarded the tall prince narrowly. "Perhaps you would like to take the lead."

Prince Kaden refused to back down. "Perhaps I will. It would be a definite improvement over —"

"Shut up, Kaden," Tara snapped. "This was my idea, so if you want to blame someone, blame me."

Kaden turned on her. "I do blame you."

"Kaden, stop it," Laraina said. "If it weren't for Tara, Aurelia would be dead."

"If it weren't for Tara, Aurelia wouldn't have been in that position in the first place!"

"Don't talk about me like I'm not here!" Aurelia yelled.

Tara and the others stared at her in surprise.

Aurelia's eyes slid to Trevillion. "You needed to come here. Your brother..."

A startled expression broke through Trevillion's mask. "You saw?"

She nodded. "I saw, and I heard it... him." She shuddered.

"Saw and heard what?" Kaden asked, his hand flying outward in exasperation. "What are you talking about?"

Aurelia went to push her hair out of her face, saw how dirty her hand was, and thought better of it. "The ghosts. Jovan's brother. You didn't see them?"

"No," Kaden said. "I saw flowers. That's it."

"Me too," said Laraina.

"And me," Dominic added.

Aurelia looked back at Trevillion. "I'm sorry."

"Sorry for what?" Trevillion asked softly.

"Sorry for the pain you have had to bear."

"Thank you, but it is nothing you need to be sorry about. My brother said I was naïve." Trevillion looked away. "He was right."

Laraina caught her breath and pointed at a nearby tree limb. "Spiders! Up there. I think they might be coming this way."

Trevillion looked back at Kaden. "The path is yours to choose."

"Of all the idiotic..." Tara stepped between them, facing Trevillion. "Would you mind?" she asked with a wave of her arm.

"As you wish," he said, his face impassive.

He led the way into the murk. Aurelia hurried after him, with Dominic and Laraina falling in behind her. Kaden followed, his lean face hard and set. Tara brought up the rear.

After another hour, the muck grew shallower, the ground firmer under their feet.

Tara stopped suddenly and listened. "Do I hear water running, or am I just imagining things?"

Dominic cocked his head. "It does sound like water."

"The river," said Trevillion. "It can't be much farther."

With renewed vigor, they forged onward. The malodorous yellow mist swirled around them as they hurried toward the beckoning sound. Several minutes later, they broke through the trees. A few feet away lay the Nournan River. Wide and deep and slow-moving, the Nournan flowed from the easterly Cyranel Mountains, through Tralyxa and Faragellyn, and all the way south into Mardainn, eventually emptying into the East Amberin River. The midafternoon sun reflected off its smooth, glassy surface, turning it to a ribbon of gold.

Tara stepped out onto the firm, grassy bank and just stood for a moment, letting her eyes grow accustomed to the bright sunlight. A soft breeze, cool and clean, gently swayed the new spring grass. She took a deep breath and drank in the fresh air.

Beside her, Laraina did the same. "Ah, this is wonderful."

"Yes, isn't it," Tara agreed.

"I never would have believed it," Dominic declared, stretching his massive frame and inhaling deeply. "We actually made it through the Bog in one piece." He smiled fondly at Tara and Laraina. "This will add some spice to your already long list of demons conquered."

Tara threw her arm around his shoulder. "You mean our list. You had a big hand in most of those battles, old friend."

Dominic grinned broadly and chuckled. "So I did, so I did."

Aurelia walked to the edge of the river. There the grassy bank ended with a four foot drop to the surface of the water. "What are those?" she asked, pointing to a group of brown lumps that looked like logs floating in the middle of the sun-gilded river.

"Those are karanaks," Trevillion answered. "They're all teeth, and you wouldn't want to tangle with one."

"Oh." She backed away from the river's edge. "They won't come up here, will they?"

"No," Trevillion said. "They are water-dwellers."

The karanaks swam in lazy patterns, their short-legged bodies and long tails undulating, their elongated heads spearing beneath the surface every so often to rise with a wriggling fish clamped in their jaws.

"I guess that means we don't get a bath," Tara observed. She looked down at herself and then at the others. "Not that we need one, of course."

"Well, now that depends on how good a swimmer you are," Trevillion said.

Biting cold shocked Tara. She wheeled toward the Bog. "Something's coming. And there are a lot of them."

Trevillion swore. "The wolves. They must have picked up our scent when the rain stopped. We need more room. This way!"

They raced north along the riverbank until they came to a wide swath, spanning twenty feet from the water's edge to the treeline. Trevillion halted and tossed his backpack to the side. The others stopped beside him and did the same. Three pairs of golden eyes stared at them from between the twisted trees.

Placing his knife in her hand, Trevillion thrust Aurelia behind him. "Get back toward the river." He motioned to Tara and Laraina. "One of you on either side of me. You two," he jerked his head at Kaden and Dominic, "behind them."

The wolves attacked. Seven of them, rangy black beasts, burst from the shelter of the trees, hackles raised, teeth bared. Trevillion positioned himself to bear the brunt of the attack. The lead wolf lunged. Trevillion leaped to the side and brought his sword down hard, slicing through the leader's skull. Tara stepped forward and slashed the second wolf's side open. Dominic, behind her, finished it off.

Trevillion barely had time to react before another two hundred pounds of snarling fury landed on his chest and bore him to the ground. The impact knocked the sword from his hand. Wrestling with the beast, Trevillion grasped it by the throat. The Bog wolf struggled fiercely, its razor sharp claws raking Trevillion's flesh, but it could not break free. With bulging eyes and frothing mouth, the wolf collapsed. Trevillion rolled to his feet, pulled a knife out of his boot, and buried it in the beast's heart.

Laraina cried out as the fourth wolf pinned her down. Prince Kaden ran to help her. Not daring to use his blade for fear of hitting her, Kaden grabbed the wolf by the tail and managed to drag it off her. Laraina scrambled to her knees and slashed the beast's throat before it could turn on the prince.

With a vicious snarl, another wolf launched itself at Trevillion. He caught the beast, fell backward, and kicked it over his head, sending it rolling in the grass. Dominic stabbed the wolf, wounding it before it could recover. Retrieving his sword, Trevillion struck the killing blow.

Guarding Trevillion's back, Tara braced herself as the remaining two wolves attacked. The first wolf leaped at her. It landed on her upraised sword, impaling itself. The force of its lunge slammed Tara to the ground. The second beast sprang. Tara jerked backward as gaping jaws snapped in her face. She ducked beneath the dead wolf, using its body as a shield. The other wolf jumped over Tara and the dead beast and came at her from the other side.

With a yell, Dominic landed between them and took the full force of the blow. The wolf knocked him backward. He lost his footing, tripping over Tara and the dead wolf. Man and beast rolled on the ground, locked together in a fierce struggle. Dominic screamed. Tara shoved the dead wolf aside. She yanked her sword, but it stuck in the wolf's rib cage and would not come free. Grabbing her dagger, she leaped to her feet and raced to the edge of the river where Dominic lay thrashing, held down by the wolf. Trevillion reached him at the same time, Laraina and Kaden a step behind. Shouting fiercely, Tara plunged the dagger to the hilt in the wolf's back. The wounded beast whirled and lunged. Tara's arm flew up to protect her throat. The Bog wolf's jaws closed around it like a vise, and then Tara and the wolf toppled over backward into the river.

CHAPTER 14

Tara gasped in a breath as she plunged into the deep river. The wolf released her arm, its legs flailing. She kicked the beast away, gritting her teeth as the wolf's claws gouged her in its struggle to reach the surface. She swam upward, away from the beast, throwing back her hair as she surfaced. Half-a-dozen karanaks sped toward her, zipping through the water like arrows.

Trailing blood, Tara swam toward the shore. The wounded wolf dog-paddled behind her. Freezing chills washed over Tara as the karanaks closed in. Frightened yelps burst from the wolf. Tara swam faster as bright crimson stained the water around her.

"Tara, hurry!" Laraina cried, crouching with Trevillion on the riverbank.

Trevillion lay flat on the river's edge and stretched out his arm. "Grab my hand!"

Something nipped at Tara's boot as she reached the shore. She grasped Trevillion's hand, and he and Laraina pulled her up onto the bank. A karanak leaped up after her, snapping its massive jaws. Trevillion kicked it back into the water. Deprived of its meal, the creature uttered a guttural snarl and swam back toward the other karanaks. Tara sat up on her knees, breathing hard, watching as the karanaks tore the wolf to shreds.

"Are you all right?" Laraina asked. "How bad is your arm?"

"It's not bad," Tara said, unable to take her eyes from the carnage.

"Raina, I think you'd better come over here," Kaden called hoarsely.

Tara swung around, met her sister's eyes.

"Dominic!" they both said, and ran to where Kaden and Aurelia knelt beside the old adventurer. The prince and his cousin rose and backed away as Tara and Laraina dropped down beside Dominic.

Laraina gasped. "Oh, gods," she whispered.

Tara stared in shock at Dominic's mangled body, a mass of blood and entrails; his breath sputtered raggedly. One look told her there was no hope. Tears slid down her face as she clasped his blood-smeared hand, already growing cold. Laraina took his other hand in hers.

Dominic's glazed eyes flicked from Tara to Laraina, then back to Tara. "You're safe," he murmured.

Tara reached for the knife in her boot. "Hang on, Dominic. Just a few minutes more. I'll try to heal you."

"No, my girl." He pulled her back to face him. "It's too late for me." A smile crossed his ravaged features. "Just let me be." He closed his eyes and let out a long, sighing breath. His hand went limp.

"Dominic, hold on," Tara cried, gripping his hand as if she would will the life back into him. "Dominic! No!" She pressed her hand against his face, felt the stillness of death. "No," she whispered.

Tears streaming down her cheeks, Laraina wrapped her arms around her sister. Tara stared in disbelief at Dominic's unmoving form. "No." Laraina hugged her hard.

Prince Kaden removed his cloak and draped it over Dominic's torn body. He squeezed Laraina's shoulder, then he and the others moved away and left the sisters alone.

A few minutes later, Laraina roused and wiped her eyes. "Come on, sister. We need to bandage our wounds. We're neglecting the others."

Tara closed her eyes and tried to pull herself together. Laraina's words filtered through her numbed mind. *Our* wounds, she had said. Laraina was hurt. Tara snapped her mind into focus. "Why didn't you say you were hurt?" She examined her sister and found several cuts and gashes, some still oozing. A pool of blood had formed on the ground beneath her own lacerated forearm.

Laraina rose. Tara took the hand she offered and pulled herself to her feet, moving stiffly as the pain from the gouges in her legs seared along her nerves. She glanced down at Dominic's shrouded body, steeled herself, and followed Laraina along the bank to where Trevillion, Aurelia, and Prince Kaden had gathered. Trevillion was bandaging claw scratches on Kaden's arm with some cloth he had dug out of one of the backpacks.

Laraina sat beside Kaden. "How bad is it?"

"It's nothing. A scratch." Kaden eyed Laraina's wounds with concern. "Raina, you're still bleeding." He turned to Trevillion. "Never mind about me. She needs the bandages."

Trevillion tied off the cloth around Kaden's arm. He looked from one sister to the other. "You both need them."

"So do you." Tara eyed his blood-stained clothes.

"The blood is not all mine." He searched the backpacks for more bandage material. "Some of it belonged to the wolves."

Tara took a deep breath and let it out slowly. "Why don't you all let me heal you? We'll never survive another wolf attack, injured as we are. And our wounds will slow us down."

"What about the dream?" Laraina asked. "You said whatever the evil thing is that's in the Bog can reach you if you use your healing power."

"The dream will come anyway," Tara said, "because my body will be healing itself."

"Out here on the riverbank, the presence is not as strong," said Trevillion, "and we are not that badly hurt. If you can split your focus between healing and defense, you should be able to block the evil out of your mind."

"You mean the way you block me out?" Tara asked.

Trevillion smiled faintly. "More or less."

"How do you do it?"

"In this case, it would be like hitting something, mentally," Trevillion said. "You feel the presence coming toward you, and you strike outward with your mind, closing yourself to it, instead of opening. Does that make sense?"

Tara nodded. She remembered how, after healing Aurelia, she had fallen into the dream. When the evil presence had seized her, the pain had been so great that instinct had taken over, and she'd somehow managed to thrust the presence out of her mind. Now if she could just figure out how she'd done it...

Trevillion handed her his dagger, hilt first.

Tara tested the blade's sharpness. "Who wants to go first?"

"I'm not hurt," said Aurelia. "The wolves didn't reach me."

"I don't need it," Kaden said. "I'll keep watch." He rose and then sat down again a short distance away, facing the Bog.

"Heal Laraina first," Trevillion said.

Tara placed the blade across her palm, then stopped. She dug into her pocket and pulled out the ring she had found in the dungeon. She held it out to Trevillion. "In case I end up back in the dungeon," she said. "I don't want to take this with me."

Trevillion hesitated, then took the ring and stuffed it in his pocket.

Tara sliced her palm and placed her bleeding hand over an open gash on her sister's arm. She closed her eyes and let the power rise within her, bracing herself against the jags of pain from Laraina's wounds. The vile presence rushed toward her like a black wave, threatening to drown her in its icy depths. Choking down her rising panic, Tara struck outward and flung up a wall against it. With one part of her mind she held the wall, and with the other she healed her sister. The presence pounded relentlessly on the wall, weakening it. Tara sensed the presence growing stronger, feeding on her fear. Focusing more energy on her sister, she healed the last of Laraina's wounds, then disengaged from her. Chinks appeared in the wall as the presence began to break through. Tara concentrated all of her power on the wall, trying to close the widening rifts. The presence reached through the openings, snagging the edges of her mind. Panic seized her, and she lost control. The wall crumbled.

A sharp pain lanced across her palm, and she felt the pressure of warm flesh against her hand. *Steady. I am here.* She recognized the whisper-soft voice of Trevillion in her mind. The pain of his injuries spasmed through her, then his essence mingled with hers as their blood mixed, and this time, she didn't try to stop it. She let his strength flow into her, help her shore up her fragmented wall. An angry shriek echoed through her mind as the presence was beaten back. She inhaled deeply and let her healing power course through Trevillion's veins. His wounds healed quickly, as did hers. Sensing his well-being, Tara knew she should withdraw before the presence clawed its way back into her mind, but she didn't want to let go. She didn't want to lose the intimacy of the moment.

Forcing herself to break the connection, she opened her eyes. She met Trevillion's dark gaze. He sat opposite her, their knees touching, his hand holding hers against his bare chest. His eyes smoldered with an emotion that sent hot shivers dancing over her skin. Mesmerized by his expression, she leaned toward him.

Laraina cleared her throat.

Tara jumped back, startled. Laraina was sitting beside her, had been there all along. Heat rose in Tara's face as she pulled her hand away from Trevillion's chest.

"I see you're both all right," Laraina said dryly.

Trevillion smiled.

Tara blushed again. "I'm fine." She rose, looking anywhere but at Trevillion. She saw Aurelia looking daggers at her. Kaden still sat with his back to them, watching the Bog. Then Tara's eyes fell on Dominic's cloak-draped body. A sudden thought struck her. She turned back to Trevillion. "Will Dominic suffer the same fate as your brother and the others who died in the Bog? Will he become like the phantoms we saw?"

Trevillion shook his head. "No, I don't think so. He died out here on the riverbank, not within the confines of the Bog. His soul should be free."

Tara looked back at Dominic, relief and sorrow and guilt rushing over her. Tears stung her eyes again. She blinked them away. She heard Laraina rising behind her.

"So he will be safe if we bury him here?" Laraina asked, her voice catching.

"He should be," Trevillion said. He stood and came forward.

Tara's nerves tingled as he approached.

Aurelia hurried over, stopping him. She smiled. "Please, allow me." She pointed to a spot on the ground next to where Dominic lay and said, "*Gravadasa deprinorum!*"

A grave-sized hole appeared in the riverbank next to Dominic's body.

Laraina looked from the hole, to Aurelia, then back to the hole. "You did it." She couldn't keep the surprise out of her voice.

Aurelia tossed her head and smiled at Trevillion. "Of course I did."

"You'd better check the hole first and make sure nothing's going to jump out and attack us," Tara said, annoyed with Aurelia and with herself for letting Aurelia's actions provoke her.

Aurelia stalked to the hole and looked in. "See? It is a perfectly good hole. You should be thanking me for saving you the trouble of digging." She tossed her head again and stood with her hands on her hips.

"Thank you," Trevillion said with a respectful nod.

"What about the dirt?" Tara asked.

"Dirt?" Aurelia looked confused.

"Dirt to fill in the hole after..." Tara stopped, unable to say the words. "...afterward." She clenched her fist to keep back the tears.

Aurelia looked down at the empty hole. "Oh." She shrugged. "I can fix that."

Trevillion and Prince Kaden wrapped Dominic in his cloak and, using the rope, carefully laid him to rest.

"Goodbye, old friend," Tara whispered.

"Goodbye," Laraina sobbed. She covered her face with her hands.

Tara hugged her, and they stood with bowed heads, offering up a silent prayer for his soul.

Aurelia pointed at the hole again and spoke a few words. Dirt filled the hole. A covering of grassy sod appeared on top. "There, see? I said I would fix it."

"So you did," Tara said. "And nothing strange happened. I'm surprised, and impressed. Thanks."

Aurelia smiled, pleased with herself. "You're welcome."

"We should get moving," Trevillion said, eyeing the line of trees, "before another pack of wolves catches our scent."

Tara followed his gaze, staring hard at the black depths between the twisted trunks. Faint prickles of unease rose on her skin. "I agree. The sooner we get away from here, the better." She glanced upward, squinting into the late afternoon sun. They had another two, maybe three, hours of daylight left. They should be able to travel a long way in that amount of time. She slipped her arm around Laraina and gave her a squeeze. "Come on." Tara led her sister over to where they had left their gear. The group shouldered their packs, and with Trevillion in the lead, headed north up the riverbank. Tara took one last look back at Dominic's resting place before hurrying to catch up with the others.

An hour's journey up the river brought them past a wide, shallow pool carved out of the west bank of the Nournan by flood waters. Foam and driftwood edged the pool, swirled in by the current.

Aurelia caught Trevillion's hand and pulled him to a stop. "Look at the water, there. It's not very deep." She looked up and down the river. "And I don't see any of those kara-whatever-you-called-them swimming around. Can we take a bath? Please?"

"They're called karanaks," Trevillion said. "They prefer the deep water, but if they see you in the shallows, they'll come after you."

"Well, we'll take turns. Someone can keep watch. It won't take long," Aurelia said. "*Please?*"

"I'd like one too," said Laraina. "I don't think I've ever been so filthy and disgusting. I'm willing to chance it."

Trevillion looked at Tara.

Tara's face grew hot at the thought of being naked in the water with Trevillion so near. She shrugged in what she hoped was a nonchalant manner. "We should be all right as long as someone keeps an eye out for the karanaks. I don't feel any immediate danger near us."

"All right," Trevillion said. "Ladies first. Stay near the edge and don't take too long." He turned to Kaden. "I'll take this end. You take the other." Trevillion sat on the south end of the pool with his back turned, positioning himself so he could see downriver and still watch the Bog. Kaden moved to the north edge and sat, facing upstream.

Aurelia hopped into the knee-deep water. She gasped. "It's freezing!"

Laraina and Tara followed her into the pool. "Of course it's freezing," Tara said. "It's spring. What did you expect?"

"I didn't think it would be this cold," Aurelia muttered with a grimace. She peeled off her muck-encrusted clothing. Light burst forth as if someone had lit a bright lantern. "Oh. I forgot I was still glowing."

"Can you turn it off?" Laraina asked. She disrobed and sank into the water.

"I'll try." Aurelia thought for a moment, then spoke what sounded like gibberish. The glow vanished. "It worked!" she said happily. "This is great. I want to try something else."

"No," Tara said. "We shouldn't press our luck. Just hurry up with the bath."

Aurelia shot her a black look but said no more.

Feeling self-conscious, Tara crouched, shucked off her clothes, and hurriedly washed off the grime. She glanced at Trevillion from time to time, but he remained with his back to them. *Good*, she thought, though she had to admit a part of her was piqued that she hadn't caught him looking. When the three women had finished bathing, they washed and wrung out their clothes as best they could, then climbed up on the bank and dressed.

Aurelia stood and shook back her wet hair. "That feels so much better." She ran across to Trevillion and kissed him on the cheek. "Thank you!" Then she pulled him to his feet and sat down in his place. "Your turn."

"You're not glowing anymore," Trevillion said.

"I didn't think the light would be needed any longer, so I undid the spell," Aurelia said with a proud lift of her chin.

"I see." Trevillion smiled. "Well done."

Aurelia beamed at him. "Thank you."

Tara resisted the urge to accidentally shove Aurelia into the river and sat down a short distance away, where she could watch the river and the Bog as Trevillion had done. Laraina took Kaden's spot on the other side of the shallows. Trevillion and the prince waded into the pool.

Sitting rigidly with her back to them, Tara concentrated on watching for karanaks. She pulled out a piece of grass and chewed on it to distract herself. She was surprised by how much she wanted to peek. Out of the corner of her eye, she saw Aurelia's head turn. Aurelia obviously had no qualms about it. Tara's fist clenched, a sudden irrational anger needling her. She found a small nub of driftwood, snatched it up, and threw it at Aurelia, hitting her in the arm.

"Ouch!" Aurelia cried, grabbing her arm.

Feeling Aurelia's glare on her, Tara fiddled with the laces of her boot.

"Is something wrong?" Kaden asked as he splashed out of the pool.

"No," Aurelia groused. She picked up the stick and threw it into the water. "The driftwood around here really drifts," she said with another glare at Tara.

"Strange, how that is," Tara said, her face a mask of innocence. She caught a glimpse of Trevillion, half-dressed, looking at her, his mouth quirked as if trying to hide a smile. She blushed and looked away.

The men finished dressing and rejoined the others.

"You're not glowing anymore," Prince Kaden said to his cousin.

"No. I undid the spell," Aurelia said smugly.

"Good for you." Kaden nodded with approval. "Your skills are improving."

Aurelia tossed her head. "My skills have always been good. I just need to use them more." She glowered at Tara. "To practice."

Tara ignored her and went to help Laraina, who was handing out portions of bread and dried meat. They ate quickly and resumed their trek up the river.

Before long, the sun sank below the treeline, casting the riverbank in shadow. The few clouds turned gold, then pink, deepening to purple as twilight fell. A crescent moon rose, spilling light onto the river, and the sky filled with countless gleaming stars.

Around midnight, they stopped to rest. The riverbank had widened again, giving them plenty of room to fight if more wolves attacked. Tara volunteered for the first watch. She knew she wouldn't be able to sleep. Guilt over Dominic's death tore at her, cut a ragged wound in her heart. She moved away from where the others were bedding down and sank to her knees in the grass. Out of the corner of her eye, she saw Laraina fussing with the backpacks and glancing at her with that worried mother hen look. Tara pretended not to see her. She didn't feel like talking; the hurt ran too deep. Looking out across the river, she drank in the cool sweetness of the wild-scented air.

Laraina approached and sat down beside her. "You're thinking about Dominic, aren't you?"

Tara gritted her teeth and looked away, blinking back the burning tears that threatened to flow.

Laraina pulled Tara around to face her. "Sister, it's not your fault. Stop blaming yourself."

"If not for me, Dominic would still be alive," Tara said. "I should have made him stay in Vaalderin." A tear slid down her cheek, and then another.

Laraina squeezed Tara's shoulder. "You couldn't make him stay. You know how he is... was. He wouldn't have come if he hadn't wanted to. You know that."

Tara wiped her sleeve across her eyes. "I should have been able to save him. He shouldn't have died."

"It was his time," Laraina said gently.

"Why now? We went through so many adventures together — you, me, Dominic, with Blackie de Runo and his band, and then with Myles and Xavier. We did things as dangerous as this... well, maybe not quite," she amended, "but no one ever died."

"We could have."

"But we didn't. We always came through. All of us." Tara ripped out a handful of grass and threw it toward the river. "Things are changing, and I can't stop them. I've lost Dominic. I'm losing you." She hadn't meant to say it, but the words had slipped out.

Laraina hugged her. "Don't be silly, sister. You will never lose me."

Tara eased out of the embrace. "Raina, you can't deny that you're changing too. You said yourself that you're in love with Kaden. Have you thought about where that will lead?"

Laraina took a deep breath. "Yes, actually. I've enjoyed our adventures and the freedom our lives have allowed." She hesitated. "But being with Kaden in Castle Carilon and watching the inner workings and all that is involved with running a castle and keeping the peace and... it's all so fascinating. I'd like to have a hand in it."

"How do you know he will let you have a hand in it? He'll have to wed at some point. Being a prince, wouldn't he have to marry a princess? What will happen to you then? You'll either be a permanent mistress with no say in anything or be turned out of the castle to fend for yourself."

Laraina recoiled. "That's not fair, sister. Kaden is not like that at all. If you weren't so busy disliking him, and every other man for that matter, because of Myles, you would see that."

"Myles has nothing to do with this."

"He has everything to do with it. Since Myles left, you have fought with every man I've been with. Myles was a coward and he betrayed you, but that doesn't mean every man is like him. You have to forget about him and stop judging every man by his standard."

Tara bit back what she'd been about to say. Her sister was right. Tara wiped more tears away and reined in her emotions. "I'm sorry. I just don't want what happened to me to happen to you."

"It won't. I'm telling you, Kaden is not like that."

"Well, you have to admit, your choices in men haven't been the greatest. Prince Fournier du Mraine, for example. He's one of the nastiest brutes I've ever met. I fear for the people of Faragellyn when he becomes king."

Laraina's gaze faltered. "He didn't seem that way in the beginning. When I first met him, he was quite charming. But then things began to change." She took a deep breath. "Yes, as far as choices go, he was a bad one, and you're right to fear his rise to the throne. He loves power. What he really wants is to be king. Sooner, rather than later. I had the impression that if there was any way he could hasten the matter, he would." Laraina shivered as if trying to shed Fournier's memory. "But as I said before, you can't judge every man by one bad experience."

"So much for the lesson of the day," Tara said, tossing another handful of grass.

Laraina put her arm around Tara's shoulders. "The only thing I worry about is what will happen to you if I stay with Kaden. The way trouble always seems to find you..." She shook her head. "The thought of you roaming around by yourself scares me."

Tara smiled faintly. "I can't imagine why."

Laraina hugged her again, then wiped a tear from her own eye. "I'm going to get some sleep. Wake me when it's my turn on watch. And remember what I said about Dominic. It's not your fault."

Tara hugged her back. "I know. But I can't help thinking —"

"No thinking." Laraina rose to her feet.

Tara rose with her. "I'm sorry for what I said."

Laraina smiled. "I know. Forget it." She walked back to where the others were sleeping and lay down.

Tara sat down again, her knees pulled tight to her chin, and stared out across the Nournan, watching the reflection of the moon as it rippled on the surface, letting the slow rush of the river soothe her frayed nerves. As much as she hated to admit it, she knew her sister was right. Since Myles had left her, she had taken an instant dislike to every man Laraina had seemed even remotely interested in. Myles' betrayal had hurt worse than any sword wound she'd ever suffered. *That doesn't mean every man is like him.* Tara thought of Trevillion and the feelings he evoked in her. The mere thought of him stirred the butterflies in her stomach and sent heat shooting through her veins. Could she allow herself to trust and love again? Trevillion seemed to care for her, but then, so had Myles.

She pressed the heels of her palms against her forehead, feeling as if her head was going to explode. Maybe when this was over, and

Laraina, Kaden, and Aurelia were safely at Castle Crystalir in Far-agellyn, she could find Blackie de Runo and his band and get back in with them for a while. They might be smugglers, but they were a good-hearted bunch, and she and Laraina had had some great times traveling with them. Memories of Dominic guffawing so hard at Blackie's antics that he had to hold his belly slipped into her mind. Other images followed, tumbling over each other like water spilling over a dam. She relived their adventures, one by one, smiling through her tears as she remembered the funny things Dominic had said and the way he used to carry on about his "lucky" hat, now lost in the Bog. She felt again the fear when she thought he was going to die of the fever, and the elation when she healed him and knew he would live. She saw his smile, heard his laughter, felt again his big bear hugs. Her head sank to her knees. Gods, she was going to miss him.

Silent sobs racked her body. Dominic's arms wrapped around her as if comforting her in spirit. She could almost hear his voice, soothing her as he had in the past.

She froze, suddenly realizing there were arms around her, real ones. She recognized Trevillion's touch, his scent, and the whisper-soft voice in her ear as he sat behind her, holding her close, her back warm against his bare chest.

He brushed her hair away from her face. "I feel your sorrow like a black cloud swirling around you."

She half turned toward him, angry with herself. "A good lot of being on watch I'm doing. I didn't even hear you come over."

"It doesn't matter. You would have known if there was danger." He handed her a scrap of cloth. "I know how hard it is to lose some-one close to you." He moved so that he could see her face. "You needn't berate yourself over Dominic's death. He died the way he wanted to."

Tara wiped her eyes. "What do you mean?"

"He told me that he hated being a merchant. He said, and I quote, 'I'll be damned if I'm going to do this just so I can live longer and end up deaf, blind, and toothless in some old home for the useless somewhere. I'm an adventurer, and by the gods, I'm going to die like one!'"

Tara smiled, brushing away another tear. "That sounds like him." She took a long breath and let it out slowly. "We did have some great adventures. He was like a father to Laraina and me. What else did he tell you?"

"He told how you met in Vaalderin."

Tara gave a hiccoughing laugh. "Yes, what a brawl that was." She sobered. "Strange, isn't it? We met when he stepped in and took a blow that was meant for me. And now we part in the same way."

"You gave Dominic the greatest adventure of his life, and you allowed him to die with dignity, protecting those he loved most. He couldn't have asked for more."

Tara was silent, digesting Trevillion's words. "I guess Dominic's death bothers me so much because I've never had to face death before," she said finally. "No one close to me has ever died. Not that I was close to that many people. Very few people cared about me." She pushed back a stray silvery lock. "I was so young when my father died that his passing didn't really affect me. I don't remember my mother at all. Once I left Wyndover and got away from those who hated me, my life became one grand adventure. The more successful I was, the more chances I took." Her voice grew softer. "I truly believed that there would always be a way out, an escape. I've cheated death so many times. Until now. This adventure is different than any I have undertaken. Things are happening that I can't control. Dominic is gone, and Raina is in love, and I'm —" She stopped, startled by what she had been about to say.

"Yes?" Trevillion asked. "What of you?"

Tara didn't answer. The words that she, herself, was thinking about love again had come so easily, unbidden. She was glad she'd caught the words before she said them and made a fool of herself.

"Would you spend the rest of your life alone and end up 'deaf, blind, and toothless in some old home for the useless somewhere'?" Trevillion said, his arms holding her gently.

"I don't know." She rubbed her eyes in frustration. It was so hard to let go of the mantle of separation she had worn for so long, keeping everyone at arm's length. She turned to Trevillion. "What about you? What will become of you when all this is over?"

Trevillion looked out across the river. "I will undoubtedly die an adventurer's death — probably a knife in the back in some godsforsaken place like Vaalderin."

Silence fell between them, lasting for several minutes. Then Tara spoke again.

"How did you survive that first time in the Bog?"

Trevillion stiffened. "You mean why did I alone survive when all the men I forced to come with me died?"

Tara pulled away from him, taken aback by his tone. "Well, yes. It's a reasonable question. You don't need to snap at me."

Trevillion looked away, his expression harsh. "I'm sorry. Apparently, it was not my time to die."

"Your brother said something like that in the Bog, or rather, his ghost did." She tried to remember Jared's exact words.

Trevillion said nothing.

Tara tried a different tack. "You said earlier that you knew what it was like to lose someone close to you. Were you speaking of your brother?" *Or someone else*, she added silently, both wanting and not wanting to know if there was some love of his life he was missing.

"Yes. Jared and I were close, once."

Raw pain edged his voice, and she knew the wound still cut deep. She put her hand over his and squeezed, felt his fingers curl around hers. "I'm sorry. It must be hard knowing he wasn't the innocent you thought."

"I idolized him and so was blind to his faults."

A word sprang into Tara's mind. "Rinpool. That was it. Your brother said you wouldn't die in the Bog because the prophecy of Rinpool had not yet been fulfilled. What prophecy did he mean? And what is Rinpool?"

Trevillion's body tensed again, and he was silent so long Tara thought he wasn't going to answer.

"Rinpool is a place of magic in the Eastern Frontier," he said, his voice still distant and cool. "It is a small pool of water with a stone border, headed by an obelisk. The obelisk is covered with runes. I don't know their translation. Those who drink the water and look in the pool when the moon shines on it see a glimpse of the future. Rinpool lies in the heart of Dharakwood, a forest of impenetrable thorn trees."

"And you have seen this place?"

"Yes."

Tara shot him a sidelong glance and caught the bitterness of his expression, his gaze lost in the smooth-flowing river. Tentatively, she cupped his face with her hand and turned him back to her. "Please tell me." Their eyes held. Her breath caught, and for a moment, time stood still. Her lips parted. His gaze went to her lips, then back to her eyes, and she thought he might kiss her. Her hand lingered on his jaw, feeling the rough stubble. He covered her hand with his, and drawing it to his lips, kissed her palm. Then, still holding her hand in his, he looked down and seemed to withdraw from her. Strangely disappointed, Tara tried to calm the rampant trembling in her body. She had really wanted him to kiss her, and the knowledge scared her. At the same time, she wondered why he hadn't.

"Rinpool. It is a long story," he said with a deep sigh.

"Tell me."

Trevillion let go of her fingers and ran his hand through his dark hair. He looked back out at the river. "Jared and I had hired on as guards for a trade caravan heading from Mandir in the East to the Gypsy Crossroads in the West. The Cyranel Mountains separate East from West, but Klyder Pass through the southern end of the mountains is generally a safe route. Just before we reached the pass, we were attacked by bandits. The Eastern Frontier has many such roving bands that kill for pleasure and take what they want. Jared and I and the other guards fought as best we could, but we were outmatched. I was stabbed in the chest." His hand drifted upward, and he rubbed a spot just below his right collarbone as if he could still feel the wound.

"Jared killed the bandit who stabbed me, but the battle was lost. Most of the caravanners were dead. We tried to escape. The southern edge of Dharakwood runs very near the pass where we were. We ran toward it, but I couldn't make it. Jared slung me over his shoulder and carried me the rest of the way. The bandits came after us. We reached the Wood right before the bandits reached us."

Trevillion stopped for a moment as if choosing his words. "Dharakwood holds magic even older than that which dwells in the Bog. The thorn trees are impenetrable, and the only way you can enter the Wood is if it opens for you. Either the branches will part and make a path for you, or they won't. Dharakwood opened for us, let us in, then closed behind us. The bandits tried to force their way in but were impaled by the thorns.

"The branches began to close in around us, but a path opened, and we were driven through the Wood by the movement of the branches. We had to keep going through the path or get impaled ourselves. I became delirious. There must have been poison on the knife. I remember Jared setting me down next to a pool of water in a small clearing. Rinpool."

"How old were you when this happened?" Tara asked.

"I was fifteen. We had no food or water, so Jared scooped water out of the pool for me to drink and used it to wash out my wound." He massaged the spot on his chest again absently.

Tara looked at the smooth skin of his chest and shoulder. "You have no scar."

"No. The magic in the water of Rinpool healed it, after a time." He ran his hand through his hair again. He seemed reluctant to say more.

"What about the prophecy? Did you see something in the water?"

He took a long breath. "I remember waking up, in one of my more lucid moments, and seeing the moon shining down through the hole in the canopy of thorns. The runes in the headstone seemed to glow, and the pool of water shone like liquid silver. I looked down into the water and, instead of my reflection, I saw a battle scene with men fighting as far as the eye could see. The fighters were blurred, but in the center was a young man on horseback, leading the battle. The crest on his shield was a red griffin."

"Like the ring? The symbol of the High King?"

He nodded. "I saw him quite clearly. He looked like me, but then again, he didn't. I tried to look more closely, but the scene changed, and I saw..."

Tara couldn't stand the suspense. "What did you see?"

"I saw you."

Tara's jaw dropped. "Me? Are you certain?"

Trevillion smiled, his hand lifting to brush her cheek and tease a strand of silver-blonde hair. "Delirious or no, there's no mistaking your face."

"What was I doing?"

"You were standing in front of a black castle, in a deep valley, surrounded by black mountains. The castle had no door. You looked back over your shoulder, at who or what I don't know. Then you turned back to the castle, touched the wall, and walked through it."

"I walked through the wall?"

"Yes."

"Did I come out again?"

"I don't know. The scene changed, and I saw darkness, twisted trees rising from slime and muck, and what looked like ghosts flitting through them, and I suddenly realized that Jared was standing behind me, looking at the water. Then the moon passed beyond the opening in the canopy, and the pool went dark."

"You saw the Bog," Tara whispered.

"Yes, though I didn't know what it was at the time. Jared wanted to know what else had appeared. He had only seen the Bog. I told him about the battle scene and the man with the red griffin standard. He knew about the High King's insignia and got very excited about the vision. I said the man sort of looked like me, but not quite."

"Perhaps Jared thought that if it wasn't you, it must be him, and that he was destined to be High King. That might be what he meant when he said a future that should have been his."

"Possibly. The man didn't look like Jared either, and I did tell him that."

"Perhaps it was you," Tara said thoughtfully. "Maybe you are destined to be the next High King."

"No. I don't think so."

"Why not?"

He shrugged. "I just don't feel that it is so." He picked up a small stick of driftwood, toyed with it, then tossed it into the water. Tara watched the silvery ripples spread out around the spot where it landed.

"Did you tell Jared about the black castle... about me?"

"No. I'm not sure why."

Tara frowned, thinking. "I've never seen a black castle, or black mountains, for that matter."

"There is a mountain range on the eastern border of the Frontier called the Black Mountains, but I have never seen them."

"I wonder what it means?"

Trevillion didn't answer.

"Is that why you helped us in Vaalderin? Because of the vision?" Tara asked.

"Yes, mostly. I never expected to see my vision in the flesh. Yet, there you were. I had to know more about you, and if your wanting to go into the Bog was related to the other image I had seen. But I also needed to know what had happened to Jared. Your appearance seemed like a stroke of Fate, compelling me to action."

"Strange, you should say that. I've been feeling for quite some time that my path is being directed by some higher power, and that my choices are not my own anymore."

"We always have choices," Trevillion said. "There will always be choices." He rose, pulling Tara up with him. "You must choose with your heart and not your head." He drew her close; his lips brushed her hair. Then he released her. "Go get some sleep. I'll take the watch for a while."

She hesitated, her mind and body in turmoil. "Thank you for telling me about Dominic."

"You're welcome," Trevillion said quietly.

Tara walked to the campsite. She felt Trevillion's eyes on her, but did not look back. She'd hoped that he would give her answers, but all she had gained were more questions. Wrapping herself in her cloak, she lay down near the others, and fell into an exhausted sleep.

*****

The bright crescent moon sifted through the few darkened clouds, painting the scarlet rocks in silver and shadows. Countless stars filled the sky. The night air blew cool and crisp, the wind filled with a thousand wild scents.

Captain Natiere stood on the edge of a rugged red cliff, drinking in the scents of the night; they flowed through him like an intoxicating draught. Beside him stood a large black wolf. Natiere crouched and stroked the dark wolf's head.

"Just beyond that ridge to the east lies the Nournan River," he said, his voice a rasping whisper. "Another day's travel, perhaps two, will see us there. From there we go north along the riverbank through the Bog and on up to Relic. The first battalion should be halfway up the river by now. From the signs I have seen, they are moving quickly."

The wolf uttered a low growl that sounded strangely like a laugh.

Natiere chuckled. "Yes, Kelya, you have been very helpful in speeding their progress. I must thank you for your assistance." He grew sober. His rough hands cupped the lean wolf's face and held it, their eyes level. "But you must promise me you and the others will not follow me up through the Bog. It is not your territory. It belongs to others more vicious and unyielding in enforcing their boundaries, and I will not have fighting among the Brothers and Sisters. Is that clear?"

The wolf leaned forward and licked the Captain's face.

The Captain smiled and gave a rare laugh without malice or sarcasm, a laugh that could almost be called joyous. "I will miss you too." He looked back out across the Scarlet Mountains to the north. "But soon I will be free. As soon as the battalion is in Relic, I will resume my pursuit of the Lady Tara Triannon and her companions. When that is done I can return to the wilds. Before I left Desta I searched for their tracks and found them heading northeast." He smiled again. "That can only mean they intended to go through the worst of the Bog, hoping perhaps it is the one place I won't follow. Witch or no, the Lady Tara has courage." He turned to the wolf. "You must admire that. If they survive the Bog, unlikely as it may seem, they will undoubtedly head for Crystalir and beg protection from the King of Faragellyn. Unless, of course, he has already been... dispatched, shall we say."

Natiere gave the wolf one last pat, then rose to his feet. The stars were beginning to fade, the sky growing lighter with the coming dawn. "It is time to go back. The men will be waking soon. Remember your promise."

The lone wolf growled in reply, then trotted off into the blood red rocks.

*****

Tara woke just after sunrise, feeling the heat of the sun's rays on her face. She sat up and stretched. She had slept well again, despite her emotional turmoil from the night before.

Laraina and Trevillion were already up. Trevillion turned and caught Tara looking at him. He smiled and raised his eyebrows in a wordless question. She smiled back with a nod, telling him she was all right. Laraina looked from one to the other, then turned away with a sly smile to wake Kaden and Aurelia.

They ate their breakfast and started up the river, heading northeast along the grassy bank of the Nournan. No wolves, or any other beasts, came near.

After two days of travel, the dead bogland became hilly, rolling with high knolls and deep hollows. The bank of the river remained firm. By the fourth day, the trees at the edge of the Bog showed signs of life. Bright green buds swelled on gray branches, and birds twittered from the heights. At dusk on the fourth day, they reached the fork where the Colin River flowed into the Nournan. Tumbling down from the north, the Colin formed a great Y-shape with the Nournan, which curved sharply to the east as it swept down through Faragellyn from its headwaters in the Cyranel Mountains.

Trevillion called a halt at the edge of the Colin River. The Colin was wide and swift and rocky with many shallows and deep spots hiding dangerous undercurrents. At this point, Tara guessed the river to be about waist deep.

"Shall we cross?" she asked.

Trevillion shook his head. "It would be difficult. The rocks of the riverbed are treacherous." He glanced up at the darkening sky. "If someone fell, they could be swept downstream, and we would have a hard time finding them before the karanaks did. There will be a better place to cross further north. We'll camp here for the night."

Shrugging his backpack further up onto his shoulders, Trevillion led the group into the woods. They found a campsite on top of a broad hill sheltered by a stand of cedar and a massive briar patch. A thin layer of clouds formed, obscuring the bright light of the moon. Laraina took the first watch while the others slept.

*****

In the deep hours before dawn, Tara woke with a stabbing chill. Sweeping back her tangled hair, she sat up and looked about. Off to her left, Jovan Trevillion leaned against a tree, on watch. His eyes met hers. She slipped to his side.

"What's wrong?" he whispered.

"I'm not sure," Tara said. "Someone's coming up the riverbank."

"Natiere?"

She shook her head. "No, it's not him."

Faint sounds grew louder until they could distinguish the muffled clank of metal, the creak of leather armor, the stomp of marching feet.

"Wake the others," Trevillion said. "I'll go have a look." He ducked into the underbrush and disappeared.

Tara ran to Laraina's side and squeezed her shoulder.

Laraina woke instantly. "What's going on?"

"Someone's coming," Tara whispered.

Laraina's eyes widened. "The Butcher?"

"No. Stay here and wake the others. I'm going to see what I can find out."

Laraina nodded.

Tara groped her way down the hillside to where Trevillion crouched in the undergrowth near the line of trees.

Trevillion pointed south. "Look."

In the distance, she saw the flickering lights of torches advancing northward along the narrow riverbank. As they drew nearer, the shadows behind them resolved into men.

"It's an army," she breathed.

Trevillion nodded. "Look at their shields. The diamond star of Mardainn. Councilman Jarnik has allied with Sulledor."

"So that's what Natiere has been up to." The full implications of what she was seeing struck her. "They're going to follow the Colin up to Relic and attack from the rear, trapping the Faragellyn Border Guard between them and General Caldren. The Guard will be wiped out, and all of Faragellyn will be open to the Sulledorns." She gripped Trevillion's arm. "We have to warn them! If Faragellyn falls..."

"The other kingdoms won't stand a chance," Trevillion finished grimly.

Hundreds of silent soldiers marched by at a fast clip, creating a long lighted trail far back into the night.

Motioning for a retreat, Trevillion led Tara back into the woods. "I will go."

"Can you get there in time?"

"With a little luck. And I can travel more quickly alone," he added, as if knowing what she was about to say.

"But —"

"You must get the others to safety. Just follow the Nournan. It will take you straight to Crystalir."

"I know, but —"

He held his finger to her lips. "You know I'm right."

"But if they catch you, they'll kill you. Or worse," she added, remembering his comment about Councilman Jarnik's torture chamber.

"They won't catch me." He sounded confident, but Tara sensed a sliver of doubt behind his words. He stepped away. "Say goodbye to the others for me."

"Jovan..."

He turned back.

Tara opened her mouth, but no words came. She didn't want to say goodbye, but she couldn't bring herself to speak of what was hidden in her heart. She raised her hand in a weak wave. "Take care."

Trevillion closed the distance between them and gave her a roguish smile. "Don't worry. You haven't seen the last of me yet." He caressed her cheek with his fingertips. "That I promise you."

He was very close, his dark eyes burning into hers. Tara suddenly found herself trembling. Trevillion's fingers slipped to her chin, lifted it. He bent his head and kissed her, lingeringly, as if he wanted to savor a moment that might never come again.

Then he was gone.

CHAPTER 15

Dusk fell rapidly, soaking the ground with dew. Ignoring the cold wetness seeping into his uniform, General Caldren lay on top of a low hill and stared through a spyglass into the distance. Not far beyond lay the Faragellyn border. The trail of the handful of soldiers who had escaped the ambush of Belgarde led straight toward it. His scouts had been tracking them for days — and should have caught them.

The General's eyes raked the darkening landscape, but detected no movement. The escapees would likely have made it across the border by now and alerted the Border Guard, costing him his crucial element of surprise. Someone would pay for this blunder.

He crept back down the hill. He was met at the bottom by a weary, bedraggled scout. The General's fingers curled around the hilt of the dagger at his belt. He could smell the scout's fear and knew what his report would be.

The scout saluted nervously. "Two of them made it across the border, sir. They were picked up by the Faragellyn Border Guard stationed in Relic."

The General's hand sliced upward, his knife thrusting deep into the scout's belly. "Thank you, I know where the Border Guard is stationed. You failed me."

The scout groaned, his breath gurgling as he crumpled to the ground. The General yanked out his dagger, wiped it on the scout's sleeve, and jabbed the blade into its sheath. He strode away without a backward glance.

As he entered the Sulledorn camp, soldiers faded out of his path, hurrying about their duties and talking in hushed tones. He threaded his way through the maze of tents and stalked into the pavilion. His scout commander stood bent over several maps spread out on a table.

"We've lost the element of surprise!" the General bellowed. He launched himself at the soldier and gripped him by the throat. "I'll have your guts ripped out for this!"

"We've only... lost it... for the moment," choked the commander, struggling to disengage himself from the General's fierce grip. "We still have some wildcards... left to play."

The General released him and threw him aside. He paced the length of the tent. "Yes," he mused, "we do, providing Jarnik's troops arrive on time and Du Mraine keeps his bargain."

The commander recovered his composure and rubbed his bruised throat. "That should produce quite an uproar — the high and mighty King of Faragellyn brought down by his own son."

"Yes." The General smiled at the thought. "It adds the crowning touch." He spun on his heel and strode from the tent.

*****

"Tara, where are you?"

Laraina's strained whisper brought Tara back to her senses. The first thing she noticed was the silence. The Mardainn army had moved past them up the river. With Trevillion ahead of them, she hoped. She closed her eyes and felt once more the touch of his lips. A wild surge of emotion swept over her again, stealing her breath.

Laraina bounded up beside her. "There you are. I was beginning to think you'd been captured. Was that an army or was I imagining things?" Laraina glanced about. "Where's Jovan?"

Tara cleared her throat, trying to collect her scattered thoughts. "That was the Mardainn army." She hoped her voice didn't sound as strange to Laraina as it did to her. "They must have allied with Sulledor. It looks like they're going to attack the Faragellyn troops from the rear. He — Jovan — has gone to warn them. He thinks he can get there first."

"Oh, no! If they succeed — if Faragellyn falls..."

Tara nodded. "I know."

Laraina looked up the river. "Jovan said that the General and Councilman Jarnik were in league. It looks like he was right. Do you think he can do it?"

"Do what?"

"Get there first."

"Oh. I don't know." Tara tried to focus her mind. "He's got a lot of ground to cover and the army was moving fast. He won't have much chance to eat or sleep." She rubbed her temples. "He might make it." *Or he might not.* Visions of Trevillion being captured and tortured or killed outright flooded her thoughts. She wished she could have gone with him.

"Aurelia's not going to like that he's gone," Laraina said. "But at least we're out of the Bog, thank the gods for that. And we know this territory well. We no longer need a guide. All we have to do is cross the Colin and then follow the Nournan east, straight to Crystalir. Simple."

Laraina paused. Looking closely at Tara, she added, "And the Butcher is standing right behind you."

Tara heard her sister speak, but the words floated around her like formless mist. She could not get her mind off Trevillion.

Laraina caught Tara's arm. "Are you all right? You haven't heard a word I've said."

Tara started at Laraina's touch. "What? Of course I heard you. You said we had to follow the river to Crystalir."

"I also said the Butcher was standing behind you."

"What?" Tara whirled, her hand on her sword. She turned back and glared at her sister. "What are you trying to do, scare the life out of me?"

Laraina raised an eyebrow. "Are you sure you're all right?"

"I'm fine," Tara growled. "Come on." She started back up the hill to the campsite. Laraina stared after her, then followed.

At the top of the hill, Kaden and Aurelia met the sisters with obvious relief.

"It's about time," Kaden said. "What in the Abyss is going on down there?"

"Where's Jovan?" demanded Aurelia.

Laraina held up her hands for quiet. "That was the Mardainn army out of Desta. We think they've allied with Sulledor and are going to attack the Faragellyn troops from the rear, probably somewhere near Relic."

Kaden paled. "Mardainn and Sulledor? It can't be."

"I don't know why else they would be going up the river," Laraina said softly.

Kaden swore and pounded his fist against the bole of a thick pine.

"Where's Jovan?" Aurelia persisted.

"He's gone to warn them," Laraina answered.

"He's gone?" Aurelia cried. "He deserted us? I don't believe it."

"He had to," Laraina said. "If the Faragellyn soldiers get caught between the Sulledorn and Mardainn armies, they won't stand a chance. We don't need his help now anyway," she added. "Tara and I know this area well. We'll be in Crystalir in a couple of weeks."

"You will, but I won't," Aurelia declared. "I'm going to Relic."

"You're going to Crystalir," Tara corrected.

Aurelia stamped her foot. "I am not."

"Yes, you are," Tara said. "One way or another."

Aurelia started to object, but thought better of it and said nothing.

"Good," said Tara. "Now I suggest you lie down and go back to sleep."

With a toss of her head, Aurelia retreated to the spot where she had been sleeping and curled up again.

Laraina's eyebrows shot up as she watched Aurelia. "How did you do that?" she whispered to her sister.

Tara shrugged. "We've only got another hour or so before dawn. You might as well get some sleep too. I'll keep watch."

Laraina nodded. She followed Kaden to a dry patch of ground near Aurelia, and they lay down next to each other.

Tara settled against the trunk of a great oak. She felt Trevillion's absence keenly. She tried not to think about it, but she couldn't help reliving the moments of his goodbye. His touch, his kiss, had let loose a tumult of emotion like nothing she'd ever experienced. And worse, she'd kissed him back; she hadn't been able to stop herself. Worst of all, she wanted more. Much more. Her hand curled into a fist. She'd sworn this wouldn't happen to her again. Curse his handsome hide.

A faint rustle interrupted her thoughts. She looked over at the campsite and saw Aurelia sit up. Aurelia glanced about, her eyes coming to rest on Tara. She mouthed the words, "I have to go," and pointed to the bushes.

Tara nodded, her eyes narrowing as she watched Aurelia disappear into the undergrowth. Aurelia was up to something again. Tara waited what she thought was an appropriate amount of time, then crossed to Laraina's side and touched her on the shoulder.

Laraina sat up. "What's wrong?" she whispered.

"Keep watch while I go retrieve the brat."

Laraina looked around. "Where is she?"

"She said she had to go. She hasn't come back yet." Tara rose from her crouch.

"Tara, don't —"

"Don't what?" Tara asked, not bothering to hide her irritation.

Laraina folded her arms across her chest. "You know what I mean. No murdering or maiming."

Tara smiled grimly. "I won't do anything to her that she doesn't deserve." She slipped across the camp and into the underbrush.

Moonlit shadows danced around her as she forced her way through the thicket and started down the hill. The haunting cry of an owl echoed through the trees. At the bottom, she searched the mix of rotting leaves and pine needles for Aurelia's tracks, finding them easily. Aurelia's trail led off into the woods. Tara shook her head. She couldn't believe that Aurelia, foolish as she was, would be stupid enough to try to go to Relic by herself. Or would she?

The shadows deepened as Tara moved further into the dark forest. Giant trees, as old as the mountains, lofted above her like indomitable towers, their interlocking branches shutting out the faint light of the approaching dawn. Night sounds, skitterings in the undergrowth, and the swift fluttering of awakened birds rose and fell around her, but she saw no sign of Aurelia.

Then a soft light flared near the ground a few yards ahead. Tara halted. The light seemed to be coming from behind a low bush. She crept forward and peered over the top of the bush. Aurelia sat cross-legged on the ground, her hands spread about two feet apart. Light flared again between her hands, and an image appeared — a man running through a forest. Tara's breath stopped. It was Jovan Trevillion.

"What is that?" Tara stepped into the open.

Aurelia's head whipped around, and the light vanished. She scowled. "Curse it all! Look what you did. I lost it."

Tara snorted. "You left camp *and* you're conjuring. You're lucky I don't knock your head off. Now what were you doing?"

"I was trying to see Jovan, to see if he was all right." She thrust her chin out defiantly. "I was worried about him."

"I see." Tara hesitated, her mind battling with her heart. "Can you do it again?"

Aurelia looked at her in surprise. "I don't know. I had a hard time getting it to work the first time. I've never been able to do it before." She glanced at Tara again, then held out her hands once more. She closed her eyes, concentrating, and whispered a few words. Light coalesced between her outstretched palms, but no image showed through. The light faded and went out. Aurelia dropped her hands and opened her eyes, her face a model of frustration and disappointment. "It's not working."

"Would it help to have something that belonged to him?" Tara asked.

Aurelia considered. "It might."

Tara undid the clasp from her cloak and handed it to her.

Aurelia examined it. "This insignia. I saw it on the uniforms of the soldiers that attacked me in Carilon." She looked at Tara suspiciously. "What are you doing with it?"

Tara squelched the anger that rose at the implication. "Jovan gave me this cloak. You saw him do it. It once belonged to his brother, who was a Sulledorn soldier."

Aurelia's eyes widened. "The one in the Bog?"

"Yes. Wait! It won't show Jared, will it? Being a previous owner?"

Aurelia shrugged. "I don't know. Let's find out." Holding the clasp, she thrust out her hands and chanted the spell before Tara could stop her.

Light blossomed. An image formed, clear and bright. Tara saw Trevillion running easily through a long stretch of trees. He didn't appear to be under any duress. The image flickered, and the light winked out.

"It didn't look like he was in trouble," Tara said.

"No, it didn't," Aurelia agreed, wiping sweat from her brow with a handkerchief. She fingered the clasp another moment, then handed it back to Tara. "Thanks."

"We need to get back to camp. Raina probably thinks I'm digging a hole to bury you in."

Aurelia rose to her feet. "I'm sure you would like to."

"Sometimes." Tara motioned for Aurelia to go ahead of her.

"Well, the feeling is mutual," Aurelia grumbled as she started back toward camp.

Tara laughed. "I bet it is."

"You probably thought I was going to Relic."

"The thought did cross my mind."

Aurelia flung up her hands. "What would be the point? You'd just drag me back."

"Yes, I would — bound and gagged and slung over my shoulder."

"You're such a mean person."

Tara bristled. "I am not. It would be no more than you deserve. You lied about having to go."

Aurelia spun around. "I did not lie! I did have to go. I just didn't say where, or what I had to go and do. I can't help what you assume."

Tara stopped. She smiled in spite of herself. "Fair enough. I'll give you that one." She turned Aurelia around and headed her back toward camp. "But you can be sure I won't make that mistake again."

They met a grim-faced Prince Kaden and Laraina at the bottom of the hill leading down from the campsite.

"There you are," said Laraina. She looked Aurelia over as if searching for injuries.

"Where in the Abyss have you been?" demanded Kaden.

"I had to go," Aurelia said.

"Apparently, she had to go, fifty yards away," Tara added. She brushed past Kaden. "Let's get the packs and get going, since we're all up anyway. There's enough light to see."

They collected their gear, then made their way back down the hill and stepped through the undergrowth to the line of trees that marked the edge of the forest. The banks of the Nournan River were deserted. The satiny surface of the water reflected the pale rose and lavender of the sunrise.

With Tara in the lead, they marched past the fork where the swift-moving Colin swept into the Nournan and continued northward along the Colin, traveling for another mile before finding a place shallow enough to cross.

Tara signaled a halt at the edge of the rushing water. "We'll cross here and —" Something on the far bank caught her eye. "Raina, look." She pointed across the river. "Footprints. Lots of them." Tara crouched and examined the sandy soil. Faint impressions marred the smooth sand. The constant lapping of the water had all but washed them away. "Well, well. It looks like Crystalir is in for a surprise."

"You don't think the Mardainn army went to Crystalir instead of Relic, do you?" Laraina asked.

"No, I don't think so." Tara rose. "There would be more of a trail if the whole army had gone through. They must have split up. A bunch of them, I can't tell how many, crossed here and are headed east."

"They can't be very far ahead of us," Laraina said.

Tara agreed. "It shouldn't take long to catch them and see what they're up to."

Laraina took the rope out of Kaden's backpack, and the four looped it around their waists and tied themselves together. They joined hands and, with Tara leading, stepped into the river. The swift current swept around their knees as if it would whisk their feet out from under them.

"My legs are freezing!" Aurelia complained. She slipped on the treacherous rocks and nearly fell.

"Fall in, and the rest of you will be freezing," Tara said, as Prince Kaden helped Aurelia regain her balance.

They managed to cross without mishap. They traveled southeastward until they were once more within sight of the Nournan. Then they veered to the east, following the river, but keeping just inside the line of trees.

As dusk drifted over the forest, they stopped to rest in a grove of fragrant evergreens. A layer of dry needles covered the forest floor. Some two hundred yards away in the edge of the woods, the Mardainn soldiers had pitched their tents. The thirty-man troop had been easy to follow; they hadn't bothered to hide their trail, obviously thinking themselves alone in the woods.

Laraina dug into her backpack, handing out their supper rations. "We don't have much left," she said, keeping her voice low.

"I'm sure the Mardainn soldiers will share." Tara collected their water flasks. "I'll go find some water. The river is too muddy to drink."

Laraina nodded. "Be careful. At least, this far from the Bog, there are no karanaks."

Munching a piece of bread, Tara disappeared into the trees.

*****

Laraina nibbled on her meal of dried fruit.

Kaden sat beside her. "What did she mean 'The soldiers will share?'"

"We should be able to pick up some more supplies tonight," Laraina said.

"From the soldiers? You're going into their camp?"

"Tara and I will go on a raiding party."

"A raiding party," Kaden repeated.

Laraina held her finger to his lips. She could see the anger building behind his words. "Crystalir is still two weeks' travel from here. We're almost out of food, and we need to slow them down. It won't do any good to warn the king they're coming if he doesn't have time to prepare."

"So the two of you are going to attack and subdue thirty men by yourselves?"

Laraina opened her mouth to speak, but Kaden didn't give her a chance.

"Raina, I care about you! One of these days you're going to get caught. Then what will you do?"

"Escape, of course." Tara strode up and handed them their filled water flasks. "A little after midnight," she said to her sister.

Laraina nodded.

Kaden ran his hand through his hair as if he would yank it out by the roots. He jumped to his feet, pulling Laraina up with him. "Excuse us," he said to Tara and Aurelia, and led Laraina off into the woods. Once they were out of earshot, the prince put his hands on Laraina's shoulders and faced her squarely.

"Raina, I won't let you do it. You're going to get killed. There has to be another way."

Laraina shook her head. "You don't need to worry. Tara and I have raided many camps without being caught."

Kaden's grip tightened. "But there is always a chance. One time is all it takes. One mishap. Like Dominic. How many adventures had he had before this one? He survived the whole bloody Bog, right up until the last minute. Now he's dead. One mishap. How do you know that won't happen to you?"

Laraina stiffened. "No one knows when their time is up." She tore out of his hold, fighting the anguish over Dominic that threatened to bring tears. "I am an adventurer. This is how I live — how I have always lived."

"Because of your sister. I thought you were tired of adventuring. I thought you wanted more."

She faced him. "I do want more. But until this adventure is over, I have to be me — the me I am now. And you have to trust that I know what I'm doing."

"And if we survive this adventure?"

"I'll go wherever you like and do whatever you want to do."

He studied her a moment. "What about her?" He jerked his head at the grove of evergreens behind them.

Laraina looked away, hiding her uncertainty. "Tara can take care of herself, as Dominic was forever telling me."

Kaden moved close, his fingers gentle on her cheek as he turned her face to his. "Would you leave her?"

Laraina hesitated. "I promised our father on his deathbed that I would watch over her."

"I think you have fulfilled your duty."

She looked away again. In the time she and Kaden had spent together in Carilon, he had given her a glimpse of a different way of life. He had shared his thoughts and honored her opinions as he grew into his role as heir to the throne. Her two-month taste of castle life and politics had left her hungry for more. But what of Tara? And what of her own future? *He'll have to wed at some point. Being a prince, wouldn't he have to marry a princess? What will happen to you then?* Tara's words rang in her ears, feeding the doubt in her mind.

"Raina." Kaden's voice had grown softer, as if he understood the battle going on inside her. He slipped his arms around her.

Her hand drifted to his chest, stroked it; the muscles beneath his worn shirt tightened under her fingertips. She didn't want to lose him.

He drew her against him. "If I asked you to give up adventuring and come back to Dhanarra and be my queen, would you do it?"

Laraina's eyes met his. "Are you asking?"

"Yes."

Laraina stared at him. Ripples of cautious joy surged through her, warming her from the inside out. "What about your people? I'm not Dhanarran, and I'm not royalty. How do you know they will accept me?"

Prince Kaden smiled. "They already like you. And when I tell them how courageous you are and how you saved my life, they will welcome you as their own."

She studied his face, hardly daring to believe his sincerity. The warmth inside her bubbled over. "Then the answer is yes."

Kaden's hand slipped to the nape of her neck. "I'll hold you to that." His lips closed over hers.

*****

Tara sat against a tree and, for the first time in her life, thought seriously about her future. Things were changing too fast; she herself was changing. How different she was from the Tara who had left Carilon just a few short weeks before. Death had touched her. Dominic... A choking wave of grief washed over her, and she fought back tears. Dominic was gone, and nothing she could do would bring him back. Laraina, too, was gone, but in a different way. She had found her place in life beside Prince Kaden. They were all so different. Kaden was no longer a pampered pleasure seeker. He'd handled the devastating loss of his father and shown surprising mettle. Not once had he complained about his own discomfort. His foremost thoughts were of helping the Dhanarran people. While she might scoff at his naiveté and disagree with his decisions, she had to admit he deserved more respect than she'd given him. And Aurelia... Well, Aurelia was still a brat, but she had matured.

Tara picked up a twig, twisted it in her fingers. *What of you?* Trevillion's question haunted her. *Would you spend the rest of your life alone and end up deaf, blind, and toothless in some old home for the useless somewhere?* Not a pleasant prospect, but few soldiers of fortune lived to see old age. What did she want out of life? The traditional family with children had never enticed her. Neither had castle life, nor the court politics her sister found so intriguing. Tara liked travel and adventure, the rush of adrenaline. But what fun would such a life be alone? An inner voice whispered she didn't have to be alone. Thoughts of Trevillion flooded through her. Her lips burned again with his kiss. She was in love with him. She could deny it all she liked, but the fact remained that she was irreparably in love. She squeezed the twig, bent it in half. Where was Trevillion now? He had said they would meet again, but would they?

There were strange forces shaping her life, changing it in ways she did not understand for reasons she did not know. The twig snapped in two. She tossed it aside in frustration. Where would it all end?

*****

Shortly after midnight, Prince Kaden and Laraina reappeared in the pine grove. Laraina's eyes glowed with a warm light that Tara did not miss. And though she was glad for her sister, she couldn't help but feel a twinge of... what? Jealousy? No, isolation. She felt like an outsider. The close bond that she and her sister had shared for so long was breaking. They were drifting apart, and Tara had never felt so alone.

Prince Kaden stepped into the grove and sat down beside his sleeping cousin. Laraina proceeded directly to her sister's side.

"Ready when you are," she said with a smile.

Tara rose, summoning a smile in return. "Let's go."

They left the grove and stole through the darkened forest to the edge of the Mardainn camp. The waning moon shone in a sky etched with stars. Dew sparkled on the grass along the riverbank.

The soldiers had bedded down just inside the edge of the woods. A single sentry leaned against a tree on the rim of the forest, yawning.

"I assume you have a plan?" Laraina whispered.

"Do you still have the flask of homemade brew you won from Blackie in that card game?"

"I think so." Laraina rummaged through one of her belt pouches and pulled out a metal flask.

"Then I have a plan."

Laraina looked at the flask. "One swallow of this stuff will turn you into a raving lunatic."

Tara smiled. "Exactly." She pulled a dagger out of her boot, then hesitated, thoughts of Dominic slipping through her mind. She grew sober. "Be careful," she said and started forward.

Laraina stopped her. "*You* are telling *me* to be careful? Are you feeling all right?"

"I'm fine. I was just thinking about Dominic. I've lost one family member. I don't want to lose another."

Laraina squeezed her arm. "You won't. Let's go."

Moving silently through the forest, they tiptoed between the bedrolls and crept up behind the nodding sentry. Tara whacked him over the head with the hilt of her dagger. Laraina caught him as he fell and lowered him gently to the ground. Together, they propped him up in a sitting position against the base of the tree. Tara picked up his water flask and handed it to Laraina, who, with swift comprehension, took out her flask of rotgut and poured a little of the fiery liquid into it. Then she returned the soldier's flask to its place. Tara nodded and smiled.

Without a sound, the Triannon sisters raided the camp. Laraina poured a bit of the brew into each of the soldiers' water flasks, while Tara scrounged up enough food to last for two more weeks. When the sisters were through, they covered their tracks and slipped back into the woods.

Relief crossed Kaden's face as the sisters reentered the pine grove.

Laraina sat down beside the tall prince and bubbled with quiet laughter. "I'd like to see what happens when they drink that stuff."

"We will," said Tara. "We'll follow them until we're sure it's going to work. The water will dilute it, of course, but it should still have some effect on them."

"Do you remember..." Laraina lapsed into another fit of muffled laughter. "Do you remember what happened when Blackie drank a few swallows of that stuff to prove it wasn't poisonous?"

Tara grinned. "Do I. I don't think he'll ever live it down." Laughter took hold of both sisters, and once started, they couldn't stop. Tara collapsed on the ground beside Laraina, and they laughed until the tears streamed down their cheeks. Prince Kaden regarded them as if they had both gone mad.

The air grew colder as the night hours passed. The heavy dew turned to frost. Tara awoke just as the first pale streaks of light signaled the approaching dawn. Nodding to Laraina on watch, she rose and slipped away, creeping through the still forest to the edge of the Mardainn camp. Loud voices reached her ears as she crouched in the brush.

A burly soldier, the leader of the troop, was furiously upbraiding the sentry that she and Laraina had knocked out. The unfortunate sentry sat on the ground, rubbing his head. Tara could hear only bits and pieces of the conversation. The leader ranted about sleeping on the job, while the sentry vigorously protested his innocence.

Poor man, Tara thought. She almost felt sorry for him.

After delivering a severe reprimand to the hapless sentry, the leader strode to the center of the camp and bellowed orders. Instantly, the campsite crawled with half-dressed soldiers preparing to move out. Tara hurried back to the sheltering grove of evergreens.

Laraina glanced up as Tara entered the grove. "See anything interesting?"

"Not yet," Tara said, "but I'm afraid we got that sentry in a bit of trouble."

Laraina laughed. "Sleeping on the job, was he?" She shook her head. "He ought to be ashamed."

Tara smiled. "They're getting ready to leave, so we'll have to get going if we want to keep up with them."

They woke the others and gathered their gear. Laraina doled out the last of their old supplies. "We can eat as we go." She slung a pack over her shoulder.

"Ugh." Aurelia spat out a bite of bread. "This stuff is stale. I thought you were going to get more food last night."

"We did get more," Laraina said, "but this is still edible. There's no sense wasting it."

"Well, here. You can eat it." She handed her portion back to Laraina. "I'll wait until we can eat the new stuff."

"Suit yourself," Laraina said.

"And no conjuring up anything else in the meantime," Tara added.

Aurelia shot her an annoyed look. "Why not? My spells have worked fine."

"Lately, yes," Tara said, "but we can't chance any relapses. After we get to Crystalir, you can cast all the spells you want."

"I can think of a few I'd like to cast right now," Aurelia grumbled. She stomped after Kaden, who had followed Laraina into the woods.

Tara smiled and fell in behind Aurelia, taking up the rear guard.

The sun rose hot over the treeline, drying the grass and burning off the light mist that clung to the forest. Not a cloud hung in the soft blue sky. No breeze stirred the still air. Tara chuckled to herself as she walked. She had never known the weather to cooperate so well. The soldiers marching out in the open along the riverbank were going to be very thirsty by the time they stopped for a break.

In the woods, the temperature was perfect. Tara breathed in deeply the cool scents of evergreen and damp leaves. She loved the woodland, especially in the spring. All around her, spring beauties and violets had burst into bloom, along with trillium, adder's tongue, and several other species she had no name for. Twittering sparrows darted about, gathering materials for their nests. The forest teemed with new life, and Tara's spirits rose. This was where she belonged. In the wilds. She felt a kinship with the land, the lakes, the rivers, the open sky. Alone or not, she would always feel at home out here. She could never be happy confined to a stuffy old castle. Never.

Shortly before noon, the Mardainn soldiers stopped for their midday meal. Tara and the others crept through the trees until they were close enough to observe. The men were aligned in two stiff rows along the riverbank, unmoving as if carved in stone. They had marched straight through the morning, their disgruntled leader not allowing them so much as a drink or a step out of line. As soon as they were permitted, the sweating soldiers made a beeline for the shade of the forest and broke out their water flasks. Long cool draughts disappeared down their throats as the soldiers drank their fill. Tara tried not to laugh at the strange expression on the face of one of the men nearest to them.

The puzzled soldier nudged his neighbor. "Water taste funny to you?"

"Yeah, a little bit," the man replied. "It's not bad."

"I've had worse," said another.

"It tastes good," said a third. "Cheers!" He raised his flask in a mock toast and took another long drink.

"Sir, some of our supplies are missing!" The supply officer's strident shout silenced the entire troop.

"What?" bellowed the troop leader. He strode across to where the supply officer was hastily recounting his inventory. "Let me see." The leader looked through the packs. "So we have a thief among us." He glared at his men. "Which of you is responsible for this?"

The soldiers glanced at each other with mystified expressions, but no one spoke.

"If I don't get an answer in the next five seconds," the leader yelled, "I'll whip the hide off every last one of you!"

His men squirmed.

"It wasn't one of us, sir," one of the soldiers blurted out.

"Oh, well then, perhaps you could tell me who else it could have been, out here in this godsforsaken wilderness?" the leader roared.

"Begging your pardon, sir," spoke up another soldier, whom Tara recognized as the sentry she had clobbered, "but I swear someone hit me over the head last night. Whoever it was must have stolen the supplies."

The leader regarded the sentry narrowly. Then his gaze shifted to the surrounding forest. He started to speak, but was interrupted by a piercing giggle. Several of the men were chuckling boisterously. The leader grasped one of them by the front of his shirt and hauled him up until their faces were inches apart.

"Just what do you find so amusing?" he demanded.

"Nothing, sir," the soldier replied, a silly grin on his face. He giggled again, then clapped his hand over his mouth.

The soldier's good humor proved contagious. In a matter of minutes, the entire troop was convulsed with laughter.

The leader threw the offending soldier away from him and stared at his formerly well-ordered troops. One soldier had shinnied up a tree and was swinging by his knees from a branch. Another was attempting to stand on his head, and still another was dancing with a sack of beef jerky. Then they began to sing. Thirty voices clamored together, belting out several different tunes. The cacophony echoed through the forest.

Singing at the tops of their lungs, the rebellious soldiers left the woods and danced along the grassy bank of the river. Two of them picked up a third by his arms and legs and tossed him headfirst into the water. Several others followed and, before long, half the troop was floating downstream.

The leader shouted, but no one paid the slightest attention. He seized the nearest soldier by the collar and half strangled him. "What is the matter with you? I order you to stop this at once!"

The soldier shook his head and raised his hands in a gesture of helplessness. "I'm sorry, sir," he squeaked, "but I can't help it."

The leader grabbed the water flask gripped in the soldier's hand. He sniffed it and took a sip, then spit it out with a grimace. Cursing vehemently, he slammed the flask to the ground.

Racing through what was left of his troop, the leader seized and emptied as many water flasks as he could get his hands on. One soldier refused to give his up, which resulted in a tug-of-war until the leader lost his temper completely and punched the man. The soldier recovered in a flash and launched himself at his commander. As they rolled on the ground, locked together, the rest of the troop gathered around them, either cheering on their comrade or placing bets on the outcome. Another fight erupted, and soon the remainder of the troop was lost in a wild free-for-all.

Laraina laughed and turned to her sister. "That should keep them busy for a while."

Tara nodded, grinning broadly. "Let's go."

Shouldering their packs, they headed eastward into the forest.

CHAPTER 16

"Captain Natiere, sir!"

The tense, unnaturally high-pitched voice of the scout pierced the gloomy stillness; the dissonant sound bounced eerily off the line of black, moss-covered trees marking the edge of the Bog.

"What is it?" snapped the Captain.

"We found a body, or at least, we think it was a body, once. We're not sure. It's bad."

"Stop babbling!" thundered the Captain.

The scout cringed. A frightened murmur swept through the battalion.

"Where is it?" the Captain asked more calmly.

"Over there, at the line of trees." The scout pointed to a place along the edge of the Bog, several yards upriver.

"Keep moving," ordered Natiere.

The soldiers quickened their pace, hurrying northward along the firm, grassy bank of the Nournan River.

Keeping one eye on his men, the Captain strode to the spot the scout had indicated. Sprawled at the edge of the line of trees, half in, half out of the Bog, was a carcass. He knelt and examined the grisly remains. The few scraps of torn cloth scattered around the body identified it as a Mardainn soldier, obviously a member of the first battalion dispatched to take part in the ambush at Relic. Embedded in the soft ground beside the corpse were traces of wolf prints, larger than any he had ever seen. He turned toward the Bog. His sharp eyes searched its murky depths, his heightened senses taking in the dark oppressiveness, the fetid odor of the noxious yellow mist, the incessant drip of the saturated moss; beyond that, all was silence. The Captain shifted his gaze, studying the varying sweep of the riverbank, noting the wide swath of trampled grass outside the straight and relatively narrow path of the passing army. An ugly battle had been fought here. Blood still stained the broken ground. There was no way of telling how many men had been lost. The casualties had either been eaten or dragged off into the Bog.

Natiere rose and strode back toward his men, the last of which were trotting by. As he fell in beside them, he spotted something moving just inside the edge of the Bog. He stopped. Five pairs of golden eyes peered out at him from the murk.

A flurry of frightened cries erupted from the men at the end of the column. Panic whipped through the battalion, and the soldiers fled.

Captain Natiere stood alone.

Five black beasts emerged from the gloom. He faced them, unmoving. The Bog wolves advanced, growling low in their throats, their golden eyes locked on Natiere.

"Well met, my Brothers and Sisters," the Captain said.

The wolves halted. Raising their heads high, they sniffed the breeze, their ears pricked forward in an unmistakable air of curiosity and attention.

"You have left your mark on the last group of men to pass through here," said the Captain, "as was your right. They intruded on your territory, and that made them fair game. But these men are under my protection, and I would ask that you find sustenance elsewhere and let them pass unharmed."

The black wolves regarded him silently. The leader bared its teeth, its jaws dripping blood and saliva, but the beast did not attack. Throwing back its head, the wolf let out a savage howl. The other wolves joined in. When the last echo died away, the fearsome pack turned and vanished into the Bog.

For three days and three nights, Natiere pushed his army forward, allowing them only snatches of rest. His men didn't complain. They were as keen as he was to leave this malevolent place behind. The intermittent howls of the Bog wolves hounded them, but the wolves stayed hidden behind the trees.

Early the next day, the battalion came upon another battleground. Six dead wolves lay along a wide span of riverbank, their carcasses rotting in the sun. Natiere walked among them, his heart rending at the loss. The battalion gave them a wide berth. Natiere let them go on without him. Kneeling beside one of the wolves, he removed a shred of leather stuck in its claws. He crumpled it in his fist. The bit of cloth belonged to no Mardainn soldier. His eyes narrowed, cold rage filling him. The silver-haired witch and her companions were responsible for this carnage. He could feel her aura still lingering amid traces of magic. They would pay for the murder of his Brothers and Sisters.

The Captain rose and pointed at an empty patch of trampled grass. "*Gravadasa deprinorum*," he whispered. A deep, rectangular hole opened in the earth. One by one, he lifted the bodies of the wolves and lowered them into the hole. He spoke a few more words, and dirt and grassy sod filled and covered the grave. "Rest well, my kin." Bowing his head, he whispered a gypsy prayer for their souls. He stood a moment in silence, then followed after his men.

*****

Tara, Laraina, Kaden, and Aurelia traveled through the forest, keeping within sight of the Nournan. The days remained warm, the nights cool and clear, washed clean by an occasional spring shower. Shallin Wood continued to burst with life. Tender new leaves unfolded on branch and vine, and soft gray pussy willows reared their heads.

With Tara in the lead, the group made good time. They saw no sign behind them of the Mardainn soldiers they had waylaid. Tara kept thinking about Trevillion and considered asking Aurelia to use her scrying spell to find him again, but her head won out over her heart, and she kept her fears to herself.

At sunset on the thirteenth day, the trees thinned, then gave way to the five-mile clearing that surrounded Crystalir, the Faragellyn capital and fabled seat of the High Kings. The city lay on a rise in the center of the clearing. A high, thick wall of rose-colored crystal, its mirror-like sheen reflecting the landscape, enclosed the variegated-stone dwellings within. At measured points along the wall, crystal watchtowers thrust into the sky, each a different color of the rainbow. Bright-hued flags with various emblems flew from the tops of the towers and billowed in the breeze.

Beyond the wall, shining against the backdrop of forest and sky, stood Castle Crystalir. Rising from the heart of the city, the castle was built of the same crystal stone as the wall and watchtowers, the colors mixed together like jewels spilled from a treasure chest.

Tara and the others stood out of sight behind the trees, watching in silence as the last light of the setting sun reflected off the gleaming towers in a dazzling display of iridescence. As the sun dipped below the horizon, the colors became soft and muted, blending gracefully into the twilight.

"It's beautiful," Aurelia said in a hushed voice. "It's like rubies and sapphires and emeralds and more, all melted together."

Laraina stirred and let out a long sigh. "No matter how many times I see it, it still takes my breath away."

Rubies, Tara thought, only half listening to the conversation. She suddenly remembered the ruby ring with the High King's insignia she had brought out of the dungeon during her last dream. She had given the ring to Trevillion for safe-keeping in case she ended up in the dungeon again. She wondered how safe it was, or rather, how safe *he* was.

"Who built the castle?" Aurelia asked.

"The Dwarves from the Cyranel Mountains," said Laraina. "Centuries ago, a war in the Eastern Frontier began spilling over into the West. Since the Cyranel Mountains divide East from West, the Dwarves were caught in the middle. They sided with the Westerners and were instrumental in pushing back the Eastern invaders. The war brought all the Western Kingdoms together, and they chose a High King to rule over them and keep the peace. That first High King commissioned the Dwarves to build a city using materials gathered from every corner of the West; it would stand as a symbol of the unity of the people. The flags on the towers represent the kingdoms that contributed."

"But there is no High King now," Aurelia said.

"No, there isn't," Laraina agreed. "The last High King died some two hundred years ago. There were no known heirs, and so the kingdoms fell apart. They fought among themselves and renounced their alliances. It was every kingdom for itself, much like it is now."

Tara glanced at her sister. "You're just a walking history lesson, aren't you?"

Laraina looked away. "As I said before, I learned a lot of history the last time I was here."

"So you did." Tara considered. "It would be nice if we could find a way in without anyone seeing us. The fewer who know we're here, the better, until we know who we can trust."

"Well, that's easy enough," Laraina said.

Tara looked at her in surprise. "It is?"

"Sure. Crystalir is as full of secret passages as Castle Carilon. There's an entrance just north of here."

"How do you know that?"

Laraina looked uncomfortable. "Fournier showed me."

"Oh." Tara resisted the urge to see Kaden's reaction. "Well, I'm glad our stay there was worth something. Hey, wait a minute." Tara stopped, thinking. "So that's where you went when they —"

"Tara, can I talk to you for a minute?" Laraina interrupted. She grabbed her sister by the arm and dragged her off into the woods.

"I'm not sure this is such a good idea," Laraina whispered when they were out of earshot. "What am I going to do if he's here?"

"Who, Fournier? He won't be."

"Are you sure?"

"Of course I'm sure. He'll be with the Border Guard in Relic."

"I hope so." Laraina shivered. "He would cause a lot of trouble if he was here."

"It would make things interesting, wouldn't it?"

Laraina glared. "That's not funny."

Tara sobered. "Sorry. I shouldn't have said that. Garrett should be here."

"Who?"

"Garrett, Fournier's younger brother."

"Oh. Right. I'd forgotten about him."

"I don't wonder," Tara muttered under her breath.

"What was that?"

"Nothing. Does this passage you know of go anywhere in the castle or just to Fournier's room?"

"Just to his room," Laraina said. "He wouldn't show me any of the others. He only showed me that one out of necessity."

"I see. Well, we'll just have to go to his room and work things out from there. Hopefully, no one else will be in it."

"You won't say anything to Kaden, will you?"

"Of course not. It's none of my business."

Laraina threw her arm around Tara's shoulders and gave her a quick hug. "Thanks."

The sisters hurried back to where Kaden and Aurelia were waiting.

Kaden cornered Laraina. "Don't tell me you were with Fournier du Mraine," he said, his contempt for the Faragellyn prince evident.

"I see you and Fournier have met," Tara said.

Kaden snorted. "He is an arrogant, pig-headed fool."

Tara smiled wryly. "How about that? We actually agree on something."

"That's wonderful," Laraina snapped. She turned on Kaden. "Yes, I was *with* him. It's part of my past, and I don't want to talk about it." She stalked away through the trees.

Tara and Kaden glanced at each other.

"After you," said Tara.

Prince Kaden followed after Laraina, with Aurelia and Tara behind him.

Darkness fell rapidly over forest and city. Along the wall, watchfires appeared, sending brilliant spears of rainbow color shooting across the towers.

Tara squinted into the dusk. "How much farther?"

"Not far," Laraina said tersely.

"Is there only one entrance?" Tara asked.

"No. There are four in all, one each to the north, south, east, and west of the city." Laraina warmed to the subject. "Actually, it's quite interesting. The Dwarves built the secret passages into the castle as escape routes. The eastern tunnel supposedly connects with a network of Dwarven tunnels that leads to the Dwarven city of Ilgresta. But it's so full of twists and turns and traps and pitfalls, that if you didn't know the way, you'd never get through."

Laraina paused to get her bearings, then headed northwest. "The High King himself was the only one who knew the passages existed, and he memorized them. No record of them was ever written down. When the time came, he told his son, the heir to the throne, who, in turn, memorized them and told his son. The knowledge was passed down from generation to generation until it was lost with the last High King who died with no heir.

"It remained lost until the present King of Faragellyn's father discovered a passage by accident. He explored the tunnels and, in keeping with tradition, told no one but his eldest son. He has since died, so now only the present King, Jacques du Mraine, and his son Fournier know the secret."

"That means Garrett probably doesn't know about the tunnels," Tara said. "We'll have to enlighten him."

"Garrett?" Laraina asked. "I thought we were going to see the king."

"We are," Tara said, "but it's going to cause quite a stir if we barge into his bedroom unannounced at this hour, and that's the last thing we need. Garrett should be able to get us in without anyone else seeing us."

"If the king will see us," Laraina muttered.

"Why wouldn't he?" Kaden asked.

"We didn't exactly leave Crystalir on the best of terms," Laraina said bitterly. "The entrance should be right around here somewhere."

She stopped in front of a gigantic oak tree, several feet in diameter. Reaching up into the crotch of the tree, she stuck her hand in what looked like a squirrel hole and pressed the release mechanism. A narrow door in the side of the oak popped open. The massive trunk was hollow. Wooden stairs led down into the earth. Ducking her head, Laraina stepped inside the tree and beckoned for the others to follow. The four joined hands and descended into the passage. The door in the tree swung shut with a faint click. When they'd groped their way to the bottom of the stairs, Laraina stopped and lit a candle she'd taken from a niche in the earthen wall. Then she led them into a maze of tunnels.

Two hours later, the four emerged from a winding passage into a cold, dark bedchamber. Tara heard Laraina release a long breath and knew her sister was relieved to find the room empty.

Laraina set the candle on a stand by the bed. "What now?" she whispered.

"I'll find Garrett," Tara said. "His room used to be the next one down the hall. Stay here. I'll be right back."

Tara hurried across the room and opened the door a crack. The torch-lit hall was deserted. Edging out of Fournier's room, she tiptoed down the corridor to the next door. Carefully, she eased the door open, and stepped inside.

Warm air struck her; a crackling fire burned in the grate. Tara closed the door and let her eyes drift over the shadowed chamber. Someone lay sleeping in the bed near the window on the far side of the room. She hoped it was Garrett. She moved across the chamber to the edge of the bed and looked down. She smiled to herself. Their luck was still holding. Prince Garrett du Mraine lay on his back, lost in the deep, untroubled slumber of youth.

He hasn't changed much, she thought. *He ought to be... what... eighteen or nineteen by now?* His thick blond hair still waved and curled of its own accord. If anything, he looked even more like his older brother. Fortunately, the similarities ended there.

She laid her hand on Garrett's shoulder. "Garrett, wake up," she whispered.

Garrett started awake. His vivid blue eyes widened. "Tara! What? How...?"

Tara raised her finger to her lips, warning him to silence. "It's a long story. There's going to be trouble, and I need to talk to your father *now*. Can you get me an audience?"

"Of course." He threw back the covers and leaped out of bed, seemingly unbothered by the fact that he was in his underclothes.

Tara turned her back while he dressed.

"Where's Laraina and how did you get in here?"

"Raina's in Fournier's room with a couple of friends. We came in through a secret passage."

"A secret passage! So that's how they —" He stopped. A sheepish grin played over his face. "I always wondered about that."

Tara smiled. "Me, too."

Prince Garrett finished dressing and hastened to the door.

"There's one more thing," Tara said, following after him. "No one else must know we're here."

"All right," Garrett whispered. "I'll be back in a few minutes." He pulled the door ajar and looked out. The hall was clear. They stepped out into the silent corridor. Tara pointed to Fournier's room, indicating that she would wait for him there. Garrett nodded and disappeared around a corner.

Tara slipped back into Fournier's chamber.

"Was he there?" Laraina asked anxiously.

Tara nodded. "He's gone to talk to his father. He'll be back short-ly."

They did not have long to wait. Within minutes, Garrett re-turned, all traces of sleep gone.

"This way." Garrett motioned for them to follow.

They followed the young prince down several long corridors to a darkly polished wooden door. Garrett knocked once and entered. He ushered the others inside and then closed and locked the door behind them.

Glowing lanterns lit the room. A warm fire burned in the hearth. Books lay everywhere — on the finely-carved end tables, on the brocaded chairs drawn up to the fire, even on the thickly-carpeted floor. The walls of the small chamber were lined from ceiling to floor with books of all sizes; the shelves sagged from the weight.

"Please excuse the untidiness," said a resonant voice. A figure emerged from a curtained alcove. "I was conducting some research."

The figure strode forward into the light. King Jacques du Mraine of Faragellyn was fully as tall as Prince Kaden, but slimmer, more wiry; he moved with the quickness, ease, and confidence of a seasoned warrior. He was garbed in a floor length robe of dark blue velvet, his iron gray hair and beard cropped short. His eyes were startlingly blue.

The king crossed the room. Prince Garrett stood to the side, an apprehensive look on his face.

"Prince Kaden," said Jacques du Mraine. "Well met." He clasped Kaden's hand warmly. "It has been many days since we last spoke."

"Yes," said Kaden, "and I wish we were here now under better circumstances."

"Indeed." The king turned his piercing gaze on the Triannon sisters. "I see you bring trouble with you." His voice grew several degrees colder. "The circumstances must be truly dire."

"We are only here out of necessity," Tara said.

"They are here because of me," said Kaden. "They risked their lives to bring me and my cousin, Aurelia, here to safety after General Caldren and the Sulledorns invaded Dhanarra. The Sulledorns have taken Castle Carilon." His voice grew rough. "They murdered my father."

The king put his hand on Kaden's shoulder. "I am sorry to hear about your father. He was a good friend, and I swear to you his death will not go unavenged. Please allow me to express my deepest sympathies."

Kaden bowed his head. "Thank you."

The king turned to Aurelia. "And you, young lady. You must have the strength and courage of ten lions to have survived such an ordeal. I commend you and offer my sincerest condolences."

"Th-thank you, my lord," she stammered in awe.

"I learned of the Sulledorn invasion only this morning," the king continued. "A messenger from the Border Guard in Relic brought word that Belgarde had fallen. The Guard rescued two men who had escaped the fortress. I did not know about Carilon or the other Dhanarran towns and villages between Sulledor and Belgarde, but feared the worst. I have sent Colonel Lemard to Relic with as many men as I could muster. Fournier is there and will do his best to hold until Lemard arrives." He sighed and rubbed his brow. "Unfortunately, the army is not at full strength. We had released many men from service after the signing of the peace treaty."

Kaden flushed. "I'm sorry. I should have foreseen this. I should have been less trusting."

The Faragellyn king waved him to silence. "You may have orchestrated the treaty, but we all signed it. All the kingdoms are at fault. We believed what we wanted to believe and let ourselves be deceived. That cannot be changed. Now we must concentrate on defeating the Sulledorn army and ridding ourselves of one lunatic General."

Feeling as if they were about to be dismissed, Tara spoke up. "There's more."

"More?" Jacques du Mraine's eyes narrowed.

"Mardainn has allied with Sulledor. A battalion of Mardainn soldiers followed the Nournan up through the Bog and is heading for Relic to attack from the rear. They are probably already there. A small group of about thirty men broke off from the battalion." She held his gaze. "They are coming here."

The king looked surprised. "Here, you say?"

Tara nodded. "Yes."

Du Mraine turned to Garrett. "Have my Guard assemble in the East Tower. Tell them I will be there shortly."

Garrett nodded and left the room.

The Faragellyn king turned back to Tara. "Tell me more." He gestured to the book-piled chairs. "Please, sit down."

They removed the books and sat. Tara recounted their story from the time they'd left Carilon to their arrival in Crystalir. The king listened intently, without interruption, a smile twitching at the corners of his mouth when she described their encounter with the Mardainn soldiers.

When Tara finished her story, the Faragellyn king regarded them with quiet amazement. "That is, indeed, quite a tale, but there is one thing I must know."

"What is that?" Tara asked.

"How did you get into the castle?"

Tara hesitated. She saw no point in lying to him. In fact, she had the distinct impression he knew very well how they had done it. "We came in through a secret passage."

"I see," said the king. His gaze shifted to Laraina. "That explains a great many things."

Laraina blushed, but her eyes met his. "It is the only one I know, and that is the truth."

Jacques du Mraine smiled faintly. "I had my suspicions." He sobered. "However, I think that episode is best forgotten. We have other matters to attend to."

"It seems to me," said Tara, "that the best thing to do is to wait until the Mardainn soldiers come, be ready for them, and catch them in the act. They may be a bit more cautious because of what happened in the woods, but if no one knows we're here, the traitor will assume the plan is proceeding as scheduled. Of course, I'm assuming they are intending to overthrow Crystalir the same way the Sulledorns took Carilon. What puzzles me is how they expect to cross five miles of open space without being seen."

"Yes," the king said slowly, "how indeed." He paced to the end of the room and back. "I find it difficult to believe that any of my guards or servants would betray me."

A bitter expression crossed Prince Kaden's face. "So did I."

"What of Barony and Tralyxa?" Tara asked. "Do they know what has happened?"

"I have sent word to Lord Hiradant in Cierra and to High Priestess Evrelynn of Tralyxa, but it will not have reached them as yet," the king answered. "And now we have Mardainn to contend with as well. I had not counted on that. Mardainn has always remained neutral in the past. I only hope your friend Trevillion was able to reach Relic in time to give warning."

I only hope he reached Relic alive, Tara thought grimly.

The door opened and Prince Garrett reentered the room.

"Garrett will show you to your rooms in the Northeast Tower," the king continued. "It would be best if you would remain there until this business with the soldiers is taken care of, so as not to alert the traitor, if indeed there is one."

"Thank you," Tara said.

"No," said the king with a smile, "thank you for the warning."

"We will do as you ask," Laraina said.

They rose and followed Garrett out of the room.

The young prince led them through a maze of silent corridors and up a broad staircase to the Northeast Tower. He ushered them inside a large, luxuriously-furnished suite of rooms.

"I apologize for the mustiness," Garrett said, "but these rooms are not often used." He started a small blaze in the fireplace. "There is plenty of water for baths should you care to indulge."

"Oh, can we *please?*" Aurelia asked, a look of longing on her face.

Garrett smiled at her. "With or without a bath, your beauty would still shine." He stopped, looking embarrassed.

Aurelia stared at him, wide-eyed.

He cleared his throat and continued. "By the time you are through, I should be back with some food and clean clothing." He took Aurelia's hand and raised it to his lips. "It was a great pleasure to meet you." He held her hand a moment longer, then hurried from the room.

Laraina looked at Tara, raising her eyebrows. Tara rolled her eyes and went in search of the promised bath.

When they were as clean as soap and water could make them, the four emerged from their chambers and, dressed in soft robes, gathered in the large front room of the suite. The cheery fire burned steadily; the air was pleasantly warm and spiced with the fragrance of hot beef stew and woodsmoke. The polished oak table in the center of the room had been covered with a fine linen cloth and was now laden with steaming bowls of stew, fresh loaves of bread, slices of cold meat, and blocks of cheese, along with a pitcher of warm mead to wash it down.

Prince Garrett finished arranging the food and poured four glasses of mead.

"Mmmmm. Smells delicious," Aurelia said.

"I don't know about the rest of you, but I'm famished," Tara said as they all sat down at the table. "Garrett, you're a prince."

Garrett laughed. "Yes, I know. If you need anything else, I'll be glad to get it for you."

"But we do need something else," Aurelia said. She jumped up, ran over to him, and linked her arm in his. "We need you to stay and talk with us."

"Oh... well... all right." He allowed himself to be led back to the table. Aurelia cleared a place beside her, and he sat. "I am truly honored," he said. "It isn't often we have such royal guests."

"A royal pain is more like it," Tara muttered under her breath.

Laraina kicked her under the table. "This smells wonderful. It'll be nice to have hot food for a change."

They ate their fill. Prince Garrett seemed content to just sit and watch Aurelia, who alternately blushed and smiled at him. When they had finished, Garrett kissed Aurelia's hand once more and took his leave. Aurelia giggled and sighed and went off to bed without another word. The others soon followed.

It was very late the next morning when they finally arose. Stretching luxuriously, Tara stepped into the front room and found the four new sets of clothing Garrett had left for them along with a hearty breakfast that would easily have fed ten people. She gathered up a soft, cream-colored shirt and forest green leather leggings and tunic, went back to her room, and changed quickly. She returned to the table, surprised that she could still be hungry after all she had eaten the night before.

A few minutes later, the others emerged. After changing into their new garments, they joined Tara for a leisurely breakfast. Delighted with her cornflower blue silk dress, Aurelia spent the remainder of the morning in front of a mirror, fussing with her hair as she waited impatiently for Garrett.

Prince Garrett made his appearance around mid-afternoon. He knocked once and entered the suite, bearing a loaded lunch tray.

Aurelia rushed to his side. "Let me help you," she said and took one end of the tray.

Tara groaned. "More food. Garrett, what are you trying to do to us?"

Garrett grinned. "Never let it be said that a guest of the king went hungry." He and Aurelia set the tray down on the table.

"Any news?" Tara asked.

The young prince shook his head. "Nothing yet, but my father thinks the soldiers will come tonight. I can only say that they'll be in for a nasty surprise if they do."

"Good." Tara sampled a piece of cheese from the lunch tray. "I'd like to see their faces when they find out their plans have been spoiled."

Aurelia sidled up to Prince Garrett and slipped her hand in his. "You won't be in any danger, will you?"

He turned toward her, his blue eyes widening as he took in her new appearance. "No, I... that is... you look wonderful." He blushed furiously.

Aurelia rewarded him with a dazzling smile. "Oh, thank you." She pirouetted before him. "Do you really think so?"

"Yes, I... yes," he stammered.

"Oh, I'm so glad." Aurelia linked her arm in his and drew him over to a richly upholstered sofa. "Tell me about Crystalir."

"I'd be happy to." The young prince launched into a detailed account of the history and traditions of the famed City of the High Kings.

Aurelia listened with rapt attention, forgetting all about the lunch tray.

"You missed a great meal," Tara said as she rose from the table an hour later.

Prince Garrett paused in his rhetoric, suddenly realizing what time it was. With a startled cry, he leaped to his feet. "I must go, but I'll be back again tonight." He kissed Aurelia's hand, picked up the breakfast tray, and hastened out the door.

It was late in the evening when Prince Garrett returned, carrying yet another food-laden tray. He seemed distracted.

"Everything is set," he said. "My father asks that you remain here until it is over. I'll be back later." With a nod to Aurelia, he headed for the door.

Aurelia ran forward. "Garrett, wait."

He stopped.

She laid her hand on his arm. "Can't you stay, just for a few minutes?"

He shook his head. "I'm sorry, I can't. I still have some things to attend to."

"But I'm afraid for you." She looked up at him, her blue eyes anxious.

"Don't worry. Everything will be fine." He clasped both her hands in his and raised them to his lips.

From a tower outside, a bell clock rang the nine o'clock hour.

Garrett jumped and dropped Aurelia's hands. "Please excuse me. I must go." He bolted from the room.

Tara stared after him. "He's really nervous about something. I wonder what's going on out there."

"I don't know," said Laraina, "but we agreed to stay here, remember?"

Tara smiled. "You mean you agreed." She sat down and picked up a chicken leg. "I made no such promises."

*****

Tara stood by the window of her darkened chamber and stared into the gloom. Midnight had come and gone. Thick black clouds smothered the feeble light of the moon that hung low over the slumbering city of Crystalir. Watchlights flared all along the rim of the rose-colored outer wall, reflecting off the crystal towers and sending bright spears of color into the murky darkness. The night watch had been doubled, and the gates were under heavy surveillance. But would it be enough to stop the traitor and avert the same tragedy that had befallen Carilon?

Shivering, Tara turned from the window and paced the room. They had not heard from Garrett since late evening. Uneasiness gripped her, a strong sense of foreboding, just like she'd felt in Carilon on the night of the attack.

An icy chill shot through her, startling in its urgency. She rushed to her sister's room and burst through the door. "Raina, wake up!"

Laraina and Prince Kaden bolted upright. "What happened?" Laraina gasped.

"Something's gone wrong. They need help!" Tara ran back to the door.

"Wait!" Laraina cried. "We can't go out there! Garrett said to stay here."

"No time to argue." Tara dashed out the door and was gone.

*****

Laraina reached for her clothes. Why did her sister always do this to her?

Kaden slid out of bed and pulled on his breeches. "Next time I'm going to lock that door."

"Stop grousing and hurry up." Laraina stomped into her boots. "She said they needed help."

"How could she know that? Besides, you told the king we would stay here."

"Well, I can't let her go out there alone."

"You said she could take care of herself."

Laraina knew he was right, but she couldn't just sit by and do nothing. "Stay if you want. I'm going."

With an angry curse, Kaden grabbed his pillow and slammed it against the wall with such force that it exploded in a great cloud of feathers.

"Fine." Laraina caught up her sword and ran from the room.

*****

Tara raced down out of the tower to the upper staircase. She slid down the banister and vaulted to the ground at the second floor landing. The clash of weapons rang out from the direction of the king's rooms.

She dashed to the end of the passage and peered around the corner. The door to the king's chambers stood wide open. Mardainn soldiers locked in combat with the king's Elite Guard filled the hall.

Sword drawn, Tara leaped into the fray. The battle raged for several minutes. Laraina appeared and joined in, followed by Kaden. Then the Mardainn soldiers, their numbers drastically reduced, surrendered and were escorted to the dungeon by the Elite Guard.

Tara spotted Prince Garrett striding out of the king's chambers. "Your father... is he...?"

"He's fine." Garrett mopped his brow. He looked weary and somehow older.

"Garrett!" Aurelia's frightened cry spun them around. Tears streaming down her face, Aurelia threw herself into Garrett's arms. "Are you hurt?" she demanded.

"No. I'm all right." He brushed his thumb across her cheek. "Please don't cry."

"You're not hurt?" She searched his clothing, looking for wounds.

"I'm fine," he said gently.

"What happened?" Tara asked.

Garrett straightened up. "Not here. Come." With Aurelia clinging to his arm, he led them to his room. Inside, Garrett closed the door and faced them.

"The Mardainn soldiers gained entrance through a secret passage in my father's chamber," he said grimly.

"How could they possibly have known —" Tara stopped, realizing the implications. "Are you saying...?"

"Who else could it have been?" Garrett closed his eyes.

"Are you sure there is no other explanation? I know your brother liked his position of power, but would he actually go so far as to plot his own father's death?"

"He would," Laraina said bitterly.

"You said your father was safe," Tara said. "He wasn't in the room?"

"No," Garrett answered wearily. "He must have suspected."

He was interrupted by a knock on the door. One of the king's Elite Guard entered. He bowed to the young prince. "His Highness, the King, wishes to speak with you, my lord." His gaze shifted from Garrett to the others. "All of you. If you would follow me."

The guard led them to a small room on the east side of the castle. Jacques du Mraine looked up from the map he was studying as they entered the chamber. He, too, looked as if he had aged. Straightening his wiry frame, the tall king motioned for the group to sit down.

"Firstly, I must thank you," he nodded to Tara, Laraina, and Kaden, "for your assistance during the battle... in spite of my request," he added with a slight smile, "although I cannot say I was surprised. Secondly..." He paused. A look of pain marred his weathered face. When he spoke again, his voice was rough. "I presume you know by now that my son, Fournier, was responsible for this. I had suspected him of coveting my throne. He has been under surveillance for several weeks. I'd hoped that my suspicions would prove false, but as you can see..." He bowed his head. Then he faced them again, his voice and expression controlled.

"Fournier is currently in charge of the army in Relic under the secret supervision of Colonel Benton. If Fournier abuses his authority, the colonel has orders to do whatever is necessary to ensure the safety of the men. I suspect that Fournier's plan was to surrender quickly when Mardainn attacked from the rear in exchange for my death at the hands of the Mardainn soldiers. He would then return to Crystalir, claim the throne, and join forces with Sulledor and Mardainn against Barony and Tralyxa, neither of which could survive such an attack."

He paused once more to gather his thoughts, then continued.

"But it seems you have thwarted him on both ends. I've just been informed that your friend Jovan Trevillion reached Relic in time to warn them of the Mardainn attack. Fournier was forced to fight the Mardainn soldiers instead of surrendering to them. The messenger also informed me," the King added slowly, "that in the ensuing battle, Trevillion was killed."

The group stared at him in shock.

Tara found her voice. "Are you sure?"

"I only know what the report said," he answered gently. "I am sorry."

"The messenger — where is he? Can we talk to him?" Tara felt as if a great hand had closed around her heart and squeezed the life out of her.

The King shook his head. "He is already on his way back. I am truly sorry." He glanced out the window. "It is nearly dawn. You must get some sleep. Rest assured, you are welcome in Crystalir for as long as you wish to stay."

They rose and made their way back to their rooms in stunned silence.

CHAPTER 17

Captain Natiere pulled back the tent flap and stepped into the gloomy lamplit pavilion. General Caldren was seated on a wooden bench, poring over the dog-eared map spread out on the table before him. He rose and beckoned the Captain inside.

"A man by the name of Jovan Trevillion arrived in Relic just as the Mardainn soldiers were about to launch their surprise attack. You failed me."

Natiere kept his face expressionless. "I had no orders concerning Trevillion."

"What of the others?"

The Captain shrugged. "If I were to guess, I would say they were most likely in Crystalir."

"You lost them?" snapped the General.

The Captain's black eyes narrowed. "If you recall, it was by your order that I was forced to abandon my pursuit — a pursuit I wish to continue. You have no need of me here."

General Caldren slammed his fist on the table. "How did he get here so quickly?"

"He took a short cut," Natiere said, his voice tinged with both amusement and genuine respect. "He and the others went straight through the Bog."

The General stared at him. "They went *through* the Bog?"

"Yes."

"You said that wasn't possible."

"It isn't."

Neither man spoke for several heartbeats. Then the General abruptly turned away and paced the length of the tent.

"So Jovan Trevillion has come back to haunt me. He should have died in the Bog with the rest of them twelve years ago. If I had known he was going to cause this much trouble, I would have made more of an effort to have him eliminated. A mistake on my part." He spun about. "Find him and kill him."

The Captain met his gaze. "I think not."

"You think not?" The General kicked over the table, sending maps and battle plans flying. "*You think not?* May I remind you that you are under oath to serve me. I spared your life. I could just as easily have had you executed!"

The Captain snorted. "For ridding the world of vermin? I hardly consider that a crime."

General Caldren bristled. "The man you killed was a member of my army."

"He was scum — the last of the bandits that tortured and killed my family and left me to die."

The General's hand sliced the air. "Yes, yes, I've heard that story. You had a gruesome childhood. You were seeking revenge. That does not excuse you. You murdered one of my men and you will pay the price. One way or another."

"I agreed to serve you because it suited me," the Captain snarled. "For four years I have done so. No more. I will take care of the

Dhanarran prince and the Triannon sisters. Then I will consider my so-called debt paid."

General Caldren stepped forward until his and the Captain's faces were inches apart. "And if I refuse to release you from your bond?"

Captain Natiere's voice grew chillingly soft. "Then you should consider that debts cannot be collected by dead men." He strode from the tent.

*****

Tara Triannon sat on a window ledge of the Southwest Tower, one leg dangling precariously over the side. A three-quarter moon was rising; the crystal city shimmered in its silver light. Oblivious, Tara stared into the darkness.

Three days had passed since the news of Trevillion's death. Thoughts of him haunted her day and night. His face was forever in her mind. She could still hear his voice, feel his touch.

She closed her eyes and tipped her head back against the smooth crystal wall. *Jovan.* The anguished thought drifted outward on a wave of heartbreak.

I am here.

The whisper-soft voice slid into her mind, faint, but clear. Her eyes snapped open. "Jovan?" She searched the moon-painted court-yard below, but saw nothing.

Tara, why are you in such pain?

She closed her eyes and opened her mind. *You're alive? Where are you?*

"So this is where you've been hiding."

Startled, Tara clutched the sill to steady herself.

"Will you come down from there before you fall off?" Laraina walked toward her.

Tara leaped down. "I need Aurelia."

Laraina stared. "*You* need Aurelia?"

"Yes. Where is she? Do you know?"

"I would imagine she's in bed, asleep. It's the middle of the night." Laraina shook her head, confused. "Why do you need her?"

"Jovan is alive." Tara headed down the stairs.

Laraina ran after her. "He's what? How do you know that?"

"I heard his voice in my mind." Tara jogged down the hall toward the Northeast Tower.

Laraina hurried to keep up. "You're hearing voices?"

"I'm not crazy," Tara said, annoyed at the disbelief in her sister's voice.

"But how could you... how is that possible? The messenger said he was dead."

"He was wrong. If I'd stopped to think about it, I'd have known he was wrong. If Jovan had died, I would have sensed it."

"Why? Because you're in love with him?"

Tara stopped short. "What do you mean?"

Laraina halted beside her. "Well, it was rather obvious."

"What was?"

"That you were in love with him."

Tara looked at her, surprised. "It was?"

Laraina put her hands on her hips. "I'm not blind and I'm sure he wasn't either."

Tara frowned. "Great."

"Is that why you would sense it?" Laraina persisted.

"I don't know." Tara started off down the hall again. "There seems to be some sort of link between us. It must be because I healed him, though that's never happened with anyone else I've healed. There is something different about him." She pulled open the door to the tower and bounded up the stairs with Laraina following. She swung by her own room and grabbed the clasp from the cloak Trevillion had given her, then continued on to Aurelia's chamber.

Laraina caught her arm as she reached for the door latch. "Knock first," she said sternly.

"Fine." Tara knocked on the door. When there was no reply, she knocked again.

"Who's there?" Aurelia's sleepy voice called.

"It's Tara. I have to talk to you."

They heard rustling inside, then the padding of feet. Aurelia opened the door. She brushed back her tousled blonde hair. "*You* want to talk to *me?*"

Tara held out the clasp. "I need you to do what you did in the woods that time."

Aurelia slowly reached out and took the clasp. "Why? He's..." Her voice caught, and she bit her lip.

Tara shook her head. "He's alive. I need to know if you can see him."

Aurelia beckoned them inside. "I can try."

Laraina looked from one to the other. "What are you talking about?"

"I'll explain later." Tara pulled Laraina into the room and shut the door.

Aurelia sat down on a braided rug, crossed her legs and rested her elbows on her knees. Holding the clasp with her fingers, she took several deep breaths, then closed her eyes and spread her hands apart. Light formed between her palms, growing brighter.

"What is she doing?" Laraina whispered.

Aurelia scowled. "Shhhhh! I can't concentrate."

Faint shadows formed in the bright glow Aurelia had created, wispy images with no substance. Her hands began to shake, and the light went out. She tried again with the same result. "I can't reach him." She sounded tired.

"Could he be too far away?" Tara asked.

"Distance shouldn't matter," Aurelia said. "It could be that his spirit is too weak..." She left the thought unfinished.

Tara knew what she was thinking. "He *is* alive. I'm sure of it."

Laraina looked at Tara. "When are you leaving?"

Tara smiled. "You know me too well, sister. As soon as I tell Garrett and get some supplies together, but —"

"No buts," Laraina cut in. "If you think I'm going to let you go to Relic alone while the Butcher is still out there looking for us — or have you forgotten about him?"

"No, I haven't forgotten him," Tara said. "What about Kaden?"

"Kaden." Laraina exhaled heavily. "He'll insist on coming with us. I wish he would stay here. I'm worried about him. He wants revenge on General Caldren. He's become obsessed with the idea. He's been closeted with King du Mraine for the last three days going over battle plans."

"He's in way over his head. He has no experience."

"I know." Laraina wrung her fingers. "If anything were to happen to him I don't know what I'd do."

"You could stay here."

"No. Absolutely not. You're not going out there alone."

Tara said nothing.

Laraina confronted her. "I want your word that you won't go sneaking off without me."

Tara laughed and gave her a warm smile. "You have it, and thanks."

Laraina smiled back. "Good. I'll go find Kaden. Hopefully, he's done with the king and has gone back to the room to get some sleep. Of course, if he's there, he's probably wondering where I am."

She shook her head. "I can't win." She squeezed Tara's shoulder and left the room.

Aurelia rose. "What about me?"

"You're staying here," Tara said.

"You can't leave me behind."

"Yes, we can. We would prefer that you stay alive." Tara stopped, surprised at her own words. She certainly hadn't felt that way at the beginning of their escape from Carilon.

Aurelia, too, seemed surprised and closed her mouth on the retort she'd been about to make.

"Anyway," Tara continued briskly, "You're staying here. Thank you for trying to find Jovan."

Aurelia hesitated. Tara tensed, expecting a battle. Aurelia held out the clasp. "You're welcome. I hope you're right."

"I am." Tara took the clasp and left the room, closing the door softly behind her. Aurelia hadn't put up much of a fight. Ten-to-one she would cause trouble before the night was out. Tara pocketed the clasp and headed down the hall.

*****

Laraina hurried back to her room. Could Jovan Trevillion really be alive? Tara had said she'd heard his voice in her mind. Laraina didn't like the sound of that. People who heard voices were generally a few quarts short of a bushel. Was her sister losing her mind? These powers of Tara's... they were changing her. Laraina shivered. She found them very unsettling. The knowledge that her sister held magic scared her. She wasn't sure why. She had always known of Tara's danger sense and quick healing ability, but she had never considered them magical. More like intuition and a strong constitution. Aurelia's magic didn't bother her. Then why did Tara's magic agitate her so? The answer was obvious. Her sister was no longer a familiar presence for her to lean on. Laraina had always felt that she was the one taking care of Tara, but she knew down deep that they had leaned on each other equally. Now everything was changing. Tara had said as much earlier, and she was right. Laraina remembered what her sister had said about the gods of Fate forcing them into paths not of their own choosing. Tara was fast becoming a stranger, and Laraina didn't know how to bridge the gap. And while she might be ready for them to live separate lives, she didn't want to lose their close relationship. The knowledge that Tara had finally fallen in love again, thank the gods, gave Laraina some comfort; Tara wouldn't have to be alone. Laraina was fairly certain Trevillion loved her sister. She'd seen the signs. Laraina paused in midstride. What if Tara was wrong and Trevillion really was dead?

Shaking her head in confusion, Laraina rounded a corner and nearly ran into Prince Kaden.

Kaden caught her by the shoulders. "There you are. I was looking for you." He looked at her closely. "Are you all right?"

"Yes... no... yes," Laraina said distractedly. "I'm just confused."

"What about?" Kaden's face darkened. "No, let me guess. Your sister —"

Laraina stiffened and pulled away from him. "Stop right there. I'm tired of your tirades against Tara. You two have done nothing but fight. I won't have it anymore." She crossed her arms over her chest. "Tara is going to Relic to look for Jovan. She says he's alive. I'm going with her, and no, you can't change my mind. I think you should stay here —"

"No," Kaden interrupted with a firm shake of his head. "Absolutely not. If you think I'm going to let you go out there alone while the Butcher is still —"

Laraina chuckled, her anger dissolving as her tired mind latched onto the irony.

"What's so funny?"

"I just said those exact words to Tara not five minutes ago."

Kaden ran his hand through his hair and took a deep breath to calm himself. "How does she know he's alive?"

Laraina hesitated. She really didn't want to say that her sister was hearing voices. "Tara said she communicated with him mentally."

"Has she done this before? Why didn't she say something earlier instead of acting like she believed he was dead?"

"Apparently, it just happened. She tried to have Aurelia reach him with her magic, but Aurelia couldn't get through. She doesn't know why."

"Your sister asked Aurelia to use her magic?" Kaden asked, his face incredulous.

Footsteps sounded in the hall behind them. They turned and saw Garrett hurrying toward them.

"Kaden. I'm glad I caught you," Garrett said as he came up beside them. "Things are coming together more quickly than we thought. We can leave in an hour."

"Leave?" Laraina pinned Kaden with a glare. "What is this about?"

"This is why I was looking for you," Kaden said. "Garrett and I are going to Relic. Garrett will be replacing Fournier as head of the army. We have a battle plan worked out. I was going to ask you to stay here and keep an eye on Aurelia."

"Aurelia will be fine," Laraina said. "Tara and I can go with you. It will be safer if we travel together."

Garrett nodded. "I met Tara in the hall a few minutes ago. She is already on her way down to the stables. I just need to say goodbye to Aurelia and then I will be down."

"We will meet you there," Kaden said.

Garrett nodded and headed off down the corridor.

"We will need to say goodbye to her, too," Laraina said.

"Yes, but we should give Garrett some time first. Come." Kaden led Laraina back to his room. Once inside, he closed and locked the door. Then he turned and slipped his arms around her. "I'm sorry for what I said about your sister." He kissed her forehead. "Whatever happens, know that I love you."

"Why do you say it like that?" Laraina eased back and, staying within the circle of his arms, drew him toward the window near the bed where she could see his expression in the moonlight. "You sound like you're going off to die." She searched his face. "Just what are you planning to do?"

Kaden smiled faintly. "I've never fought in a battle before. I don't know what will happen. But I wanted you to know how I felt, in case..." He looked away.

She turned his face back to hers. "Nothing will happen."

"You told me one never knows when their time is up."

"Nothing will happen," she repeated. She smiled. "I love you, too."

His arms tightened around her, and he lowered her onto the bed, his lips seeking hers in a hungry kiss.

*****

Tara swung a saddle over the back of a dark chestnut gelding, tension threading through her as she cinched it down tight. She'd collected a few things from her room before coming to the stables and had tried to reach Trevillion again. She had opened her mind, stretching outward over the distance, but had gotten no response. He had to be alive. Why couldn't she reach him?

Prince Garrett entered the stables, flanked by six of the king's Elite Guard. Laraina and Kaden arrived shortly afterward. They readied their horses in silence.

As they waited for a stablehand to finish loading the packhorse, Laraina led her mount over to where Tara stood, fidgeting with her horse's reins. Laraina patted her horse on the neck. "We get to travel in style this time."

Tara nodded. "If we follow the path the army took, we can be in Relic in a week."

"A lot faster than walking," Laraina agreed. She lowered her voice. "Did you try contacting Jovan again, however you did it before?"

"Yes."

"And?"

"Nothing."

"You couldn't reach him?"

"No."

Laraina put her hand on Tara's arm. "What if you're wrong?"

"Have my instincts ever been wrong before?"

Laraina hesitated. "No."

Tara held her gaze. "They're not wrong now."

"Mount up!" Garrett said.

Tara swung up onto her horse's back. "Let's go."

Surrounded by the Elite Guardsmen, Garrett, Tara, Laraina, and Kaden rode out of the stable, the moon lighting their way toward Relic.

CHAPTER 18

They traveled west at a swift pace. The sun rose behind them, spilling light through the forest canopy overhead. Pushing their mounts hard, they stopped only briefly to eat and rest.

As the chill of dusk settled over the trees, the group halted at the edge of a small gurgling stream. The tired horses lowered their heads and drank. Tara shifted in the saddle to ease her cramped muscles, her thoughts once more on Trevillion. If only he would answer.

The sharp staccato of approaching hoofbeats rang on the hard ground from the direction of Crystalir. Tara looked at Garrett. He shook his head, mystified. Moments later a horse and rider burst into view on the path behind them.

"Aurelia!" Prince Garrett exclaimed.

"I might have known," Tara said.

Aurelia reined in her laboring horse and pulled up alongside Garrett.

"What are you doing here?" Garrett said in consternation. "You must go back."

"Yes, you must," Kaden agreed. "You can't come with us."

"I will not go back," Aurelia declared. "I refuse to be left behind like a little child."

"Aurelia, it's too dangerous," Garrett argued.

"It's no more dangerous for me than it is for you. What if something happened to you? Do you expect me to sit around and wait, worrying myself sick that you might be hurt or killed and I might never see you again?" Aurelia's eyes brimmed with tears.

"Being a bit overdramatic, aren't you?" Tara asked. "Relic is a battleground. It's no place for you." She wanted to send Aurelia straight back to Crystalir, but part of her leaped at the thought of Aurelia using her spell to try to locate Trevillion.

"We'll lose two days if we take her back," Laraina pointed out.

"She can't come with us," Kaden repeated.

"Please," Aurelia begged. "I'll do anything you say, if you'll just let me come with you."

"Why not send her back with some of the Guard?" Laraina glanced at the six Elite Guardsmen surrounding them.

"I'll need their help to arrest Fournier and his personal guards," Garrett said. "My father wanted to keep the arrest quiet. We don't want to disrupt the army any more than we have to with a battle coming."

Tara shrugged. "The choice is yours, but I'm not going back. As Raina said, we'll lose two days. That's more than I'm willing to spare."

"We need to get to the army," Garrett said. He looked back toward Crystalir, obviously torn.

"Then she'll have to come with us." Tara turned to Aurelia. "I hope you realize what you're getting into. We may all die in Relic."

"It can't be any worse than the Bog," Aurelia said.

"It will be if the Butcher catches us." Tara reined her horse around and started again for Relic.

Aurelia urged her mount forward, galloping after Tara before Garrett or Kaden could object.

Six days of hard riding brought them to the edge of the shallow, swift-flowing Colin. They plunged across the icy river and continued onward, leaving behind the ancient forest of Shallin Wood. Rolling hills passed under their feet. The deep fertile valleys were lush with new spring growth, their pristine beauty as yet untouched by the ravages of war.

Tara kept trying to reach Trevillion, but the whisper-soft voice her mind longed to hear remained silent. Aurelia volunteered to use her scrying spell to search for him, but she too was unsuccessful.

At sunset the next day, the group reached the outskirts of Relic. Although termed a city, Relic was actually an immense fortress surrounded by a large town and an ever-expanding collection of small villages, populated by tradesmen and farmers.

Garrett reined in his mount. Tara and the others drew up beside him. The Elite Guardsmen circled them, staying close.

"Look what they've done." Garrett's eyes swept the landscape.

The city lay in ruins. Tara followed his gaze, taking in the burned, looted buildings and trampled gardens. Silence reigned, eerie and forlorn, like a graveyard in winter. The smell of charred wood lingered in the cold air. Tara searched the stillness for signs of danger and for any aura of life. She found neither.

"Perhaps it's not as bad as it seems," she said. "I see no bodies, human or animal. Your father said they had warning. Maybe they made it to the fortress before the Sulledorns came."

"I hope you're right," Garrett said.

"Your Highness, it is not safe to stay out in the open like this," one of the Guardsmen said.

Garrett motioned the group forward, and they galloped toward the keep.

They reached the battered fortress uncontested. At the gate, Prince Garrett gave a shout that echoed harshly in the darkening twilight. A face appeared over the parapet.

"Who goes there?" the man called down. He held a torch high over his head and looked more closely at his visitors. Then he turned away, bellowing orders. Instantly, the massive gates began to swing inward. They hurried inside. The gates clanged shut behind them.

Confusion reigned inside the muddy courtyard. Every inch of space was filled by the townspeople, the possessions they brought with them when they'd fled their homes, and their myriad livestock. Horses, cattle, sheep, goats, pigs, and chickens milled and darted about, leaving behind the pungent odor of their dung. Tara ducked her head against the cacophony of anxious voices and the constant bellow and bleat of the nervous animals.

Glad she was on horseback, Tara pushed a cow aside with her foot and followed Garrett as he forced his way through the throng to the open stable door. Two harried grooms hurried up to them. Recognizing Garrett, the grooms bowed hastily and grasped the horses' reins.

"I need Colonel Benton or Colonel Lemard," Garrett shouted above the din.

"They're inside, my lord," one of the grooms yelled back, gesturing toward the fortress. "I'm sorry, I don't know exactly where."

Garrett nodded. The frazzled grooms bowed again and rushed away with the horses.

Keeping close to the stable wall, the group crossed to the main entrance of the fortress and stepped inside. The broad entry hall was as crowded as the courtyard, but at least there were no animals. The hall's high ceiling was lost in shadow, its stark gray walls unadorned save for a line of burning torches and a large coat-of-arms at the far end. Garrett pointed to the left, and they slipped through the mob to the main staircase and ascended to the second floor.

"I have to find either Colonel Benton or Colonel Lemard," Garrett said again as he reached the top. "Kaden, I'll need you with me."

Kaden nodded.

Prince Garrett took Aurelia's hand and, accompanied by Kaden and the six Elite Guardsmen, they started down the hall toward the east side of the keep.

A voice rang out behind them. "Prince Kaden!"

Two disheveled men approached. One leaned on a crutch and limped badly; the other man's left arm and shoulder were swathed in bandages.

"My lord!" The man with the limp stared at Kaden as if he were seeing things. "They said you were dead!"

"Not yet." Kaden strode back toward them.

The man with the limp saluted. "Lieutenant Ramisen, my lord, from the garrison at Belgarde. This is Corporal Ambrose." He indicated the man beside him.

Kaden called to Garrett. "Go on without me. I'll be there in a few minutes." Kaden turned back to Lieutenant Ramisen. "Tell me what happened."

Lieutenant Ramisen launched into a vivid account of the battle at Belgarde.

Laraina touched Kaden on the arm. "We're going to look around."

Kaden nodded. "Be careful."

Tara and Laraina walked down the hall. "I'll go this way," Tara pointed to her left, "and see what I can find out."

"I'll go that way." Laraina nodded toward a hallway on the right. She squeezed her sister's arm. "Don't worry. We'll find him."

They separated and began exploring the fortress.

*****

Forcing herself to think positively, Laraina made her way along the passage. Low moans from wounded soldiers drifted through the hushed corridor and mingled with the fading clamor rising from the ground floor. The astringent odor of disinfectant stung her nostrils. Exhausted medics hurried from room to room, treating the injured men. Laraina considered asking one of them where Jovan Trevillion was, but decided against bothering them, at least until she had looked around some more.

She wended through countless hallways, passing through room after room overflowing with wounded, but saw no sign of the man she sought. Apprehension knotted her stomach. Maybe for once, Tara was wrong. She turned down another corridor, this one quieter, with fewer wounded. She searched every room, but still no Trevillion.

The last door opened into an empty chamber. On the far side near the window, a large wooden table stood covered with papers. Curious, she walked over to it. Maps, notes, messages, and numerous other documents were strewn haphazardly across the hard surface. She sifted through them, barely noticing the sound of footsteps in the hallway until they stopped and came back. She turned and found herself gazing into the startlingly blue eyes of Prince Fournier du Mraine. He stood in the doorway, his large frame nearly filling it.

"Well, now," he said, "this is a surprise."

Handsome as ever, Laraina thought bitterly.

He came toward her, his blue eyes devouring her. "It's been a long time."

"Has it?" she asked coolly. "I don't remember."

He bent to kiss her, but she turned away. His eyes grew steely. He grabbed her arms and pulled her to him, kissing her forcibly.

She wrenched out of his grasp and slapped him hard, raking her nails across his cheek. Rage contorted his face. He swung at her, but she anticipated his move and dodged it, stepping smoothly around to the other side of the table.

Fournier regained control of himself and faced her across the table. "You learned your lessons well," he said, a familiar mocking smile playing over his lips.

"Never let it be said I was twice a fool."

Fournier wiped the blood from his face. "I see your temper hasn't improved any either."

"Neither has yours," she retorted.

"What brings you to Relic, may I ask?"

"Nothing that would interest you."

"Oh, but you're wrong," he countered. "Everything you do is of interest to me."

"Well, then," she began, seized with a desire to wipe the arrogant smile off his face. "It might interest you to know that I have just come from Crystalir. I'm afraid your plan didn't work."

The smile disappeared. He tensed, his hands gripping the table. "And just what do you mean by that?"

"Just what I said." She smiled sweetly. "Tara and I reached Crystalir in plenty of time to warn your father about the Mardainn soldiers coming up the river, who are now, I might add, residing quite uncomfortably in the dungeon."

Fournier's knuckles whitened. The muscle in his cheek began to twitch. Laraina knew that sign. Fournier was dangerously angry, but she didn't care.

"It might also interest you to know," she added, "that your father has a similar welcome planned for you when you return."

An ugly expression crossed Fournier's face. "You will be sorry. No one interferes with my plans and lives." He leaned across the table. "Before I get through with you, you'll wish it had been the Butcher who caught you instead of me." He stepped sideways, moving around the table. "And when you're dead, I'll find that cursed sister of yours who I'm sure must be around here somewhere, and I will do the same to her." He laughed smugly. "How I'll enjoy that."

"Then why wait?" asked a cool voice behind him.

*****

Fournier whirled. Tara stood just inside the door, leaning against the wall, arms folded. She watched him closely. "You might be interested to know," she said, emphasizing the words, "that Colonel Lemard is looking for you. He has orders to arrest you and take you back to Crystalir. It seems your father wants to give you a chance to explain yourself before he hangs you for treason."

Fournier walked toward her, the muscle in his cheek twitching visibly. "Do you always eavesdrop on other people's conversations?"

Tara smiled. "Of course. You learn a great deal that way."

Fournier stepped closer. Tara blocked the door, drawing her sword and holding it so that the tip rested on the floor. He reached for his sword, then stopped. He raised both hands in protest.

"This isn't necessary." He moved forward again. "I'm sure we can come to some sort of understanding, for old times' sake."

Tara allowed him to advance until he was almost on top of her. Then she flicked her wrist, and the sharp point of her sword came to rest under his chin. He stopped as it pressed against his throat.

"I understand you perfectly," she said.

Running footsteps thudded in the corridor. Colonel Lemard appeared, flanked by four rugged soldiers. Fournier snarled. Tara pressed her blade into the soft flesh of his throat. "Try it."

Fournier backed away and turned toward the window, but Laraina was there, sword in hand. Fournier hesitated and the soldiers pounced. They wrestled Fournier to the floor and disarmed him, then hauled him to his feet.

Out in the corridor, Garrett arrived with three Elite Guardsmen. Fournier spotted him and went still. The brothers faced each other in silence. Then Garrett spoke.

"Why?"

Fournier gave him a pitying smile. "Power, boy. The spoils go to the strong." With a deft movement, he twisted his right arm free. "You will not have what is mine!" Fournier flicked his arm, and something flashed outward from his sleeve toward Garrett.

A cold shock of warning spurred Tara forward and she shoved Garrett aside. A knife whistled past him, nicking his cheek before striking one of the Elite Guardsmen. Garrett cried out, his hand flying to his face. He stumbled to his knees as the Guardsman grunted and fell.

Cursing, Fournier thrashed like a mad beast, nearly breaking free from his captors. The four soldiers fought to hold him down.

"I thought you disarmed him!" Colonel Lemard ran forward to aid his men. Tara and one of the Guardsmen dashed to Garrett's side and pulled him back out of the way. The other Guardsman helped pin Fournier to the floor.

"I will kill you all!" Fournier shouted.

One of the soldiers whacked Fournier over the head with the hilt of his dagger. Fournier collapsed, unconscious. Breathing heavily, the soldiers lifted him and carried him out of the room.

Tara and the Guardsman helped Prince Garrett to his feet. Colonel Lemard hurried to the prince's side; the other Guardsman checked his injured comrade and shouted for a medic.

"Your Highness, how bad is it?" the Colonel asked solicitously.

"Not bad," Garrett said with an effort. Blood seeped between his fingers covering the knife cut on his face. "Go with your men. Make certain my brother is locked up in the dungeon."

Colonel Lemard saluted and left the room.

Laraina tore a square of fabric from the bottom of her tunic and handed it to the prince.

He grimaced as he pressed it against his wound. "Thank you." He turned to Tara. "And thank *you* for saving my life."

Tara nodded. "You're welcome."

Two medics rushed in with several orderlies. One of the medics bent over the fallen Guardsman, while the other came straight to Garrett's side. He took one look at the wound and ushered Garrett out the door. The Guardsmen went with him, one in front, one behind. The orderlies lifted the injured Guardsman and followed, along with the second medic.

Tara turned to her sister. "You all right?"

Laraina nodded. "I'm just ashamed I ever had anything to do with him."

Tara placed a comforting hand on her shoulder. "Don't torture yourself. He's not worth it."

"Did you find Jovan?"

"No. I know he's here. I can feel him. But I can't tell where he is. It's almost as if he's shutting me out, hiding his location."

"Why would he do that?"

Tara shrugged, frustrated. "I don't know."

Running footsteps echoed along the corridor. Tara and Laraina turned as one, their hands on their weapons.

Prince Kaden burst into the room. "Thank the gods!" He hugged Laraina hard. "Are you all right?"

"I'm fine," she answered. "What did you find out from those soldiers from Belgarde?"

"Belgarde fell the same way as Carilon," Kaden said. "Someone opened the gates in the middle of the night. They never had a chance. A few of the men managed to escape, but only Ramisen and Ambrose survived. They were picked up by the Faragellyn Border Guard and brought here. The townspeople were evacuated and moved to the fortress. The Sulledorn army arrived shortly after. They've destroyed most of the city, but they haven't been able to breach the outer wall yet. They're camped in a valley just west of the city. Lemard is worried they're going to try the same trick here."

"With all the noise and chaos in the courtyard," Tara said, "it would be easy for someone to slip into the gatehouse."

"Exactly," Kaden said. "Lemard has the gatehouse under twenty-four hour guard. He and Colonel Benton have been watching Fournier du Mraine and his personal guards, hoping to catch them in the act. Lemard was sure they were going to try something tonight, but after this... I don't know. If nothing happens tonight, he expects the Sulledorns will attack at dawn and try to overpower us by sheer force of numbers."

"They'll be able to do it too," Tara said, "if we don't get help soon. The Woodsmen from Tralyxa and Barony's Horsemen would —"

Pounding footsteps sounded in the hall again. Aurelia darted into the room, her face smeared with tears. "Come quickly! Fournier's escaped!"

"He was out cold not ten minutes ago," Tara contended.

"He came to and he went crazy," Aurelia cried. "He stole a sword from one of the guards and wounded Colonel Lemard and killed several of his men. Then he escaped through a secret door in the dungeon wall. Garrett went after him. He said it was his duty to bring Fournier back. Please, you must hurry! Fournier will kill him!"

Tara headed for the door, Laraina and Kaden right behind her. "You stay here. We'll —"

"I'm going with you," Aurelia declared determinedly.

Tara stared hard at her for a moment, then capitulated. "All right. Come on."

They raced through the halls of the keep, plunging down several flights of stairs to the dungeon. Its massive iron door stood open. The damp stone corridor swarmed with soldiers treating injured men and hastily putting together makeshift stretchers. Tara and the others dodged through the crowded passage into the gloom of the dungeon labyrinth. Following a trail of lighted torches, they soon found the hole through which Fournier had escaped. Two grim-faced soldiers guarded the opening. The tunnel beyond was pitch black.

Tara seized a torch and they stepped into the narrow passage. The air stank of mold. The cramped tunnel extended some fifty feet before ending in a blank wall. The group stopped short. Tara raised the torch higher. A rusted iron ladder, concealed in a niche in the wall, led to an open trapdoor in the ceiling. Two faces appeared in the square opening, drawn by the torchlight. Tara recognized them as two of the soldiers she had seen with Colonel Lemard. She climbed the ladder and, handing her torch to one of the soldiers, pulled herself up through the trapdoor. The others clambered up behind her.

Bright moonlight poured through the dusty windows of the spacious building they'd entered. *A warehouse*, Tara thought. Looted like the rest of the city. Stacks of wooden crates, those that hadn't been smashed, tipped precariously. Torn sacks of corn seed lay scattered on the floor, along with loose bundles of straw. Farm implements had been knocked over and broken. A few odd pieces of leather harness dangled from wooden pegs along the shadowed walls, and several lengths of rope hung from the rafters where sacks of vegetables and cured meats had been cut down.

They worked their way to the front of the building, following the path Fournier had cleared in his violent escape. The warehouse door stood wide open, nearly torn from its hinges. Tara stopped at the door and looked out. She neither saw nor sensed anyone near. Signaling the others forward, she jogged west down the moonlit street. The others followed, their booted feet crunching on the gravel.

Shouts filled the night, somewhere ahead of them, and the clash of weapons rang out. They raced toward the sounds. Then a wounded cry lanced through sudden stillness. Tara's gut turned to ice. She knew that voice. Prince Garrett. She rounded a corner and stopped, holding her arms out straight to keep the others behind her. Three men lay unmoving on the far side of the street. One of them was the young prince.

"Garrett!" Aurelia ducked beneath Tara's arm.

"No, wait!" Tara snatched at her, but Aurelia twisted away and dashed across the street. She dropped to her knees beside the fallen prince. Cursing, Tara pulled out her sword and ran after her.

Weapons drawn, Laraina and Kaden followed more slowly, looking for Fournier. Reaching Garrett's side, Tara knelt and searched for a pulse. Blood soaked the left side of his shirt and the gravel beneath him. Aurelia sobbed and gripped his hand. Tara let out a breath of relief. His pulse was weak but steady. An icy chill whipped down her spine. She whirled.

"Raina! Behind you!" Tara sprinted toward her sister and pointed to a shadowed alley.

Fournier du Mraine sprang from the alley. Laraina turned, but Fournier struck first, his razor-sharp blade biting deeply into her shoulder. With a cry of pain, she reeled into Kaden. He caught her as she fell. Aurelia screamed as Fournier raised his weapon to strike again. Tara leaped between her sister and Fournier as he began his downward swing, blocking him smoothly and countering, driving him backward.

"You!" Fournier roared. "You have been nothing but a thorn in my side. A thorn that is about to be crushed!" He attacked with murderous fury. Tara parried and dodged and thrust, watching for an opening. Fournier feinted left, then swung at her head. She ducked, her blade slicing across his abdomen. He hissed in pain and swung at her again. She side-stepped, slipped on the blood-stained gravel, and landed on one knee. With a shout of triumph, Fournier lunged. Deftly, Tara rolled to the side. She thrust upward with all of her strength and planted her sword deep in his chest. Fournier's shout slid to a groan as he fell.

"Enjoy the Abyss," Tara said grimly as she retrieved her weapon from his corpse.

"Over here!" Kaden called. He'd set Laraina down next to Prince Garrett.

Tara rushed over and dropped down beside her sister. "Raina?" She touched Kaden's cloak, knotted tightly around Laraina's shoulder, and her hand came away red.

"She passed out," Kaden said. "I can't stop the bleeding."

Tara slashed her palm on her sword blade and slid her hand under the cloak bandage. She closed her eyes and, bracing herself against the pain from Laraina's injury, let the healing power sear through her in a hot, rushing wave. Laraina's body twitched as the power swept through her, healing the worst of the deep wound.

A new sound reached their ears — the crunch of running footsteps, a great many of them, coming from the west. Sulledorn soldiers drawn by the fight. Tara sensed the danger even before she heard the sound. Leaving Laraina half healed, Tara gathered the power back into herself, fought off her dizziness, and placed her still bleeding hand over Garrett's chest wound. He moaned as the power slammed into him, coursing through his veins. She gritted her teeth until the pain from his sword wound passed.

Moments later, Tara released Garrett, blood oozing from the wound in her palm. "The Guardsmen?"

"They're dead," Kaden said.

Laraina stirred and tried to sit up. "What's happening?"

"I've healed you and Garrett as much as I could," Tara said. She kept her eyes averted to hide the swirling of their silver-blue color. "The Sulledorns are coming." Her vision cleared, her dizziness fading more quickly this time. She picked up Laraina's sword and handed it to Aurelia. "Get them back to the fortress. I'll keep the Sulledorns busy for a while."

"I-I will." Aurelia's voice wavered, but her gaze was steady. She helped Laraina to her feet. Kaden hefted Garrett over his shoulder, and they headed back toward the keep.

Tara smiled to herself as she ran toward the approaching Sulledorns. Perhaps there was hope for the girl yet.

CHAPTER 19

Captain Natiere rose abruptly from where he'd been crouching, drinking from a small stream. A black wolf padded up to him, ears pricked forward, sniffing the breeze. Natiere looked toward the Relic fortress, its dark bulk rising in the moonlit distance. He let his eyes unfocus, seeing with his mind.

"She is here," he whispered to the wolf. "The witch has left the safety of the keep. She is out in the city."

He sensed the charge of magic in the air, breathed it in. She would not escape him this time. He motioned to the wolf. "Come with me."

The wolf growled softly, and six more shadows eased out of the vale. Natiere and the wolves skirted the Sulledorn camp and slipped toward the ruined city.

*****

Dizzy and weak from blood loss, Laraina forced herself to keep moving. They had to get back to the fortress. Aurelia supported Laraina as best she could, with the sword Tara had given her still gripped in her hand. Kaden bolstered Laraina from the other side, keeping one hand at her elbow, his other arm wrapped around Garrett's legs. Draped over Kaden's shoulder, Garrett hadn't shown any sign of waking. The rising clamor of shouts and swordplay drifted back to Laraina from the west, and she knew the chase was on. Sick with pain, she closed her eyes and prayed that her sister would be all right.

It seemed hours later when they finally reached the storehouse with the secret passage. Aurelia called to the two guards still posted by the open trapdoor. "Come quickly! We need help!"

The guards looked up, startled. They glanced at each other, then drew their swords.

"What in the Abyss...?" Kaden said.

As the soldiers advanced, Laraina caught a glimpse of their faces in the moonlight and recognized Fournier's personal guards.

"Oh, no," she whispered.

"You're not the same soldiers who were here before," Aurelia burst out.

"They're Fournier's guards. Aurelia, give me my sword." Laraina struggled to stand on her own.

"No. Tara gave it to me."

Fournier's guards closed in.

Shouting Garrett's name, Aurelia swung the blade wildly and charged at them. Surprised, they leaped to the side. One of them backed into a tier of crates, which crashed to the floor. Potatoes scattered in all directions. The guard stepped on one, slipped, and fell, his sword flying from his grasp. Aurelia lunged at him. He dodged and scrambled to his feet. Brandishing her sword, Aurelia chased after him. He retreated before her.

"Aurelia, behind you!" Kaden pointed at the second guard, slipping in behind her. Kaden had set Garrett down and was drawing his weapon.

The man Aurelia was pursuing stopped in front of her. She swung at him hard. The weight of the sword threw her off balance.

She spun all the way around and hit the man behind her in the leg. The soldier howled in pain, and she nearly dropped her sword in surprise. She swung again at the injured guard and her blade caught him in the forearm. He howled again; his weapon slipped from his hand. Aurelia leaped at him, stabbing at him with her sword. The wounded soldier backpedaled, tripped over a sack of grain, and fell with a crash into a collection of metal pails.

Rough hands grabbed her from behind. The other guard yanked her back against him, pinning her with one arm while snatching her sword away. He spun around to face Kaden, using Aurelia as a shield. Before the guard's blade reached her throat, Aurelia stomped on his foot. He yelled, lifting his foot and loosening his grip. She twisted free, pointed at him, and shouted a magical phrase. White feathers flew into the air. The sword clattered to the floor. A great white goose honked and flapped where, moments before, the guard had stood.

Kaden lowered his sword. "You did it."

Aurelia tossed her head. "When I say goose, I mean *goose*." Glaring at the other wounded guard, she raised her finger and pointed at him.

His eyes widened, and he clambered behind a stack of crates. Kaden grasped him by the collar and dragged him to his feet. "Any more of Fournier's men in the tunnel?" Kaden pressed his blade against the guard's neck.

"No," the guard answered, keeping his eyes on Aurelia.

"Someone's coming," Laraina said. Running footsteps sounded in the tunnel below.

Moments later, a helmeted head popped up through the trapdoor. The soldier took in the scene, his gaze lingering on the honking goose. "Prince Kaden. Lady Aurelia. What happened?"

"An ambush," Kaden said. "Garrett and Laraina are hurt. We'll need help getting them down."

The soldier shouted back down the tunnel for more help. Then he and his men climbed up to the floor of the warehouse. Kaden handed over the cowed guard, who was shoved down through the trapdoor. Aurelia led the soldiers to where Garrett lay.

Laraina stood near him, leaning on a crate. She smiled at Aurelia. "Well done, as Tara would say."

Aurelia smiled back. "Thanks." She retrieved Laraina's sword, wiped it clean on a burlap sack, and gave it back to her.

The soldiers lifted Prince Garrett and carried him to the trapdoor, carefully lowering him through to the men waiting below. Aurelia followed as they bore him away to the hospital rooms.

Leaning heavily on Kaden, Laraina followed the path the soldiers had cleared. A wave of dizziness swept over her.

Catching her to him, the tall prince bent down and lifted her in his arms. He carried her to the trapdoor. There he set her down and, with the soldiers' help, they descended the rusted ladder to the tunnel below. Lifting her in his arms once more, Kaden made his way back through the dank corridors of the dungeon labyrinth and up a flight of stairs to the main floor of the castle. More soldiers parted the milling crowd of townspeople who'd been awakened by the ruckus and gave Kaden a clear path to the main staircase.

Laraina closed her eyes, gritting her teeth against the pain. Tara's healing power had stopped the bleeding and mended the deepest part of her injury, but the wound still hurt badly.

"Kaden! Laraina!"

The shout came from behind them. Laraina's eyes shot open at the sound of the familiar voice. Kaden stopped and turned, setting Laraina down on her feet. "Jovan!" she cried.

Limping slightly, Jovan Trevillion ran up to them from the direction of the dungeon. Red-stained bandages swathed his broad chest and ribs, visible beneath the disheveled and torn Sulledorn uniform he wore. His gaze fastened on Laraina's bloody clothing. "What in blazes happened? Are you all right?"

Laraina nodded. She hugged Trevillion with her good arm. "Tara was right. She said you weren't dead."

"Well, not yet anyway."

"Change sides?" Kaden asked, eyeing Trevillion's Sulledorn uniform. He drew Laraina back beside him, supporting her with his arm as she leaned into him.

Trevillion ignored the barb. "It's easier to spy on the enemy when you look like them."

"Kaden!" Aurelia hurried down the stairs from the second floor. "Colonel Lemard in the infirmary needs to talk to you." Her eyes widened as she spotted Trevillion. "Jovan!" She rushed forward and threw her arms around him, knocking him back a step. "I'm so glad to see you! We thought you were dead."

He returned her hug. "It's good to see you, too."

She pulled back and gasped, noticing his numerous bandages. "I didn't hurt you, did I?"

"I'll survive." His mouth quirked as if trying not to smile.

"I did it, you know," Aurelia said. "I turned one of Fournier's guards into a goose."

Trevillion's eyebrows rose. "You did?"

"Aurelia, you can tell him about it later," Kaden said. "Will you please let Colonel Lemard know I'll be up in a moment?"

Aurelia rolled her eyes. "Yes, yes, I will tell him." She smiled at Trevillion. "I can't wait for you to meet Garrett." She darted back across the main floor and up the stairs.

Trevillion looked with concern at Laraina's blood-soaked shoulder again. "Are you sure you're all right? Where is Tara?"

"I will be. Tara healed some of it."

"She healed you?" Trevillion said, suddenly tense.

"Yes. She's out in the city playing decoy with a troop of Sulledorns so we could get back to the fortress."

Trevillion swore. "She's out there? Alone?"

Laraina's gut clenched. "Yes, why?" She already knew the answer.

"Natiere is out there. He can sense the use of magic."

"Oh, no." Laraina took a step toward the dungeon. "We have to find her before he does."

"You stay here," Trevillion said, as Kaden pulled Laraina back against him. "You're hurt. I will find her."

"But so are you," Laraina objected.

"I will find her," he repeated, his dark eyes intense, "and that is a promise." He turned and headed down the dungeon stairs.

*****

Tara slipped into a looted shop to catch her breath. She tore another strip of fabric from the bottom of her tunic and wrapped it around the makeshift bandage covering her bleeding hand. Because she hadn't completely healed her sister and Garrett, the wound on her palm hadn't closed. The bandage had soaked through and was dripping blood. The last thing she needed was to leave a trail of red droplets for the Sulledorns to follow. She clamped her jaw against the pain and started down the moonlit street, her footsteps crunching on the gravel.

She headed toward the fortress, keeping to the shadows. The acrid smell of burned wood still tainted the air. Jagged remnants of blackened buildings pierced the night sky like unburied skeletons in a vast battlefield. She scanned them for hidden dangers. The

Sulledorn soldiers still searched for her. She could see them, here and there, hunting through the ruins. The Sulledorns didn't worry her as much as the other enemy stalking her. She tried to stifle the icy shivers crawling over her skin. The Butcher was near. She sensed him closing in like a wolf about to rip into its prey.

A hoarse shout shattered the stillness. She cursed under her breath as she spied two groups of Sulledorn soldiers bearing down on her. She ran, zig-zagging in and out of the ruined buildings, the Sulledorns chasing her. She heard someone bellowing orders, telling the men to spread out and surround her. Darting into what had once been an alehouse, she spotted an open pantry door next to the main entrance. She leaped over the bar and ducked into the pantry, pulling the door almost shut behind her. The Sulledorn soldiers raced into the alehouse, knocked aside broken tables and chairs, and continued on out the back.

As soon as they were gone, Tara slipped from the pantry, climbed back over the bar, and peeked out the front door. There was no one in sight. She dashed across the street into an alley behind an old barn.

Shouts erupted all around her. "Great," she muttered. She dodged into another alley and ran. A few minutes later, she collapsed behind a blackened cottage, her lungs burning, her breath gone. She had managed to evade the soldiers, but she knew it wouldn't be for long. She could hear them searching the buildings nearby, working methodically now. What she needed was a good place to hide.

Dragging herself to her feet, she surveyed her surroundings. There wasn't much to choose from. Two more burned-out cottages, another barn, and a tall granary. The cottages didn't look like they would afford much shelter. The barn was a possibility, but she would have to cross a great deal of open space to get to it. Her gaze shifted to the granary. It was smaller than the barn and likely to be empty at this time of year. She looked around again, searching for other options. Her eyes slid back to the granary. She had the strangest impulse to go there. Something about the building drew her.

Several soldiers strode into view and began examining the charred houses. Tara ducked back into the shadows. *The granary it is*, she told herself grimly. *If it's locked, I'm in trouble.* Crouching low, she slipped around to the door. She reached for the door handle, then stopped, perplexed by her odd compulsion to go in. She heard more soldiers approaching. She reached for the door again. To her amazement, it opened by itself. A hand shot out, caught her arm, and pulled her inside. The door closed behind her. In the dim light she saw the insignia of an eagle and crossed swords on the shoulder of the man holding her arm. A Sulledorn soldier. She kicked him hard in the shin and wrenched her arm from his grasp, her hand closing on the hilt of her sword.

The man let out a muffled oath.

Tara's heart raced at the familiar voice. "Jovan? Is that you?" she whispered.

"Of course it's me. Who did you think it was?"

Tara snorted. "How should I know? My friends don't usually go around wearing Sulledorn uniforms."

Trevillion massaged his smarting shin.

Tara knelt beside him. "I'm sorry. You're supposed to be dead, you know."

Trevillion laughed softly. "So I've been told." He straightened up, pulling her up with him. Then his arms went around her and his lips found hers in a kiss that scattered all thought to the wind. Tara leaned into him, lost in the kiss, her arms sliding around his waist, up over his back, her fingers searching for the warmth of skin under the torn fabric of his uniform. Instead she felt damp cloth... and bandages.

She pulled away. "You're bleeding!"

"Not badly." He kissed her again.

Loud voices and crunching gravel broke them apart. "They're coming," Tara said breathlessly. She looked for a place to hide.

The granary was nearly empty; most of the grain had been used up over the winter. A few piles of loosely-stacked bags of wheat, barley, and seed corn remained, leaning against the near wall.

"Over here." Catching Tara by the hand, Trevillion led her to the largest pile.

She noticed his uneven stride. "You're limping. I'm sorry I kicked you."

"It wasn't you. I was stabbed in the leg in a fight with a Sulledorn."

"And I just made it worse."

"No, it was the other leg." He dragged aside some of the bags, reconstructing the pile to contain a cave-like niche in the center.

"Get in," he said.

Tara balked. "What about you?"

"I'm a Sulledorn, remember? Get in."

Reluctantly, Tara climbed into the hole. Trevillion shoved a stack of bags in front of her to conceal the hideaway. Peering through a chink, Tara watched him snatch up a torn sack of barley and scatter its contents across the dusty floor to cover their footprints. Then he tossed the empty bag into a corner and stepped behind the door.

As if in response, the door flew open. Trevillion was ready for it, his hands raised to catch the heavy door before it slammed into him. Five Sulledorns trooped into the granary and poked around. Trevillion joined them. He searched the area where Tara was hiding and stirred up as much dust as he could. Tara held her nose to keep from sneezing.

"There's nothing here, sir," one of the soldiers said in a choked voice. He sneezed.

The man in charge agreed. "Move out."

The soldiers headed for the door. Trevillion fell in behind the last man. As the Sulledorns strode from the granary, he ducked behind the door and pushed it shut. He stood with his ear to the door, listening.

Tara sneezed, unable to stifle the impulse any longer. She shoved a pile of bags aside with her feet and climbed out of the hole.

"They're still out there," Trevillion said, "but it sounds like they're moving away."

She sneezed again.

"I'm glad you didn't do that earlier."

"You didn't make it very easy." Tara looked at his back. She touched the blood-encrusted uniform, spreading apart the torn fabric to see the bandages beneath. Fresh blood had stained them scarlet. She started to undo the cloth around her palm. "Let me heal you."

He spun and caught her hand. "No, you can't. Natiere can sense magic. If you use your healing power, he'll find you."

Tara's hand dropped to her side. "How do you know that?"

"I found out the night you called out to me. I was in the Sulledorn camp, eavesdropping on a group of soldiers. I heard your voice in my mind. Your pain was unbearable. I had to know what was wrong."

Tara looked away. "I was mourning your death. We were told you'd been killed in the battle with the Mardainn soldiers."

"I was wounded. I let everyone assume I was dead, so I could infiltrate the Sulledorn camp. Colonel Benton and the chief medic were the only ones who knew otherwise. When you broke the mental link, I realized Natiere was walking right toward me."

"Laraina interrupted me," Tara murmured.

"I'm glad she did. Otherwise, I might not have seen him coming. I was concentrating on you."

"How did you escape?"

"I was on the opposite side of a wagon from him. I don't know if he actually saw me or not. I beat it out of there, and he didn't follow." Trevillion cupped her cheek. "That's why I couldn't answer when you called again."

"You didn't want the Butcher to find you."

"No. I didn't want him to find *you*. I was afraid if he could feel your magic through me, he would somehow be able to trace it back to you and know where you were." Trevillion drew her to him, held her close. His lips touched her hair. "I couldn't take the chance of his finding you. I'm sorry."

"You're alive, and that's what matters." Tara eased back.

Trevillion quirked a smile. "I had hoped you would stay in Crystalir. I liked knowing that the Butcher was here, and you were there, with a lot of distance in between."

Tara laughed. "You should have known better."

"Yes. The gods forbid you stay where you're safe." He listened at the door again. "I don't hear them anymore."

As he reached for the door handle, Tara put her hand against the door, holding it shut. "I want to know about your wounds. How bad are they? And I want the truth."

He hesitated, then drew a line with his finger across his upper chest and another down his right side. "I have gashes here and here, one on my back, and the one on my leg. The chief medic sewed them up, but they still bleed a bit."

"You're not giving them time to heal. Can you fight?"

"One can always fight." Trevillion cracked the door open, then shut it quickly. "They're coming out of the barn across the way."

"You know, I had the strangest urge to come into this building," Tara said. "It had to be because you were in here, but I've never felt anything like it before. What did you do? How did you find me?"

"Finding you wasn't hard. I followed the shouts of the soldiers. I saw you once or twice, heading this way, so I ducked in here and tried to reach you without using the mind link. That must have been what you felt. I just hope Natiere didn't sense it as well."

"I felt him coming after me earlier. I think he's hovering somewhere, waiting to trap us."

"Getting back to the fortress will be no easy trick." Trevillion eased the door open again. "I don't see anyone. Let's go."

Thickening clouds clogged the starless sky. The shrouded moon, a pale circle behind the dark overcast, dipped toward the band of clear night along the western horizon. Taking advantage of the shifting darkness, Tara and Trevillion worked their way back toward the keep, dodging handfuls of Sulledorn soldiers still searching among the ruined buildings.

As they neared the fortress, a group of soldiers patrolling a wide open street halted their progress. Tara and Trevillion crouched behind a low, half-burned wall.

"I count ten of them," Tara whispered.

"There's not much cover here. We'll have to backtrack and go around them," Trevillion said.

A freezing chill gripped her. She seized Trevillion's arm. "Someone's coming." She had barely gotten the words out when four Sulledorns strode into view behind them. The Sulledorns ran forward, drawing their weapons and shouting to the other soldiers.

As one, Tara and Trevillion whipped their swords free and sprang over the wall, running toward the line of soldiers blocking the street. The soldiers closed in, surrounding them. Tara pulled a dagger out of her boot and flung it at the nearest soldier. It struck him squarely in the chest, driving to the hilt. He fell backward with a cry. Spinning on her heel, Tara kicked a stinging flurry of gravel into the next one's face. His hands flew up to ward them off, leaving his body unprotected. Tara ran him through. She saw two more hit the ground and knew Trevillion was holding his own, in spite of his injuries. Standing back to back, they fought off the assault. Two more soldiers retreated from the skirmish, wounded by Tara's blade.

Trevillion grunted in pain and backed into her, knocking her off balance. She caught herself and turned toward him; he was on one knee, still parrying blows. Sensing movement behind her, she twisted to the side, but not far enough. A slash of pain seared across her back just below her shoulder blades. With a muffled cry, she dodged away, keeping close to Trevillion. The soldier swung at her again. The blade whistled past her midsection. Leaping forward, she kicked him in the belly and shoved him backward into another soldier. They fell in a tangle of limbs.

Trevillion regained his feet and fought with both sword and dagger. Warding off blows, Tara feinted in one direction, then lunged at her attackers. Her blade bit into flesh, and a soldier fell, clutching his ribs. She ducked beneath another blade, then reversed tack and buried her sword in the soldier's side. Before she could recover her weapon, another soldier's blade caught her in the elbow and sliced down her left forearm. She cried out as a fiery pain shot down her arm. Her fingers went numb; her sword slipped to the ground. The soldier slashed at her head. Tara dropped and launched herself at his knees, knocking his feet out from under him. She rolled to her feet and caught up her sword in her right hand. The soldier regained his footing and came at her.

Tara froze as a deluge of icy cold swept over her. A feral howl pierced the night. Poised to attack, the soldier stopped. His head swiveled toward the source of the sound. More howls bit the air.

"He's coming," she hissed. "We have to get out of here!"

"Too late," Trevillion said.

A massive figure stepped out of the shadows and blocked their path. The brilliant moon, hovering just above the horizon, revealed him clearly; its silver light softened the ragged scar that snaked down the left side of his face and gleamed off the polished broadsword in his gnarled hand. Captain Natiere. The Butcher.

Trevillion thrust Tara behind him as the Butcher strode forward. Seven wolves loped out of the ruins and surrounded them.

Natiere pointed at the Sulledorns. "Leave or die."

The soldiers fled.

Tara stood with her back to Trevillion, watching the wolves. She shook her left arm, spattering drops of blood on the gravel as she tried to shake the feeling back into her numb fingers.

Natiere stopped about fifteen feet away. "Lady Triannon, I have been looking forward to this meeting."

Tara moved up beside Trevillion. "Sorry, I can't say the same."

Trevillion stepped in front of her again. "What do you want, Natiere?"

The Butcher's black eyes settled on Trevillion. "I had no quarrel with you until you killed my Brothers and Sisters."

"Your brothers...?" Trevillion asked guardedly.

"The Bog wolves. You killed them and left them to rot on the riverbank."

"*They* were trying to kill *us*," Tara said over Trevillion's shoulder. "We didn't have much choice."

"You trespassed on their territory," Natiere rasped.

"Because *you* were trying to kill us," Tara shot back.

Trevillion half turned toward her, keeping one eye on Natiere. "I think he is angry enough without your provoking him."

A smile crossed Natiere's face, and he chuckled, the gravelly sound swelling into a full-bellied laugh. "*Silvestri witana, ilesst courandi matas ilesst beliera.*"

Tara recognized the first two words. He had said them to her before in Castle Carilon. 'Silver-haired witch,' according to Aurelia's translation. The other words were a mystery. Tara glanced at Trevillion. "What did he say?" She didn't expect an answer.

Trevillion's eyes narrowed. "*Ili tarissta pasi mi denor bostir.*"

Tara glared at him. "What did *you* say?"

Trevillion didn't answer as he and the Butcher stared each other down.

"So be it." Natiere moved into a fighting stance.

Trevillion stepped forward.

Tara jumped in front of him. "What are you doing? You can't fight him. You're already bleeding from —"

Her words were lost as Trevillion's lips closed over hers in a hard kiss. He released her and strode past to where Natiere stood waiting. She whirled to follow, but the wolves closed in around her, snarling and snapping, forcing her back.

The two combatants faced each other. The clash of steel struck Tara like a physical blow. Wounded as he was, Trevillion was no match for Natiere. She had to do something. She thought she had lost him once. She wasn't about to let it happen again.

Trevillion slipped on the loose gravel and nearly went down. Natiere's blade flashed and a streak of bright red appeared across Trevillion's ribs.

Swinging her sword in front of her, Tara rushed at the wolves standing between her and the combatants. The wolves ducked beneath her blade and snapped at her legs, their teeth catching, not flesh, but the cuffs of her boots. The wolves behind her bit into her cloak and pulled her backward. More wolves shoved against her, buckling her knees. Teeth caught in her sleeves and yanked her over. She fell flat on her back, her arms held out straight by the wolves. A large, black wolf put its front paws on her chest and growled at her.

"Tara!" She heard Trevillion call out.

"I'm all right! They're not hurting me." Which was the strangest thing she could imagine. She looked the black wolf in the eye, saw intelligence there. "I don't want to kill you, Wolf, but if I have to, I will." She gathered her strength. "Now get... off!" She snatched her arms back, ripping the fabric out of the wolves' teeth, and with a rolling shove, knocked the black wolf off from her. Sword out, she spun in a low, crouching circle, holding the wolves at bay. She really didn't want to hurt them, since they were so deliberately not hurting her.

Keeping up the rapid whirl, she made it to within a few feet of Trevillion and the Butcher. Dizziness forced her to a stop, and the wolves darted in, pushing against her and tugging once more on her clothing.

The black wolf latched onto the sleeve of her sword arm. She jerked her arm back, but couldn't get free. "Curse you, Wolf, let go of me!"

The clash of swords ceased as both Natiere and Trevillion turned toward her, surprised. Trevillion staggered back a few steps, barely keeping his feet.

Natiere spoke a word, and the wolves released her. Teeth bared, they surrounded Trevillion. Trevillion dropped to a defensive crouch.

"I asked them not to hurt the lady," Natiere said. "I will not ask the same for you."

"I want no mercy." Trevillion kept his eyes on the wolves. "And I will give none."

"Jovan, listen to me." Tara moved between him and Natiere. "Don't hurt the wolves, unless they attack you first."

"I won't let you fight him alone," Trevillion said heatedly.

She shot him a beseeching look. "Please, just trust me and do as I ask." Shaking off the cold shivers slithering over her skin, she faced the Butcher.

"I did not want to fight you this way," Natiere said, circling.

Tara kept him in front of her. "What do you mean?"

He gestured toward her left arm, still oozing blood. "There is no challenge in fighting an injured opponent."

She smiled grimly. "On the contrary, wounded and cornered enemies are often the most dangerous."

He lunged at her, harrying her with blows. She parried them all and launched an attack of her own, forcing him backward. He spun around and swung at her again, the tip of his blade lancing across her thigh. She sucked in a hissing breath at the sharp sting. Natiere circled again, nodding to her with what looked like approval. "You fight well off-handed."

"Not well enough," she muttered. She flexed her left hand, trying to will the feeling back into her fingers.

He feinted this way and that, as if testing her. "You didn't harm my wolves. Why?"

Tara watched him carefully. She had underestimated his quickness and agility. "They didn't harm me. I don't kill for pleasure."

"What do you kill for? Money? Loved ones?" Natiere's black eyes flicked to Trevillion, then back to her.

She leaped forward and swung at Natiere. He fended off the attack, but didn't strike.

She backed away. "What do you want from me?"

"I want you to look at me."

"I did that once. I didn't like what I saw."

Natiere's voice grew soft. "Look again, *mi achina*."

Tara frowned. "You've called me that twice now. Why?"

Natiere's blade flashed. She parried and ducked underneath it, whirling to face him again.

"You are all the gypsy said you would be."

"Gypsy? What gypsy?" She fought off two more blows, dancing to the side out of reach.

Natiere backed off. "The gypsy warlock who forced me to live, when I wanted to die. He showed you to me in a dream."

Tara stared at him. "You saw *me* in a dream?"

"Yes. He said you would be my redemption and my downfall."

"That makes no sense. I cannot grant redemption. Only the gods can do that."

"All things are possible, Lady. Look at me."

Tara wavered. His voice compelled her to look, but his magic... If she went into his mind, would she be able to get out again? Or would he just kill her where she stood?

He took a step toward her.

She stepped back. "You expect me to trust you?"

He stopped and lowered his weapon. "I will not strike while you are within. You have my word."

Tara heard a strange note in his voice, almost a plea. In spite of herself, her eyes slid upward and locked with his.

"Tara, no! Don't let him in!" Trevillion yelled from somewhere behind her.

She heard the wolves snarl in warning. "No, Jovan, stay there. It's all right." Cautiously, she opened her mind, reaching outward. Shudders ran through her as she touched Natiere's mind. Then wave upon wave of horror, agony, and paralyzing fright pummeled her, drowning her in a sea of terror. Unable to stop, she slipped deeper, seeing images through the eyes of youth, of loved ones tortured and pain-racked and... such atrocities...

Tara dropped her sword, her hands flying to her head as if to block out the visions. She wrenched her mind out and stood, gasping for breath. After a moment, she lowered her hands. An aching throb settled behind her eyes. "By all the gods," she whispered. "What happened to you?"

"Bandits," Natiere said quietly. "Bandits who like to torture and maim before they kill."

Tara looked at Natiere's face. "The bandits gave you that scar?"

"No. I gave myself that scar in remembrance of what was done to my family."

"I'm sorry."

"You needn't be. I repaid the bandits tenfold."

Tara caught her breath as realization dawned on her. "All those mangled bodies you left behind — those were the bandits?"

A frightening smile crossed Natiere's face. "I hunted them down. Every last one. They took from me the life that should have been and left me with this one." He raised his blade.

Tara snatched up her sword. "Killing me won't change what has happened."

"No." He resumed his fighting stance. "Killing you and the others will fulfill my debt to General Caldren, and I will be free of him."

"The General is a murderer and a madman. He does not deserve your allegiance." Tara's vision blurred, and she shook her head to clear it. Blood loss was weakening her, fraying the edges of her consciousness.

Natiere watched her, his black eyes inscrutable. "I gave my word. I am honorbound."

"Then you are a murderer, just as he is. Where is the honor in that?"

Natiere attacked with a swift rain of blows. Tara parried and dodged, twisting and turning with every sword thrust, deflecting his blade with her own. Sliding on the blood-slicked gravel, she backed away from him.

"Why did you... want me to see... your past?" she asked between breaths.

He smiled faintly. "To show you I am not the monster I might seem."

"If you weren't a monster, you would let us go. And what do you care what I think?"

Natiere didn't answer. "If you can best me, I will let you go." He pressed forward, slicing and jabbing with rapid strokes. She fought him off, felt his blade cut into her left shoulder. She gasped in pain. The cobbled streets and broken houses whirled around her. A loud roaring sounded in her ears, and she fell. Sensing his downward strike, she twisted to the side. His sword struck the gravel, sent it scattering. In the back of her mind, she heard snarls and yelps from the wolves. Fighting her dizziness, she scrambled to a crouch. Natiere swung again. She dodged the blade, then leaped toward him in a rolling somersault, landing at his feet. She swept upright, directly in front of him, and drove her sword deep into his chest. His arm curled around her, drawing her against him as he fell. His massive body crunched on the red gravel. Tara landed on top of him, her face inches from his. He caught her gaze and held it. The intensity of emotion staggered her. She braced herself, but he did not try to force a mind link.

"Well done, Lady." His voice dwindled to a hoarse whisper. He raised his other hand and brushed her cheek. "*Urani metrissta elann...*" His eyes drifted shut. The arm holding her fell away.

Shaking, Tara levered herself up from his chest. Trevillion lifted her to her feet and drew her away as the wolves rushed past. They milled around Natiere, whining and licking his face.

Trevillion gathered Tara into his arms. "Can you run? The wolves may come after us."

"Wait." She turned back to Natiere. "Is he dead? I couldn't tell."

"He's dead. He must be. And we will be, too, if we don't go now."

"But... if he's alive..." She looked at Natiere, his body hidden by the anxious wolves. Part of her wanted him dead but another part ached with compassion, and she wondered if she had been in his position, what would she have done?

"He's dead. Let's go."

Confused by her ambivalence, Tara allowed Trevillion to lead her away. "The wolves are ignoring us."

"For now." He herded her into a shambling jog.

They headed toward the fortress. Tara took several deep breaths, trying to shrug off her pain. Trevillion stumbled once, and she caught him. Slowing to a stop, they leaned against a building to rest. Tara swept her gaze over the streets behind them and saw no wolfen shadows in pursuit. She looked worriedly at Trevillion, at his blood-soaked shirt, his arms laced with claw and teeth marks. "Can you make it? Maybe I should heal you now."

"No. We need to get back. Yes, I can make it." He took her good hand in his.

They hurried down countless streets, cutting through empty buildings until, finally, they staggered into the warehouse with the secret passage. A group of Faragellyn soldiers, guarding the trapdoor, helped them down the ladder. More soldiers cleared a path for them up out of the dungeon and across the crowded first floor. Tara and Trevillion climbed to the second floor, then stopped to catch their breath.

Passing townspeople, eyeing their blood-smeared clothing, called for a medic, but Tara waved them away. "Thank you, but it's not necessary." They looked at her doubtfully and hurried away. She glanced after them as a sudden thought occurred to her. "I should have asked if anyone has seen Laraina."

"Laraina is here, and Kaden and Aurelia," Trevillion said.

"You saw them? Are they all right?"

"Laraina was hurt. Kaden and Aurelia were fine. They were headed for the infirmary. They told me you were out in the city."

Tara sagged against the wall. "Thank the gods, they made it back. What about Garrett?"

"I didn't see him, but Aurelia mentioned him, so he must be here."

A messenger boy ran by, a note gripped in his hand. Trevillion flagged him down.

The boy stopped beside him. "Sir?" He couldn't keep from staring at Trevillion's wounds.

Trevillion gestured back down the hall. "After you have delivered your message, go to the infirmary and find Laraina Triannon. Tell her Tara and Jovan are back in the fortress and that we are fine."

"Yes, sir," the boy said with a dubious frown. He hastened off down the stairs.

Tara gave a short laugh. "Yes, we're in great shape." She pushed away from the wall. "I need to heal you." She swayed slightly. "And me." Trevillion steadied her. "Is there somewhere less conspicuous we can go?"

"This way." He led her up another flight of stairs to the third level. By the time they reached the top, they were both panting. "Over here." He crossed to a door just down the corridor. They went inside and he closed and locked the door.

Tara looked around. "Where are we?"

"Officers' quarters. Colonel Lemard's room. He's in the infirmary, so I know he won't be up here." Trevillion drew her over to the fireplace. She sank onto a rug of thick brown fur, a weary ache in her limbs. Trevillion knelt on the hearth, took some logs from the woodbin and stacked them in the grate.

Gingerly, Tara pulled off her tunic, leaving her undershirt. She glanced at Trevillion and felt the butterflies somersault through her gut. The thought of healing him again scared and tantalized her at the same time. The last time she'd healed him, after the fight with the Bog wolves, she had let him inside her mind, let their souls join, igniting a passion she'd seen echoed in his eyes. Entranced by his expression, she'd leaned toward him, and only Laraina's presence had stopped her from kissing him. Would it be the same this time? A strange tightness rose from the pit of her stomach, squeezing upward until she found it hard to breathe. But what about the dream? The creature wouldn't be as strong this far from the Bog, but it could still reach her through the dream. She shuddered at the memory.

Trevillion turned away from the warm blaze he'd started and sat down facing her. "Are you sure you're up to this?"

She nodded, forcing back her fear.

Trevillion stripped off his shirt with a grimace and dropped it into the fire. With shaking hands, Tara eased the torn bandages from around his chest, revealing many crisscrossing gashes. Two had been stitched, but much of the stitching had pulled apart. Blood seeped from the wounds.

Tossing the bandages into the fire, she unwrapped the cloth covering her cut palm. She placed her hand over the wound nearest Trevillion's heart, took a deep breath, and closed her eyes. The power flared and almost got away from her. Working through the pain and exhaustion, she regained control and sent the power coursing into him. He put his hand over hers and drew her in; his steadying presence bolstered her, held firm while she healed them both. Her weariness dissipated, swept away by a sudden wild euphoria. The connection deepened and she let it go, melting into him both mentally and physically. He slipped his arms around her and kissed her. Her senses reeled, the heat of her emotions fanned by the power still flowing between them.

His hands slid upward, cupping her face as he released her from the kiss. She opened her eyes, her breath coming fast. She felt the tension in his body as he held himself in check, looking askance. He was giving her a chance to back out, to break the connection. Did she want to? She twined her arms around his neck and pulled him back down to her, drawing him with her as she sank backward onto the soft fur rug. Her whole body trembled as his hands caressed her, loosening her clothing, his lips tracing lines of fire over her skin. She whispered his name as they moved together, rising with him to an explosion of passion that stole her breath and dazed her senses. She basked in the ripples of pleasure surging through her body, ebbing into languorous bliss. His lips closed over hers again in tender kisses; her fingers trailed through his hair and over his muscular shoulders, their souls and bodies one. Slowly, she eased the power back into herself.

Trevillion shifted his weight and settled beside her, his arms still around her. His lips brushed her hair. "Sleep, Love. I will be here." He reached back and pulled a blanket from the bed, and wrapped it around them.

She rested her head on his chest. His warmth enveloped her and her eyelids grew heavy. "I love you," she whispered, and drifted off.

CHAPTER 20

Tara dragged herself off the cold stone floor. Her head throbbed with every pulse as she struggled to her knees. The light from four torches flickered dimly; yellowish slime dripped from the rough-hewn walls. She closed her eyes and sagged back on her heels, cursing silently. The dream dungeon.

She lurched to her feet and realized her clothes were in disarray. Warmth stole through her as she remembered why. With stiff fingers she laced her shirt and leggings. Trevillion had said he would be with her; she wished he'd meant physically.

Brushing aside a dusty cobweb, she faced the blackness that cloaked the depths of the passage. Nothing. No sound filtered through the cloying stillness. Her skin crawled. Where was the creature?

Turning away, she stumbled toward the tall iron door at the other end of the hall, then stopped, staring. The figure of a griffin, blood-red with wings extended upward in profile, was set into the door. The torchlight glimmered off its finely-carved surface, making the half-eagle, half-lion form look alive and breathing.

The griffin's eagle eye, a dark molasses brown, seemed to shift, as if focusing on her. Cautiously, she walked toward it and slid her fingers over its lion body. The carved wood felt cool to her touch, yet smooth and soft, almost like fur... and somehow familiar.

A scraping sound ripped icy warnings down her spine. She spun about. Her eyes searched the blackness, but she saw no movement, nothing. She turned back and, with a wary glance at the red griffin, swung the door open.

Beyond lay the familiar maze of tunnels. She slipped through and closed the door. Another griffin — or was it the same one? — stared at her from this side of the door. The griffin's dark eye seemed to watch her, but she sensed no threat.

A screeching hiss rent the moldy air. Something slammed into the back of the door. Stifling a scream, Tara flung herself into the nearest side passage. The creature hammered on the door, its claws scraping the iron and wood. Tara ran through the dimly-lit corridors. Then the pounding ceased. A furious shriek echoed through the passageways. Clapping her hands over her ears, Tara sank to one knee, the shriek reverberating in her head like a cannon blast. Pain ratcheted through her skull and her vision dimmed. Gathering within herself, she forged a mental wall. Another shriek ripped through her mind like claws digging into exposed flesh, tearing at the wall. She screamed, her control slipping.

Tara! The whisper-soft voice pried into her mind. *Love, I'm here. Let me in!*

Jovan? She grasped at the voice, clung to it.

Let me in, Love. You're blocking me out, too.

Struggling to regain control, Tara opened her mind a crack. The creature lunged for the hole, but Trevillion was quicker. Tara inhaled deeply as his strength flowed into her, helping her seal the rift and drive the creature back. With a savage screech, the creature released her. The pain in her mind eased. She closed her eyes and focused inward, regrouping behind the shield of Trevillion's strength.

When the last curdles of sound died away, she opened her eyes. She stared at the door-lined hallway. *I'm still here.* She'd expected to be back in the room in the officers' quarters, on the fur rug, in Trevillion's arms.

I know. I'll get you out.

Another thought slipped into her battered mind, freezing her where she crouched. *It knows where I am.*

So do I. Stay there. I'm coming.

Rising panic spurred Tara to her feet. *I can't stay. It will find me.* Her head whipped back and forth, watching the doors up and down the passage. *It's coming. I can feel it.* She took a few jogging steps down the hall.

No! The voice stopped her. *Stay where you are. Trust me.*

Tara forced herself to stand still; it took every ounce of willpower she had. Her ears strained for the insidious scraping noise that signaled the creature's approach. Then she heard it, wafting faintly in the dimness.

A door behind her opened. The stink of carrion filled the hall, gagging her. She tried to run, but her limbs refused to move. Arms came around her from behind. A jolt like frozen lightning snapped down her spine, shocking her into motion. She dropped to the ground and rolled sideways. The creature's arms closed on air.

A shriek like that of an eagle rang through the corridor. Feathered wings beat vigorously, whipping the dust like a gale-force wind. A massive red shape leaped toward Tara from her other side. She threw her arms up to protect her head and flattened herself on the floor.

The creature let out a roar as a huge red griffin, talons extended, flew over Tara and attacked it. Their bodies clashed with a sickening thud. Back and forth across the hall the beasts thrashed, shaking the walls with their battle. Tara scrambled to her hands and knees and backed away.

The griffin caught the creature in its talons and threw it out the open door, slamming the door shut before the creature could recover. Then the eagle head turned toward Tara. The griffin's dark eye caught hers and held her motionless. Trevillion's voice eased into her mind again. *Tara.* Folding its wings, the griffin shimmered and stood upright, its shape shifting into human form. Tara stared as Trevillion crossed the distance between them and pulled her into his arms. The passageways spun around her in a dizzying blur. She closed her eyes and wrapped her arms around his neck to keep from falling.

"It's all right. I've got you," he whispered.

Slowly, the whirling sensation faded. Tara opened her eyes. Firelight played along the darkened walls of the bedchamber. She felt the fire's warmth, smelled the burning wood. Colonel Lemard's room in the officers' quarters. They were back. She leaned her aching head against Trevillion's chest and tried to stop trembling.

Trevillion's arms tightened around her in reassurance, then he held her back, his eyes seeking hers. "Are you all right?"

She nodded. "Thank you. Are you?" She looked him over but could see no wounds.

"I seem to be." He flexed his arms. "I hurt a little bit here and there, but nothing shows."

"How did you —" She spied the ring with the red griffin on the third finger of his right hand. She caught his hand and lifted it, running her thumb over the griffin. "The ring... but... how?" Dizziness overtook her again, and she gripped Trevillion's arm.

He lowered her to the rug. She sat with her head between her knees. Trevillion sat behind her and massaged her back and shoulders. "I'm not sure what happened, exactly. You had just gone to sleep. I felt a hard lump beneath me — the ring. I took it out of my pocket, more for comfort's sake than anything, and I had a sudden urge to put it on. I must have done so, though I don't remember doing it, and found myself in your dream dungeon. You were there on the floor. I tried to reach you, but couldn't."

Tara sat up slowly. "I'm sorry. I didn't mean to shut you out." She shook her head in disgust. "I have a hard time controlling my fear when I'm in there."

"I can see why."

"Now that you've seen my dungeon and the creature, can you tell me anything about them?"

"Nothing more than you already know."

Tara faced him. "But you knew the dungeon was in the Bog and that the creature was the presence that ruled there."

"It was just a guess," Trevillion said, his dark eyes unreadable.

Tara looked away, staring into the fire. "Why do I always have the feeling you know more than you're saying?"

"I thought you trusted me."

Tara felt the subtle shift in his manner, the slight tenseness, the withdrawal. She looked back. Her eyes searched his, trying to see beyond the expressionless mask. "Don't shut me out. I do trust you. I just can't get past this feeling that you're hiding something. You shape-changed into a griffin. How did you do it?"

"I don't know."

"And you still say you don't have magic?"

"The ring has magic, not me."

Tara turned her back. Why did he have to be so infuriatingly stubborn? She was sure he had some kind of magic hidden within. Her instincts were never wrong.

The silence lengthened. Trevillion let out a long exhale and swore under his breath. She sensed anger in him, but not directed at her. He swung around in front of her and gently clasped her shoulders. "Tara —" He stopped, then began again. "There are so many things I would tell you..." He looked away as if wrestling with something. He met her eyes again. "But I can't speak of them." He held his hand up to stem her questions. "And I can't tell you why. I can only ask that you trust me a little while longer."

Tara watched him wordlessly, suspicions rising and falling as her head warred with her heart. She needed answers if she was going to survive her nightmares, answers he wasn't willing to give. "I need to know more about the dream. If you could just tell me something..."

"Love, I can't. I know trust does not come easily for you, but I need you to trust me. Please?" He cupped her face, his thumb brushing over her cheek. "I don't want to lose you."

She closed her eyes, her bones growing weak, even from such a small touch. *You must choose with your heart and not your head.* Trevillion's words whispered through her memory. She knew that if she turned him away now, she would regret it forever. She opened her eyes. Her breath caught at his expression, the depth of feeling he made no effort to hide. She cleared her throat. "I meant what I said before. I do trust you."

He drew her close, pulling her onto his lap, his arms circling her tightly. "I promise I will tell you what I can, when I can."

"Then that will have to do," she said softly and kissed him. They tumbled backward onto the rug, and for a long while, all thought ceased.

The clamor of battle preparations finally roused them. Trevillion glanced out the window. "It will be dawn soon. The Sulledorns will attack just before sunrise, if they hold to their plan."

Tara forced herself to think. "I need to find Laraina, and we should see what we can do to help whoever's in charge. With Garrett, Benton, and Lemard all out of commission, I don't know who that will be. One of the lieutenants, maybe."

"You need to sleep, to recover from the dream."

"There's no time."

Trevillion's arms closed around her. "Sleep for an hour. Then we will go."

"But —"

"Sleep. I will wake you when it's time."

"All right. For a few minutes." Tara curled up against him and closed her eyes.

*****

Cold noses nuzzled and nudged. A wet tongue licked his face. A warm body lay on his side. He felt its weight on his arm and hip, though he could not yet see it. Around him, a soothing coolness salved the excruciating pain in his chest.

Awareness returned in full, and Natiere opened his eyes. The large, black wolf licking his face gave a joyful yip and began lapping more vigorously.

"Kelya," he croaked. The whispered word, forced through lips crusted with blood, quivered in the frosty air. He cleared his parched throat. "I am glad... to see you as well."

The black wolf ceased her ministrations and barked softly. A young wolf stepped gingerly off from Natiere's side. The rich, earthy smell of mud and growing things filled his senses. He shifted his head, his scarred cheek resting on a pillow of green moss. Pain stabbed through the wound in his chest. He bit off a groan, gritting his teeth until the spasm passed. He couldn't see much of his surroundings in the thin, predawn light. Reeds, dried and stiff, edged the mudhole in which he lay. Dark boles rose upward, closing him in. Willow fronds, sprouting new leaves, brushed his face. A small brook burbled off to his left.

He recognized the marshy grove of willow and ash in which he had been hidden. The grove lay just beyond the outskirts of Relic. The wolves must have dragged him here after he fell in his battle with the silver-haired witch. Wonder and gratitude filled him as he pondered the monumental effort it must have taken.

Carefully, Natiere tested his limbs. Every movement brought agony. "Kelya," he called softly. The black wolf's ears pricked, and she came toward him. "I need a small stick."

The wolf bounded away and came back shortly with a thick, broken twig. She dropped it before him.

"Thank you." He stretched forward and picked it up with his teeth. Biting down hard, he slowly lifted himself onto his hands and knees, elbow-deep in mud. Pain seared through him, radiating outward from the sword still protruding from his chest, and he nearly passed out. Hovering on the edge of oblivion, he reached deep within. *Wolfgren, gypsy warlock... Spirit of the Wolves, I call on you. You saved my life as a youth... gave me strength far beyond most men. I call on that strength to sustain me now.*

He rocked up onto his knees. Gripping the hilt, he yanked the sword out and tossed it into the trees. Warm blood poured from the wound. His head swam. He fell forward into the muck and knew no more.

Sometime later, consciousness returned, and with it, a burning thirst. He lifted his head from the mossy pillow, igniting the pain. The black wolf padded up to him, whined, and licked his face again. "Kelya... water..."

The black wolf spun away, picked something up in her mouth, and ran toward the stream. The young wolf on his back stayed where it was, pressing Natiere firmly into the mud, the healing substance that had stemmed his bleeding and cooled his fevered body. Kelya returned, pulling his hat along the ground with her teeth. She slid it up to him and gave an anxious yip. He drank. The cold, sweet water refreshed him, washed away the taste of blood.

"Once again, I thank you," he whispered. His vision grayed. He closed his eyes and let the darkness overtake him.

*****

The combined armies of Sulledor and Mardainn attacked at dawn. Black clouds hung low; the sullen sky reflected the grim faces of the Faragellyn soldiers lining the ramparts of the Relic fortress. Each soldier was keenly aware of how vastly outnumbered they were, and how slim their chance of survival.

Prince Kaden of Dhanarra prowled the walkway along the western parapet, his sword drawn, his eyes fastened on the advancing troops. With Prince Garrett, Colonel Lemard, and Colonel Benton incapacitated, he had taken command. The Faragellyn soldiers had accepted him, albeit reluctantly, after he had shouted down their objections and outlined the battle plans he, Prince Garrett, and King Jacques du Mraine had formed back in Crystalir. Though still too weak to fight, Laraina had managed to convince her sister and Trevillion to back him, much to his surprise. Their support had helped sway the men. He owed them for that. This would be his first real battle — and most likely his last if help did not arrive soon. He wondered for the thousandth time if King du Mraine had been able to secure aid from neighboring Barony to the north and Tralyxa to the southeast.

A young soldier appeared in front of him and saluted nervously. "All is in readiness, sir."

Prince Kaden nodded. "Take your position."

The young soldier saluted again and hastened to his post. Kaden swept a glance back across the far battlements, wishing he had more men, soldiers instead of farmers and tradesmen conscripted from the townspeople. Tara and Trevillion had taken up posts on the north and south walls. He knew they would hold as long as they could. As much as he hated to admit it, they were the best fighters he had.

The clank of armor and the stomp of marching feet drifted through the dead air as the enemy troops closed in. Prince Kaden turned and surveyed the line of archers positioned along the walkway, their bows strung, arrows nocked. Tension ran high. He could see the sweat dripping from the brows of the men as they awaited his command. The men lacked confidence in him. He could feel their uncertainty as strongly as if they'd slapped him in the face. He couldn't blame them, really. He knew his own reputation — a pleasure seeker who spent more time in the bed chamber than the council chamber. The fact that he had engineered the now worthless peace treaty did not help his cause either. His eyes narrowed. None of that mattered now. He was not that man anymore. His gaze shifted back to the steadily advancing troops, their banners hanging limply in the still air. Somewhere out there was the deranged man who had ordered the death of his father and forced him to flee his own castle. General Caldren. Kaden's lean face grew hard and set. He had a score to settle.

A sharp blast from a battlehorn shattered the air. Enemy soldiers, their shields wedged tightly together over their heads, wheeled a massive battering ram toward the gate. Kaden watched impassively, concealing his inner turmoil, as the rest of the army lined up just out of arrow range, bringing ladders and grappling hooks to the forefront.

The gate to the fortress had been solidly reinforced, and two of Colonel Lemard's most trusted men had barricaded themselves in the gatehouse. The secret passage in the dungeon had been sealed shut. Kaden only hoped that there were no more hidden doors scattered throughout the dungeon labyrinth. He had posted guards at the dungeon entrance as a precaution, even though he could ill afford to spare the men. The women and children had all been moved from the courtyard to the keep; those unable to fight were told to lock themselves in.

Another trumpet blast rocked hard on the echoes of the first. Whooping and roaring, the enemy soldiers charged.

"Now!" Prince Kaden yelled.

Arrows flew, volley after volley, sailing through the air with deadly accuracy. Countless Sulledorns fell, their throats pierced, but still more came on. Mardainn archers returned fire, sending the Faragellyn soldiers ducking for cover.

Thunder rolled across the leaden sky as the Sulledorn-Mardainn army surrounded the fortress. Ladders, some wood, some metal, with Sulledorns clinging to the tops, were heaved up against the high stone walls. The Sulledorns leaped through the crenels onto the walkway, slashing into the Faragellyn defenders as more Sulledorns climbed upward. A hammering thud rang out above the shouting and thunder as the battering ram crashed into the gate.

Kaden cut through two Sulledorns and shoved another back over the wall. "Now!" he shouted again. He heard the order repeated along the battlements behind him.

His men rushed forward with steaming cauldrons of boiling oil, what little they had, and dumped the contents over the walls. The enemy soldiers, doused by the hot liquid, screamed and jumped or fell from the ladders. Prince Kaden seized a lighted torch and tossed it over the side. Flames snaked along the ground, roaring upward as men and ladders burned. The Sulledorn army fell back. Black smoke billowed above the ramparts, blotting out the darkening sky.

The stench of scorched flesh thickened the air. Fire raged on all sides of the stone fortress, licking outward toward the ravaged city.

Lightning sliced through blackened clouds, striking the earth not far from the fortress. Thunder cracked as the ground shivered. Pebble-sized hailstones pelted down, dinging against helm and armor, stinging exposed skin.

The Faragellyn defenders fought off the Sulledorns that had made it over the wall and, with battle roars of their own, threw the corpses back over the side. Then they knocked down the metal ladders and the wooden ones not yet burned through. Kaden saw a few Faragellyn soldiers down, but not as many as he had expected. Medics gathered up the injured and carried them back to the keep.

For all its violence, the storm passed quickly. The sky lightened. Prince Kaden moved to the edge of the wall and looked out through the thinning smoke. The oil fire still burned, though greatly subdued.

The enemy soldiers had regrouped and were massing for another attack. Their battering ram had been damaged. A portion of their ladders had been destroyed. But now they had another weapon. Rolling ponderously over the gravel, massive catapults were dragged into position.

In tightly-shielded phalanxes, the enemy advanced. Just as the Faragellyn archers prepared to shoot, a large stone whizzed over the parapet. The archers leaped back out of the way. Rocks and debris crashed over the ramparts on all sides, felling many Faragellyn defenders. With the Mardainn archers providing cover fire, the Sulledorns rushed the fortress. They set up more ladders and swarmed up over the walls.

Prince Kaden met the onslaught with savage determination. A single thought burned in his mind — revenge. If General Caldren entered this fortress, it would be as a prisoner of war or a dead man.

Dodging arrows and flying debris, Kaden lunged at his foes, his sword thrusts swift and deadly. He heard the battering ram pounding and hoped the gate would hold.

A boulder crashed into the northern parapet, taking out three merlons and twice as many men. Another boulder, bigger than the last, smashed into the wall just below the first strike point, weakening the wall. Kaden rushed to the breach. Two Sulledorn soldiers leaped from a ladder planted in the gap. Hurdling bodies half-buried in rubble, Kaden charged into them. He knocked one of them backward and jabbed the second in the shoulder, angling his sword into the joint between the armor plates. The soldier groaned and fell back. Kaden's second swing cut the soldier's throat. Shoving the dead soldier away, Kaden ducked as the other Sulledorn's blade whistled past his head. Rounding on him, Kaden kept low and cut the Sulledorn's feet out from under him. The Sulledorn fell, clutching his bleeding leg. Kaden made certain he did not rise. Then he turned to meet the next wave of Sulledorns coming up the ladder.

Trevillion appeared beside him with a rope tied to an iron hook. Slugging a Sulledorn off the top of the ladder, Trevillion looped the hook around a ladder rung. He shouted back down the parapet. The rope grew taut and yanked sideways, pulling the ladder over. The Sulledorns yelled as they crashed to the ground.

The battle intensified as the day wore on. Kaden worked his way around the parapet, fighting, exhorting his men. The Faragellyn soldiers rallied around him. Though their numbers were dwindling, the Faragellyn defenders held their own. None of the Sulledorns made it down to the courtyard alive. The walls of the fortress, battered and pockmarked, still stood tall. The wooden gate, reinforced with crisscrossing bands of iron, had cracked and bent, but not broken.

With a final thrust, Prince Kaden dispatched the Sulledorn in front of him and dropped back into his fighting stance, ready for the next onslaught. To his surprise, the walkway was clear. Cautiously, he stood, his panting breaths rasping in his ears. He was long past winded. Weak sunlight spilled down through ragged gray clouds. He guessed the time to be around noon. Exhaustion melted him, and he sagged against the parapet.

Pain ripped into his left shoulder. He stumbled backward with a cry and fell, a burning arrow shaft protruding from just beneath his collarbone. A Faragellyn soldier raced to his side, shouting for a medic. The soldier tore off his outer tunic and smothered the fire. Then he drew his dagger and cut away Kaden's shirt and leather armor where the arrow had pierced.

"Pull it out," Kaden ordered through clenched teeth.

The soldier hesitated, then grasped the shaft and yanked. Kaden screamed. The arrow would not budge.

"I can't get it," the soldier cried. "It must be caught on a bone."

Through a pain-filled haze Kaden heard running footsteps. Trevillion knelt beside him. He looked at the wound. Gesturing to the soldier, Trevillion slipped his arms under Prince Kaden's shoulders as if to lift him. "Let's get him to the keep."

"No!" Kaden rasped. "I will not leave the fight."

One of the townspeople, a blacksmith who had been pressed into service, ran up to them. "The Sulledorns are pulling back. They're leaving."

"What? Where are they going?" Kaden demanded.

"They are heading east toward Crystalir."

"They're forcing us to come out and fight them," Trevillion said grimly.

"We can't!" the blacksmith said. "We're outnumbered ten to one."

"We have to, or they will massacre every village between here and Crystalir." Kaden tried to move his arm and couldn't. The arrow had lodged in his shoulder and locked up the joint. He nodded at the soldier and Trevillion. "Help me up. Assemble the men in the courtyard. We're going out."

"We?" Trevillion lifted him upright. "You need a medic. You won't last five minutes out there."

Kaden clenched his fist. "These are my men now, and I'm going out with them. Now *go!*"

Trevillion gave him an inscrutable look. "As you say."

The soldier saluted. "Yes, sir!"

They moved off in opposite directions, gathering the men. The blacksmith held Kaden's arm, steadying him. "What can I do, my lord?"

Prince Kaden looked at the blacksmith with his well-thewed arms. "I want you to pull out this arrow." He braced himself against the parapet.

"I will try." The blacksmith grasped the shaft. He gave a sharp tug, but the arrow remained stuck fast. Kaden sucked in a hissing breath. The pain sickened him, and he barely kept his stomach from heaving its contents.

The blacksmith eyed him solicitously. "Should I try again?"

"No," Kaden whispered. "Break it off as low as you can. I will deal with it later."

The blacksmith stared at him in mingled disbelief and admiration, then carefully snapped off the protruding end of the shaft. Kaden grimaced, but managed not to scream. The blacksmith picked up the tunic the soldier had used to put out the fire and wrapped it around the wound, forming a sling. "I'm no medic —"

"It's fine. Thank you. What is your name?"

"Gindras, my lord."

"Thank you, Gindras. Now, if you will come with me." Kaden staggered a few steps and nearly fell.

Gindras caught him. "Let me take you to the keep."

"No." Kaden pulled away. Grayness clouded his vision. He shook his head to keep from fainting. He searched his memory and recalled the image of his murdered father, lying in bed, bloodied and staring. Anger burned through the fog in his mind. Gripping his sword, he made it across the walkway and down the stairs to the courtyard without stumbling. Gindras trailed close behind him.

Prince Kaden faced the Faragellyn defenders gathered in the courtyard. He saw those in front take note of his injury and look at each other. "I know we are outnumbered," he said, raising his voice so all could hear. "And I know if we go out there, we may well all die this day. But if we do not fight, every man, woman, and child in all the villages from here to Crystalir will die in our stead." His eyes swept the crowd of soldiers and townspeople and saw what he wanted in their faces — respect, determination, resolve. They were willing to follow him into battle, even if it meant their deaths.

"General Caldren killed my father," he continued. "He is mine. When I find him, I swear on my father's life that he will kill no more. I have no fancy strategy. We must stay together and fight as we have never fought before." He turned and faced the gate, raised his sword high. "For Dhanarra!" he cried.

"For Faragellyn!" The shout rose up behind him.

The gate creaked open and they rushed into battle.

CHAPTER 21

The battle lasted longer than Tara had thought it would. The Faragellyn soldiers fought well and hard. She, Trevillion, and the blacksmith, Gindras, wielding a wicked-looking mace, had stayed close by Prince Kaden, fending off countless attacks as they plunged into the middle of the Sulledorn-Mardainn army. Once the Faragellyn soldiers left the fortress, the enemy had turned back, as expected, and the fighting spread rapidly through the wreckage of the destroyed city.

In the chaos, Tara found it hard to tell friend from foe. The rain and sweat-dampened colors the soldiers wore blended together until all appeared the same. The battle seethed around her in a blur of motion with no beginning or end. She watched for General Caldren, but didn't see him. She hoped he wouldn't come near. If Kaden saw him, she knew the prince would try to attack, and he was in no condition to tackle the General. She skewered a Sulledorn who swiped at her with his blade, then glanced back at the prince again, making sure he was still close behind her. She'd promised Laraina she would do her best to keep him alive. Pain and weariness lined his face, but he stood his ground. He had more guts than she'd given him credit for. Defending him, though, was getting more difficult. She cut down another Sulledorn and shoved a third backward toward Trevillion who ran him through. Exhaustion had slowed Kaden's reactions. It was only a matter of time before...

Gindras' mace thudded into a Sulledorn's midsection and sent the Sulledorn flying backward. Two more Sulledorns lunged at him. He parried one blow, but missed the other. The Sulledorn's blade cut deep into his arm. With a cry, he stumbled sideways.

Kaden's sword came up, too slowly. The Sulledorn leaped at him, his arm cocked back as if he would take Kaden's head off with one swing. Tara whipped her dagger out of her belt and flung it at the Sulledorn attacking Kaden. It sank into his back. The Sulledorn grunted and fell on top of the prince, knocking him flat. Kaden hit the ground and lay gasping, the wind knocked out of him. The Sulledorns pressed forward, forcing Tara and Trevillion back, almost on top of him. Then Tara caught another sound, as sweet as any music she had ever heard — the blare of a battlehorn.

The Sulledorns pulled back, surprised, and turned to face a new foe. Gindras shoved the dead Sulledorn off Prince Kaden and helped him to his feet. Tara looked to the southeast and saw, over the Sulledorns' heads, a forest-green flag with bow and lute insignia approaching. The banner of the Woodsmen of Tralyxa.

The twang of bowstrings shook the air. Shouts and screams rang out in a cacophony of confusion. Arrows flew and found their marks. Sulledorns fell by the dozens. Then, with a thousand rasps of metal, the Woodsmen, clad in green and gold, drew sword and dove into the fight. Unnerved by the ferocity of the attack, the Sulledorn-Mardainn army broke apart. A cheer went up from the Faragellyn defenders, and they fought with renewed vigor.

A pounding like thunder rose above the uproar. The ground began to shake. Tara whirled toward the sound and saw horses, an army of them. Whooping and yelling, the Horsemen of Barony swept down out of the north and charged into the midst of the Sulledorn-Mardainn army. Blades flashing, they rode roughshod over the panicking troops. The Mardainn combatants broke ranks and fled. The Sulledorns fought fiercely, driven by the murderous threats screamed at them by General Caldren. But they were no match for the combined strength of Barony's Horsemen and the Woodsmen of Tralyxa.

Tara heard the voice shouting at the Sulledorns and knew it had to be the General. Kaden heard it too and, with a strangled cry, staggered toward the sound. Tara ran after him, Trevillion and Gindras right behind her. Kaden stopped and gestured them back. "No! This is my fight. Stay out of it."

"Caldren will kill you!" Tara reached toward him, but Trevillion held her back. Prince Kaden gave Trevillion a nod, then headed toward the source of the shouting.

Tara turned on Trevillion, who still gripped her arm. "What are you doing? We can't just let him go off to die. Laraina will kill me."

"He may die, he may not. He has the right of vengeance. You can't take that from him."

"But —"

"We can keep the other Sulledorns away from him." Trevillion released her and ran down the gravel street after Kaden. Grumbling under her breath, Tara followed, with Gindras on her heels.

*****

Oblivious to the isolated battles being fought around him, Prince Kaden stumbled down the street, moving toward the bellowing voice. The pain in his shoulder burned like white fire, but he refused to let it stop him. Gods willing, he would have his vengeance this day. He gripped his sword tighter. *Father, this is for you.* The path before Kaden cleared. One man stood alone. His snow-white hair streaked with red, General Caldren had planted himself in the middle of a blood-spattered street. He screamed at his men to come back and fight. Kaden's exhaustion evaporated in a surge of adrenaline, and he rushed forward. Two of Barony's Horsemen bore down on the General, but Kaden waved them off. The General whirled. Recognition burned in his hate-ridden eyes.

They ran at each other. The clash of their weapons sent shock waves down Kaden's arm, but he did not loosen his grip. Their blades arced and slashed. The General countered Kaden's swing and backhanded him across the face. Kaden reeled backward, tasting blood, but kept his feet. The General leaped after him, his sword rising and falling with savage blows. Kaden parried and scrambled away, crying out as the General's blade sliced into his wrist and side. Pain wobbled him. His vision tunneled, dizziness throwing him off balance. He shook his head, saw the General coming at him again. With a wild swing, Kaden tried to fend him off. The General deflected his blade and kicked him in the gut. Kaden doubled over with a groan. The General kicked him again, sent him spinning to the ground. Landing on his side, Kaden curled in around himself, cradling his bruised ribs. The General lifted his foot over him and stomped downward. Kaden whipped onto his back, caught the General's foot, and shoved backward, planting the General on his backside.

With an angry roar, the General sprang at him. Kaden hauled himself upright and brought up his sword, too late. The General's blade jabbed into his injured shoulder, just below the protruding arrow shaft. Pain exploded behind Kaden's eyes, and he screamed as he fell. Time seemed to stop as he lay on the ground, moaning. He heard footsteps running toward him and someone calling his name. As if in slow motion, he saw the General raise his sword and, gripping the hilt with both hands, thrust it point-down at him. At the last second, Kaden rolled onto his side. The blade drove through the gravel into the dirt beneath. Kaden rolled back and jammed his own sword deep into the General's exposed armpit. He struck bone, and a dark crimson stain spread down the General's dented armor. Kaden yanked his sword free. The General staggered backward and fell. Kaden lurched to his feet. The General tried to rise. Gathering the last of his strength, Kaden raised his weapon and, with one blow, severed the General's head from his body. It thudded to the gravel; the General's body collapsed beside it, blood draining away.

Kaden dropped to his knees. He stared at the General's face, frozen in a defiant sneer. Tears filled Kaden's eyes, tears for his murdered father. His gaze swept over the annihilated city littered with the broken bodies of the dead and dying. So much death and destruction caused by the twisted aspirations of a madman. The blood began to pound once more in his head. Overcome with exhaustion, he crumpled to the ground.

*****

When Captain Natiere opened his eyes again, the sky was dark. Soft moonlight sifted down through the willow leaves, shadowing the great trunks of willow and ash that grew out of the marsh. Rime edged the brittle reeds. The mud beneath him had grown cold, hardening around him. But he was not cold.

The wolf curled on Natiere's back and legs gently rose and leaped off him, sensing he was awake. Kelya licked his scarred cheek, then disappeared into the trees. The other wolves lay nearby. He could see their dark shapes nestled here and there in patches of dried grass. Natiere breathed in the frosty air, the sweet spice of herbs and mint. The dull ache in his chest sharpened. He clenched his fists and with infinite slowness, pushed himself onto his knees. Blood oozed from the wound. He scooped up handfuls of mud and plastered them thickly over the wound, stanching the flow. When the pain eased, he folded his cloak lengthwise and wrapped it around himself, tying the ends snugly together to keep the packed mud in place.

The wolves rose and gathered around him, pressing up against him. Leaning heavily on their shoulders, he moved one knee forward, then the other. More slowly than a snail, he crawled to the nearby stream. The clear water sparkled in the moonlight as it swirled over a bed of polished stones.

Carefully, he lowered himself to the ground. He dipped his hands in the icy water, rinsed them, and splashed water on his face, washing away the blood. Then, cupping his hands, he scooped water up to his parched lips. He drank his fill. Hunger rumbled through his stomach, and he wondered how much time had passed since his duel with the silver-haired witch.

Kelya slipped out of the shadows and dropped something beside him — a freshly-killed rabbit. She sat on her haunches, watching him. Stifling a groan, Natiere eased himself back onto his knees. He stroked the dark wolf's head, scratched her ears. "Thank you," he rasped, his voice barely a whisper. He looked up and saw the rest of the wolves standing nearby. "Thank you all." The wolves lay down with their heads on their paws, ears twitching at the sounds of the night.

Natiere picked up the rabbit, skinned it, washed the meat in the creek, and ate it raw. The cold meat settled heavily in his belly. As he chewed, his thoughts turned again to his duel with the witch. She had beaten him fairly, despite being injured and fighting off-handed. His estimation of her rose several notches. He closed his eyes and remembered their brief, but turbulent, mind link. He had shown her the pain and horror of what he was, had experienced the warring emotions in her, the revulsion and compassion. She felt sorry for him, he knew. His lip curled. He did not want her pity. He ripped off another bite with his teeth. What did he want? He searched within himself, peeling back the layers of his psyche, and was surprised by the answer. He had never sought human companionship. He dealt in death, not life. And that had never bothered him. Even the thought of his own death did not trouble him. He had exacted his vengeance. He had no family, except the wolves, to mourn his passing. He had no real reason to live or die. Until now.

The long buried soul of the boy he once was had crept from its tomb within and filled him with a sudden yearning to be what he was not. He had wanted the witch — Tara — to think of him as an equal, a human being, instead of the reviled monstrosity he'd become. He'd wanted her to somehow return him to humanity or kill him and end the hollowness of his existence. The gypsy had said she would be his redemption and his downfall, which he assumed meant his death. So why was he still alive? He did not feel like he had been redeemed. In truth, he did not think redemption possible, though many of his crimes against humanity were in retribution. He fully acknowledged that many others were not. Long ago when he first embarked on his quest for vengeance, he had accepted that his soul would burn in the Abyss as a result. He'd grown indifferent to his fate.

But now, death did not appeal to him. He wanted more from the Lady Tara. With every link and mental touch, she assuaged a fragment of the horrific burden he carried and made him feel more like a man and less like a beast. He finished his meal, washed his hands, and drank. No, he was not ready to die just yet. He turned carefully and looked back across the grove to where he had tossed Tara's sword. He wanted a rematch.

*****

Tara Triannon stood at the window of her chamber on the west side of the fortress, looking out over the devastated city of Relic. The sun was setting, a red-orange glow on the horizon. A cool, moist breeze blew softly through the open window, bringing with it the smells of the funeral pyres — ashes, wood smoke, and burnt flesh. She could see the fires burning just beyond the edge of the city. Three days had passed since the resounding defeat of the Sulledorn-Mardainn army. For three days she'd helped drag the dead to the wagons that carried them to the pyres. She sagged against the stone sill, exhausted. She should go to bed, she knew, and rest before the evening's festivities. She needed sleep. But her mind was too restless, too unsettled.

In the morning, a portion of Barony's Horsemen and some of the Woodsmen of Tralyxa would depart for their homelands. The rest would remain behind to help with the reconstruction of Relic and the retaking of Carilon and Belgarde. According to all reports, General Caldren had left only token forces at both Dhanarran fortresses. Laraina was recovering quickly. Prince Garrett, too, had awakened and was on the mend. His father, King du Mraine, had sent word that he was to stay in Relic to oversee the rebuilding process. Then he would return to Crystalir. Aurelia, of course, would accompany him. It was widely rumored that a wedding would soon be in the offing.

Tara sighed heavily as her thoughts shifted to another wedding that loomed on the horizon. As soon as Carilon had been retaken, Prince Kaden and Laraina would be married, and then in a grand ceremony, Kaden would officially succeed his father as King of Dhanarra. Laraina would be a queen. No more would they roam the Western Kingdoms in search of adventure. Tara felt a dull ache settle in the empty places inside her. She would miss her sister dearly. Another deep sigh escaped her. She missed Laraina now. Her sister already seemed so distant, so caught up in other things.

And Tara didn't even have much time to get used to the idea. Prince Kaden was impatient to reclaim his throne and would talk of nothing else. He refused to give his wounds time to heal, and she knew it would only be a week, two at the most, before he and his army left Relic to battle the remaining Sulledorns. The medics had removed the arrow from his shoulder, but the arrow and the General's sword had done so much damage that the medics doubted he would ever regain full use of his arm. Kaden had declared vehemently his arm would be fine. But Tara sensed his fear and uncertainty, and knew deep down he didn't believe his own words. She knew, too, that Laraina wanted her to heal Kaden's shoulder, but couldn't bring herself to ask. Tara had mixed feelings about healing him. Kaden hadn't asked and she knew he wouldn't. He had thanked her for saving his life during the battle, but beyond that he seemed to avoid her whenever possible. Why should she suffer through another nightmare for his sake?

Her thoughts slipped to the nightmares and the strange turn they had taken. Trevillion had shape-shifted into a griffin in the last one. The event still boggled her mind. In fact, he had rescued her the last three times she'd encountered the dream creature. The question dogged her — what would happen the next time if he wasn't there? Would she be able to get out on her own? She hadn't done a very good job of it so far. If she healed Kaden, she would have to do it without Trevillion's knowledge. He had already made it plain he didn't think Kaden's arm worth the risk. What did he know that she didn't? Whatever it was, he wasn't able to share it.

She pressed the palm of her hand against her forehead, trying to still the whirl of thoughts. Trevillion was the crux of the matter. As much as she'd fought it, she'd gotten used to having him around. All right, she admitted, she wanted him around. She was in love with him. And she thought he loved her. He had asked her to trust him a little while longer. How long was "a little while"? And what then? She wondered if he had other "unfinished business" to take care of.

And then there were the visions from Rinpool he'd described. One had her entering a black castle. Was that something that might come to pass? Was Trevillion really destined to become High King? He hadn't thought so.

A knock on the door interrupted her brooding. Before she could move, the door opened and Jovan Trevillion stepped into the room.

"What's wrong?" he asked, closing the door and striding over to her.

Her heart began to pound. "Nothing. Why do you ask?"

His hands cupped her face, then dropped to her shoulders. He held her gaze. "I can feel it when you're upset."

With an effort, Tara looked away. "I'm not. I was just thinking."

"About your sister. About Kaden. About your dreams. I know."

Tara looked back at him, her eyes narrowing. "How do you know what I'm thinking?"

He smiled briefly. "What else would you be thinking about?" He drew her to him. "Laraina can't wait to start her new life. You should be happy for her. Kaden's injury is not life-threatening. He will survive as he is. You must not risk another dream unless a life is at stake. I can't believe Laraina would ask you to —"

"She hasn't asked. And I am happy for her. I just feel... lost... without her. I don't know what to do about the dreams."

Trevillion brushed his thumb over her cheek and lifted her eyes to his. "We will find an answer to your dreams."

"You sound so sure." Tara's voice betrayed her uncertainty.

"I am."

She slipped her arms around his neck. "Thank you for staying."

Trevillion's mouth quirked upward. "Someone has to keep you out of trouble."

"Good luck," Tara retorted.

Trevillion's lips closed over hers in a warm, lingering kiss.

Sometime later they broke apart and looked out the window. The sun had sunk below the line of hills, leaving scatterings of bluish-purple clouds to welcome the night. The fires continued to burn like beacons against the darkening sky. Tara leaned back, and Trevillion crossed his arms around in front of her, holding her against him.

"You're exhausted," he said softly. "You need sleep."

"Did you find Natiere's body when you were clearing out the streets in that area?"

Trevillion hesitated, but only an instant. "No."

"Neither did I."

"Someone else must have picked him up."

Tara turned her head until she could see Trevillion's face. "He is dead, isn't he?"

Trevillion met her gaze, his expression veiled. "You drove your sword into his chest. He couldn't have survived."

Tara tried to read beyond the mask. "What did he say, right before the fight? 'Silvestri witana' I know is silver-haired witch. Aurelia translated that for me before. But what was the rest?"

Trevillion hesitated, longer this time. "He said your courage matched your beauty."

Tara stared at him. "He said that?"

"Yes."

"What was it that you said? And how did you know the language?"

"I said he would have you over my dead body, or words to that effect. It is an Eastern gypsy tongue. I am from the Eastern Frontier, as you know."

"Apparently so was he." Tara looked back out the window, strange feelings running through her as Natiere's words echoed in her head. The Butcher thought her beautiful and courageous. He had challenged her, but treated her with courtesy. And he had let her go. She knew that if he had really wanted to kill her, he could have, easily. How bizarre the whole situation was. She found herself wondering what he would have been like if his family hadn't been attacked by bandits. Surprised by her turn of thought, she gave herself a mental shake. She had other questions she needed answered. What else had he said — a gypsy had shown her to him in a dream and that she would be his redemption and his downfall. What, by all the gods, did that mean?

"Natiere said he had seen me in a dream, just like you saw me in your vision in Rinpool. Do you think that's possible?"

Trevillion stirred. "I don't know. I wouldn't worry about it." He slid his hands gently up and down her arms and over her shoulders. "The 'victory feast,' as Kaden called it, will be starting soon. Are you sure you want to go? You look like you are asleep on your feet."

Tara roused herself from the blissful stupor the motion of his hands was creating. "We have to at least make an appearance." Fireworks erupted across the sky in brilliant hues of red, orange, and green. As they fizzled and dissipated, more explosions of color burst into bloom. "Looks like the festivities are starting now."

They watched for a while, then she turned from the window. "We should get going." She caught Trevillion's hand and led him to the door. She reached for the door handle, then stopped, looking back at him. "Natiere said one more thing, right at the end. *Urani metrissta elann.* What does it mean?"

Trevillion's eyes slid away from hers.

She turned him back to face her. "Please tell me."

"It means 'until we meet again.'"

Cold prickles goose-pimpled Tara's skin, and she shivered.

"Forget Natiere," Trevillion said, tension in his voice. "He is dead. General Caldren is dead. We've defeated the Sulledorn army."

He smiled as if shedding his worries and swung the door open. "We have much to celebrate. Let's go."

Trying to shelve her misgivings, Tara preceded him out the door and down the hall.

The great hall was filling up with people as they entered. Soldiers and city folk trooped in together, talking, joking, releasing long-held tension. The long tables, previously used as temporary beds for the wounded, were now covered with all manner of dishes for the feast — roast pigs, ducks, chickens, racks and legs of lamb, sides of beef, heaping mounds of potatoes, tender vegetables, dozens of loaves of bread, and bottles and bottles of wine and mead. The savory aromas woke Tara's appetite and her stomach growled, reminding her that she hadn't eaten much all day.

"Smells delicious," she said, moving toward one of the tables.

"Mmmmmm." Trevillion nodded in agreement. "This was a good idea after all."

Tara saw Laraina, standing, beckoning to her from the head table. Prince Kaden sat on her left, a grim expression on his face despite the laughter and levity in the air. His embroidered tunic hid his heavily bandaged shoulder. Next to him sat Prince Garrett, pale and weak, but smiling. Aurelia sat at his elbow, talking earnestly to him. His eyes never left her face.

"Looks like we have to sit up front," Tara said, none too happy with the idea.

"I'd rather sit down here somewhere." Trevillion glanced around.

"Me too. But I guess, if we must." She nodded to Laraina and worked her way through the crowd to the head table, with Trevillion following.

Laraina met her with a hug. "I'm glad you came. I wasn't sure you would."

"I wasn't sure myself."

"Please sit by me," Laraina said. "Everyone expects it. What?" She turned to Kaden who had said something to her from the other side.

Tara moved to sit. Then, hearing Aurelia's laughter, she stopped and put her hand on Trevillion's arm. "Will you excuse me a minute? There's something I have to do."

He nodded. A puzzled look crossed his face, but he said nothing.

Tara slipped over behind Aurelia and touched her on the shoulder. "Can I talk to you for a minute?"

Aurelia looked surprised, but rose from her seat and followed Tara to a relatively quiet corner.

"Is something wrong?" Aurelia asked tentatively.

Tara smiled and shook her head. "No. Laraina told me what you did, how you stood up to Fournier's guards at the fortress. I just wanted to say — well done. And thanks."

Aurelia beamed, looking very pleased with herself. "You're welcome. It was quite an experience." She gave a rueful giggle. "I can honestly say that swordfighting is not for me. But ever since you healed me, my spells have been working, so I must thank you again for that. I can't wait to restart my training."

"Best of luck to you." Tara grinned. "If I ever need someone turned into a goose, I'll know who to ask."

Aurelia laughed and followed Tara back through the throng to their table, and they sat down.

Prince Garrett rose and called for order. When the room quieted, he raised his wine glass in salute. "We are here to celebrate the resounding defeat of General Caldren and the Sulledorns."

Shouts and thunderous applause rocked the hall. After a few moments, Garrett lifted his hand for silence. "The kingdoms of Alltyyr have come together to defeat our common enemy, and I am proud to be a part of that alliance — an alliance which I hope will continue for years to come."

Cheers and more applause erupted from the crowd.

"But our great victory would not have been possible without the courage and determination of these five seated with me — Prince Kaden and Aurelia of Dhanarra, Tara and Laraina Triannon, and Jovan Trevillion. Their heroic efforts saved us and will be long remembered in story and song."

Prince Garrett bid his five companions to rise. Tara and Trevillion stood reluctantly along with the others.

A deafening mix of clapping, foot stomping, and shouting shook the walls of the great hall. Tara and the others bowed and sat down. When the noise subsided, Garrett spoke again.

"A toast to them and to those who are no longer with us, for with great victory comes great loss, and we are left to mourn those who will not return to us." He bowed his head. Silence filled the great hall.

As they sat with eyes closed, Laraina caught Tara's hand and squeezed it, and Tara knew that her sister, too, was remembering Dominic. Tara heard Garrett speaking again and raised her head.

"Let us remember our fallen family and friends with joy and not pain, and let us celebrate their lives along with our victory." He nodded to Aurelia, Kaden, Laraina, Tara, and Trevillion. "To you —" He turned and his gaze swept the hall. "— and to all of you, I give my most heartfelt thanks for your courage and sacrifice. May this new peace endure." He raised his glass again and drank. Everyone cheered and did the same. Aurelia hugged him as he sat down. He kissed her, eliciting whistles and ooohhhhs from the crowd.

Tara caught Trevillion's eye, and they smiled at each other, their fingers twining together under the table as the celebration began.

END BOOK I

ABOUT THE AUTHOR

Lori L. MacLaughlin traces her love of fantasy adventure to Tolkien and Terry Brooks, finding *The Lord of the Rings* and *The Sword of Shannara* particularly inspirational. She's been writing stories in her head since she was old enough to run wild through the forests on the farm on which she grew up.

She has been many things over the years – tree climber, dairy farmer, clothing salesperson, kids' shoe fitter, retail manager, medical transcriptionist, journalist, private pilot, traveler, wife and mother, Red Sox and New York Giants fan, muscle car enthusiast and NASCAR fan, and a lover of all things Scottish and Irish.

When she's not writing (or working), she can be found curled up somewhere dreaming up more story ideas, taking long walks in the countryside, or spending time with her kids. She lives with her family in northern Vermont.